Critical acclaim for
DOING HARM

"Best medical thriller I've read in twenty-five years. Terrifying OR scenes...characters with real texture."
—Stephen King

"This skillfully wrought debut gets high marks for building tension to a breathtaking climax."
—*Library Journal* (starred review)

"A terrific medical thriller—compelling, gripping, and terrifying. You'll shiver with delight." —Harlan Coben

"A classic cat-and-mouse game with a refreshing, unexpected twist...Top-notch storytelling." —Steve Berry

"A twist worthy of a surgical knot. Flawed characters standing on moral pedestals. Insight into the world of medicine and the ambitious geniuses who make life-and-death decisions. *Doing Harm* is more faction than fiction, presenting a world so close to our own that you find yourself second-guessing the characters as if they're sitting next to you. Repeatedly, I found myself breathless and troubled, yet compelled to keep reading. Brilliant." —Ridley Pearson

"This spine-chilling medical thriller has so many twists and turns, you may feel compelled to finish it in one sitting...whip-smart...the start of an impressive new career." —*Shore News Today*

"A suspenseful story, complete with heart-stopping (as it were) medical scenarios." —*The Star-Ledger*

ALSO BY KELLY PARSONS

Doing Harm

UNDER THE KNIFE

KELLY PARSONS

St. Martin's Paperbacks

This is a work of fiction. All of the characters, organizations, and events portrayed in this novel are either products of the author's imagination or are used fictitiously.

UNDER THE KNIFE

For information address St. Martin's Press, 175 Fifth Avenue, New York, NY 10010.

ISBN: 978-1-250-03350-5

Our books may be purchased in bulk for promotional, educational, or business use. Please contact your local bookseller or the Macmillan Corporate and Premium Sales Department at 1-800-221-7945, extension 5442, or by e-mail at MacmillanSpecialMarkets@macmillan.com.

Printed in the United States of America

St. Martin's Press hardcover edition / February 2017
St. Martin's Paperbacks edition / January 2018

St. Martin's Paperbacks are published by St. Martin's Press, 175 Fifth Avenue, New York, NY 10010.

10 9 8 7 6 5 4 3 2 1

For my family: ever patient, generous, and supportive in my pursuit of two careers

Acknowledgments

Writing is not a solitary endeavor. Thanks as always to my agent, Al Zuckerman, whose wisdom and mentorship continue to raise my game every day; and to my editor, Jen Enderlin, for her astute critiques and sharp eye for clean prose.

Prologue

The man stood, alone, hands in the pockets of his dark suit, gazing down into the earthen maw that had just swallowed his wife.

He was a tall man, stooped at the shoulders. Slim, with a pinched nose, prominent ears, and thin lips. He had fine hair the color of dry sand, which was parted to the side in a precise and solemn manner that made him appear much younger than his forty-odd years, like a boy made up for a school picture. His hair twitched in the warm breeze. The grass he was standing on was even and green; the headstones were silver and white.

He looked up and squinted into the brilliant sky.

Isn't it supposed to be raining?

In movies, and on TV shows, it always seemed to be raining during burials. But today, sun, sky, clouds, and breeze had colluded to produce a day breathtaking even by Southern California standards.

I wish the weather had been this nice on my daughter's wedding day, he'd overheard one of the mourners murmur to her companion right before the start of the brief ceremony. One of Jenny's friends. The CEO of a local biotechnology start-up. A very promising one. He was even considering acquiring a silent majority stake in it. She was an avid triathlete with brown, sinewy arms, mirrored sunglasses, and tiny breasts.

The triathlete was, he admitted, a shrewd businesswoman. He found it unlikely that her initial meeting with Jenny at a local gym, involving some sort of misunderstanding over a yoga mat, had occurred by chance. She had no doubt cultivated a relationship with Jenny to advance her company's agenda with him. He'd voiced these suspicions to Jenny shortly after the friendship began.

Jenny, for whom glasses had never been half-empty, had laughed, and had told him to lighten up because he wasn't *that* important, after all, and it wasn't *always* about him.

She'd touched her forefinger to her lips, and stood on her tiptoes, and pressed her finger to his lips, the way she often did to signal that a particular topic was no longer open for discussion. That was that. Debate was closed, and he'd never again questioned, out loud, at least, the triathlete's motives.

Her finger on his lips.

How he'd adored that simple gesture. The memory of it, its tactile echo—the gentle pressure on his skin, the slight ridges of Jenny's fingertips catching faintly on his bottom lip as she pulled her finger away—was almost enough to make him smile.

Almost.

He personally couldn't abide the triathlete. It wasn't a female thing. He did business with women all the time. To a certain extent, he even preferred dealing with women rather than men. Or at least disliked it less. He appreciated the fact that most women weren't fixated on some asinine alpha-male ritual du jour. Like kite surfing. Or rock climbing. Or golf. Even the fat ones played golf and boasted about it like it was some monumental athletic achievement. What a colossal waste of time.

So.

He didn't dislike the triathlete because she was a woman. He simply didn't like her. Which was of little consequence. There were lots of people he didn't like. Besides, to make that kind of comment today, not ten feet from where Jenny lay . . .

Well.

He'd bitten his lip and ignored her.

For Jenny.

She'd been well liked. Most of her friends, and there had been a good many of them, had attended the service, greeting him with handshakes, and sympathetic shoulder pats, and a few stiff hugs.

How are you holding up? Such a tragedy. Taken before her time. She was so loved. She touched so many in the short time she had. She'll be sorely missed.

He'd accepted their ministrations graciously enough, in his opinion. But he'd kept his distance during the service, standing alone, several feet away from the main group. He wanted nothing more to do with any of them. They were Jenny's friends, not his. They'd attended the burial for her sake, certainly not out of any genuine concern for him. Their relationships with him were gossamer and transitive, established and maintained through Jenny. The same went for Jenny's parents and brother, with whom he'd been cordial but who'd never known quite what to make of him. Now she was gone.

He himself didn't have many friends. Not close ones. It was a truth that didn't disturb him in the least. He viewed it with the objectivity of a scientist observing a squirming microbe under a laboratory microscope.

He withdrew his hands from his pockets and turned his attention from the sky back to Jenny's grave.

Like a black hole, its darkness seemed to defy the shimmering day, sucking in the surrounding sunlight. Or perhaps repelling it. He stared hard into the opening, peering into the dimness. He could just make out his wife's coffin, which gleamed the dull silver of a bullet.

He was seized with a wild urge to throw himself into the hole and grab the coffin; to pound on its cold, unyielding shell and scream his throat raw; to wrap his arms around it and hug it to his chest and wait for the indifferent earth to bury them both.

Because, really, what else mattered now?

Something moved in his peripheral vision.

A man, bald and short and thick, inched forward from a gleaming black Town Car parked on a nearby road. He cleared his throat.

"Mr. Finney?" His voice was reedy yet carried clearly. He and the tall man were the only living souls now remaining in this section of the cemetery.

The tall man lifted his chin and inclined his head to one side.

The thick man coughed. "Mr. Finney. You have that, ah, meeting. In forty-five minutes. At the Salk." He tapped his wristwatch. "Just wanted to, uh, remind you."

Finney did not turn around, or speak. He kept his head tilted toward the horizontal, as if he were in the aisle of a supermarket, casually holding up a cereal box to inspect its list of ingredients.

The man reeks of cigarettes, Finney thought. *He was specifically instructed that I hate cigarettes.*

Finney watched him out of the corner of his eye. The seconds ticked by. Perspiration gathered across the thick man's bare skull and glinted in the sun. The man cleared his throat, as if to speak again, then seemed to think the better of it. He retreated to the car, wheezing.

Finney straightened his head back to the vertical, so that his chin was once again aligned with his neck. Although he'd never been predisposed to quick anger, or rash thoughts, Jenny's death had kindled in him an emotional brittleness, worsened by his hopeless incapacity to process the cauldron of feelings that had simmered deep in his psyche since she'd been taken from him. Rage, raw as an open wound, bubbled over from inside him and threatened to consume him.

He drew a deep breath and held it.

Finney was not given to cliché. He, in fact, hated cliché. So he was surprised when the first coherent thought to pop into his mind as the thick man waddled away was *I'm going to kill him*: a sentiment that was, of course, a cliché.

He forced the air out of his lungs and seized that thought. Flipped it around in his mind. Mentally hefted it, turned it this way and that, considered its substance.

I'm going to kill him.

In an instant, his anger over the thick man's stupendous idiocy had turned to curiosity.

I'm going to kill him?

People casually uttered that phrase all the time, without thought or conviction. As in, *if he shows up late again for work, I'm going to kill him.* It was a sitcom catchphrase or a throwaway line for cheap villains in summer movies. It meant nothing. No substance. All cliché.

But was it really, at this moment? For him?

Because Finney knew, with the absolute certainty of a man who had grown rich from being absolutely certain about things, that at this moment he really *did* want to kill the thick man.

This insight fascinated him. He was a law-abiding citizen, after all. Well, *mostly* law-abiding. Certainly not given to thoughts of premeditated homicide. From what dark corner of his mind had this urge sprung?

The immediacy of his conviction, its vividness and power, intrigued him. Finney didn't believe in the existence of God. But if he did, he would at this moment invoke God to witness the fact that he wanted nothing more than to wrap his fingers around the man's fat throat and squeeze, really *squeeze*, until his fingers disappeared into the folds of skin, as if they'd slipped beneath fleshy quicksand; and he felt the man's windpipe crack, and heard the gratifying, high-pitched gasp of his final, foul breath.

It was an odd sensation. Not simply rage, anymore, or indignation over the man's appalling disrespect, even as Jenny was about to disappear into the ground forever.

No.

It seemed to him something greater, far more consequential: as if the mere existence of this squat, nicotine-addled creature had somehow tipped the universe out of balance, and it was Finney's mission—no, his *burden*—to right the order of things.

Finney's emotions were something that he'd always experienced from a distance, from the outside in, like they were fish in an aquarium, and he was viewing them from the other side of thick-paned glass; so it was rather like he watched, instead of felt, the murderous urge slip away, disappearing beneath the murky surface of his subconscious. It did so slowly, as if reluctant to give up its grasp on him.

He sighed.

Order.

Or a lack thereof.

Maybe that's what it was that was bothering him so much, that had been eating away at him, chewing on his insides, at all times of day and night over the last week. He hadn't slept in days, and he was exhausted. Jenny's death had set askew the natural order of things, and he sensed the unbalance in the universe around him. Newton's Third Law at work: Her death was the action, and cosmic disequilibrium the reaction.

He would have to settle for firing the thick man, who had only recently started working for him, and ensuring he never again achieved any professional rank above that of graveyard-shift janitor. The man otherwise wasn't worth the mental effort: not a single additional electrical impulse fired in a single neuron of Finney's brain.

Besides, as much as he repulsed Finney, the thick man was not responsible for Jenny's death.

That distinction belonged to another.

Because, really, what else mattered now?

The grief crashed over him without warning. It was as if his grief were a dense, poisonous liquid, and he was drowning in it, tumbling and spinning, helpless and sick. The familiar feeling, the *hated* feeling, rose in his throat.

He was going to cry.

He closed his eyes and balled his hands into fists, fighting the tears, as he had done repeatedly since her death. Even so, he felt them pooling in the corners of his eyes. Soon, here in the bright sunlight, in front of the thick man and the world, he would be sobbing like some pathetic child.

He could not, he *would not*, let that happen. He squeezed his eyelids and fists together harder.

Morgan.

He stirred.

It was Jenny, her voice as distinct and clear as if she were standing right next to him.

Jenny told him it was okay to cry.

He knew that it was the kind of thing that in life she would have encouraged him to do. Out of the mouths of lesser women, such advice would have sounded trite—the pedestrian psychobabble of daytime talk-show hosts and banal self-help books. But not from Jenny. Never from her.

It's okay, she whispered.

He thought it over. Should he cry? Do what she'd empowered him to do when she was still alive? Acknowledge all of his emotions: the good and the bad? As she would surely want him to do now if she were standing here at his side?

But Jenny wasn't here. Not really. And as much as he loved her—*had* loved her, he corrected himself—he was finished with these foolish sentiments. For good. He would no longer wallow in self-pity, as if he were some pig rooting through the foul muck of its pen.

No.

He *had* to be done with them. Because emotions were weak. Because acknowledging them meant he would never escape the searing pain of her loss. He needed to purge himself of this ridiculous mawkishness.

His fingernails had grown long and firm during the distraction and grief of the past several weeks, through her illness and its bleak finale, and they bit into the soft skin of his palms. It hurt.

It hurt a lot.

Good.

He made slight scraping motions with his fingers to force the nails deeper, drawing blood as he felt them break the surface of the skin, and concentrated on the physical pain to distract himself from the psychological.

Morgan.

She sounded more distant now.

In a way, it should be straightforward. Like closing a business deal, or solving an engineering problem. He just needed to approach things analytically: think it through with the precision, the elegance, of a mathematical equation. He would refocus his energies, redirect these irritating emotions into more meaningful and productive pursuits. But what kinds?

Scrape, scrape, scrape. His fingernails sunk into the compliant flesh. His clenched hands shook. He could feel his palms becoming slick with blood. He pictured it oozing through the gaps between his fingers and dripping onto the ground beneath him. Red dew drops on green grass.

The revelation came to him in a moment of sudden, perfect clarity.

Of course.

The answer was simple.

The grief receded, limping away like a wounded animal.

He relaxed his fists and opened his eyes. The urge to cry was gone. He examined with indifference the four crimson streaks running in series across each of his palms: the eight fingernail-inflicted stigmata trickling tiny red rivulets. He drew a handkerchief out of his pants pocket, wiped his hands clean of the blood, and dropped the soiled handkerchief on the ground, not knowing, or caring, who would pick it up.

He listened for Jenny.

Nothing.

Because, really, what else mattered now?

There was, actually, one thing.

A singular task that required his attention.

A task to which he would bend every fiber of his psyche until completed.

He removed a small notebook from his suit-coat

pocket. It was old, with a worn, black-leather cover. Most of its pages were covered in writing. Some had been carefully scotch-taped to preserve their integrity. He flipped toward the back, to the first blank page, and drew a mechanical pencil from the same pocket. He clicked the pencil three times to extend the thin cylinder of lead beyond the tip of its sheath.

He began to write.

He bore down hard. Twice, the pencil lead snapped. Twice, he replaced the leading edge with three sharp reports—*click, click, click*—of the mechanical pencil. He wrote slowly and with exacting penmanship. When he was finished, he inspected the name he had written.

Dr. Rita Wu.

He stared at it for a moment, then drew an empty box next to her name, as if she were an entry on a to-do list. He closed the notebook and returned both it and the mechanical pencil to his coat pocket.

I'm going to kill her.

And he knew, with absolute certainty, that he would.

But first he would make her suffer.

The way Jenny suffered.

And he would rob her of something precious.

The way I've been robbed of something precious.

And balance would return to the universe.

Finney turned and walked back to the car, beside which the thick man waited.

He did not look back.

One Year Later

RITA

There was darkness.

And then there was her name.

"Dr. Wu?"

A voice probed the dark, cleaving it like a search-light. The darkness was familiar and, in its familiarity, comforting; the voice, intrusive and discordant, was not. Rita drew away from it and embraced the dark, as if she were a little girl pressing herself against her mother's leg.

But the voice would have none of it.

"Dr. Wu?" It was a woman.

Darkness still, but sensations were resolving themselves, bit by bit, from nothing.

"Do you want me to go get some help?" A second voice, also female. Breathier. Huskier.

"No. She's breathing. And she's warm. She's just asleep. Grab some blankets, though, will you?"

"Okay." Receding footsteps. A crisp, artificial *click*,

like someone tugging on the latch of a refrigerator. A puff of warm of air.

. . . sounds like an operating-room blanket warmer . . .

Approaching footsteps. "Got some."

"Dr. Wu?"

A hand was on her shoulder, nudging her toward consciousness. There was a thick, coppery taste in her mouth, as if she'd been sucking on pennies, and a pain in her head, enveloping her left temple and snaking toward her left ear. Without opening her eyes, she perceived that she was lying flat on her back, on a padded surface. Her arms were lying at her sides.

"Dr. Wu?" The hand shaking her shoulder applied more pressure.

Rita opened her eyes. The darkness surrendered itself to blinding brightness. The pain in her head blossomed into an agony—an ice pick driving its way through her left eye and punching its way out the back of her skull.

She gasped. God, how it *hurt*. The light was a rabid dog clawing at her eyes. She squeezed them shut and groaned. Her stomach lurched, as if the light had reached through her eye sockets, down her throat, and given her gut a good, hard tug.

Oh, God.

"Dr. Wu?" The first voice, which a dim recess of her clouded brain now registered as familiar, sounded worried, but also more insistent. "Are you okay?" Pause. "Can I help you?"

The pain made it difficult for her to concentrate. *No, not just the pain.* Something else, too. Her brain was a jumbled slurry of inputs and outputs, scrambled up in a way that pain alone could not explain, as if all of her trains of thought had been dumped into a blender at high speed.

Why? some part of her mind asked.

Who cares? another replied.

She let herself slide back toward the void.

"Dr. Wu." Commanding now, and louder. Unconsciousness, inviting as it was, was no longer an option.

Rita opened her eyes and groaned, squinting against the light.

"Wendy," said the first voice. "Move the spotlight out of her face."

"Sure," said the breathy woman.

The light dimmed and, with it, the pain in her head.

Rita blinked and looked at the anxious face peering into hers. In a more alert state, she might have been surprised. Astounded, even. But all she could muster now was a vague sense of puzzlement.

Lisa Rodriguez, one of her operating-room nurses, was the owner of both the first voice and the hand now resting reassuringly on Rita's shoulder. Lisa wasn't, of course, *hers* in the strict sense of the word. But Rita, like many surgeons, used possessive pronouns to describe people and things in the operating rooms she supervised. *Her* nurses. *Her* patients. *Her* surgical instruments.

Lisa was standing next to her. Or, rather, *over* her, as if Rita were one of her own patients, stretched out on a table in her operating room, over which she and Lisa traded scalpels and gossip most working days.

What's going on?

Lisa's blunt features, framed by a pale blue surgical cap that corralled her curly black hair, registered equal parts astonishment and concern.

Standing behind her, and to one side, was another woman, also an OR nurse—

(*Wendy*)

—a skinny young woman with a long face. A single tuft of blond hair, glowing with a peroxide lacquer, poked out from underneath her blue cap and tumbled halfway down her forehead. With her puffy, bouffant surgical cap and emaciated frame, she looked like a mop standing on end. She was carrying some folded white blankets, tucked under one of her arms.

Wendy looked just as astonished as Lisa but not nearly as concerned.

In fact, something less seemly seemed to flicker behind Wendy's eyes (*pleasure? glee?*), which were as blue as her surgical cap and ringed by turquoise eye shadow. Both women were dressed in dark blue scrubs.

Just like the scrubs we wear in the operating room.

"Lisa?" God, she could barely form the word. Her tongue was concrete.

Where am I?

Without sitting up, Rita turned her head to one side and spotted dark floor tiles lying about three feet below her. She turned her head to the other side and saw the same thing. She concluded, dully, that she was lying on some kind of padded surface suspended off the floor at about waist height.

She started to sit up . . .

. . . but something circling her chest, something flat and broad, seized her and yanked her back down again.

"Hey."

The rear of her head snapped down on the padded mat. *Ouch!* The impact worsened her headache, and she moved her hands up to cradle her aching forehead.

Or tried to.

But she couldn't.

Because her arms were pinned to her sides.

"*Hey!*"

A new emotion. Not panic—her senses were still too blunted to generate panic—but Rita felt an abrupt unease that raised her from one level of semiconsciousness to a slightly-less-semi one; and she perceived, for the first time, that she lacked all control over her current situation. Rita *hated* not being in control. Ever. She struggled to free her arms.

"Here," Lisa said. "Let me help you, Dr. Wu."

She watched as Lisa, in one smooth motion, reached down to Rita's side and grasped a shiny metallic buckle through which wound a black band. It looked like an enormous seat belt. Lisa lifted the buckle and loosened the black band, which was pinning Rita's torso and arms to the foam pads she was lying on.

Funny, Rita thought, as Lisa pulled the band free from the buckle and freed her from the pads. *It looks just like the restraining straps we use to secure patients to our operating-room tables.*

Another coincidence. Like the blue scrubs.

A moment later, as Lisa loosened a second black strap binding her thighs, Rita realized, with an uneasy swirl of emotions, that it *was* one of the restraining straps for an operating-room table.

The same table on which she was now lying.

"*What?*" Rita straightened her head and tipped her chin to her chest to stare at her feet.

That was when she noticed she wasn't wearing any clothes.

Dr. Rita Wu, an assistant professor of surgery at the University of California, was strapped to an operating-room table.

Naked as the day she was born.

Without the faintest idea of how she'd gotten there.

SPENCER

Spencer Cameron stepped outside, closed his front door, and breathed in the early-morning air of late November in coastal San Diego. It was still dark, but faint red-and-orange embers licked the sky behind the mountains to the east.

The predawn temperatures were cool, and Spencer wore black, full-length running tights with fluorescent-yellow reflectors stitched down the sides and a lightweight, black athletic shirt equipped with similar reflectors along its long sleeves. The skintight fabric strained against his massive chest, shoulders, and thighs as he stretched out his limbs and torso. He slipped headphones in his ears, tuned his iPod to NPR, and adjusted his knit running beanie over his curly, dark brown hair so as to shield the exposed portions of his ears and scalp from the mild chill. He took off at an easy jog down the street.

A stout, middle-aged woman walking a small brown

dog of indeterminate breed appeared, heading in the opposite direction. She jumped back and froze as Spencer lumbered toward her. The dog, in contrast, seemed to decide that the best defense was a good offense: No larger than a good-sized rabbit, it lunged at him, drawing its leash taunt and yipping in the high, piercing frequency of small dogs.

Spencer stifled a scowl—he didn't love dogs, especially microscopic ones that disturbed the peace of his early-morning runs—but waved gamely.

See? I'm friendly!

He didn't recognize the woman or her dog. But that wasn't unexpected. Although he'd lived here for years, there were plenty of folks in the neighborhood he hadn't yet gotten around to meeting. His grueling work schedule—early mornings, late nights, and long days sandwiched between them—didn't make it easy.

"Good morning!" he called, flashing a cheery smile.

The woman, bundled in a bulky grey sweatshirt embroidered with a University of Southern California logo, acknowledged him with a slight nod but remained rooted in place and looked at him askance as he passed, holding her dog at bay. Furious, the dog scrambled along the perimeter of its leash, growling truculently and straining in vain to launch itself at Spencer.

In a parting gesture of amity, he cut the woman and her dog an extrawide berth, smiling and waving one last time, before refocusing on his run. He didn't blame the woman—or her pet rat, for that matter—one bit. Even in broad daylight, his immense frame routinely attracted curious stares, and he pictured how he must have appeared from their perspective: a man big enough to be an NFL lineman, clad in black and wearing a knit skullcap, charging at them out of the early-morning shadows of an otherwise deserted street.

Aside from the dog lady, the neighborhood was still, and he was alone. As his muscles limbered up, he pushed the pace, accelerating to a brisk trot. He needed to. He was still in pretty decent shape, but it had never been easy for him to keep the paunch at bay, even back in the old days, and it was only getting harder now that he was closing in on forty.

He swerved to the left to avoid a row of trash cans at the curb, changing his heading by pushing off with his right leg. His right knee protested with a twinge of discomfort that fell just short of outright pain. That knee had been acting up recently.

Should probably get it looked at.

A sagging midline and creaky joints.

Old-man problems.

In his headphones, a newscaster was recapping the morning's headlines: bland iterations of the ones from the day before, with little or no bearing on his life. The newscaster's voice faded into so much white noise. His mind wandered.

Forty years old.

Had it really snuck up on him this quickly? That was the problem with being a doctor: By the time you soldiered through your education and training, and finally found a real job, it was practically time to retire. All told, his own training had taken him, what . . . twelve years? But he loved neurosurgery, from the time he was a kid he'd wanted to be a brain surgeon, so his sacrifices had always struck him as irrelevant. He didn't even think of them as sacrifices. They were choices, his choices, and he didn't regret them. He didn't believe in second guesses. Monday morning quarterbacking was worthless.

And yet.

Second guesses and doubts were what lately had been slipping into his head. They nibbled at his psyche, exhorted him to reconsider some of his irrational life choices. The ones he'd made in his love life.

The ones about Rita.

But what *wasn't* irrational about love?

It had been nearly a year now, one year since she'd clawed his heart out of his chest for no apparent reason other than that she could. People said time healed all wounds. *What a crock.* Time healed *nothing.* But was a year time enough, if not for healing, to at least accept the way things were? To acknowledge that Rita really *was* done with him and for him to move on with his life?

Rita.

Spencer couldn't help but envy his friends who'd shifted smoothly into the next phases of their lives. Sometimes, alone late at night on his phone, after a few beers, Spencer would scroll through pictures of his friends' young families on Facebook. There were always *firsts.* Lots of them. First smile. First steps. First day of ballet class. First day of soccer. First day of school.

Spencer, single and sad and loyal, pointed and clicked, liking each and every one.

Rita.

UNDER THE KNIFE   21

But wait. He had his *freedom*. Right? He could do whatever the hell he wanted, whenever the hell he wanted. He wasn't tied down. He didn't have a steady girlfriend. He got to play the field. He was living the dream. *Right?* Isn't that what all guys were supposed to want?

After all, forty was when the other guys who'd settled down were supposed to flip into midlife-crisis mode. Rage against conformity. Ditch the wife and kids. Have a fling with a pretty little thing just this side of statutory. Buy a really cool car. Wear skinny jeans.

But Spencer liked conformity. He craved normality. He went to church on Sunday; paid his taxes every April; visited his parents back in their small town in Washington State every Thanksgiving, Christmas, and Easter; bought Girl Scout cookies once a year from the uniformed girls staked out in front of the supermarket, then bought some more from their mothers selling them at work. These things made him happy.

Nor was he the kind of guy who'd ever run out on a family. He'd be grateful to have a family. What he wouldn't give to post pictures on Facebook of his own smiling, walking, dancing, soccer-playing, school-age children.

He could indulge himself in an attractive young woman, he supposed. He was a good-looking guy—he wasn't vain about it, or anything, but it presented certain advantages he wasn't going to ignore. He lived and worked near the local college, so there were plenty of nubile coeds running around. One lithe, flirtatious barista at his neighborhood Starbucks, with glorious coffee-colored eyes and sheets of lustrous chocolaty hair, had made her intentions pretty clear. But she looked like she was barely out of her teens, if that. She belonged with a guy her own age.

And the really cool car? Well, that would just be plain irresponsible. Why waste that kind of money? He was perfectly happy with his nice, practical, environmentally sound Toyota Prius, thanks.

And trendy skinny jeans were not an option. Even if he had the inclination to try to squeeze into a pair, which he most certainly did not, his thighs were each as big around as a tree trunk.

That's all great, Spencer. Good for you. So, let me in on a little secret, Dudley Do-Right: If you're such a boring, stand-up citizen, what the hell are you doing stalking your ex-girlfriend? The one who told you she wants nothing more to do with you?

He gritted his teeth.

It's not stalking, he answered himself. *Not really.*

Is it?

He was sweating now, and his scalp itched underneath his knit cap. His chest and legs burned, but it was a pleasant burn. There was a nice onshore breeze, rich and moist, carrying with it the scent of the Pacific, half a mile away. He inhaled deeply, savoring it, timing it with the controlled breathing of his run.

A car turned onto the street ahead. It accelerated away from him, careening from one side of the street to the other, coughing newspapers from its open passenger-side window, the driver a dark silhouette.

Spencer, who preferred to read his news on his phone, didn't understand the appeal of newspapers, which were supposed to have gone the way of the dodo

by now. It astonished him how many of his neighbors
still insisted on having one delivered. The final pay-
load, tossed to a home just short of an intersection at
which the car cornered hard to the left before speeding away, fell short of the driveway, landing in the
gutter.

The home was a cozy, Mediterranean-style one-
story with native Southern California landscaping
and cheerful red-ceramic roof tiles. On his morning
runs, Spencer always passed by it; on days he didn't
run, he altered his driving route to include this street,
just to drive by it, even though other routes were faster.

Because it was Rita's house.

He sighed to himself.

So maybe it *was* stalking. Kind of.

He frowned.

Something about Rita's house this morning felt
wrong.

RITA

"Lisa," Rita croaked. Rita hugged herself and struggled to sit up. She felt something small and cold and
metallic, hanging on a chain from her neck, knock
against her bare chest.

Her father's dog tags.

So she wasn't *completely* naked.

She lurched to one side, almost toppling off the
table.

"Careful." Lisa grabbed her by the arm and helped
her to a sitting position. "Hey, Wendy." The blond-haired

nurse was standing a few feet away, still holding the folded blankets and gaping at Rita. "*Wendy.*"

"What?" Wendy asked distractedly.

Rita's teeth began to chatter.

"The *blankets*, Wendy."

"Oh. Right. The blankets." She handed both blankets to Lisa, oblivious to Lisa's glare.

Lisa snapped each blanket open with a practiced flick of her wrists, then wrapped one around Rita's shoulders and chest and the other across her midsection.

"Thank you." Rita huddled within the blankets, grateful for the warmth. Her shivering slowed, then stopped. She pressed her hand to her aching head, rubbed her temples with her fingers, and tried to scrape together her thoughts, which felt like leaves tumbling in the wind.

"What's going on?" said Rita.

"I—well, I was going to ask you the same question, Dr. Wu. Are you all right?"

I don't know. Am I?

"I'm . . . Where am I?"

Lisa and Wendy exchanged a look.

"Room 10," said Lisa.

"Room 10. Room . . . 10. You mean . . . in the operating room? *My* operating room? At Turner?"

"Yes."

"What am I doing here?"

Wendy looked at Lisa, and Lisa looked at Rita.

"I don't . . . I mean, we just found you lying here, Dr. Wu, with the lights out. This morning. When we came in for work. Scared me half to death." Lisa paused. "How long have you been here?"

"What time is it?"

"A little after six in the morning."

"What . . ." Rita licked her lips. They were dry, and scraped against her tongue like sandpaper. "What . . . uh, day?"

Wendy made a gargling sound that resembled a gasp. Lisa pursed her lips. "Monday. It's Monday, Dr. Wu. November 27."

"When did you get here?" Lisa said. "Did you . . . *sleep* here?"

Fragments of Rita's memory were pulling together now, bits and pieces starting to form a picture.

I remember coming here last night, on Sunday the twenty-sixth. I came here to check on the auto-surgeon.

"Dr. Wu." Lisa leaned in close. Rita could smell her shampoo, or conditioner, or whatever it was; some kind of flower scent. "Are you okay?"

Rita tasted bile in the back of her throat and swallowed it back down.

"I'm fine." No, she wasn't. She was a pretty long way from fine. She glanced around, trying to gain a better feel for her situation, to process what exactly was going on. But her thoughts were fuzzy and insubstantial, like cotton candy. She felt—

(*hungover she felt hungover but that was* IMPOSSIBLE *she couldn't be hungover because she didn't drink she hadn't had a drink for over a year*)

—like she was going to throw up.

How the hell to process all this? So many different things at once: surreal; crazy; humiliating. She didn't know where to begin. A part of her (okay, *most* of her) wanted to run screaming from the room. Two nurses had just found her passed out on her own operating-room table, *naked*, and she couldn't remember how she'd gotten here.

Situational awareness.

She needed situational awareness. That's what her father would have called it.

Her father.

She reached up and touched her father's dog tags, which dangled around her neck. He'd been a pilot, flying a P-3 Orion for the U.S. Navy all over the Pacific hunting Russian and Chinese subs. He'd talked about situational awareness a lot, especially with his pilot buddies, in her family's backyard, where they'd swapped stories and grilled in the cool Southern California dusk, some still wearing their olive-green one-piece flight suits.

In her mind, she still smelled the grill smoke, drifting across their tiny backyard, heavy with hamburger juice and beer hops. *Situational awareness.* She'd heard her father and his buddies banter the term around so much that she'd finally looked it up one day in junior high, in one of the aviation textbooks in her dad's study. Not too long before he'd died.

Situational awareness: the ability to calmly assess a dynamic, dangerous environment and determine appropriate responses to avert disaster.

She liked that. She hadn't understood it, not at first, but she'd liked it so much that she wrote it down on a small piece of paper she carried around with her. She'd pull it out of her pocket every once in a while and read it to herself. In time, she memorized it, and thought she began to understand it, and applied it to lots of different things. Cross-country meets. Driving. Walking alone at night between her dorm and the college library.

And, eventually, to surgery.

The ability to calmly assess a dynamic, dangerous environment and determine appropriate responses to avert disaster.

In the OR, Rita thought of it as the delicate art of preventing big chunks of shit from colliding with big fans. She knew she was good at it. Very good. It was something she prided herself on, a skill that had guided her out of some tough scrapes in the OR over the years. She believed in it, heart and soul.

Still, when all was said and done, situational awareness hadn't helped her father out much when his plane ran into that mountain.

What was going through his mind, seeing that mountainside fill the cockpit windshield an instant before oblivion? Had he had time to calmly assess the environment?

She hoped not. She preferred to think that he didn't have time to see it coming, because that way he wouldn't have had time to feel fear or to worry about the daughters he was about to leave behind.

And this situation, the one she was in now: Was it her mountain, filling the cockpit window?

She shivered again, but not from cold, and rubbed the goose bumps that were sprouting on her forearms despite the blankets.

Panic: It felt like some sinister vine unfurling up from her belly, moist tendrils thickening and tightening in all directions. She knew that, in a few seconds, if she didn't do something to stop it, the spreading panic would choke off her capacity for reason, leaving her with only the urge to run screaming from the room.

She took another deep breath, closed her eyes, reached up with one hand, and grasped her father's dog tags.

Don't panic.

Not now.

Not *ever.*

Instinct told her, practically screamed into her face, that something huge was at stake here, that one false step now would leave her *well and truly screwed, lovely Rita.*

Leave it to weaker women (*or men*) to fold. Completely lose it. Start weeping, maybe, or slide into some catatonic state. Not her.

She was *not* weak, had *never* been weak.

No weakness.

She seized on that thought.

No weakness.

SPENCER

Spencer squinted into the gloaming ahead.

The car.

That's what was wrong. It was still there.

That piece-of-crap white Ford Fiesta, parked squarely in front of Rita's house. The one that had first shown up last week.

Whose car is that?

He'd been on vigil over her house for the last year. He knew every car on her street, had memorized their comings and goings, and which ones belonged to which houses. Before it had appeared five days ago, he'd never seen this car. Ever.

So whose was it?

Probably nothing. A car belonging to someone visiting a neighbor, maybe. And yet some indefinable thing about the piece-of-crap Fiesta bugged him. Why? Maybe because in this upscale neighborhood of upscale foreign cars in car-centric Southern California, piece-of-crap Fiestas—piece of crap *anythings*—stuck out like sore thumbs. Or maybe because, with plenty of empty spaces around the other houses, why was the Fiesta the only one parked in front of *her* house?

He slowed, then stopped as he reached her darkened house. He picked up the newspaper in the gutter and lobbed it into the driveway, in which Rita parked her late-model BMW. The driveway was empty.

She must already be at the hospital.

Rita usually left for work early, even by surgeon standards, and surgeons started their days while most everyone else was still in bed. Today was Monday, and he knew that Rita operated on Mondays. When operating, Rita liked to arrive at the hospital no later than 6:00 A.M.— a habit, he knew, that helped her feel focused and calm before her operations.

Today, Rita also had that big operation, the one everyone was talking about—with the new, automated surgical system. She'd been working her fingers to the bone on that for years. She was probably already at work to get a jump on what was going to be one of the biggest days of her career.

A stand of bushes near the front door shook, and a fat grey cat emerged from them. No, not a cat: an opossum. A big one, its long, ratlike tail trailing behind as it waddled onto the front sidewalk, sniffing at the ground. Spencer spotted them around the neighborhood from time to time, at night. He wasn't squeamish but didn't like them, with their big black eyes and creepy tails. The feeling appeared mutual: the opossum spotted Spencer and hissed through a mouthful of sharp teeth before shuffling back into the bushes.

He studied the Fiesta for a few moments before breaking back into a run. He didn't want to appear as if loitering, or draw attention to himself by lurking in the dark outside her home. Neighbors talked. Besides, he was probably just being paranoid.

But was he?

He craned his neck around for one last glimpse before turning a corner.

Forget it.

But he couldn't. The Fiesta had latched onto his thoughts like a tick.

The road he was running along bent right, to the north, for another half mile. Then the houses on the left abruptly gave way to an empty embankment that sloped steeply down away from him, and the onshore breeze stiffened.

He'd arrived at the ocean.

Up ahead was one of the local surf spots. Here, sand and rock greeted the Pacific in violent collisions of spray and sound. The waves were enormous; and the local newscaster in his ear was reporting that a storm churning offshore was expected to hit San Diego later today.

The surfers, too, had heard about the storm and the monstrous waves announcing its impending arrival. A crowd of them was up ahead, milling around on the ocean side of the street: men and women of varying ages, from sleek preteens sneaking in a quick surf before school to leathery and lean middle-agers. Many were squeezing into black neoprene wet suits and pulling surfboards from the beds of pickup trucks or off specialized racks mounted on the tops of their cars. Others were arriving on skateboards and bikes, their boards tucked under their arms. The ones not already paddling out into the thunderous surf gathered in eager clumps on an elevated vantage point in a little beachside park, nursing cups of steaming coffee and gaping at the undulating ocean. Occasionally, one would point out a particularly choice wave, and the rest would hoot.

Spencer had never understood the appeal of surfing, which to so many in San Diego equated to a religious experience. To him it seemed like a cult. He'd tried it a few times. It was fun enough, he supposed, but couldn't see the big deal.

Still, he *could* appreciate that those were some big-ass waves, and that big-ass California waves often heralded big-ass California storms. Case in point: The newscaster was now speaking of flash-flood and mud-slide warnings.

Will be a good night to stay indoors.

He left the surfers behind. The sound of crashing

waves diminished as his route followed the coast north, then turned east, back toward his modest house a mile inland.

His right knee was hurting now, not just acting up—a minor jolt of pain shot up his leg with every third or fourth step.

This was new. Where had it come from?

Forty. That's where, idiot. You're getting old, Spencer.

So what was causing it? Bursitis, maybe? Medial collateral ligament strain? Stress fracture?

Gotta get that looked at.

He glanced at his watch. He had surgery this morning at Turner, and he wanted to squeeze in some free weights and push-ups before showering and changing for work.

He ignored the pain in his knee—and the mental image of the Fiesta in front of Rita's—and ran faster.

RITA

Rita's first code—not the first one she ran, but the first one she saw—was carved into the circuitry of her brain, an event as indelible as any she'd known.

Because it was the first time she realized she wanted to be a surgeon.

She clung now to that memory with a fierceness that made her think of a movie she once saw about fishermen (one of them was George Clooney) caught in a monster storm out in the middle of the ocean. Like she was one of those guys, flung overboard, flailing in the mountainous waves; and the memory was a life preserver thrown from the ship, the one tiny thing in the universe preventing her lungs from filling with icy water and dragging her to the bottom of the North Atlantic.

As the memory took shape, it began to crowd out her panic, filling her mind with the sights and sounds of this singular occurrence in her life.

She'd been a third-year med student, fresh out of the classroom and terrified by the prospect of treating real, honest-to-God patients. She'd been working a twenty-four-hour shift, the very first time she'd spent the night in a hospital, and it was late at night. Or maybe early in the morning: Who could tell after sixteen-plus hours of scrambling from one perplexing task to the next, one far-flung corner of the hospital to the other, with barely time for a pee break? No exaggeration. She was having trouble finding sixty seconds for a routine biological function she'd always taken for granted.

I mean, who doesn't have time to pee?

She'd been screamed at by a brilliant but scary female cardiology professor who told Rita she was just *too damn timid, for God's sake* and asked her if that *was, like, an Asian-girl thing or something*; urinated on while trying to put a bladder catheter in a semiconscious drunk; felt up by a leering, ninety-year-old bed-bound troll pretending (she was sure) to have dementia; and almost impaled by an intern fumbling with a hypodermic needle as thick around as a broom handle.

Then, when she'd finally stolen a minute to put her head down, she'd gotten lost looking for the student sleeping room. *God*, but she'd been tired. She'd begun to understand why sleep deprivation was used as torture. Even waterboarding, she'd reflected, had to be easier than this. She was spent, emotionally strung out, and wondering if she'd made the right career choice.

So there she was, wandering the hospital in the middle of an interminable night (morning?) *looking for a bed like a zombie hunting for human flesh, when she heard it.*

Shouting.

Down a corridor lined on both sides by patient rooms. Loud and desperate, with one voice rising above the others, shrieking with pain.

She stopped and looked down the hall. Her muscles and joints, every part of her, groaned with fatigue. But she was curious. What could trigger that kind of yelling in the middle of the night in a hospital?

Curiosity won out. She turned and followed the noise to a patient's room down the hall. She peeked inside.

Her exhaustion disappeared.

The room was crammed with a dozen raw recruits of the medical world. Junior residents and interns. Young nurses barely out of school. Fellow med students. Not an experienced doctor in sight—not surprising, really, because in the hierarchy of medicine, what person in their right mind with any seniority would be working at that hour?

All were pressed together around a patient's bed. Through the thicket of bodies, she caught glimpses of a small, brown man with snow-white hair—about fifty, maybe? Hard to tell, because he gave the impression of a younger person who looked much older.

His eyes.

That's what she remembered most. The whites turned dirty yellow (Jaundice, *she'd thought to herself,* it's called jaundice, a sign of liver failure), *and wide with terror. His shrieks had been the ones carrying down the hall.*

He was lying on the bed, writhing and screaming in a foreign language, several gloved pairs of hands trying to restrain him. His flimsy hospital gown slipped off his shoulders to reveal an abdomen swollen to the size of a basketball and a neat, vertical line of metallic staples that ran like a zipper from his sternum to his belly button, marking the site of a recent surgical incision.

The man interrupted his howling long enough to vomit bright red blood, which splattered across his bare chest in a pattern that reminded Rita of the finger paintings on display in the lobby of the children's hospital next door.

She looked away, repelled; then, intrigued in the way of a driver slowing to get a better look at a traffic accident, pushed her way into the room. The air was heavy with odors: sweat, urine, feces, ammonia. A young doctor she judged to be an internal medicine resident stood at the head of the bed, squeaking instructions to the interns and nurses. He seemed more scared than the patient. He had an adolescent whisper of chin hair and a brush of acne highlighting his cheeks, as if a kindergartner had streaked red crayon across them.

The interns and nurses did their best to follow Dr. Acne's instructions. All kinds of things were going on

that Rita didn't understand. None looked good: needles jabbed into veins, wires connected to electrodes,
IV bags of medicine hung. The med students stood and
stared. Rita sensed that Dr. Acne and the interns
meant well but didn't have a clue. It had been the second week of July, right after med-school graduation,
and most of them, she knew, were almost as green at
this as she was.

Suddenly, the patient heaved a long, plaintive wail
and collapsed backward, unconscious, a thin stream
of blood dribbling from a corner of his mouth.

Dr. Acne froze, mouth agape, staring down at his
motionless charge. The room paused, collectively
holding its breath as everyone processed this: coma-
tose patient and dumbstruck leader. All eyes fixed on
Dr. Acne as they awaited further instructions.

None came.

And the room erupted then into chaos as everyone
just did what they thought might help, which involved
a lot of shouting and arm waving.

Rita was pushed to the side of the room by a mass
of bodies and pressed up against a wall. She remembered thinking that this was like watching a bunch of
ants swarm aimlessly after a petulant kid has stamped
on their hill: all frantic motion with no purpose.

Until another doctor swept into the room.

And changed everything.

Including the course of Rita's life.

The first thing she noticed about him was that he
was not tall—five-six, maybe, and shorter than Rita.
She could barely see the top of his head through the
crush of people.

But in her memory he was gigantic: a towering Greek demigod with brown hair that tumbled to his shoulders in thick waves and an impregnable air of confidence. The moment he'd stridden into the room, it was his.

Announcing himself as the chief surgical resident in charge of the patient, he divided the crowd like Moses parting the Red Sea, and emerged from the melee at the patient's bedside. In one smooth motion, he bodychecked Dr. Acne, who tumbled into the surrounding group with an expression of relief.

The surgeon folded his arms, looked coolly around, and within seconds had the undivided attention of every person in the room, which was now deathly still, save for the erratic rasps of the unconscious patient.

The room's attention thus commanded, he began to issue orders in a calm British accent, which, to her bland American ears, had made him sound really smart.

And really cool.

The room flew back into motion, but smoothly now, fluidly. She watched as he molded order from chaos, the junior doctors and nurses acting as a synchronized extension of his will. Under his command, you'd have thought they'd been doing this for years—an experienced, world-class orchestra responding to a renowned conductor.

Rita loved every moment of it: staring at him, mesmerized, studying every word, gesture, body movement. It dawned on her that someday, like that surgeon, she wanted to be the one in charge. She wanted to be him: the one person everyone else looked to. Unshakable. Imperturbable.

This, she realized, was what being a doctor was really all about. She could deal with all the other crap—bigoted professors and horny old men and exhaustion—if it meant that one day she got to do what this surgeon was doing.

Unfortunately, despite the renewed vigor of his treatment, the patient continued to spiral downward, and within minutes stopped breathing. The surgeon deftly slipped a breathing tube down his throat. The patient's heart stopped shortly thereafter.

Chest compressions commenced. Under pressure from them, the stitches and staples in his abdominal incision burst apart with a series of pops, the incision split open, and his intestines spilled onto his abdomen. Glistening and smooth, bathed in pink fluid (peritoneal fluid, Rita had recited sickly to herself), they'd convulsed in intermittent waves, like giant albino earthworms, until the surgeon barked an order, and someone covered them with a large sterile dressing moistened with saline.

That was enough for Rita. She was tough. But human intestines were just too much at that stage of her career.

She clapped a hand to her mouth and stumbled out the door. Out in the hall, she leaned against a wall and bent over, hands on her knees, breathing hard, until the nausea had passed. When she straightened up and looked around, she found herself alone. Everyone else was still in the room with the code.

So she was the only one who saw the surgeon emerge. He strode to a nearby sink, glanced over his

shoulder, and calmly threw up into the basin. Repeatedly. In great, heaving bursts.

She looked on, fascinated. It was an impressive
amount of puking. But more impressive was how quiet
he managed to be. She hadn't known it was possible
to empty one's stomach so violently yet so silently.

He went on like that for a while. When through, he'd
washed his hands, splashed water over his face, drank
out of the faucet, and turned around.

His eyes met Rita's.

He wiped his mouth with the back of his hand and
grinned. He had perfect teeth: two rows of gleaming
white enamel. He didn't seem the least bit embarrassed. Or ruffled.

He asked her name and what year of med school
she was in.

Mortified, she wondered how he knew she was a med
student. Was it that obvious? Did she look that clueless? That stupid? She ran her hands self-consciously
down her sides.

Oh. Right, she thought. The short white coat.

Only med students wore short white coats.

Rita told him her name.

"Rita. Lovely. Just like the Beatles song."

She felt heat rushing to her cheeks. That's exactly
what her father had always said. Lovely Rita, meter
maid. His eyes were an intense shade of bluish green,
like pictures you see of the Mediterranean; and he had
somehow managed not to get any vomit in his hair,
which was coifed, but not too coifed. Like a rock star.

A really cool rock star.

"Right. Well, Rita, you and I aren't missing anything out here," he said. "Because that poor man is certainly not going to pull through. I told them to keep at it for a while, though. Have a go at it. Good for them to practice."

He pointed at the sink into which he'd just puked.

"Touch of the flu," he said. "I know, I know." He waved his hand in the air dismissively. "I'm not supposed to be here. I should be home, in bed. I should at least be wearing a bloody mask. But that wouldn't exactly instill confidence in the troops now, would it?"

He tipped his perfectly dimpled chin toward the patient's room. "Can't have the doctor leading the whole bloody charge looking like he belongs in isolation on the TB ward."

He pulled a paper towel from the bin above the sink and wiped his mouth. "You see, Rita: we surgeons, when we get sick, we don't lie in bed, whining like small children. We get the job done." He grinned, a high-wattage affair that made her cheeks burn fiercely. "Right. Do you know what I'm going to do now, Rita?"

Rita shook her head.

"I'm going to steal an IV—a big one, fourteen- or sixteen-gauge—from the supply room and stick it in my arm." He pointed to the crook of his elbow (That's where the antecubital vein is, she remembered. We use it to give IV fluids). "Then I'm going to run a liter of LR into me."

(LR. Lactated Ringers. A hydration fluid.)

"Maybe two," he continued. "Surest way to replace fluids and stave off dehydration. Wouldn't you agree?"

To this, she didn't have a response.

He slid his hands in his pockets and leaned rakishly against the wall. "Are you interested in surgery, Rita?"

Rita replied indeed she was though she hadn't completed any surgery courses yet, and had never considered it before. But one of her fellow students had once advised her, in a hushed and conspiratorial tone, to always answer in the affirmative whenever a resident or attending asked if you were interested in their particular medical specialty. It helped your grade.

He nodded. "Do you think you have what it takes? To be a surgeon?"

Rita was a fierce—some who knew her well would even say insane—*competitor, and in college had been a nationally ranked cross-country runner for a Division I team. Back in college, puking during and after big races had been no big deal. She figured the same principle applied here.*

She said yes.

He sized her up, then nodded. "Brilliant. I'm going to tell you a secret. Do you know what the trick is? To being a surgeon? To being a truly good *surgeon?"*

She answered she didn't.

"Never look weak. That's it." He gestured toward the door of the patient's room, through which Dr. Acne and a trickle of others had started to emerge. "If they sense weakness, everything else falls apart."

Dr. Acne spotted him and began to walk over.

He smiled again at her, dazzlingly. "Never look weak, Rita."

She couldn't help herself: She giggled and returned the smile like she was some idiot teenager. The feminist in her looked on, appalled. She never giggled. Particularly for a boy.

"Right, then. Have a good evening, Rita."

She looked on as he gave a few final instructions to Dr. Acne—something about calling time of death, and death certificates—and then watched him stroll away.

She never found out his name and never saw him again. When she enrolled in her first surgery course, a few months later, he was gone.

But by the time he'd disappeared around a turn in the corridor, she'd decided then and there that she wanted to be a surgeon.

More than anything else she'd ever wanted.

Since then, she'd never looked back.

Never look weak.

With each passing year, for every tough situation Rita had found herself in, her appreciation for this essential truth grew. *Never look weak* meant maintaining your cool no matter what kind of crazy, dangerous stuff came through the door, since everyone—other doctors, nurses, patients—depended on you to stay calm.

Never look weak.

You couldn't teach it. You either had it, or you didn't.

And Rita *definitely* had it.

Which brought her back to her present predicament, the solution to which boiled down to those three words she'd learned in the middle of that night watching the surgery resident throw his guts up into a sink after trying to bring a patient back from the brink of death.

Never look weak.

Yes. It was that simple.

She was a *surgeon*.

She needed to get over whatever the hell was going on, to take command and seize the offensive. She hadn't gotten this far, been this successful, by being weak, or, God forbid, showing weakness to those around her. Ever. Instinct dictated that vulnerability equated to failure.

Never look weak.

She needed to come up with an explanation for her predicament. Something reasonably credible.

Disoriented or not, sick or not, naked or not.

Now.

FINNEY

If Finney were a lesser man, he would have perhaps allowed himself the satisfaction of a smile.

Just a small one, to savor the moment, to anticipate the fulfillment of plans a year in the making, and the rewards promised by the accomplishment, *finally*, of his goal.

But he was not a lesser man.

Self-congratulatory gestures were beneath him. His thin lips retained the geometric purity of a straight line as he spoke into the small microphone affixed to the collar of his shirt.

"Sebastian."

The response in his earpiece was immediate. "Here, boss."

"I need to temporarily cut your feed."

A beat. "Why?"

Finney liked Sebastian, insofar as he was capable of liking a man like him. Sebastian was good. Sebastian had come to him by way of the highest recommendations from discreet parties and had never failed to impress.

Truly, though, the man could be a royal pain in the ass sometimes. He had a tendency to ask the most exasperating questions and to forget his place. Like now. Why should it matter to Sebastian why Finney wanted to cut the feed?

"Because I want to, Sebastian."

I want to be alone with her.

"Are you sure, boss?"

"Yes."

"For how long?"

"Not long. Just until she's primed for embedding."

A pause. "I don't think that's a good idea, Mr. Finney. We really shouldn't deviate from the plan."

"We agreed that I'd be the one to prepare her for embedding. We don't both need to be involved."

"Technically, yes. But redundancy is always good, boss. What if something unexpected happens? I think we should stick to the original plan."

"Duly noted, Sebastian."

Finney was holding a tablet. He touched an icon on the screen.

I want some alone time with her, Sebastian.

For the time being, it was going to be just himself and the good Dr. Wu.

He was going to enjoy this.

But he still didn't smile.

SEBASTIAN

"Boss? Boss?"

No answer.

Asshole.

Finney had cut his audio feed.

Asshole!

What was he playing at? Why didn't Finney want him to know what he was saying to the surgeon chick?

He was already in position, so Sebastian waited where he was.

He had no choice.

RITA

Rita opened her eyes and let go of her father's dog tags.

The throbbing in her head was still there, but her panic was gone.

She drew herself up straight and set her jaw in what she thought (*hoped*) was a commanding way, as if performing complex surgery rather than swaddling herself in blankets like a Red Cross disaster refugee.

"I'm fine. Just a little tired. I must have dozed off."

"Dozed off?" Lisa asked, puzzled. "But . . . what were you doing here?"

A mental scene from last night, hazy at the edges, played out in Rita's mind, a snippet of an event that she was reasonably certain had happened.

"I came in last night to prep for this morning's surgery."

Wendy spoke up excitedly. "You mean—you were here all night?"

"Yes. I must have fallen asleep."

"You . . . fell asleep?" Lisa said. She was trying to stifle her incredulity. "Here? In the operating room?"

More of Rita's memory was returning. Yes, she was pretty sure she'd walked, under her own power, into operating room number ten last night to check on the auto-surgeon system. She remembered turning the system on, testing its components, and running through the pre-op checklists as she'd done thousands of times before.

And then . . .

She hadn't the faintest idea of what had happened next.

No weakness.

She shrugged. "You guys know me. I like to come in and prep for the big cases the night before. Our auto-surgeon case this morning is as big as they get. I worked a little later than I planned last night, and I got tired. That's all."

There. That sounded okay. Rita knew she had a reputation for working late hours in the OR, and her involvement with the auto-surgeon was common knowledge. She must have dozed off. It was plausible.

Wasn't it?

"So you decided to . . . sleep here?" Lisa said.

"Yes."

"On—the OR table?"

Rita hesitated, then said: "Yes. I must have—I

mean, I put my head down for a second, but I guess I drifted off."

"Naked?" Wendy tittered. She appeared to be enjoying herself. What an interesting way for her to kick off a Monday morning.

"I sleep naked at home," Rita said.

No, I don't.

At least, not when alone in bed; and she'd been alone in bed since ending things with Spencer last year.

Spencer.

She found herself wishing he were here.

No weakness, lovely Rita.

"Sometimes, I sleepwalk," she ventured. That *was* true. It didn't happen often—once every few years since high school. She'd gotten used to it: waking up in the middle of the night in odd places throughout the house. One time last year she'd found herself in the kitchen at three in the morning with the refrigerator door wide open and a plate of leftover pasta sitting on the counter.

She forced a laugh, which sounded to her like a braying donkey. "I must have undressed myself without realizing it. God, how embarrassing."

Lisa and Wendy looked unconvinced. Rita admitted to herself that her story strained credulity. But she'd heard of sleepwalkers doing crazier things—even drive a car—so why couldn't she have undressed herself?

Hell, she even started to believe the story herself, a little.

What do the psychiatrists call that? Believing in imagined memories? Confabulation.

"How did you strap yourself down?" said Wendy.

Rita blinked. "What?"

"You were strapped to the table, with your arms underneath the straps. How did you tighten the straps? After you were lying down? With your arms, like—trapped?"

"Well." She nibbled on her lower lip. *No weakness.* "The buckle for the strap was near my right hand. I'm right-handed. You only need one hand to tighten these buckles. Right?"

"But why would you strap yourself down in the first place?"

Rita shrugged, hoping it looked nonchalant. "Who knows? People do strange things while they're sleep-walking, then, uh, have absolutely no memory of it. Strapping patients to these tables is something we do just about every day. It makes sense that my brain is, um, hardwired for it, and that I might go through the motions even when I'm asleep."

She laughed (*brayed*) again. "Haven't either one of you guys ever done something weird in your sleep?"

At first, neither said anything. But after a few moments—long enough for Rita to wonder if the two of them were buying it, or at least feigning belief for politeness' sake—Wendy decided to try her luck one more time.

"But, then, how did you—" she began.

When Rita was a girl, there'd been this boy her age who'd lived down the street: a lumbering, sullen kid who'd tag along after the older boys as they'd skate-boarded and smoked cigarettes in back of the local

Circle K minimart. She and her friends had avoided him; he'd, in turn, ignored them.

Until one summer afternoon when they were nine, and she'd been playing with a few neighborhood girls on the small patch of browned grass that had served as her family's front yard. She'd been standing next to her bike when the boy had appeared and, without explanation, knocked her down and tried to make off with her bike.

Her reaction had surprised herself as much as anyone else. To this day, she remembered her fury, her little-girl righteous indignation that someone, even this bigger boy, *would try to take away her bike*, with the flowered Barbie basket hanging on the front panel— still remembered the frightened screams of her friends as she'd launched herself at him, and pinned him in the spiky brown grass.

She'd flailed at him with her small fists until her father had come out and dragged her away. The boy, stunned but unhurt, had run home crying and never bothered her again. Her father had carried her inside, cleaned her up, and placed her on his lap.

You're a little spitfire, lovely Rita. You don't let people walk all over you. That's good. Just like your mom. But you've got to learn to control that temper.

She'd burst into tears. The injustice of it! She'd wanted to tell him that she didn't *have* a temper, whatever *that* was. It had been the boy's fault, not hers: If he'd just left her alone, she wouldn't have had to hit him. She buried her face in her father's chest (*his dog tag, his metal dog tag underneath his T-shirt, she felt it press against her cheek*) and promised she wouldn't do it again.

But she did do it again.

Many times, over many years. Trips to the principal's office, notes sent home from school talking about her *anger-management issues*. Her parents would sigh and give her a good talking-to, and tell her not to do it again; and then she *would* do it again, and the cycle would repeat.

It wasn't until high school, after both Mom and Dad were dead, that she realized that the word *temper* didn't fit. She had a short fuse, no doubt. But temper implied blind rage without purpose. Her anger sprang from an emotional reaction to a perceived injustice: like that time in high school when, during a close race, one of her cross-country rivals had wielded some sharp elbows to beat back Rita's final surge. Rita had fumed: not because the other girl had won but because she hadn't won fairly. She hated cheaters. Their ensuing argument had escalated into a screaming match. Physical intervention from girls on both teams prevented the two of them from trying to rip each other's lungs out.

Afterward, the anger-management classes her school had required Rita to take as a precondition for remaining on the cross-country team weren't as bad as she thought they'd be. The counselor who ran the classes was an idealistic twentysomething with a psychology degree from Stanford. Nice enough. She liked to say *super* a lot, and make liberal use of exclamation points in everyday speech. *Super great job, Rita! I'm super impressed! You're making* super *progress!*

Rita did as told; and, eventually, she'd *super* managed her anger.

Anger management.

It was a useful skill. But as she'd clawed her way up through the professional ranks, Rita had soon discovered that a measured display of righteous anger could be productive for a career woman—a sad commentary on modern society, maybe, but true: People *always* moved faster in her OR when they thought she was pissed off, much more so, she thought, than with her male counterparts.

So she'd cultivated her anger—or indignation, or whatever. She'd repurposed it. Domesticated it. Groomed it. Kept it on as a pet. When necessary, she'd let it run loose for a while, do its thing, then tuck it away again before it could do any real damage.

Now was one of those times she needed to let her anger out of her subconscious for a little romp. Wendy was her subordinate, and she was having just a little too much fun this morning at Rita's expense. Who did she think she was?

"Wendy!" she snapped. The acoustic peculiarities of the cavernous OR propelled Rita's shout from one end of the room to the other and back, magnifying its effect. Wendy and Lisa flinched, Wendy more so. "Enough already with the twenty questions! We've all got work to do this morning. Move on. Okay? You found me here, and I'm awake now. Just get *over* it!"

Rita put her hand to her temple as the pain in her head spiked briefly to an almost intolerable level. She made a mental note not to raise her voice again until she was feeling better.

"Wendy," Lisa said into the uncomfortable silence. "Why don't you go over to the storeroom and grab the surgical trays from the sterilizer?"

Wendy thrust out her lower lip and slouched out of the room.

Lisa shook her head. "Ugh. Sorry about that." She placed a hand on Rita's shoulder. "How *are* you feeling, Dr. Wu? For real?"

Hungover.

The thought shocked Rita before it had finished forming in her mind.

Impossible.

She hadn't had a drink in over a year.

Unthinkable.

"I'm okay, Lisa. Really."

Lisa made a face and pointed to Rita's left ear. "What's that?"

"What's what?"

"You're bleeding." Lisa retrieved a package from a nearby cabinet, ripped it open, and plucked out a square-shaped piece of white sterile gauze. She dabbed it to Rita's ear. She had a light touch, but the motion still made Rita wince with pain.

Lisa held up the gauze to Rita's face. It was spackled with bright-red spots.

Rita frowned. "What?"

"It looks like it's dripping from inside your ear. Here." She placed the gauze in Rita's hand and gently guided it to her left earlobe. "Put some pressure to it. I'm going to get your clothes."

"My clothes?" Rita said, holding the gauze in place.

Lisa looked stricken. She pointed to a pair of scrub

pants and matching top neatly folded on a nearby table, on which were lying a pair of white panties, bra, cell phone, hospital ID badge, and eyeglasses. A pair of white sneakers, with a grey athletic sock tucked into each of them, sat on top of a nearby stool. "Yours?"

Rita blushed. "Yes."

Lisa carefully laid the cell phone and ID aside, picked up the clothes, and brought them over to her. She checked Rita's ear again. "I think it's stopped." She tossed the blood-dappled gauze in a red trash can. "I'll guard the door."

Rita stood up, unsteadily, and dressed herself as Lisa stood vigil at the door, at one point shooing away Wendy and another nurse.

Once dressed, Lisa handed her a scrub cap. Rita touched her shoulder-length black hair, which felt like a bird's nest and probably looked worse. In violation of OR sterility protocol, her hair wasn't properly covered, which, if possible, left her feeling even more naked and vulnerable.

She took the cap, slipped it over her head, and tucked her hair underneath the expandable elastic edges. "Thanks."

"Your operation this morning. Are you going to be—all right for it?"

No weakness.

"Uh, sure." Rita slipped her cell phone in the back pocket of her scrubs, smiled wanly, and wondered if she really was in any kind of shape to cut into another human being this morning.

So, she suspected, did Lisa, whose concern etched deep lines in her forehead and drew the corners of her mouth downward. Lisa was one of the best nurses Rita had ever worked with: smart, confident, compassionate. They'd been together almost ten years. In the way of an outstanding caddy counseling a professional golfer, Lisa knew more about Rita's surgical skills—what she was capable of and, more importantly, what she *wasn't*—than Rita.

But Rita also knew she could not back down. Not now. Lisa opened her mouth to say something, but Rita talked over her.

"I'm good. I'm, uh, just going to head over to the locker room. Maybe take a shower, grab some coffee. Clear my head."

"I'll walk you over to the locker room."

"No, thanks, Lisa. I'm good."

"I have to go over that way anyway." She folded her arms and thrust out her left hip. She wasn't going to take *no* for an answer.

"You sure?"

"Absolutely."

"Okay. Thanks." Rita clipped her ID badge to the front of her scrub shirt and put on her glasses. They were stylish, with thick black frames. She winced as the left end piece slid over her sore left ear. She usually wore contacts, except when she worked late nights at the hospital.

She and Lisa stepped into the corridor outside. Rita kept her head down. The last thing she wanted was to attract attention.

"Good morning, Dr. Wu! Hi Lisa!" A passing nurse flashed them a sunny smile. She was carrying a box of

bladder catheters. "Big day! The auto-surgeon operation today, right? Off to an early start this morning?"

"Um. Good morning, Becky. Yes."

"Hi, Becky," Lisa said.

"Good for you," Becky chirped. "I mean, gosh. The
auto-surgeon operation. *Gosh*. Everybody in the hospital's heard about the auto-surgeon. *So* exciting, Dr.
Wu. Good luck! Have a terrific day!"

"Thanks, Becky."

Becky sped away, cheerfully greeting a male nurse
several paces down the hall. His reply was clipped and
surly. He was staring at his cell phone and mumbling.
A short distance beyond him she spotted Wendy, a
conspiratorial grin playing about her lips, engaged in
an animated dialogue with another nurse, who was listening with a rapt expression that oscillated between
surprise and morbid fascination. They didn't see Rita
or Lisa. Rita couldn't hear what Wendy was saying, but
she had a good idea what the topic of the conversation
was.

Me.

She realized with dismay that she was still a long
way from the women's locker room and that the corridors between here and there were teeming with early-
morning staff preparing the operating rooms for a
busy working day.

Lisa seemed to read her mind. She grabbed her
lightly by the elbow and spoke in her right ear. "Let's
go the other way."

Rita nodded numbly. She had no personal experience with walks of shame. But she'd seen plenty of

girls who had as she'd jogged to cross-country practice on Saturday mornings in college: as they'd slouched home in revealing dresses or blouses with tight jeans, high heels slung over shoulders, eyes fixed on the ground. Back then, Rita had felt nothing but contempt for those girls. Right now, wanting nothing more than to blend in with the walls, she was feeling a whole lot less judgmental.

They reversed direction and entered a relatively empty hallway. Lisa kept her hand resting on Rita's elbow, for which Rita felt grateful: She was still feeling wobbly. Operating room ten was one of the farthest away from the locker room. A walk of what couldn't have been more than a few minutes seemed to stretch into hours. Eventually, a thick red line appeared on the floor ahead of them.

Finally. Thank God.

The red line demarcated the end of the designated operating-room area, in which scrubs and surgical hats were mandatory, and the beginning of everything else. This morning, the red line felt to her like the tape at the end of a grueling marathon. She could see the entrance to the women's locker room just beyond.

Lisa let go of her elbow as they stopped at the red line. "You sure you're okay?"

"Yes."

Lisa folded her arms.

"*Yes*, Lisa. I'm fine. And, um . . . you won't, ah, *mention* this to anyone. Will you?"

Lisa shook her head. "No."

"Thanks, Lisa. I—well . . . just, thanks."

Lisa offered a small, unenthusiastic nod as Rita darted into the women's locker room.

RITA

The place was empty. The early nursing shift had already changed into scrubs and was at work in the operating rooms; the women surgeons had not yet arrived. Her timing was perfect.

Thank God for small favors. She could use a few more this morning.

Rita placed her phone on one of the spare wooden benches that squatted between the rows of lockers. She located her locker, dialed the combination, and yanked at the handle, which refused to yield. Chagrined, she reset the dial and tried again. It would not open.

It took three more ineffectual attempts, each more frantic, for her then to realize that she was trying to open the wrong locker.

God, what's wrong with me?

She took a deep breath, then located and opened her *actual* locker, from which she procured a bottle of Advil and a plastic bottle of water. She washed a few of the Advil down. Her stomach protested with an audible groan.

Rita sat down heavily on the bench next to her phone, took off her glasses, and laid them on the bench.

She took a sip of water and tried to size up her situation.

You mean—you were here all night?

How are *you feeling, Dr. Wu? For real?*

"I don't know," she said aloud. She cradled her head in her hands and closed her eyes.

Her phone vibrated with an incoming text, rattling the wood and propelling it in electronic spasms toward the side of the bench. Without moving her head or opening her eyes, she reached out, grabbed the phone before it toppled off the edge, and hit the reset key. Silence again enveloped the room.

Minutes later it vibrated again. With great effort and no enthusiasm, she lifted her head to look at the screen and read the text. It was the pre-op area, informing her for the second time (the previous message having been the first) that her first patient of the day, Mrs. Sanchez, had checked in, and that she and her family were waiting to speak with her before her operation.

Rita's stomach clenched, and she tasted bile in the back of her throat.

God, but she felt horrible.

How could she possibly operate this morning?

No weakness.

She'd trained herself to ooze strength from every pore of her body, and canceling the operation would look weak. Backing down was not in her nature. She couldn't let a little nausea stand in her way.

Her phone buzzed again. This time an incoming phone call.

Goddamn pre-op nurses!

She stabbed the *accept call* icon without checking the incoming number.

"I'll be right there!" she barked.

"Rita?"

"Oh. Darcy." It was her kid sister. "Sorry. I thought you were . . . Sorry, Darcy."

Wait—what's Darcy doing up at this hour? Since crashing at Rita's a few days ago, Darcy hadn't been getting up much before noon.

"Darcy? Why are you awake? Is everything okay?"

"Yes. I mean, I think so. It's just that—"

"Okay. Good." Rita's phone vibrated: another text from pre-op. "I'm glad you're okay. Look. Now's a really bad time. I've got work stuff right now. Can I give you a call back in a few minutes?"

"Um . . . okay. I guess. But—"

"Thanks. I'll—wait! Darcy?"

"Yeah?"

"Do you, uh, remember what time I left the house last night? To go to the hospital?"

"Oh. Um . . . around seven, maybe? After we finished dinner?" She paused. "Hey, Rita, something kind of weird happened to me—"

"Gotta run. Call you later. I promise." She hung up without waiting for Darcy's response.

So she'd definitely come to the hospital last night on her own. The question was, what had happened then?

She looked at her locker and thought of her fumbling attempts to open it.

No weakness.

She thought of the operating-room table . . .

. . . (*naked I'd been naked*) . . .

. . . and the big gaping hole in her memory . . .

. . . (*I'd been NAKED*) . . .

. . . and the pain and fuzziness in her head . . .

. . . (*hungover but I couldn't be because I DON'T DRINK ANYMORE*) . . .

. . . and the blood dripping from her ear . . .

. . . (*what was THAT all about?*)

. . . none of which made any sense.

And she asked herself again: Could she really operate this morning?

That chief surgery resident she'd met, so many years ago: *He* would have operated. He puked in a sink, but he still ran that code.

"He ran that code," she murmured.

But he really shouldn't have, lovely Rita, her father's voice answered.

She rubbed her face with both hands.

You can't operate this morning, lovely Rita. God knows what you'd do if someone handed you a scalpel right now.

No, she didn't know. And she didn't want to find out.

She had to cancel it because it was the right thing to do.

To her surprise, she experienced a surge of relief. She'd expected shame: shame over her weakness at not sucking it up and getting the job done, despite feeling like crap. Instead, it was as if a burden had been lifted from her shoulders.

There's no weakness, lovely Rita, in doing the right thing by your patients.

No, she thought. *There isn't.*

She picked up her cell and dialed the pre-op area, trying to think of what she was going to tell her patient.

"Good morning, Dr. Wu."

It was a man's voice.

Clear. Distinct. Close. To her left.

Rita was so surprised she dropped the phone before her call had connected, and knocked the water bottle off the bench. It spilled on the floor next to the phone.

What was a *man* doing in the woman's locker room?

When she spun her head left, in the direction of the voice, she saw no one.

"Can you hear me, Dr. Wu?"

The voice was like marble. Smooth and cold, and so close it was as if he was speaking directly into her left ear. Maybe her injured ear was distorting her sense of direction, somehow inhibiting her hearing. She cupped her left hand behind her left ear, trying to get a sense of where he was.

"Can your hear me, Dr. Wu?"

"Yes," she answered, swiveling her head from left to right, her hand positioned behind her left ear like a radar dish. "This is the ladies' room, you know. You're not supposed to be in here."

There was something else about the voice, too, which unnerved her.

She'd heard it before.

"I know, Dr. Wu. That's why I'm not in the ladies' room."

That's weird. No matter what direction she turned, she always heard the man directly in her left ear, as if she were wearing headphones with a broken right speaker.

And how did this guy know her name, anyway? Another weird float in this morning's parade of disturbing events.

"Look, perv, this isn't a joke. I'm calling security."

She grabbed her car keys out of her locker, palmed them in her right hand, and wrapped her fingers around them, positioning the longest key so that its sharp tip protruded through her closed fist.

Thank you, YMCA women's safety class.

Her headache and unhappy stomach forgotten beneath a wash of adrenaline, she walked the length of the room, tensed, searching the rows between the lockers, brandishing the key like a miniature spear.

Nothing.

"Don't worry, Dr. Wu. I'm not a pervert."

Where have I heard that voice before?

She crept into the adjacent bathroom. The row of sinks was silent and unattended. She bent over and checked the stalls. All empty.

She straightened up and put her hands on her hips, puzzled. She was alone.

Except for his voice.

"There's no point in checking the toilets. Or anywhere else. I'm not in there. I'm also not interested in seeing you, or your female colleagues, in any state of undress. Although, as I understand it, you awoke in a rather awkward position this morning."

Her stomach constricted into a tiny knot.

She dropped the key.

"What—do you mean?" Sweat erupted across her forehead and upper lip. She wiped it off with the back of her hand as she bent over, retrieved the key, and placed it in her pocket.

"Aren't you wondering how you ended up on the operating table?"

How does he know about that?

"Look." She struggled to keep her voice steady. "I don't know what you're talking about. And I don't know what kind of sick game you're, ah, playing. But you're not supposed to be in here. And I'm getting security. Right now."

"Don't you want to know who I am, Dr. Wu?"

"No."

"My name is Morgan Finney."

She stopped dead in her tracks, halfway to the door.

"*What?*" she whispered.

Rita grabbed the edge of a nearby sink to steady herself.

Oh my God.

"Do you remember me?" he breathed. "Do you remember *her*?"

How could I possibly forget?

She was clutching the sink with both hands.

Because this time, there was no stopping the panic.

She was terrified.

RITA

"Dr. Wu?"

Rita stood at the sink, a hand on each side of the basin, drawing breath in short, ragged bursts, her lungs clawing for air. She was shaking all over, trying to hold her panic at bay.

I'm hallucinating.

She had to be. That was the most reasonable medical explanation.

But why was she hallucinating about *him*?

"Dr. Wu?"

She'd seen plenty of patients over the years hallucinate. She'd listened to their lucid conversations with people who didn't exist, and as they'd described imagined events in their lives in more detail than she could remember the real ones in hers.

There'd been this one patient: a young man suffering from a severe form of inflammatory bowel disease that had caused him so much pain, he'd needed to have a portion of his intestines removed to obtain relief.

She'd first met him in an exam room. He had bright, penetrating green eyes beneath a widow's peak and wore a yarmulke. His mother had accompanied him: a thin, fretful woman who waved her hands around as she spoke.

He was direct, confident, and forceful without being overbearing. He asked Rita penetrating questions about the surgery that conveyed a firm grasp of the issues and kept Rita on her toes.

He was, without doubt, a really smart kid.

And a hopeless schizophrenic.

It had begun during his second year of med school: inappropriate outbursts in class; an abrupt academic tailspin; long-standing social connections severed without warning. A classic pattern for schizophrenia onset in an otherwise healthy, white male in his early twenties.

Is that what the psychiatrists told his parents? she'd wondered, gazing at the young man's mother, who'd pawed the air anxiously as she'd posed her own questions. *That his age of onset and initial symptoms fit the textbook definition of schizophrenia?*

Would they have cared?

She doubted it. He'd been an only child and a source, no doubt, of great pride: graduation with distinction from an Ivy League college, acceptance into a top-notch med school. How must they have felt, watching all their hopes trampled underneath the weight of his paranoid delusions?

His pathology focused on his firm belief that he was Moses—or, rather, a modern version of Moses. He'd explained to Rita that Moses's second coming had been foretold in Scripture, and that he was Moses re-born. Rita had never heard of a second coming for Moses and told him as much, so he'd pulled a dog-eared copy of the Old Testament from his back pocket and quoted to her passages marked in four different shades of colored highlighter and annotated with dense scrawls in the margins.

His mother had smiled tiredly and twisted her hands.

He hadn't ranted, or raved. He'd made his case with the eloquence of a skilled trial lawyer. And he'd made *perfect sense*. By the end of the interview, it made her question, if only a little, if he was right, and everyone else (including herself) was wrong.

I know you don't believe me, he'd told her, his green eyes drilling into hers. *I don't care. I don't need you to believe in me.*

Rita had looked at the man's mother, who'd nodded and raised her hands in a noncommittal gesture. Indulgence? Capitulation? Rita couldn't tell.

His surgery had gone well, and he'd gotten better. She hadn't seen Moses for a long time. She'd wondered sometimes how he was doing, and what it was like to live in his self-formulated version of reality.

Well, now maybe she was finding out.

"Dr. Wu?"

Or was she? The voice in her head calling itself Morgan Finney sounded so *real*, and exactly how she remembered him. How could it be a hallucination? It didn't make sense.

Or did it? After all, that was the whole point of a delusion: It was completely real to the person suffering from it. Maybe she was developing schizophrenia, like Moses, a disease that would slowly choke her off from reality and from everyone she cared about.

Darcy.

Spencer.

The thought terrified her.

Waking up naked in an operating room, with no memory of how I got there.

Now a voice talking to me in my head.

Is this how psychosis starts for me?

Is this how it started for Moses?

Maybe, but . . .

But she knew schizophrenia was unlikely in her case. It could, she suppose, be some type of early-onset dementia, like Alzheimer's. But she didn't think Alzheimer's usually gave people these symptoms, at least in its early stages.

A holdover from last night, maybe? A year later, her experience with Morgan Finney still pressed heavily on her conscience; and his voice, surfacing with last night's flotsam, implicated her remorse in whatever was going on.

Delirium.

That's what it must be, she decided. An acute change in mental state, typically caused by fevers, or surgery, or intoxication—

—(*alcohol, couldn't possibly be alcohol*)—

—or some other type of stress on the body.

She saw it often in her patients after surgery, especially the elderly ones. At night, it happened with enough regularity that doctors and nurses had an informal term for it: *sun downing.*

"Dr. Wu?"

Delirium was common. Delirium wasn't serious. Most important, delirium was temporary.

Delirium. Okay. So, now what do I do?

Diagnosis was the first step, she reasoned. *Physician, heal thyself.* That's what Spencer liked to say.

(*Spencer—wish he were here*)

It was just a matter of convincing herself that she was chatting with an errant series of electrical signals in her brain rather than a real person.

All in my head. Not real. Just delirium.

She took a few deep, controlled breaths. Her breathing rate slowed—not quite to normal, but closer to normal. The shaking in her body continued but with less violence.

"Dr. Wu."

Not happening. Delirium.

"You can still hear me, can't you? Answer me, please."

All in my head.

"Dr. Wu."

All in my head.

"We need to talk about my wife. Jenny Finney."

She opened her eyes and stared at her hands, still gripping the sides of the sink. Her knuckles had turned bone white. Her breathing sped back up; her heart hammered at the back of her sternum, as if trying to break free of her chest.

"What did you say?" she whispered.

All thoughts of ignoring him—of rationalizing whatever was happening into nonexistence, or writing it off as some kind of temporary medical condition— had evaporated at the mention of that name.

Jenny Finney.

"Thank you. I thought you could hear me."

She clutched the sides of the sink as if holding on to her sanity. She worried that she really *was* breaking with reality.

The voice claiming to be Morgan Finney seemed to be reading her thoughts.

"I realize that this situation, what's happening to you this morning, must be difficult for you to grasp, Dr. Wu. That it might seem like you're losing your mind. But you're not. You're completely sane. My name is Morgan Finney. I really am speaking to you right now. I'm not just an imaginary voice inside your head."

"Stop talking," she whispered.

"There are some very rational explanations involved."

"Stop talking. Please. Stop talking." She closed her eyes and leaned her forehead against the mirror over the sink. It was cool and, under the circumstances, even a little pleasant. "Stop talking."

"It's important you hear me out."

"Please. Just stop talking."

"It's very important you not lose control."

"STOP TALKING."

He paused, then said, "You can't wish me away, Dr. Wu."

Something occurred to her. "Okay," she said warily, pushing herself away from the mirror and opening her eyes. "If you're really talking to me right now, it has to be through some kind of speaker system, or radio, right? Which means other people can hear you. If you're real."

As if on cue, the locker-room door opened—not the one she'd entered from, but a separate door, near the sinks, that led to a different part of the hospital. Through it trudged another surgeon, one of Rita's colleagues. At first, Rita couldn't decide which the woman's scrubs sported more of: wrinkles or blotchy stains of various shades of black and red. She settled on wrinkles.

"Oh. Hi, Rita."

Rita released her grip on the basin and stood up straight as the woman approached the sink next to her and turned on the faucet. She felt pinpricks in the tips of her fingers as blood rushed into them. She opened her mouth to speak, but nothing came out.

The woman looked at her curiously.

"Aren't you going to say hello, Dr. Wu?" the voice in her left ear said.

"What?" Rita said.

"Hi," the woman repeated.

The voice said, "*Hello.* Say hello to her, Dr. Wu."

"Did you hear that, Lucy?" Rita said.

"What? Hear what?"

"That voice."

"What voice? You mean—mine? My voice?"

"*His* voice," Rita said.

"What are your talking about?"

"I . . ."

Lucy looked baffled, and it occurred to Rita that she was the only one in the room having a three-way conversation. This did not bode well for her sanity—

(*I don't care,* the boy who would be Moses had said. *I don't need you to believe in me.*)

—so she decided to keep the information to herself, at least for now.

"Never mind," Rita said. "Sorry. My mind's a little fuzzy. Long night."

Lucy, a thickset, taciturn surgeon, nodded solemnly. She looked exhausted. "Me too." Her voice was deep— almost as deep as the one knocking around inside Rita's head.

Lucy splashed water from the faucet over her face and short brown hair as she studied Rita's ashen complexion in the mirror.

"Yeah. Yeah, you definitely look the way I feel right now: like hell. Maybe even worse." She guffawed, a sonorous growl from low in her throat. "Every part of me aches."

She turned off the faucet, dried her face with a paper towel from a wall dispenser, and ambled to a row of lockers in the adjacent room.

"Follow her, please, Dr. Wu," the voice (*Finney, might as well call him Finney*) said.

"Why?" Rita said to Finney.

"Trauma call," Lucy replied, opening her locker and peeling off her scrubs.

Rita trailed her into the locker room's main area. Lucy's locker was a few rows over from hers. Rita's locker door remained ajar; her cell and eyeglasses were still lying on the bench, next to some personal belongings Lucy had removed from her locker and was rooting through.

"Um . . . Bad night?" She picked up her glasses and put them on.

Lucy nodded. "Yeah. A couple of MVAs. And a GSW to the abdomen. A guy was showing off his semiautomatic pistol to his buddy, and it went off by accident. Supposedly. Hit his buddy twice in the belly. One of the bullets tore the ileocecal junction to all hell. Yours?"

Lucy had picked the empty water bottle off of the ground, the one Rita had knocked over earlier, and was frowning at the soggy spot on the carpet near her foot. Rita nodded. Without comment, Lucy handed her the bottle, which Rita tossed into a nearby recycling bin.

"Up all night sewing bowel. The resident I was working with sucks," Lucy said. "Worthless. Practically had to hold him by the hand all damn night." She kicked her dirty scrubs into a pile on the floor and grunted. "They're gonna have to burn these."

"Take your notebook out of your locker," Finney said.

"What?" said Rita.

"They're going to have to burn these," Lucy said, raising her voice and increasing her enunciation. "My scrubs. God knows what I got on them last night."

"That notebook you keep in your locker," Finney said. "Take it out."

Rita reached in and retrieved her notebook. It was the kind students and scientists use to record scientific observations and data, with a black-and-white-checkered pattern across the front, its pages filled with hand-drawn sketches and personal notes Rita kept on all of the surgeries she performed.

"Open it."

Rita complied. Tucked inside the pages of the notebook was a sealed envelope.

This isn't mine. I didn't put this here.

"Look inside the envelope."

She broke the seal and opened it. A four-inch-by-six-inch color photograph slipped out and onto the floor. She bent over and picked it up.

It was her.

Jenny Finney.

Rita would never forget that face. How could she? Near the end, in the SICU, it had been distorted beyond recognition, swollen by pounds of retained body fluid and hidden beneath the harsh plastic of a breathing tube.

But in this picture it was brimming with health and life: round, freckled, friendly, and stamped with laugh lines. She was dressed in tan shorts and a white polo shirt, sitting with her legs crossed on a green lawn, eyes pointed somewhere off to the right of the photographer. She was laughing, revealing mildly crooked front teeth, and reaching up with a slender, freckled hand to push wayward strands of long red hair behind her ear.

Lucy, having donned a pair of jeans and a light grey

T-shirt that read IF I AGREED WITH YOU, WE WOULD _BOTH_ BE WRONG in bold black lettering, glanced over Rita's shoulder at the picture. "Friend of yours?"

"No. Not really. Former patient."

"Huh. Nice, uh, smile." Lucy grunted and turned away, slipped into a pair of flip-flops, and placed her personal items back into her locker.

"Yes," Finney said flatly. "It was. There, Dr. Wu. Tangible evidence of my existence. Confirmed by an objective third party. Do you believe in me now?"

"Yes," Rita whispered, staring at the picture.

"God, what a night." Lucy hadn't heard her. She was buckling the belt of her jeans. "All I can think about is a long, hot shower, a big pancake breakfast, and bed." She finished and closed her locker. "Can't wait to get home. Hey." Her face brightened, and she favored Rita with a rare smile. "Good luck today, by the way, with that auto-surgeon thing."

She slapped Rita on the shoulder, apparently unconcerned whether Rita's haggard appearance signaled problems that might impede her surgical skills.

(_Hell, a moment ago she said I look like hell_)

"Thanks, Lucy."

"I'd stay and watch but—you know." She shrugged. "I'm totally beat."

"No worries."

They faced each other in awkward silence until Lucy shrugged again. "Well. See ya."

"Bye, Lucy."

Lucy tossed her soiled scrubs in a nearby laundry bin and exited.

Rita was, once again, alone in the locker room.

But not really.

"Do you remember her? The woman in the picture?" Finney asked.

"Your wife," Rita answered in a hushed voice. "Jenny. I operated on her last year. I—I took out your wife's ruptured appendix."

"Yes," Finney said. A pause. "And then she died."

"Yes," Rita whispered.

"She died terribly."

A second, longer pause.

And then he said, "Because of you, Dr. Wu. She died because of you."

SEBASTIAN

The man stood a discreet distance from the entrance to the women's locker room, fiddling with the laminated hospital ID badge dangling from the left breast pocket of his scrub shirt. The badge read, ROBERT RODRIGUEZ, PERIOPERATIVE TECHNICIAN, and beside the name was a small color picture of the man in which an unabashed grin spread underneath a generous crop of black hair in a stylish pompadour.

The badge's owner was currently not smiling. The man, who called himself Sebastian, peered, tight-mouthed, at the locker-room door.

This is the tricky part, he thought.

From what he could tell, before Finney had cut his feed, the implant had successfully activated. Now was when the subject realized what was going on and accepted the nature of the device.

Or didn't.

Sebastian sucked his teeth.

When he'd taken this job a year ago, Finney had provided him with the dossiers and videos of the early test subjects: those unlucky enough to have been the first to receive the implants.

Poor bastards.

Although, come to think of it, the ones who'd come later hadn't been all that much better off.

He'd studied the files and videos, had spent hours poring over them, taking detailed notes, leaving no item unexamined in gathering and processing as much information as he could. He always did that, with every job he took. He was a professional, and he always acted as one.

He had not been hired to ask where the test subjects came from, so he didn't. But he'd traveled the world several times over, and recognized in their haggard faces a mixed bag of races representing a good swath of Southeast Asia and Indonesia. Political prisoners, probably, their participation quietly arranged through confidential, and no doubt lucrative, contracts with governments for which human rights weren't high on the agenda. Men, mostly. But also some women.

And, much to his distaste, even a few children.

The device's designers had, he knew, implanted the original models in monkeys. The monkeys were nothing special: run-of-the-mill, lower-order primates that liked nothing more than to eat, shit, and screw. From a technical standpoint, the implants had seemed to work fine, and the monkeys took to them okay. After a brief recovery period, they continued to eat, shit, and screw as if nothing had ever happened to them, except to occasionally paw at their left ears.

But the monkeys couldn't describe how they were feeling. Hence the need for people, who could tell you exactly what was going on inside their heads and hopefully respond to the device in the manner in which its designers had intended.

And most of them did. The device worked well, and it worked the way it was supposed to.

But there was a wrinkle no one had anticipated: A certain proportion of the subjects went completely apeshit once the device was activated, a descent into insanity that was as irrevocable as it was unpleasant, and a psychosis that persisted even after the designers had deactivated the device. Some had practically torn their own ears off, and one guy had gazed tranquilly into the wall-mounted camera in his cell as he sank an eight-inch-long wooden shank into his left ear canal.

Christ, what a mess *that* had been.

Another had smashed her head with rhythmic and inhuman force onto the concrete floor next to her bunk. She hadn't lasted long, either.

Then there was the teenager.

Pretty, in a melancholy way. Within ten minutes of her device's activation, she'd collapsed into a corner of her cell in the fetal position, her lips opening and closing every so often without making any sound, as if she were mouthing a silent prayer.

She'd otherwise never moved again.

Watching the video of her, curled up on the floor, had reminded him of an experiment he'd once read about: rats in boxes subjected to random electric shocks wired through the boxes' metallic floors. There was no way for them to escape the shocks because there was no way to escape the floors.

There were levers in the boxes, and the rats could push them, but it didn't matter because the levers weren't connected to anything, they were useless; and the shocks came fast and furious no matter what the rats did: push the lever, didn't push the lever—the little fuckers got their asses electrocuted regardless. Eventually, they just gave up, lay down, and died.

Learned helplessness. That's what they called it.

Fucking spooky was what it was.

The girl made him think of the rats.

The device's designers had been nonplussed. After all, the monkeys had never gone crazy. So they'd observed, and pondered, and redid their calculations. They'd made some design modifications before slapping the new, improved models in more subjects' ears, turning them on, and talking into their brains. Then they'd observed some more.

Some subjects still continued to go ape-shit.

Which had pissed the designers off to no end. After all, going ape-shit defeated the whole purpose. It hadn't mattered to them that it happened in only a minority of cases. They were engineers. The inexactitude, the uncertainty of it, had irritated them. They'd wanted to strip everything down and start over. But they had deadlines to meet, and since the device took hold safely *most* of the time, they threw up their hands and decided to move forward.

Another glitch, in addition to the ape-shit thing: electronic interference from outside sources. One of the subjects had sworn he'd heard late-night sermons in Tagalog from a Baptist minister transmitting out of Manila (enough, Sebastian thought, to drive *anyone* insane). Another's device had stopped responding entirely after the installation of a nearby cell-phone tower. But interference wasn't a big deal: more a rare inconvenience that the designers would engineer out of the next version.

Although, given the nature of this particular job, Sebastian didn't know how many of the device's designers were still alive, or at the least knowledgeable as to the purpose to which the device was currently being put, despite their apparent lack of concern for international laws banning human medical experimentation.

Not paid to know. Don't want to find out.

He did know, though, that there'd been a consensus among them that it was the smarter, more sophisticated targets—like this surgeon—who stood the best chance of keeping their sanity—if they came to understand and accept the nature of the device. That was critical.

So they'd developed a protocol, a method of doling out information in a way that didn't overwhelm the subjects. You reasoned with the smarter ones, talked them off the ledge, explained to them how the device operated. Spoon-fed them small bites of material. You didn't overload them because mental overload led to madness. Using the protocol, the smart ones generally did okay.

But not always.

So he watched the door, and he waited.

He waited to see if she would go insane.

And he wondered, not for the first time, how he

himself would react if he awoke one morning to some unseen stranger whispering into his brain.

He glanced about and noted that the activity around him was increasing as the hospital staff prepared the operating rooms for the coming day. Men and women in dark blue scrubs hustled by, some pushing heavy equipment, others carrying bundles of surgical instruments wrapped in sterile packaging. All jostled for space in the corridors.

He was glad for the dark blue scrubs, which with the light blue scrub hats provided a dichromatic, shifting sea into which he could disappear. Perfect cover. A casual observer would never have looked twice at him, so perfectly did he blend in with all of the other blue-scrubbed, blue-capped figures all around him.

Everything about him was a careful study in normality. His trim, powerful frame disappeared into the folds of his baggy scrubs, which he'd deliberately selected to be one size too large. Its oversized sleeves concealed the knotted musculature of his upper arms. He was neither handsome nor ugly. His straight black hair, tucked underneath his surgical cap, was clipped medium length and parted into a forgettable style that looked nothing like the sculpted pompadour in the picture on his ID badge. His face, composed of softened intersections of overlapping smooth lines, was nondescript and of ambiguous ethnicity: for the rare individuals who got a good look at him, some thought he was Asian, others might swear Latino. The truth he kept to himself.

He checked his watch.

This was taking a lot longer than it was supposed

to. It made him uneasy. He was beginning to feel exposed.

Stupid.

Leaving the surgeon naked like that.

Unprofessional.

A thing that could attract too much attention.

It was one thing to drug her up and dump her senseless on the operating table. That played effectively into their strategy. But stripping off her clothes was something else: a needless exercise that introduced a reckless, pseudosexual element into the job. A complex, ambitious operation like this one (almost *too* complex and ambitious for his liking) left absolutely *no* margin for error. Best keep things simple. Buck-ass nakedness was an extra variable that this equation definitely did not need.

He shifted to a different vantage point on the other side of the hall and pretended to text someone.

It had been Finney's idea to abandon her naked. He'd been adamant about it. And Sebastian had worked for Finney long enough to know that it wasn't some weird sexual thing. Finney didn't get off on that kind of shit. Other sick fucks Sebastian had worked for over the years had. But Finney was different: For him, it was all about control. He'd wanted to humiliate her.

In this Finney had succeeded. She'd looked pretty freaked-out, walking from the operating room to the lockers earlier with the nurse. Still, they had to be careful, or she'd go over the edge and end up like the pretty teenager, curled up on the dank cement in a corner of her cell.

Or worse.

So he waited. Which was all he could do.

He didn't like the way Finney had insisted, without explanation, on turning off Sebastian's audio feed, how he was made to stand watch outside the locker-room door like a chump. This hadn't been the plan. And if something didn't happen soon, he was going to have to move to safer ground before someone took an interest in him.

This behavior was a fucking disturbing development. This was the first time Finney had blown Sebastian off. Finney usually listened to Sebastian's advice in these matters because that's what he'd hired him for. Now that their yearlong project was coming to fruition, Sebastian worried that Finney was starting to get carried away, letting his personal feelings cloud his judgment. He'd seen it before. Many times. This kind of job required total professionalism—a single-mindedness of purpose devoid of emotion and thoughtless impulse, or it could unravel and blow up in their faces.

Sebastian knew all about Finney, and Wu, and the history they shared. He never took a job without first doing his homework. This business with Finney's wife . . . well, that could screw with anybody's mind. Still, Sebastian had believed Finney would hold it together. But he also knew not every wound got better with time. Emotional wounds could fester, as Sebastian knew from personal experience.

His hand stole to his chest. Through the thin cotton of the scrub shirt, he touched the metal dog tag hanging around his neck.

All these years he'd carried it.

Alfonso's tag.

Screw it. It is what it is.

He'd known this job would be tricky when he took it. Whining now would do no good. He'd never blown a job. Ever. He goddamn wasn't going to start now.

Besides: He had his sister to think about, and Sammy and Sierra. So he was all in, and he would make this work. Make it work for all of them. Their futures, for better or for worse, were tied up with Finney's.

It was just him and Finney. From the beginning, Sebastian had been convinced it was the right way to go. More assets meant more help, but it also meant more opportunities for secrets to be spilled. And there were some big-ass, incriminating secrets involved here.

Three may keep a secret, if two of them are dead. It had been Alfonso who'd introduced him to *Poor Richard's Almanac*, which Sebastian thought was brilliant.

Even Benjamin fucking *Franklin knew you couldn't trust anyone.*

Three may keep a secret . . .

Alfonso.

. . . if two of them are dead.

He could have trusted Alfonso.

Alfonso, who'd turned down a spot in Officer Candidate's School after acing the qualifying exams because he'd decided that *every officer is by definition a prick, and I don't want to turn into a prick* . . .

Alfonso, who'd died in his arms, in a shitty little hovel at the other end of the world, at the hands of a twelve-year-old boy.

He moved a few paces down the hall and, with practiced casualness, leaned against a wall, eyeing the women's locker-room door.

He fingered Alfonso's dog tag again and thought of the one he'd left hanging around Wu's neck earlier that morning.

RITA

"You remember her, then," Finney said in her ear.

"Yes," she said. Surprisingly, she was starting to regain her composure. The physical evidence of Finney's existence she now held in her hand was injecting a bit of reality into this unreal situation.

She placed the picture back in her locker. "Okay. I'll accept for the moment that I'm not having some kind of psychotic break." She glanced up toward the ceiling, as if he were some kind of ghost, or deity. "If you're not in here, where are you? How are we having this conversation? Why can I hear you only in my left ear?"

"Let's just say that I've altered your ability to hear in your left ear."

"How?"

"Through a minor surgical procedure."

"Is that where the blood came from? And the pain?"

"Yes."

"What kind of procedure?"

"I'm not inclined to tell you."

"Who performed the operation?"

"I'm not inclined to tell you that, either."

She chewed on her lower lip. *Did he do it, or some-one else? Did I have to be naked for it?* As far as she could tell, aside from her ear, and the pain in her head, nothing else had been . . . *done* to her.

"Why can't I remember anything?"

"A side effect of the procedure."

Situational awareness, lovely Rita. She needed more information.

"Did you give me . . . drugs? Sedatives?"

No answer.

"Okay. Is it like a cochlear implant, or something?"

"Cochlear implants are glorified hearing aids," he said, as a teacher would to a slow student. "I'd never deal in something as clumsy as a cochlear implant."

In spite of the circumstances, and her feelings of helplessness, his arrogance—the way he dismissed her question out of hand—rubbed her the wrong way. She was, after all, a *surgeon*.

Screw you, you condescending bastard, she thought.

Then another thought immediately surfaced: *Can he read my mind?*

The concept terrified her.

Impossible.

But was it?

Because here you are, lovely Rita, talking to this man inside your head.

The idea that he might be able to read her mind made her consider cutting off her left ear.

Seriously. In the hopes of removing whatever it was he'd put there, or at least doing enough damage to it so that it couldn't work.

She knew that cutting off her own ear was not

a thing a rational person would do. That it meant psychosis.

She didn't care. She would NOT have him rummaging around inside there, dissecting her emotions, eavesdropping on her thoughts. So she coolly began to plan out the steps: disinfect the skin with betadine, numb it with lidocaine, incise it and the underlying cartilage with a scalpel—a number fifteen blade should do just fine.

After a few moments, he said, "Dr Wu? Hello? Did you hear what I said? Can you still hear me?"

She hesitated. Two possibilities here: Either he couldn't read her mind; or he could, but was pretending he couldn't. She decided, for now, that he couldn't.

Probably.

She laid her ear-removal plans aside, and said, "But I've never heard of anything like this. It just doesn't seem possible."

"Do you recall what I do for a living?"

"I—well. Hmm." She knew he was rich although she couldn't remember why. Biotechnology, maybe? The biotechnology industry was big in San Diego.

"Suffice to say I have sufficient resources to develop and produce this kind of device," he said. "As well as the intellect and experience to oversee its development."

He paused before continuing. "Is it really that much of a leap, what you and I are doing right now? Think of all of the recent, remarkable developments in biotechnology and medicine. Stem cells for growing brand-new organs. Microscopic machines that seek out and destroy cancer cells. Face transplants. Your patients, and the public, seem to take these kinds of things for granted."

"Is it . . . permanent? This thing?"

No answer.

"Okay, then," she said. "Can I still hear out of my left ear?"

"Yes."

"I'm really the only one who can hear you?"

"Yes."

"And . . . you can hear other people around me?"

"Obviously."

"How can you hear me?"

"Vibrations, mostly," Finney said. "Carried through your skull. You might recall it's why your voice sounds different to you than it does to everyone else."

She conceded it made sense. If all of this was happening in her imagination, if she truly was experiencing a psychotic break, her psychosis had concocted a scenario with airtight logic and more creativity than she would ever have given herself credit for having.

Except for one incongruity: "But . . . you knew when Lucy had finished cleaning herself up at the sink . . . and then when she'd walked over to her locker. How did you know that? You couldn't have figured that out just by listening."

"Your glasses, Dr. Wu."

She touched the frame. "What about them?"

"You left them lying on the bench next to her locker when you went to the sinks."

"I don't understand . . ."

He sighed. "I would have thought these things would have been more obvious to you. Perhaps I've overestimated you. I watched your colleague enter the room, Dr. Wu, with your glasses. The camera I've installed in them is quite hidden and allows me to see what you see."

"But I thought you told me earlier you weren't interested in seeing any of us, umm . . . naked."

"I said undressed, not naked." His tone remained even. "Your stocky surgical colleague wasn't naked. Besides which, I certainly could have done without seeing the parts of her that I did. In any event, interest—or my lack of it—in seeing naked women is irrelevant to our purpose."

"*What* purpose?"

"We'll discuss that shortly."

"What if I call security? Or the police?"

"And tell them what, exactly, Dr. Wu?" Finney's voice was soft. "That, after being discovered passed out naked on your own operating-room table, you heard a voice in your head? The voice of a man whose wife previously died under your care? How do you think that will sound to security, or to the police?"

She knew exactly how it would sound.

Like I'm a paranoid, psychotic schizophrenic.

She'd probably find herself locked up on the inpatient psych ward before lunchtime.

Maybe I belong there.

She could feel herself slipping, starting to lose her mental footing again, sliding toward blind panic, and perhaps psychosis. Like Moses.

"Why?" she whispered.

"You need to speak a bit louder, Dr. Wu."

"Why are you doing this to me?"

He was quiet for several seconds.

"Did you know she was pregnant, Dr. Wu?"

Oh, God.

Her legs had become rubber. She collapsed heavily onto the bench, closed her eyes, pressed the flats of her palms against them, and rubbed.

Of *course* she'd known.

"Yes," she whispered. She stopped rubbing, but kept her hands pressed over her eyes, as if hiding behind them.

"Two months," he said. No emotion, just a flat recitation of the facts. "Two months along. Our first. We hadn't told anybody yet. Not even Jenny's parents. They'd been planning on coming for a visit, and she'd wanted to surprise them. But then she got sick. The appendicitis. You must have done a pregnancy test before the surgery, right? When she came into the emergency room."

Yes, I knew. Finney seemed to have forgotten the detailed conversations Rita had had with him before his wife's emergency appendectomy, explaining the substantial risks the anesthesia and surgery would pose to the pregnancy.

He fell silent for a long time, then said: "She was so excited. I'd never seen her so excited about anything, ever, the way she was about the b—the pregnancy."

(Baby he almost said BABY God he's making this HARD)

"It was all she could do to keep from telling everyone she knew, as soon as the doctor confirmed the home test," he continued. "We would be out to dinner with her friends, and it would be obvious she wasn't drinking alcohol, and her women friends would, ah, giggle and wink at each other. They'd ask her why she wasn't having any wine. Women always seem to be . . . attuned to those kinds of things."

Oh God, why is he talking about this?

"Jenny would laugh and change the subject. She'd also sit on her hands. Yes. I remember that very distinctly. She'd place her hands underneath her legs. I think—because she was happy. She always sat on her hands when she was excited about something. Like . . . like a child would."

Oh, God.

"It's all she talked about when we were alone." He sounded distant. Distracted. "Getting a room ready. Buying baby clothes. Toys. Strollers. Names, of course."

She waited for him to continue. When he didn't, she said, from behind her hands, "I'm sorry. I'm so very sorry."

Oh God dear God this can't be happening to me.

A beat. An ominous one.

"Not nearly as sorry as I was."

Another, longer, even more ominous beat.

"As sorry as I *am*, Dr. Wu." The slight emphasis he placed on the word *am* felt like a punch to her stomach.

She dropped her hands from her face and stared up at the ceiling. "But my ear. If someone were to look inside there, or scan my head, with a CT, or an MRI—"

"My technology is for all intents and purposes undetectable. A medical examination will reveal some inflammation, perhaps a little bleeding around your tympanic membrane. The same goes for a head CT or MRI. Minor findings easily explained, if necessary, as the self-injurious behavior of a paranoid schizophrenic."

She felt exhausted. Weak. Defeated.

Afraid.

No way out. There's no way out.

But the question was: no way out of *what*?

This grieving, unbalanced (*crazy?*) husband of a former patient had trapped her, in an elaborate and perfectly executed—what? *Setup,* she supposed. But *why*? Setup for *what*? What did Finney want from her?

"What do you want?" Rita asked.

No answer.

Her cell phone trembled on the bench, announcing the arrival of another text message.

"What do you want from me?"

Another minute of silence, her cell rumbling every fifteen seconds or so, as if expressing indignation over being ignored.

Having received no response from Finney, Rita picked up her phone and read the message. It was the nurse in the pre-op area, insisting for the third time that she come and see Mrs. Sanchez.

"I want you," he finally said, "to operate on Mrs. Sanchez."

SPENCER

Spencer was halfway to work and still thinking about that damn Ford Fiesta in front of Rita's.

It was just a car parked on a street, he told himself. He was being paranoid. He had to get his mind off it.

Raj. I'll call Raj.

The clock on his dashboard read just after 7:00 A.M. He'd long ago settled on 7:00 A.M. as an arbitrary cut-off time, on weekdays, for calling people who weren't surgeons. On weekends he stretched it out to eight.

"Call Raj," he said.

"Calling Raj," his hands-free phone replied.

After several rings, he heard a drowsy, interrogatory grunt that Spencer accepted as a greeting: "Huh?"

"Hey, man," Spencer said. "Good morning."

"Spencer?" Raj groaned. "Shit. Dude, it's barely even light outside."

Spencer grinned. "Day's a wasting, man." Like many men of a certain age, Spencer and Raj downshifted a gear in the maturity department when around one another, which in their case meant peppering their conversations with obscenities, *dude's*, and *man's*. Raj, who, like Spencer, was single, was more enthusiastic in this pursuit than Spencer, probably because he was closer to thirty than to forty and less inclined to embrace adulthood.

"Speak for yourself." Raj yawned. "*Brain surgeons,* dude. What the hell do you want?"

"The MRI data. Wondering if you had the results yet from yesterday's supercomputer analyses—the ones you ran during our designated time."

"Of *course,*" Raj said, exasperated. "Didn't you check your e-mail? I sent it around 3:00 A.M." Raj was one of those enviable people who required little sleep.

"No."

"You woke me up at the crack of dawn for *this*? *Come on*, Spencer. What are you, like, ninety years old? Even my *grandmother* knows people don't talk on the phone anymore."

An elegant, silver-haired woman driving a red Tesla abruptly cut Spencer off, inches separating her rear bumper from his front. Spencer leaned on his horn. He caught a glimpse of mirrored designer sunglasses sizing him up in the Tesla's rearview. Then, with languid grace, the woman stretched a fine-boned hand out the driver's side window and extended her middle finger. Spencer suppressed an unchivalrous urge to respond in kind, and growled, "I didn't have time this morning to check e-mail before I left for work."

"Not my problem."

"Come *on*, Raj. Just tell me."

A pause. "Are you wearing it?"

Oops. Spencer's eyes darted to the leather satchel (a gift from his parents last Christmas) in the front passenger seat. *Shit.*

"You're not wearing it, are you?" Raj said.

"No."

"Why?"

Because I was thinking about the Fiesta. Which he'd never admit to Raj because he'd then have to explain what he'd been doing outside his ex-girlfriend's house at six in the morning. Besides which, Raj wasn't brimming over with warm and fuzzy feelings toward Rita.

"I, uh, forgot."

"Come *on*, man. We *need* those data. Your name's on the patent, too. You should care about this as much as I do. Put it on now, and I might tell you about the results."

Spencer *really* wanted to hear about those super-computer results. He'd been waiting for months. Besides, Raj was right: He should be wearing the damn thing. There was no excuse.

He pulled his Prius to a stop behind the red Tesla, which was idling at a red light.

"Okay. Just give me one sec."

Intermittently casting glances at the traffic light, Spencer opened a side pocket of the satchel and removed a tan-colored, circular object the size and thickness of a quarter. He peeled a removable strip from one side of it, revealing an adhesive backing. He pushed the object, adhesive side down, to the skin behind his right ear, where it stuck fast, like a Band-Aid.

He felt around on top of it with his forefinger until he located a small knob sticking up along one edge of its circular border. Using his fingernail, he pushed the knob along a tiny linear track that ran from one side of the circle, through the object's center, and ended at the opposite side.

"All set," he said, once the knob had clicked into position at the opposing edge of the circle. "I just turned it on."

"Let me check the integrity of the EEG signal."

All of a sudden, the Prius's satellite radio, tuned to a classical station, started to fade in and out. Spencer tried a different station. Same story. "Hey. Raj. My satellite radio isn't working."

"Yeah. The same thing happens in my car when I'm

wearing it. The signal sometimes screws with satellite and wireless. Need to work on that."

Spencer drummed his fingers idly on the steering wheel, waiting for the light to change, and for Raj to confirm things were good on his end. EEGs (or, more properly, *electroencephalograms*) were devices that mapped the electrical currents of the brain. Neurologists used EEGs to diagnose diseases like epilepsy. Existing EEGs were big and bulky, and required numerous electrodes placed over the skull with wires connecting them to a recording machine.

The EEG that Spencer now wore, designed and built by him and Raj (well, Raj, mostly), required only a single wireless electrode placed behind the right ear. This electrode transmitted brain-wave signals directly to a server in Raj's lab, and Raj could monitor these signals with an app on his phone. It was slick stuff, with tons of commercial applications. Already a few biotech companies were sniffing them out, but he and Raj needed more proof that it actually worked before they could start trying to close deals.

"Okay. We've got a nice signal," Raj said. "Recording as we speak. Has anyone ever told you that you have beautiful brain waves?"

"Sweet talker. I bet you say that to all the neurosurgeons."

"Only the cute ones. I see you're on Torrey Pines Road. Heading north."

"How did—"

"The signal from the EEG's like a GPS. Shows your exact location. Hadn't I mentioned that before?"

"No. But—cool, I guess. In a disturbing, Big Brother kind of way."

"Oh, *please*. No different than your cell phone. Do you have the extra EEG pads I gave you?"

"Yes." As he drew a second EEG pad from his satchel and shoved it into his pocket, the light turned green, and the red Tesla shot away like a dragster. Spencer scowled and slid his Prius forward at a sensible speed. "Just in case I find someone else stupid enough to wear one. So. The MRI data? How do they look?"

"Awesome. Hold on a sec." Raj groaned, and Spencer heard bedsprings squealing. He was getting out of bed. "This generation of software can take existing images and sharpen them *way* better than we'd ever hoped. *Huge* improvement."

"Really?" Spencer was skeptical. The previous version of their MRI software had been pretty damn impressive.

In addition to being longtime buddies, Raj and Spencer were research collaborators, both professors at the University of California. Spencer was no slouch in the IQ department, and he jokingly pointed out to friends that what Raj did for a living wasn't exactly brain surgery. But they both knew that Raj's intellect, armed with an MD from UCLA and a PhD in applied physics from Cal Tech, could run circles around Spencer's.

Together, they aimed to improve the diagnosis of brain tumors and other diseases with magnetic resonance imaging: MRI. Rather than enhance the MRI machines themselves—which were big, expensive things that filled up entire rooms—they were working on the pictures: the grey-hued images from which radiologists diagnosed diseases, and which neurosurgeons like Spencer used as road maps for performing brain surgery. MRIs were essentially digital photographs. And like any digital photograph, MRIs could be touched up, their pixels coaxed into sharper and more precise images.

So, like a super-advanced form of Photoshop, Raj and Spencer were writing new software to improve MRIs. They were a perfect team: Spencer supplied the surgical expertise, patients, and MRIs; Raj supplied the engineering and software-coding skills, and a few grad students for grunt work. They'd been working on this for the last three years and were getting really good at it. A few months ago, in fact, they'd scored a five-million-dollar government grant that would keep their lab going for at least another five years.

"Really. Wait till you see the images. They're *awesome*. We're able to make out structures the size of proteins. *Proteins*, Spencer! Small ones, on the order of less than fifty amino acids in length. Think about it. Think about what we could do with that!"

Over the phone, a door squeaked on its hinges, followed by a *knock* of plastic striking ceramic.

A toilet seat going up, Spencer recognized. Raj continued to talk over the sound that started, predictably, a moment later.

"Yeah. I'm thinking if I tweak the algorithms a little more, we'll be able to see early recurrent glioma. And possibly structural changes consistent with a pre-

Alzheimer's state, or early Parkinson's. What do you think?"

"Uh, sure. Okay." Spencer tried to block, without success, an image of Raj at the other end of the line, holding the cell phone with one hand while obliging his biological needs with the other. "Raj, do you *really* have to take a piss while we're talking on the phone?"

"Yes," Raj said, yawning. "Anyway. It's going to put us years ahead. A goddamn work of art, if I do say so. Those envious pricks at Hopkins (like Coleman, re-member *that* asshole?) are going to *shit* when they see this." *Flush.* "When we submit to a journal . . . Oh, shit. *Shit.*"

"What?"

"The storm!" Raj was practically shouting into the phone. "Dude, I totally forgot about that storm."

"What are you talking about?"

"That offshore storm! It's all over Twitter."

He didn't know how Raj had pulled off that feat of multitasking: checking his Twitter feed while talking on the phone and taking a piss. He didn't want to know. Raj had always been incapable of doing just one thing at a time. His mind always seemed to be racing in at least five different directions, even, Spencer suspected, during the few hours he slept.

"Oh. Right. What about it?"

"Consistent swells with ten-foot faces. Ten feet! And breaking totally clean. I've got to get down to Black's, dude."

Black's Beach was a popular surf spot at the base of

steep cliffs. Turner Hospital and the university campus sat at the top of the cliffs overlooking Black's. Spencer's understanding was that, back in the seventies, Black's had been some kind of hippie nude beach. These days, though, it drew properly attired surfers, sunbathers, families, and the occasional paunchy old man wearing nothing but a G-string and leering grin. It went without saying that you never made eye contact with those guys, who wandered the shoreline like enormous, bronzed crabs. Ever.

Raj was a surfer, and, despite his ungainly physique, a damn good one. Raj preferred the most direct route to Black's from his campus lab: clambering down steep, switchbacking trails carved into the precarious sandstone of the four-hundred-foot-high cliffs, surfboard tucked underneath his arm. Spencer thought he was nuts, risking his life for a couple of seconds perched atop a damn six-foot piece of fiberglass.

"Thought you would have heard about that by now. I saw a bunch of guys down at Calumet this morning on my run. It was packed."

"I'm not surprised. I'll get in a quick surf, then head over to the lab." Raj's enthusiasm and energy spilled through the receiver; it sounded as if his four hours of sleep would suffice. "Probably only a few good hours of waves left."

"You want to meet for lunch?"

"Sure. Sushi? At that place near Higdon Park?" The view from there, a sweeping one of the Pacific, was phenomenal.

"Okay. How about one o'clock?"

"Great."

Spencer was approaching the mouth of a steep canyon. "Raj. I'm about to drive through the canyon, so I'm probably going to lose you. I'll look over those data, and we'll talk more at lunch. Sound good?"

"Yeah, sounds—" But then, as Spencer had anticipated, the connection was gone.

Spencer grinned. This was great news, and it shoved the memory of the tumbledown Ford Fiesta parked in front of Rita's house out of his mind. He couldn't wait to see Raj at lunch.

As he wound his way along the four-lane road through the canyon, two lanes in either direction divided by a concrete median, the grey-haired woman in the red Tesla, having switched lanes several more times, got caught in a knot of traffic, and ended up behind him and one lane over.

This presented him, he realized wickedly, with a golden opportunity to cut *her* off, and trap her behind the knot of cars. Teach her a lesson. Show her how it felt.

He gripped the wheel harder as he began to change lanes and nudge his car into the small gap of road in front of the Tesla.

But, no.

He shifted the Prius back into his lane.

He was a better man than that. He would not cut her off. He didn't do road rage. Or any kind of rage.

Instead, he maintained his lane, turned the radio— which still wasn't working properly—off, and focused on running through the steps of his first (and only) operation that morning.

SEBASTIAN

Sebastian wondered what kind of conversation Finney and Wu were having right now, compliments of the device.

The device.

The device, truly, was a piece of work. A goddamn technological marvel.

Sebastian had never encountered anything like it; and as someone who'd had access to a lot of secrets over the years, he'd seen some weird sci-fi-type shit in his time. When this thing got out (and it *would* eventually get out), every government, crime syndicate, and multinational corporation in the world was going to want one.

There were all kinds of applications. Mostly military, of course: surveillance, field communications, interrogation.

Interrogation.

It was while developing interrogation techniques that, he knew, the designers had stumbled across the device's most intriguing—and unexpected—asset.

Not to mention its most goddamn disturbing one.

This line of research had been pursued in a different group of test subjects: all young men, of all ethnicities. They'd had the look of soldiers about them, he'd thought. They'd seemed more defiant than the others. Harder. Terrorists? Rebels? It depended on your point of view.

To his practiced eye, though, they looked to be true bad guys. Cold-blooded killers with empty stares, the kind that filmed themselves hacking off the heads of screaming prisoners in orange jumpsuits. There were more of these men in the world than Sebastian cared to count, men you didn't waste time shedding tears over, and they'd provided a steady stream of fresh material on which the designers could experiment.

The research methods differed with this group. There were interrogators. You could hear them off camera, barking questions at the subjects in various languages. From the materials provided him, it was impossible for Sebastian to tell for certain which countries were involved. Which was just as well, since that information might have landed him facedown in a ditch with a bullet through the back of his head.

He knew the device was going to render obsolete every technique of information extraction conceived since the dawn of time. The goddamn thing practically read minds.

But there were . . . side effects. Irreparable ones that, even when they befell men such as these, gave Sebastian pause.

The interrogators had first tried a direct approach: asking the same questions over and over, like a song set on an endless repeating loop. Sleep held no escape because it was a physiological impossibility while the device was receiving voice broadcasts. Eventually, the subjects told their interrogators *everything*. The longest any had lasted before talking was twenty-four hours—and that guy had ended up spending the remainder of his short life with his hands clamped over his ears, screaming in repeated, ululating bursts the answers to questions that were no longer being asked. Which made the interrogators curious: Were there other methods that were even quicker?

Sebastian suspected that they had drawn their next inspiration—pumping loud heavy metal and hard-core rap into the subjects' heads—from U.S. soldiers, who had employed similar tactics (albeit over loudspeakers) in places like Gitmo. This had an unfortunate tendency to drive the subjects insane with breathtaking rapidity, and usually before any useful information could be extracted. It was quickly abandoned. Still, Sebastian, recognizing many of the song selections, admired the interrogators their appreciation of these musical genres and gave them props for at least mixing some pretty decent shit.

Then somebody got the bright idea to transmit subliminal messages. Sebastian didn't grasp all of the underlying mechanisms, which involved advanced theories mixing psychology, biology, and engineering. He had a hunch that the device's designers didn't have a clue, either, and were just throwing around fancy words to explain things they otherwise couldn't.

Sebastian had always thought of subliminal messaging as when companies tried to get you to buy their shit—beer or pickup trucks or whatever—by flashing pictures of naked chicks, or a word like *sex*, across a TV screen so quickly your conscious brain couldn't process it, but your subconscious brain could, so your subconscious brain nudged your conscious brain and said *hey, asshole, buy that beer,* because *that beer* equated to mind-blowing sex with hot girls.

Except the subliminal signals the device used weren't pictures of naked girls but timed electrical pulses transmitted into the subjects' brains by way of the vestibu-locochlear nerve. What the designers hoped was that, in combination with spoken suggestions, these pulses would allow them access to the subconscious, like downloading data from a hard drive. The idea was to coax the subjects into divulging information in more detail, and with more reliability, than through conscious recall—to in effect obtain buried memories.

It didn't work—at least not how they'd planned. They weren't able to tap into a subject's subconscious and pluck memories out like so many cookies from a jar.

But it turned out to be an even bigger mind-fuck than what they'd hoped for: In response to the sublimi-nal signals, the subjects unintentionally *acted out* the content of the messages.

If, for instance, the designers transmitted a signal that translated roughly as *tell us how you got here*, the subjects paced around and around their cell, as if walk-ing over a distance; or they mimicked the motions of steering a car. And they didn't realize they were do-ing it.

Mind control.

The designers had blundered into mind control.

Well, okay, not mind control, *exactly*. Not like pull-ing a lever on a machine, or issuing commands like a drill sergeant to an Army recruit. You couldn't send a message that said *laugh out loud* or *stick your hand in a blender*, then kick back and watch as the subject col-lapsed into giggle fits, or ground up their fingers on the puree setting. It didn't work that way. The subjects tended to reject direct commands.

So the designers perfected their technique. They

learned to be subtler, more refined: to perform some mental sleight of hand and *trick* the subjects into doing what you wanted them to do.

It wasn't mind control.

But it was pretty damn close.

Pretty damn close.

Sebastian had seen a hypnotist once, in high school. A big fat guy with poufy hair and gold chains, in a velvet tuxedo with a ruffled shirt. He'd called himself Dr. Dream, or some such dumb-ass name, and had come to their school to put on a show. When he'd asked for volunteers, the popular kids had fallen over each other to clamber up on stage and make fools of themselves. Dr. Dream had tapped each on the forehead, and they'd responded by barking like dogs, performing air guitar, writhing like strippers—whatever Dr. Dream had told them. Some crazy shit. Meanwhile, he had sauntered back and forth across the stage, clutching a cordless microphone, tapping students on the head while crooning cheesy Vegas lounge songs.

Sebastian, only fourteen at the time, had concluded that the whole thing was total, unmitigated bullshit. He still thought so: popular kids pretending and preening, grubbing for more popularity. They'd known exactly what they were doing up on that stage. And the hypnotist? Please. He'd known ten-year-olds down on the corner that could run a better con with three-card monte than that bloated asshole.

But Finney's device was the real deal. No bullshit, cheesy-ass lounge act here. He'd seen it with his own eyes, in the tapes. Not hypnosis, not really. It was more like *persuasion.*

And this was what he and Finney had planned for Wu this morning.

The device's electrical signals would render her susceptible to spoken commands. The designers called this process—the combination of electrical signals and verbal commands—*embedding*. Once embedding was complete, Wu would experience an overwhelming desire to carry out the commands but would otherwise act and feel normally. Certain psychoactive drugs, administered before the signals, would make her mind more pliable. He'd seen to it that Wu had received healthy doses of these this morning, when he'd implanted the device in her ear.

Embedding had its limitations, and it didn't always work. Complex commands—things that required multiple steps or complicated reasoning—were out of the question because they would confuse the subject. Sometimes, too, the subjects fought back and resisted the impulses, especially if the suggestions weren't in some way connected to their personal experiences. You couldn't ask a plumber to fly an airplane, or, for that matter, a pilot to fix your toilet. It didn't work that way.

Afterward, most of the subjects didn't remember anything specific about the embedding process—just the urge to carry out the commands and a sense of having awoken from a dream. Those that did would describe vivid out-of-body experiences, or the sensation of being split in two. *It was like I was seeing and talking to my twin*, one of them had later said. Some reported buzzing sounds, and feelings of unease. Confusion. Dizziness. Vomiting. A few had had seizures.

And one other thing: You could transmit the persuasion signals only in brief, concentrated bursts. Otherwise, you risked scrambling the subject's brains to jelly.

In the videos, this had happened more than once, when the interrogators had intentionally bombarded subjects with suggestions. Just to see what would happen.

The results were always the same: pain, and screaming, which sometimes lasted hours, then silent, open-mouthed stares. Sebastian couldn't decide which was more disturbing: the screaming or the staring, the subjects' eyes fixed on something beyond the camera lens that only they could see. Those men had all died a few days later, still staring, and no one figured out why. Their autopsies had showed zilch.

Sebastian had made himself watch every one of the videos. He hadn't had to do that. He sure as hell didn't want to. He'd seen a lot of disturbing shit over the years, but it didn't get any more goddamn disturbing than this.

But he was a professional, and he always acted like one. So he'd watched the videos and learned everything he could about the device. He'd studied all of its components, specifications, capabilities, and shortcomings. Alfonso had always insisted Sebastian was good at tinkering with things. And now he knew just as much about the goddamn thing as Finney.

Hell, he thought. *Maybe more.*

He checked his watch again and tried not to think about the teenager, twitching, curled up on the floor in her cell.

Yes, there were plenty of bad guys in the world.
When did I become one of them?

RITA

"Operate on Mrs. Sanchez? You mean . . . with the auto-surgeon?"

Rita stood up. It took a surprising amount of effort. She fixed her eyes on the ceiling, as if Finney were lurking somewhere around up there, in the crawl space above the ceiling tiles.

"Yes. I want you to perform the auto-surgeon operation. This morning. As scheduled."

"That's . . . it?"

"Yes."

"Why?"

"Does it matter?"

Every neuron in her brain was screaming at her that operating this morning was the wrong thing to do.

"I don't think . . . I'm not sure I'm up to operating this morning. I was going to, uh, cancel the surgery."

Finney didn't say anything.

"I just—I want to be safe," she added.

A long silence followed. Eventually, he said, "What about Jenny? Were you worried about being safe with her?"

Her throat tightened. She bunched up her fists and drove them underneath her glasses and into her eyes.

She would not cry.

Not with *him* around.

But the problem, of course, was that he was *always* around.

FINNEY

Studying the readouts on his tablet, he denied himself, once again, the satisfaction of a smile.

She's ready for embedding.

He'd prepped her long enough. Plowed the rich soil of her mind. Now it was time to sow the seeds and convince her to operate on Mrs. Sanchez, and to set the main part of his plan in motion.

Dr. Wu hadn't been that far off the mark when she'd guessed that the device was a cochlear implant. It was, of sorts: conceived by a small, innovative start-up focused on curing deafness, which he'd happened across several years ago. He'd invested a healthy amount in it. Now the company was on the verge of revolutionizing the treatment of deafness and netting him tens of millions in the process.

Long before he'd met Jenny, Finney had also conceived of the device's other uses and quietly moved the development of these offshore: to locales under the authority of wealthy and powerful clients who'd made up in discretion what they'd lacked in scruples. He'd been aware of the medical experiments they'd conducted for him. It was unpleasant, to be sure, but necessary; he'd looked the other way because business was business, after all, and the international market for this would be huge.

After Jenny's death, he'd had to rush the device's final development, to ready it for the field ahead of the original timetable.

Now, here they were.

Ironically, Jenny had worked with deaf children in college and had delighted in the cochlear implant concept.

"You're making the world a better place, Morgan," she'd said when he'd told her about its (legitimate) application over breakfast one morning, and kissed him on the cheek. "I'm so proud of you."

He'd given serious thought then and there to ending the offshore program, had even taken a few preliminary steps to divest himself of it.

But then she'd gotten sick a few days later.

Jenny.

Much as he believed in what he was now doing, he had to concede that she would not have approved.

But she wasn't here.

Finney swiped his tablet screen with two fingers. A red circle appeared in the middle of it. He tapped it. A large "5" replaced the red circle and proceeded into a countdown. At "0" the screen burst into a pixelated riot of multicolored sine waves.

The die was cast.

He couldn't see it, or hear it, or touch it; but Finney knew that at that moment a pulse of electromagnetic energy was reaching out from his tablet, seeking its brother embedded in the substance of Dr. Wu's brain—an electronic umbilical cord that would link her thoughts with the tablet, and, by way of the tablet, with him.

A single word flashed on the screen: NOMINAL.

The connection was established.

RITA

Rita perceived a slight tickling sensation inside her skull, as if someone had removed part of the bone and passed the tip of a feather along the surface of her brain.

She pulled her fists away from her eyes. The impulse to cry had disappeared, erased by the tickling feeling, which felt so *odd*. She touched her left ear and shook her head, as if to clear it away.

But the sensation was gone.

"What was that?" she said.

"Dr. Wu," Finney said. "You need to operate on Mrs. Sanchez this morning. You can't cancel the operation. You're a surgeon."

And a strange but compelling thought rang through Rita's head, as if a part of her mind had grabbed a bullhorn and was shouting:

I've got to operate on Mrs. Sanchez this morning! Because I'm a surgeon!

Without thinking, she stood up—

(*Because I've got to operate on Mrs. Sanchez this morning*)

—intending to hurry to pre-op to tell Mrs. Sanchez it was time for the operation.

She went ten paces before she stopped.

But.

No.

She shook her head fiercely from side to side.

Where the hell had *that* stupid idea come from? Operate this morning on Mrs. Sanchez? That didn't make sense. Any sense at all. She'd already decided to cancel. Operating wouldn't be safe.

"But . . . that doesn't make sense," she said aloud. "There's no reason for me to do that."

It was so *hard* to push those words out of her mouth, an effort as intense as any of the biggest running races of her life. Which was so strange. She felt like she was trying to move concrete blocks with her tongue. Why was that?

"There's no reason for me to operate this morning," she said.

FINNEY

Finney raised his eyebrows and studied the colored displays on his tablet.

Interesting.

And annoying.

She was blocking him.

Her resistance was impressive. He hadn't expected her to shrug off the embedding so quickly, or with so little effort. Her intellectual discipline—or willpower, whatever you wanted to call it—was formidable. And, he conceded, admirable. In its own way.

The signal strength, the amount of power he was transmitting to her brain, was set to fifty percent, the level that had worked for most of the experimental subjects. He swiped the tablet with his index finger and increased the power level.

He increased it *a lot*. Not to its maximum, but close. Admirable or not, he was in control here.

Not she.

RITA

She winced as the tickling sensation reappeared in her brain.

Except now it wasn't tickling.

It was much more intense—like a buzzing, or a humming, that rattled her head like the wheels of an approaching train shaking its tracks, then vanishing with the same abruptness that had accompanied its arrival.

She felt—

(*what the hell had that buzzing been?*)

—really, *really* strange.

She raised her left hand to her left ear, and . . .

. . . and in that moment somehow stepped outside herself.

Literally outside myself was her very first, very vivid impression.

But that can't be, she thought. *I can't* literally *step outside myself.*

Still, there she was, standing in the locker room, staring at herself: Because she now saw another Rita there, as if she'd become a pair of twins. The other Rita was standing about a foot away, holding her gaze.

She raised her hand, thinking that the other Rita would raise hers at the same time, too, like a mirror image; but the other Rita stood there with her arms at her sides, staring back, acting like she was waiting for something.

With the peculiar logic of a dream, all this somehow made perfect sense to Rita.

"What's happening to me?" Rita asked the other Rita.

The other Rita, her twin, blinked but didn't answer.

"Am I speaking these words out loud?"

The other Rita said nothing.

She didn't want to just stand there gawking at herself. So Rita began to pace a slow circle around the other Rita. This also made sense, for no reason other than it just did.

"Is this happening inside my head?"

"Does it matter?" the other Rita replied.

Except the other Rita wasn't using Rita's voice.

She was using Finney's.

And she heard his voice only in her left ear.

Which her dream logic said was just fine. Right as rain.

"So you *can* talk," Rita said.

"Yes," the other Rita said.

"I guess maybe it doesn't matter whether this is happening in my head or not," Rita said. "And I guess, well, that I *could* maybe operate on Mrs. Sanchez this morning."

"Yes," the other Rita agreed in Finney's voice. "You're an outstanding surgeon."

"Yes, I am," Rita said. She was now completing her first circuit around the other Rita, who remained still.

"You've prepared for every possible eventuality," the other Rita said.

"Yes," Rita said.

"Mrs. Sanchez needs you. You need to do the auto-surgeon operation this morning," the other Rita said.

"Yes," Rita said.

"Mrs. Sanchez is sick. She needs your help."

"Yes. She needs my help," Rita said. She was now well into her second lap around the other Rita.

"You can help Mrs. Sanchez this morning with the auto-surgeon," the other Rita said in Finney's voice. "She needs you."

"Yes, she needs me," Rita said. She stopped, having completed her second loop around the other Rita. "I can help Mrs. Sanchez. This morning. Using the auto-surgeon."

Each Rita regarded the other, and in the dream logic, Rita could see both versions of herself at the same time, through two sets of eyes, and it was fine.

Just fine.

"Yes," both of them said, in unison, and the other Rita no longer spoke with Finney's voice, but with Rita's.

"I need to operate on Mrs. Sanchez using the auto-surgeon."

Both reached their left hands up to their left ears . . .

. . . and then Rita was in the hallway, outside the locker room, walking toward pre-op.

She stopped, blinked and looked around.

"How did I get out here?" she said.

No answer.

She shook her head and tried to remember what had happened. She felt as if she'd been dreaming, in the dream talking to a twin version of herself, then . . .

Then she was here. And the little bits of the dream she could recall were quickly fading into oblivion.

But how? And what had that dream been all about?

It doesn't matter, she thought. *Because I need to operate on Mrs. Sanchez. Using the auto-surgeon.*

Of that she was certain.

She started walking toward pre-op again.

Operating would be risky, yes. She knew she wasn't in the best shape this morning. But she needed to do the operation because Mrs. Sanchez was sick, and Rita needed to make her better.

"I need to operate on Mrs. Sanchez," she murmured.

"You won't regret this, Dr. Wu," Finney said in her ear.

To hell with you, some part of her wanted to tell him. *I'm getting out of here. I'm going home and crawling into bed.*

But she didn't say anything out loud, and her legs felt like they belonged to someone else as they took her toward pre-op.

Because, she thought, *I have to operate on Mrs. Sanchez.*

And Mrs. Sanchez was in pre-op.

SPENCER

Spencer's Prius glided into the multistory parking garage at Turner Hospital and settled into an empty space. As Spencer emerged, alongside a quiet side of Turner's main complex, and walked toward the hospital entrance, the new wing under construction came into view. He stared at the construction site as he passed it. He operated on people's brains for a living but had never outgrown the mindless appeal of watching lumbering construction machinery belch smoke and move super-heavy stuff around.

The new wing was scheduled to admit its first patient in eighteen months, and the site buzzed with frenzied progress. The wing was to be composed of one main, tall tower flanked by two smaller towers. Privately, he had nicknamed them the Holy Trinity, in spite of the fact that many of the rich philanthropists underwriting it were Jewish.

The three emerging towers had the look of one large domino bounded by two smaller dominoes, standing on end, the long ends facing east–west. The main tower topped out at ten stories, its final height, and high enough to provide the topmost floors (reserved for the VIP patients, naturally) with breathtaking views of the Pacific. Some of its bottom floors were already swathed with sheets of bluish-green glass that would, in time, swallow the entire complex.

The site teemed with workmen in hard hats, clambering through open spaces in the superstructure and swarming over naked girders. Some were welding steel beams, and showers of sparks tumbled from their torches; others were hammering away at walls, or laying electrical wiring; while still others assisted a large crane as it lifted an immense I-beam into place.

It was to be the jewel in Turner's crown. Three hundred luxurious beds, all in private rooms. The most advanced ICUs and operating rooms money could buy. A birthing center designed by a world-famous architect specializing in *wellness* and *spatial warmth*, whatever the hell that meant. Spencer was of two minds about the Trinity: On the one hand, the prospect of practicing medicine in a brand-new, kick-ass facility excited him; on the other, the shameless marketing trumpeting its grand opening made him wonder if they'd soon need to substitute the word *customer* for *patient* in the Hippocratic Oath.

Spencer had reached one of the employee entrances, an unmarked door on a quiet side of the hospital. He swiped his ID badge across the card reader next to the door. A light at the bottom of it turned from red to green, accompanied by a loud clicking sound. He pulled the door open and walked inside.

Just inside was a security guard squeezed into a small wooden booth. She was monitoring the adjacent ER waiting room, which was currently empty. "Norma!" he called to her. "How you doing this morning?"

"Dr. Cameron," she said, grinning. She set down her frayed paperback novel and grinned. "I'm doin' real good. How 'bout you?"

"Great. Broke up with that boyfriend of yours yet, Norma?"

Norma shifted in her seat. The booth she was sitting in swayed and groaned. She was tall, almost as tall as Spencer, and with nearly as much girth. She had an open face and friendly eyes.

"Nah. Not yet. He's still got some use left to him. But when I do, you'll be the first to know." She spoke with a slight lisp.

"I'd better. I'm not waiting around forever, you

know. *Somebody's* gotta make an honest man of me, Norma."

She threw her head back, let loose a big belly laugh, and pounded the small wooden lectern in front of her with a meaty fist. The booth around her looked ready to collapse. "You have a blessed day, now, Dr. Cameron."

"You too, Norma."

He strode a short distance down a busy corridor toward a set of stairs. As he started up them, a bolt of pain rumbled up his right leg from his knee. It grew a little worse with each step. He wondered, grumpily, if his knee was getting swollen.

But the pain diminished as he reached the second floor and left the stairs behind him. He headed toward pre-op, located next to the operating rooms, to see his patient before the operation.

SEBASTIAN

There she was.

He saw her stop just outside the locker-room door and glance around. Sebastian recognized the blank, fixed stare on her face right away and unwound the tight coil of his muscles an infinitesimal amount. He'd seen that expression before, many times.

The embedding had worked.

He observed with detached professionalism that, despite everything she'd been through, she actually looked pretty good. An attractive woman, of medium height, with intense brown eyes and an athletic build, she seemed to be holding up okay.

Still, appearances could be deceiving.

She took a few hesitant steps and stopped. Then she spun around in a small circle, and he saw her lips moving, as if she were having a conversation with herself.

That disturbed him because it reminded him of the girl in the cell, curled in the fetal position. Maybe she wasn't holding up as well as he'd thought. Training and discipline compelled him to hide his consternation.

Shit.

If she lost it now, he wouldn't finish this job, and he'd never get his money.

Sammy and Sierra's money.

But maybe she was just talking to Finney. He tamped down the uneasiness (*not anxiety, never anxiety, because anxiety, like guilt, was unprofessional*) rising in his belly and casually pushed himself off the wall to get an unobstructed view of her. He again pretended to text someone, for good measure adding a few shakes of the head, as if unhappy with what he was seeing on his screen. But his attention remain fixed on her.

Rita took a few hesitant steps, lifted her hand to her left ear, and started walking briskly away.

He was about to follow when the tiny headset hidden in his ear crackled.

"Sebastian."

Finally. About goddamn time.

He stopped and faced the wall, shielding his lips from any onlookers.

"Mr. Finney. Yes, I see her. I'm assuming that you successfully embedded the impulse to operate with the auto-surgeon this morning?"

"Yes. She's on her way to talk to the patient now."

"Took some time."

"Yes."

Sebastian waited. No additional explanations were forthcoming.

Cagey son of a bitch.

"Any problems, boss? Persuading her?"

"No."

So then what were you two talking about all that time?

"You mind, then, if I patch back into the feed?"

"No. I don't mind."

"Will you please grant me access?"

Please. Groveling to Finney like he was some little bitch. Sebastian hated that. The day this job ended and he got his money (*Sammy and Sierra's money*) couldn't come soon enough.

"Yes."

Sebastian tapped an app icon on his phone called Fruit Punch Drunk. The app looked like a game, and you could even play it: The object was to punch flying clusters of fruit before they hit you in the face. But buried within it, accessible with a combination inputted by hitting various types of fruit in a specific order, was its real purpose: to monitor the electronic signals going back and forth between Finney's control tablet and the device in Wu's head.

Sebastian had no control over Wu's device, or the inputs to it; only Finney did. Sebastian was but a spectator. He hated this. And even more frustrating was that Finney could lock him out, at any time—which was what he'd done earlier, when Wu was first waking up. Sebastian hated being kept in the dark. He was used to keeping *others* in the dark.

Now the inputs and outputs flowed across his screen as a series of colored graphs and figures, representing the electronic interactions between Finney and the device since he'd implanted it in Wu's skull a few hours ago. Sebastian chewed on the inside of his cheek as he studied the data.

"That's some pretty high signal strength there, boss."

"Nothing outside of our prior experience."

"But more than what we'd anticipated."

A LOT more.

"No. I disagree. She's requiring one, perhaps two standard deviations above the mean to maintain her directives."

Two standard deviations: that was a lot—a goddamn large amount of juice pumping into her brain. About as much as what the most resilient test subjects had been able to tolerate.

Right before they'd started to go insane.

"But right here, around 0700—the way you cranked it up so quickly to get her to respond to the commands. Don't you find that concerning?"

Because I sure as hell do.

A slight pause.

"No. Simply an . . . irregularity, Sebastian. One for which I quickly and effectively compensated. Nothing more."

Finney always talked like this, even in casual conversation. Formal. Deliberate. He liked ten-dollar words, and sentences that didn't end in prepositions.

To Sebastian it made Finney sound like a robot. Pure analytics. No emotion.

"Okay. If you say so, boss."

RITA

She was walking toward pre-op. The first operations of the day were scheduled to start soon, and the corridor hummed with activity. Nurses, doctors, and patients on gurneys crowded the hallway, heading in various directions, a blur of motion, and she weaved determinedly through it.

The left side of her head still hurt, but the pain was tolerable now; the throbbing had faded to a distant drumbeat. Her head felt clearer, as if she'd just awoken from a brief power nap, and while her stomach burned with acidy lumps of anxiety, her nausea had diminished.

Her phone buzzed. Without breaking stride, she fished it out of the back pocket of her scrubs and glanced at the screen (*Incoming call: home*) before lifting it to her right ear.

"Hi, Darcy," she said sheepishly. "Sorry. I, uh, forgot to call you back. Sorry."

"It's okay. I know you must be, like, *super* busy this morning."

"Yeah, I really am, kiddo," Rita said, preoccupied because she *needed to operate on Mrs. Sanchez.* Up ahead, she could see the automatic double doors leading into pre-op. "Is anything wrong? Everything okay?"

"I . . . think so. It's just . . . when I woke up this morning, I felt kind of, I dunno—*weird*, Ree."

"Uh-huh." Rita had almost reached the double doors.

"I don't know how to describe it." '

"Uh-huh."

"Ask her about her head," Finney said.

Rita almost dropped the phone.

She stopped a few feet short of the doors. Her chest tightened, as if someone were sitting on it, and she struggled to pull air into her lungs.

"What did you say?" Rita whispered.

Darcy: "What?"

Finney: "Ask your sister about her head, Dr. Wu."

Rita's fingers tightened around the phone—

(*Darcy how could HE know about Darcy?*)

—and she heard herself say, very slowly, "Darcy. Is, uh, is your . . . head okay?"

"Well, no, actually. I woke up with a horrible headache this morning." She hesitated. "How did you know about that, Ree?"

Oh God.

Finney murmured, "Ask her *where* her head hurts, Dr. Wu."

Rita wiped the gathering sweat from her forehead. "Where, kiddo? Where does your head hurt?"

"My left. All over. Shit, even my left *ear* hurts. But, whatever. That's not the weirdest part, Ree."

"What do you mean?" Rita's tight grip on the phone—

(*Oh God, Finney what did Finney do to my little sister?*)

—tightened.

"The weirdest part, the reason I called you, is—"

"Rita!" a man called out from behind her. Startled, Rita jerked her head away from the phone.

"Rita," he said again. She'd recognized that unmistakable baritone the instant she'd heard it, and knew who it was before she'd spun around to face its owner, making a beeline straight toward her from down the hallway.

"Dr. Montgomery," Finney said conversationally. "Of course. I've been expecting his involvement. I'm sure it didn't take long for him to hear about this morning's excitement."

In a tinny squawk projecting from her phone, which Rita was holding a foot away from her head, Darcy said, "Hello? Rita? Did you hear me? Are you still there? *Hello!* Can you hear me?"

So many different people at once; so many different voices to process at the same time.

It's enough to drive me crazy.

Rita brought the phone back up to her ear. "Ree, I have to go."

"That would be advisable," Finney said. "Dr. Montgomery is going to require your full attention."

Shut up, she spat at Finney in her mind. *Just shut up and let me think.*

"What? But, Rita—" Darcy began.

Rita covered her mouth with her hand, and said, "Darcy. I *really* have to go. I swear to God I'll call you back." She hung up and faced her boss, who was now standing in front of her, his arms folded.

"Hi, Chase."

"Good morning, Rita."

Chase Montgomery was a handsome man, in his early fifties, who had the contradictory magnetism peculiar to a certain species of fit, middle-age, Southern California white male: the lush dark hairline and strapping physique of a man fifteen years his junior but the sunbaked, crumpled face of one fifteen years his senior. Raised in Orange County, south of Los Angeles, he had a nut-brown face that was creased by years in Southern California's year-round sun. The crinkled implosion of exposed skin, and the excision of a few basal cell skin carcinomas, had failed to deter him from a hatless, SPF-free existence. He squinted a lot, even indoors, as if in perpetual bright sunshine. An avid cyclist, he was known to traverse hundreds of miles of blacktop in the steep hills outside San Diego each weekend on his high-performance bike.

Montgomery's elegant grey suit today appeared to have been poured over him, so well was it cut: stylish, but not in-your-face stylish; the same for his white dress shirt and blue-silk tie. She noticed he was wearing foundation this morning, in anticipation of the cameras, no doubt. Chase was a pro, after all—public relations and image control came as easily to him as breathing to others.

He smiled, which coaxed his wrinkles, despite the foundation, into deep chasms that radiated from the corners of his eyes and mouth and revealed his perfect, bleached-white teeth. Yes, his news-anchor smile. His press-conference smile. His everybody's-watching-so-I-have-to-look-good-for-the-cameras-and-the-whole-world smile.

She knew that smile too well and knew that she was in big trouble.

"Could we chat for a second, Rita?"

"Uh—sure."

He had already taken her with gentle but unmistakable firmness by the arm and steered her toward a small, unoccupied alcove carved into a nearby wall. As they traversed the bit of corridor leading to the alcove, he offered cheerful good mornings to several passing staff with the smoothness of a politician working the rope line at a campaign rally. His brilliant smile never once faltered, and the staff members grinned, glowing in the warmth of his attention.

But Rita wasn't fooled. She knew better. Chase wielded his interpersonal skills with the same ruthlessness and precision with which he handled a scalpel. Both talents had driven his meteoric rise.

The alcove functioned as an ad hoc storage space. A large portable fluoroscopy machine—a thick, metallic contraption the size of a large refrigerator and configured in the shape of the letter *C* (the descriptive but uninspired name for which was a *C-arm*)—guarded the entrance, providing just enough room on one side to allow passage into the enclosed space.

"In here, please," he said pleasantly. They squeezed through the opening single file: Rita first, followed by Chase, who, broad-shouldered and north of six feet by a few inches, stooped to fit into the space. It was darker and warmer than in the hallway. Boxes of equipment were stacked floor to ceiling, but there was room to move around.

The moment they were out of sight from the hallway, hidden behind the metallic bulk of the C-arm, Montgomery's lips smashed together to form a pale, slender line. He squinted at her from the shadows, his politician's smile gone.

"He looks upset," Finney observed.

"Let's talk," Montgomery said in a fierce *sotto voce*. "Do you want to tell me what the *hell* is going on here, Rita?"

"Chase, let me—"

He held up a hand. Chase always posed rhetorical questions when he was pissed off.

"First of all," he said. "You look awful. Absolutely awful. And the stories I'm hearing, Rita! Am I to understand that two nurses found you this morning in OR 10? Without, uh, without any—" A pained expression crossed his face, and for moment, he looked as uncomfortable as she'd ever seen him.

"Clothes," she finished. She spoke quickly so as to get a word in edgewise before he could cut her off again. "Yes, Chase. I wasn't wearing any clothes. But I can explain."

He extended his hand, palm up, and squinted. "By all means. Please."

She launched into the sleepwalking story she'd used earlier, this time injecting a few additional details (*I haven't been sleeping well lately . . . anxious I guess about the auto-surgeon . . . I think it finally caught up with me last night . . . happens when you take an Ambien*) in an attempt to bolster its authenticity.

Montgomery listened, squinting.

"Sleepwalking naked. I'm not sure it sounds any more convincing than when I heard it the first time,

Dr. Wu," Finney said, without a trace of sarcasm. Which made him sound sarcastic anyway.

"*Sleepwalking*, Rita?"

"I know it sounds strange, Chase. But I— There's no other explanation. I came in last night to do some final checks on the auto-surgeon. I was tired, I put my head down for a few minutes in the OR. I must have undressed and stretched out on the operating-room table without realizing it. It's the simplest explanation, right? You know, like Occam's razor."

"Hmmm." That was Finney. "Yes. Occam's razor. All things being equal, the simplest explanation is usually the correct one. An interesting argument, but I'm not sure I agree. The sleepwalking hypothesis involves several assumptions and isn't necessarily the simplest."

"Don't be glib, Rita," Chase said sharply. "This is serious." His eyes darted to the hallway beyond the protective sweep of the C-arm. "Goddammit. Your entire professional reputation is at stake here. Do you understand? How am I possibly going to keep this quiet? This whole thing—I mean, I've never seen anything like it. I've never *heard* of anything like it." He grunted. "*Sleepwalking*."

"He's going to tell you not to operate on Mrs. Sanchez," Finney said.

"Whatever happened to you last night, one thing is certain," Chase continued. "We need to cancel the auto-surgeon case this morning."

"But—"

"No." He drew a hand down his face and shook his

head. "No. Whatever happened to you this morning, it wouldn't look good. Besides, you don't look like you're in top form. We have to think of the patient. The patient always comes first, Rita."

I know that, Rita thought bitterly. *You think I don't know that, Chase?*

"You don't believe me?" she said.

Chase didn't reply. The corners of his mouth curled downward; but his eyes roved over her through the narrowed apertures of the squinted lids, paternal and sympathetic.

He looked away and ran his hand down his face.

"You don't believe me, Chase?" she pressed.

He laughed. Barked, really: a short, guttural chuckle. "Would you believe you, if you were me, Rita?"

His eyes swung back to her and searched her face. It was the way he always glared at a resident when he thought they were faking something about a patient, or trying to bullshit about some scientific paper they either didn't understand or hadn't read. It never failed to intimidate the hell out of them. She knew this from personal experience because she'd once been one of Chase's residents, and she'd learned the hard way never to bullshit him.

Or, at least, to never get *caught* bullshitting him.

"Is that really what you think happened, Rita?" he said softly.

She didn't hesitate. "Yes."

They stared at each other in silence for a full thirty seconds, like two kids playing at a staring contest. Chase finally conceded to Rita, dropping his eyes, spinning around on his heels, and running his hand down his face.

"This is fascinating," Finney murmured. "Absolutely fascinating. Listening to the two of you."

Chase began to pace, his chin cupped in his hand. The confines of the alcove prevented him from going more than five steps in any direction. Rita speculated how many circuits across the alcove, from one side to the other, it would take to make him dizzy.

"God*dammit,* Rita. Why this morning, of all mornings? Marketing's been working overtime on this for months. The media's all set up. There's a *Wall Street Journal* reporter here doing a feature. Several prominent surgeons, personal friends of mine, have flown in from the East Coast. Hell, I even convinced Linton to show up, from Boston. You sure as hell aren't doing me any favors, Rita."

She didn't attempt to reply.

"Then there's our hospital CEO, and the dean of the medical school . . . even the chancellor. All here for the auto-surgeon. If we back out now—"

His hand came down over his face, pulling and tugging.

Rita stared at him and for some random reason thought, *Well, that's a good way to smear your makeup.*

"Yes," Finney said. "This all does pose a problem."

She fought down the urge to clamp both her hands over her left ear, as if that would somehow keep him out of her mind.

God, why can't he just shut up?

Chase stopped pacing and gazed at the C-arm and the operating rooms beyond.

"The work. The amount of work we've put into this. And what are we going to *tell* everyone? It's going to look bad. Whatever we say. What *are* we going to say? We'll have to think of something. Something credible. We can say that the patient was too sick. Or not right for the surgery. Or equipment issues. Right?"

Finney said, "All potential excuses."

She wanted to scream at the top of her lungs: *God, just STOP TALKING!*

"We can spin it like that," Chase said. "Right?" The pitch of his voice rose on *right*, in a plaintive way, and his broad shoulders drooped. He ran his hand down his face again.

"You can't let him cancel the surgery," Finney said. "You have to talk him into letting you do it today, Dr. Wu."

No, I don't.

The thought had popped into her mind suddenly, and with a force that took her by surprise.

Of course I don't. I don't need to talk Chase into anything.

She squeezed her eyes shut, then opened them, as if for the first time that day. What the hell was she doing here, anyway, trying to talk Chase into doing something she didn't want to do? Something that would put a patient at terrible risk? She knew she shouldn't operate. So why were they even having this conversation?

Rita tugged at her left ear.

"No," she said aloud to Finney.

The word was loud in the small alcove.

SPENCER

Spencer's patient eyed him up and down.

"You a prayin' man, Doc?" he rumbled. A rancher—*third-generation*, he often reminded Spencer—from the arid mountains east of San Diego, he had a big barrel chest and even bigger voice.

"As a matter of fact, I am, Mr. Bogart," Spencer replied. He was standing over the man's gurney in the pre-op area.

Bogart's craggy face broke apart into a wide grin. "I knew it. You look like the prayin' type. I can always tell. Episcopalian?"

"Presbyterian."

"Close enough. Come on, then, son. We don't got all day." He reached up a rough, meaty paw, and Spencer took it. He had thick calluses, and the feel of it matched the look of Bogart's face.

"Sheila?" Bogart offered his other hand to the woman standing next to the gurney.

She was his sister, as small and mousy as her brother was large and burly. She stepped forward wordlessly, and Mr. Bogart's hand swallowed hers.

"Sheila's a pastor in our church," he explained.

Bogart's wife had passed away last year. "Goddamn pancreas cancer ate her to the bone," he'd growled during their first meeting. "Never smoked or drank a day in her life. Pesticides, Doc. It was those goddamn pesticides. Always knew those things caused cancer. Government knew, but wouldn't tell us. Goddamn feds. Guess it's my turn now, huh, Doc?"

"We don't know that, Mr. Bogart," Spencer had replied carefully. But Spencer was in fact pretty sure that yes, indeed, it was Bogart's turn. Spencer could read a brain MRI as well as anyone, and based on Bogart's, he was almost certain that he had a glioblastoma multiforme—about as bad as it got in the brain-cancer department. Chances were he'd be joining his wife within about eighteen months, no matter what Spencer did. In fact, Spencer wasn't planning on cutting out his tumor: it was too deep and too close to too many important structures that, if damaged, might leave him a vegetable for his remaining days. Spencer's goal today was simply to get a biopsy.

Sheila the sister grasped Spencer's free hand. He could barely feel it. It was like holding hands with a two-year-old. The three of them bowed their heads, closed their eyes, and Sheila began to pray in a clear, strong voice: the usual stuff, invoking God and the Lord Jesus Christ to guide Spencer's hands during the surgery. Spencer had heard variations on it many times.

He knew that an outside observer might not appreciate the importance of ritual in a surgeon's mind. But as a surgeon, he'd learned not to underestimate the power of ritual. Habit and ritual were calming to surgeons: provided reassurance and confidence, reinforced a sense of control. Spencer had colleagues who would operate only in rooms corresponding to their lucky numbers, or only on certain days of the week; or always wear the same pair of shoes while operating; or insist on using the same type of suture, sewn in the exact same pattern, with the same number of knots, when other sutures and patterns and knot numbers would have done just fine.

Since Spencer ultimately placed his faith in God, his own ritual was to cross himself and mouth a short prayer before each operation. All his operations: big and small, straightforward and complex, because he knew that, from a patient's perspective, there was no such thing as a *little* or *simple* operation.

Spencer never prayed openly in front of patients or the OR staff unless patients like Bogart invited him to join them. He otherwise hid in one of the OR supply rooms. This was in part because he didn't want to offend folks of other faiths or of no faith at all.

But it was mostly because, as a surgeon, he knew that one of the surest and quickest ways to invoke a crisis of confidence among patients and staff was to demonstrate the need for the intervention of a higher being. After all, could he imagine wanting to board an airplane after watching its captain perform the sign of the cross at the gate? Or don a yarmulke and recite Hebrew prayers? Or kneel on a carpet in the direction of Mecca? No way.

Praying: that's how he'd met Rita.

Not that Rita was religious. She wasn't. Not in the least. She'd never given religion any real thought, ever, despite her having lost two parents at a young age. She didn't even know if she was an agnostic or atheist. She didn't care, and Spencer hadn't minded. Lack of faith had never been a deal breaker for him when dating women. He'd come across more than his share of women who professed faith but actually had none, or who did but expressed it in ways he found weird, disturbing, or both.

She'd spotted him praying one morning before an operation, almost two years ago, crouched behind tall racks of equipment in the supply room.

"What are you doing?" she'd asked, as he'd stood up and crossed himself. She hadn't been confrontational, just curious. That was Rita. She didn't explain to him, then or later, what she'd been doing back there in the otherwise empty supply room, and for some reason he'd never asked.

He'd told her (he'd never been self-conscious about his faith), and they'd struck up a conversation. He'd seen her around the OR, but they'd never met. He couldn't recall what they'd talked about. All he could remember was how taken he'd been with the trim surgeon confidently planted in front of him, hands on hips, chin thrust forward, her long black hair pushed away from her lovely face by her surgical cap. The cap had seemed set back on her head at a jaunty angle. How could a shapeless paper surgical cap be *jaunty*? But it was jaunty on *her*.

Spencer had never believed in love at first sight. Still didn't. He thought it was bullshit. Great for cheesy songs and movies. But real life? No way. You could *want* somebody right away, sure. Lust after them. Spot them from across a room and experience an instantaneous attraction.

But love? Love wasn't that easy. It took time, and effort. Up to that point in his life, Spencer had been in love only once, during college, and maintaining that relationship had felt like constant work: as if feverishly writing a term paper he could never seem to finish.

And he'd watched his parents, who loved each other more than just about anyone else he knew, soldier through plenty of tough times.

So all he'd known for certain after his five-minute-long conversation in the supply closet with Rita was that he'd wanted more than anything to get to know the attractive woman with the *jaunty* cap better. So he'd asked her out to coffee.

She'd said no.

Hadn't even bothered to sugarcoat it.

No, thanks.

End of conversation.

She'd spun on her heels and stridden away, calling out something like *nice meeting you* or *see you around the OR* over her shoulder. That had been it.

Except that it hadn't.

Because he hadn't been able to get Rita out of his mind. She'd burrowed into it and stuck there, like a splinter under his fingernail.

Her confidence: That's what had hooked him more than anything, as surely as a fish biting down hard on a baited line. He'd always found confident women appealing. He'd decided that he wasn't going to take *no* for an answer. In this sense, he'd modeled himself off his parents. He knew the same had happened to his father after he'd first met his mom in a bowling alley near the small college in eastern Washington where they'd both been students. According to his parents, the bowling alley had been the hub of their social universe. Bowl was what the kids did because apparently there hadn't been much else, especially in winter. Bowl and drink. Probably screw, too, which was left unsaid:

Spencer didn't like to dwell on that because it was his parents, after all.

His mother was outgoing, popular, and vivacious; his dad was taciturn, but with a wicked sense of humor. His mom and dad agreed that at first she'd given dad the cold shoulder. She'd thought him an arrogant ass because he'd had so little to say. But dad had kept at it; and it was, she liked to say, his *sweet perseverance* that had worn her down. Spencer, being an only child, and thus the one person benefiting most from their eventual union, felt grateful for his dad's *sweet perseverance*.

So Spencer had persevered (*sweetly*, if he did say so himself) until Rita gave in and agreed to go out with him.

If it had been Rita's confidence that had first hooked him, it had been her toughness that later sunk the hook deep into him. Surgery was grueling. It could kick your ass. Some nights, Spencer was so exhausted he could barely drive himself home from the hospital before dropping into catatonia in front of the TV, nursing a warmed-over frozen pizza and a few beers.

But that schedule never seemed to get to Rita, who seemed to have a limitless reservoir of energy and was tougher and more tenacious than just about any surgeon he'd ever met—and over the years he'd run across some hard-core, hard-ass surgeons. She was absolutely devoted to her patients, practically sweated blood for them. It was obvious she loved to operate and reveled in the intellectual and physical challenges of taking people apart, then putting them back together again. But he learned that she loved the patients even more.

Devotion to their patients: They were much alike in this respect. It was one of the many reasons why he'd fallen so hard for her, the hardest by far of any woman he'd ever met in his life. And why he'd thought they'd made such a great couple.

"Doc?" Bogart said.

Until that horrible night a year ago, when Rita had told him they didn't.

"Doc? You okay?"

Spencer opened his eyes and looked up. Bogart and Sheila were staring at him.

"Oh, sorry." He cleared his throat and smiled sheepishly. "*Amen.* I get . . . ah, carried away sometimes, Mr. Bogart." He turned his smile toward Sheila. "Pastor." It wasn't an outright lie, but enough of one to make his conscience give him a sharp poke. His cheeks burned.

Lying about praying, Spencer Wallace? For shame. If you were a Catholic, that would cost you, like, twenty Hail Mary's and ten Acts of Contrition.

Bogart smiled. "I understand, son. I'd much rather have you praying *too* hard for me if you know what I mean."

After finishing with Bogart, Spencer lingered around pre-op, hoping to catch a glimpse of Rita. He counted it a good day when he was lucky enough to see her at work, and an even better day when they exchanged polite hellos in passing.

But she was nowhere to be found this morning in pre-op—which was strange since he knew she was operating today. He left disappointed but holding out hope that he might be able to sneak into her OR later during the auto-surgeon operation.

FINNEY

"No," Dr. Wu said.

This was growing tedious. She dared to defy him. *Again.*

He would not be defied.

He tapped the tablet with his finger, increased the power settings—

(because he would *not* be defied)

—and said, "Dr. Wu, you have to talk him into letting you operate today."

SEBASTIAN

"No," Wu said in Sebastian's headphone.

Wow.

God*damn* if she still wasn't fighting it. She was one tough-ass lady.

Sebastian had caught up with her before she and Montgomery had entered the alcove and was keeping an eye on things from a discreet spot nearby. He watched as the graphic displays on his phone spiked. Finney had turned the signal strength even higher and was now flirting with the established upper limits of human tolerability.

She would not be able to take much more of this.

Careful, boss. You're going to fry her brain.

Finney repeated the command: "Dr. Wu, you have to talk him into letting you operate today."

RITA

Chase spun back toward her with a surprised look on his face, as if he'd forgotten she was there.

"What?" he said. "What did you say?"

Rita didn't answer.

She couldn't, because the buzzing was back—this time with teeth rattling, skull-crushing intensity, as if someone were smashing glass bottles inside her head with a hammer. It crowded out all thought. She winced and clenched her teeth.

"What?" Chase repeated, then saw the expression on her face. His eyebrows drew together. "Rita. *Rita.* Are you okay?"

And then the buzzing was gone . . .

(*What was I saying?*)

. . . and Rita felt as if a reset button somehow had been pressed in her brain.

What were Chase and I talking about?

"Rita?" Chase said.

"You have to talk him into letting you operate today," Finney said.

Right. I have to talk Chase into letting me operate today.

It seemed the most natural thing.

Of *course* she had to talk Chase into it.

"Rita?" Chase repeated worriedly.

"You have to talk him into letting you operate to-day," Finney repeated.

I have to talk him into letting me operate today.

"I'm . . . fine, Chase." She cleared her throat. "I'm fine."

"What did you mean by 'no'?"

"Oh. I meant that we don't have to cancel the surgery this morning."

"What?" he said, squinting. "And why the hell not?"

I have to talk him into it.

For reasons she couldn't explain, Rita now felt filled with an urgency to make the operation happen this morning. *Consumed* with it. The only obstacle in her way was Chase, and her mind raced with potential ways to win him over—

(*But a second ago wasn't I AGREEING with him?*)

—to her way of thinking.

Chase was an exceptionally bright and ambitious man in a profession of bright and ambitious people. One of the smartest guys in a roomful of smart guys, and he knew it. He was a skilled and widely respected surgeon, and as political a beast as they came. The buzz was that he was first in line to take the Turner CEO job next year, when the current CEO retired. No doubt this job was the next carefully planned step in Chase's grand plan for career advancement and world domination.

No way the auto-surgeon project would have ever moved forward without his support. Nothing in the OR happened at Turner without Chase's blessing. If you were a surgeon here, any kind of surgeon, and you wanted something done, you sought an audience with

Chase, and you received his blessing. Or you didn't, and that was the end of it for you. Because his was the first and last word in surgery at Turner.

He was also a voracious competitor, driven to win in everything: publishing the most scientific papers on a particular topic, or performing more of a complex type of surgery than anyone else in the country, or winning the annual Surgery Department golf tournament. Chase was *always* keeping score.

It was a pride that could blind him to certain, disagreeable facts that might otherwise dispute his mastery of all things. She knew all this because she knew Chase as well as anyone she'd ever known. She rejected the term *father figure* as trite. It belied the complexity of their relationship, reduced it to cheap, pseudo-Freudian analysis. Yes, his presence in her life had, to an extent, replaced that of her father. But Chase was also many other things to her.

A silver-haired Olympian who'd spotted her talent from on high, swept down, pointed his finger at her, and plucked her out from the crowd.

(*Out of trouble he got me out of trouble after Jenny Finney died he fixed things but don't think about that now I can't think about that now*)

A mentor and confidant, the man behind the curtain who'd nurtured her skills, guided her career, opened doors, and introduced her to all the right people.

(*He fixed things after Jenny Finney died so no one would know but don't think about that now*)

The man who'd nominated her for the auto-surgeon project and given her every resource she needed to make it work.

(*He fixed things after Jenny Finney died*)

Chase hated losing.

So, yes: That was the way forward for her.

"Chase. Look." She reached out and placed a hesitant hand on his shoulder. "I know all of this, uh, looks weird." She chose her words carefully. "Whatever happened, last night . . . well—I can't completely explain it. I think it's safe to say I've been working too hard, and that it finally caught up with me. But I feel good, Chase."

He raised his eyebrows.

"Really!" she said. "I *can* do this. I can do it safely. Besides, the auto-surgeon is going to do most of the work anyway, right? It passed all the cadaveric models, and the animal tests, with flying colors. I'm just there to set things up and let it do its thing. It runs itself. That's what it's supposed to do. *Run itself.*"

He squinted at her, hard, and clenched his jaw.

"Look, Chase," she continued. "I'm not a, uh, media expert, or anything. But I have a feeling that if we cancel, it's going to make us look bad. Like we don't know what we're doing, or that there are major safety problems. And the university president, and the dean, and whoever else is here—they're not going to like it, either. If only because you've wasted their time."

He squinted still harder, the horizontal slits of brown skin that encased his eyes almost squeezing shut at the mention of their superiors. She could all but hear the political gears in his brain grinding away.

"And if we postpone today, Chase, it's going to put us behind schedule. Way behind schedule. Look how long it took us to find Mrs. Sanchez. She's perfect for it: perfect anatomy and body habitus. If we cancel to-day, we'll have to find another patient. I don't know how long that will take. The Europeans are nipping at our heels. Fabius, in Lyons—"

"I know about *Professor* Fabius," he growled.

She also knew that Chase in private often referred to Fabius as *that frog bastard.* As in: *There's no way in hell I'm letting* that frog bastard *beat me to the punch.*

"Okay, then you know that Fabius is almost as far along as we are, with that EU consortium he's head-ing up. We need to get this done, Chase. We need to get this done, and out there, ASAP. Or Fabius will be first. We can't afford to wait. Not even a day."

Chase's face remained inscrutable.

She took a deep breath and plowed ahead. "You pulled all of this together. It was your leadership and your vision, Chase, that made this possible." As with any political beast, she knew that ego-stroking was like heroin to him. "You've believed in me all of these years. You know me. You know that I would go for-ward only if I thought it would be safe. I can perform this operation in my sleep, Chase. *Trust me.* Trust me the way you've always trusted me."

In the hallway outside the alcove, a group of men and women laughed. It sounded full-throated and un-inhibited, unusual for so early on a Monday, and Rita wondered if they were laughing about her.

Chase's face was stone.

This isn't working. He's not going to go for it.

"That was a nice speech, Dr. Wu," Finney said. She realized only then that he hadn't interrupted her for a while.

The tight lines around Chase's eyes and mouth relaxed a fraction. Or was it a trick of the light?

"Are you sure you're feeling okay?" he asked. "You don't look like it to me. You look pale."

"Yes. I'm okay, Chase. Really."

"Huh." He worked his jaw, as if chewing on a piece of gum, crossed his arms, and leaned backward on his heels.

"You know," he said, "I remember the first time I met you. When I interviewed you for the residency program. Do you remember?"

"Yes." Rita recalled Chase in his corner office, sitting at his football-field-sized desk of polished oak. His office windows overlooked a stand of eucalyptus trees, through which she'd caught a glimpse of a blue sliver of the Pacific.

She remembered thinking how handsome and impressive he was, the wunderkind just promoted to chief of surgery, and at being surprised to see the framed vintage movie posters adorning the walls of his office alongside the diplomas and awards. *The Godfather, Part II. His Girl Friday. The Terminator. The Searchers.* Chase, she'd soon learned, was a film buff who took particular pride in his limited edition *Star Wars: Revenge of the Jedi* poster—of which, he loved pointing out to bemused visitors, only a few thousand were ever issued before the movie title was changed to *Return of the Jedi.*

"God, I remember it so well. So many applicants. So many kids wanting to be surgeons. But you: You stuck out immediately."

"Why?"

"Your confidence. I asked you where you saw your-self in ten years. A standard bullshit-interview ques-tion, to which we normally receive a standard bullshit-interview response. Do you remember what you said?"

"No."

"You pointed to me, and said, 'Sitting in your chair, sir.'" He laughed, with warmth, and the ghost of a smile lingered on his lips. "'Sitting in your chair.' Jesus, what goddamn *nerve!*"

This was the first time, in all the years she'd known him, he'd told her this story.

"God—you reminded me *so* much of myself, at your age. Full of piss and vinegar. A lot of the faculty didn't care for your attitude. I had to argue your case. Tell them you were the best applicant I'd ever seen. Talented. Smart. Gutsy." He grunted. "But they were uncomfortable around a strong woman." A strong *Asian* woman, he didn't need to say. The opinion of the old boy's club, she knew, was that a nice Asian girl like her, good at math and science (which in their Nean-derthal worldviews were the only things Asians were good at), belonged in a lab, not an OR. She couldn't care less about their asinine opinions. She never had. She could operate circles around any one of them.

He clasped his hands behind his back and turned away.

You're a little spitfire, lovely Rita.

Just like your mother.

"That's an interesting story," Finney said. He sounded curious. "Were you really like that?"

Rita swallowed. It was exhausting, trying to hold down two conversations at once, one inside her head.

"So . . . what do you think, Chase?"

"I think I don't need to tell you how important this operation is, Rita." He was still contemplating the C-arm. She noticed how rigid his back was, the tanned cords of his neck prying open the collar of his white shirt like thick fingers. The warmth had drained from his voice as abruptly as water from a bathtub. "Everyone's watching you. *Everyone.* Are you *really* up for this today?"

No, some weak part of her tried to protest.

But she needed to operate on Mrs. Sanchez.

"Yes. Absolutely, Chase."

"You realize if you screw this up—"

"I know, Chase."

"—I won't be able to protect you."

Able?

Or willing, Chase?

"I understand."

"Okay, then," he said, facing the C-arm. He suddenly sounded very tired. "Okay, Rita. We'll do it. We'll move ahead. But we delay for two hours."

He spun around and jabbed his index finger at her. "And that's nonnegotiable. I want you to go take a shower and clean yourself up. And put on some makeup, for God's sake. We need you to look good for the cameras. You have some with you? Makeup?"

"Yes," she said, and bit her lip. Under other circumstances, she might have been more pissed about the makeup thing. Despite the pretty speech he'd just made, Chase's intermittent, offhand remarks about her appearance—clothes, hair, makeup—betrayed a subtle if unintended sexism. Most of her male colleagues were like that, really—

(*except Spencer, but don't think about Spencer now, can't think about him now*)

—but Chase had on his own makeup this morning, so she had to give him a pass on that one.

He nodded. "I'll keep the visitors occupied. Reshuffle the schedule and take them on a tour of the construction area first. We've got hard hats and everything." He snorted. "The hospital CEO loves that goddamn hard hat. You can practically see his hard-on as he's slapping the goddamn thing on his head. Especially when you give him a set of blueprints to go along with it."

Chase didn't much care for the CEO. The feeling, Rita had heard, was mutual.

"And . . . later, Rita, we'll talk. You and I. You're not off the hook yet."

"I understand."

His eyes roamed over her, troubled, and he stroked his chin. He opened his mouth, closed it, and tightened his jaw. For a moment, she was worried he would change his mind.

But then he said, "I like the glasses. Keep those. They make you look more authoritative. And intellectual. Besides, your eyes are a little bloodshot. It'll be harder for people to tell with the glasses on."

"Okay."

He squeezed past the C-arm and out into the hallway, then stuck his head back through the narrow gap.

She sucked in her breath because suddenly he seemed sinister: a bodiless head, bathed in shadow and backlit by the bright lights in the hallway.

"Rita."

"Yes, Chase."

"Don't make me regret this."

"I won't, Chase. I promise."

He nodded, a single curt tilt of the chin.

Then he was gone.

Rita sank to the ground, and her knees hit the hard tile, the bone of each patella pushing against the floor through the thin fabric of her scrubs. It hurt. But she didn't care. She just sat there, kneeling and breathing hard.

What's happening to me? I shouldn't be operating today. I know that. So why do I keep doing things I know I shouldn't be? Saying things I shouldn't?

The tears came, then, without any warning, or fanfare. She felt them trace warm rivulets down her cheeks; and in her chest she felt the approach of body-wrenching sobs, something she hadn't experienced since her father died, when she was fourteen. She decided she would curl up into a little ball, right here on the cold floor behind the C-arm, and cry for as long as she needed to, and hope all this just went away.

Because why was she saying these things? Doing these things? Why was she so sure that she needed to operate, even as she knew deep in her soul she shouldn't? What was *wrong* with her?

And then he spoke.

"Good," Finney said. "Excellent. It's nice to see Dr. Montgomery is such a reasonable man."

Suddenly, the urge to sob, to give up and cry like the girl she'd been when her father died, was gone. She balled her fists and ground her teeth together.

Bastard.

Far down, down deep where all her anger-management classes had pushed it, the righteous anger seethed. It was no pet now, to be trotted out every so often to keep subordinates on their toes. No. Not now. It was raw, primal fury; and it overwhelmed—for the time, at least—her confusion and fear.

Smug bastard, she thought. *You did this to me. I'm going to find a way out of this.*

She wiped her face with the back of her hand and, using the wall for leverage, pushed herself up.

I don't know how, but I'm going to find a way out of this. Even if it kills me.

She snuck past the C-arm and into the hallway.

But first, I need to operate on Mrs. Sanchez.

With the auto-surgeon.

SEBASTIAN

He saw Wu emerge from the alcove, her cheeks red and blotchy. She'd probably been crying. She looked around. He wasn't expecting that, and inadvertently he allowed his eyes to lock with hers.

Dammit.

He'd gotten too close.

Stupid. Unprofessional.

He forced himself not to react and started to stroll toward her, frowning as if in concentration, and bending his head over his cell. He did all this while still watching her through the top of his eyes. She greeted a coworker, and then headed purposely in his direction.

Uh-oh.

But then he felt the breeze in her wake as she passed him without so much as a glance.

He relaxed and turned slowly to mark her progress.

"Sebastian. She just walked by you."

Does he think I'm a goddamn idiot?

"I see her, boss."

"This is a critical juncture. How does everything look? Any cause for concern?"

Other than the amount of goddamn juice you're dumping into her brain?

"No. None that I can tell."

"Best to keep a close eye on her."

"Agreed." He waited until she was nearly out of sight before padding after her. "What about her sister?"

They hadn't expected Wu's sister to wake up so early. When he'd broken into Wu's house that morning and implanted the device, Sebastian had dosed her (he'd *thought*) with enough sedatives to practically put her into a goddamn coma.

He'd never liked involving Wu's sister. It had complicated the logistics—

(*The teenager in the cell*)

—to have him rush from the hospital, to Wu's house, then back to the hospital.

(*Wu's sister reminded him of the teenager in the cell*)

Finney had insisted. The sister, he'd argued, provided them with additional leverage and was the perfect backup plan should Wu not respond to the embedding.

Sebastian suspected there was more to it than that.

(*The teenager in the cell.*)

Much more.

But he'd kept his mouth shut.

Because he needed to finish this job. This one last job.

For his niece, Sierra. For his nephew, Sammy.

Sammy.

Who reminded him of the kid who'd killed Alfonso.

"Leave her to me," Finney said. "For now."

Sebastian didn't like the sound of that.

SPENCER

The rowdy atmosphere of the male surgeon's locker room invoked memories of a high-school PE class. Men stood in various states of undress in front of their lockers, talking and laughing. Spencer withdrew a laundered, pressed set of scrubs from an ATM-like dispensing machine and snaked his way to his locker, exchanging greetings and backslaps with fellow surgeons en route.

He traded his blue polo shirt and grey slacks for the scrubs, and his loafers for a pair of sneakers he kept in his locker. As he stood up from tying the sneakers, somebody tapped him from behind.

"Spence! How they hangin', compadre?"

He turned around and looked down. It was one of the other surgeons, Ray Lorenz.

Ray clapped him on the shoulder, and said, "Careful how you answer that one, compadre. I'm always prepared to offer my professional opinion about your balls. Hah!"

Spencer forced his lips into a tight smile. Ray was a urologist. The personalized license plate of his late-model Porsche (for which he normally helped himself to two adjacent parking spots in the crowded garage, with the middle of the undercarriage straddling the center white line between the two parking spaces) read PP DOC. They must have loved that one down at the DMV.

"Hey, Ray. What's up?"

Ray patted down his slicked-back, ink-black hair (maybe a shade *too* black for a guy Ray's age) and cracked his neck. His beady eyes reminded Spencer of the opossum he'd seen this morning in Rita's front yard. He was an East Coast transplant, originally from somewhere in New York or New Jersey—Spencer wasn't sure.

"Terrific. Freakin' balls out *outstanding*. You?"

"Good."

"What are you up to this morning?"

"Short day. Just a quick stereotactic brain biopsy on a probable GBM."

"GBM, huh? That sucks."

"Yes."

"Yep. Most definitely sucks." Ray rocked back and forth on the balls of his feet. His smile didn't quite reach his eyes.

"And you? What's going on in your room today, Ray?"

"Three penile prostheses and a vasectomy reversal."
A beat.

"What can I say, compadre?" Ray said, breaking the
ice with a brisk clap to Spencer's shoulder. He had to
reach over his head to make it that high. "I make a few
old geezers feel like they're eighteen again. Give 'em
a few more laps around the track, a few more pokes
with the stick. Hah! For old time's sake. Know what
I'm sayin'? Besides, it pays the college tuitions. Hah!"

"I'm sure it does."

"Hey." Ray leaned in and flicked the back of his
hand against Spencer's chest in an affable, just-
between-you-and-me-a-couple-of-the-guys-talkin'
kind of way. "Hey." Ray flicked him a second time.
Spencer flinched. His personal space was important to
him, and this was a violation. "Compadre. Did you
hear a couple of nurses found some jackass passed out
naked this morning in one of the ORs? A surgeon?"

"*What?*"

"I know, right?"

"You're kidding."

"For real. I shit you not, my friend. Freakin' *nuts*,
right?"

"Who was it?"

"Don't know. But, man, I sure wish I did. Just lying
there, lettin' it all hang out. JEEE-sus!" He slapped his
knee. "Hah! I heard that Montgomery is *pissed*."

"*Naked*, Ray? Are you sure? That's just—I mean,
bizarre. You sure it's for real?"

"Compadre," Ray said solicitously. "Come *on*. Shit
like this happens. Don't you remember that anesthesiologist a few years back? The guy they found in one

of the on-call rooms, whacked out of his brains on drugs? Banging two hookers?"

Spencer hadn't known that.

"Hah!" Ray said, reading his shocked expression. "The guy was run out of town on a rail. But Montgomery kept the whole thing quiet. *Real* quiet. Montgomery's good at that. Slick as hell—one of the reasons why that golden-boy bastard is head of surgery."

"Huh."

"Then there was that trauma surgeon. Young guy. Placing central lines into drug addicts for cash, in some shitty little rental shack in Ocean Beach."

"*Really?*"

"Yeah." Ray snorted. "Montgomery kept that one real quiet, too. The *balls* on that kid."

"Where did he get the lines?"

"Stole them from the SICU. Cunning little prick. Sticking junkies at a thousand bucks a pop—until this one time when he went a little too deep on a subclavian and dropped some kid's lung. *That* poor son of a bitch ended up almost buying it. Tension pneumo, you know? Lung crushed to the size of a grape before the ER guys popped his chest with a needle. You telling me you never hear about that, either?"

Spencer shook his head.

"Huh." Ray narrowed his eyes. "Compadre, you are one straightlaced son of a bitch. You know that? You really are as clean-cut as everyone says you are."

Spencer blushed. "So . . . why do you think he did it? The central-line guy?"

Ray waved dismissively. "Who knows? Some of us get screwed up sometimes, you know? Don't get me wrong: In the great pantheon of big-time doctor fuck-ups, this one today is seriously *fucked up*. All I'm say-ing is that this shit has happened before, and it'll happen again. I mean, this job *sucks* sometimes. Every so often, one of us flames out. *Spectacularly*. Nuclear-grade meltdown."

"So . . . is that what you think happened with the naked guy?"

"Oh, yeah," Ray said, as if it was the most obvious thing in the world. He snorted, threw a rapid glance over his shoulder, and leaned in. "One thing's for sure—guy's out of a job. Might as well pack his bags today. His career? Stick a fork in it because it is fuck-ing *done*, my friend." He leaned closer and flicked Spencer's chest. "Am I right?" Chest flick. "Hah!"

Spencer took a step back and folded his arms. He didn't like being touched like that. It took him back to college and med school, when he'd worked nights as a bouncer at clubs to scrape together some extra cash. At most shifts, there'd been at least one cologne-reeking alpha stalking the entry line outside the front door, showing off for his girlfriend wobbling on foot-high stilettos and spilling out of a vaporous dress two sizes too small. Those guys were usually chest pokers, or, worse, chest *butters*, shoving up against him like stags in heat.

"Well." Ray stole a glance at the thick gold Rolex on his wrist. "Gotta go pay for another semester at Col-gate. Hah! Adios, compadre."

As Ray bounded out the door toward the ORs, Spen-cer heard him say: "Hey! *My* man! Did you hear about that naked guy they found in room 10? . . . You did? . . .

I know, right? *JEEE*-sus! Can you believe it, compadre?"

The door closed before Spencer could hear if Ray's unseen companion could, in fact, believe it.

For some inexplicable reason, Spencer's insides twisted into a knot.

I wonder who it was?

RITA

Pre-op was a large, rectangular room. Arranged around its perimeter were twenty small, private sitting areas: cubicles enclosed by walls on three sides, with a thick retractable curtain strung across the side facing the center of the room. Each cubicle contained a gurney, an IV pole, and two chairs.

Rita paused in the doorway. She was late, delayed by her conversations with Finney and Chase. Most of the patients scheduled for the first operations of the morning had already been wheeled off to operating rooms. A few of the cubicles, though, were occupied with patients and family members. Nurses in scrubs darted between cubicles like hummingbirds lighting from flower to flower.

"I remember this place," Finney said quietly. "This room. We spoke with you in here, just before Jenny's operation." A beat. "It was the last place I ever saw Jenny awake."

Oh God, does he have to keep bringing that up?

Rita leaned against the doorframe to steady herself.

Easy, lovely Rita. That was her father. His presence

in her mind was almost as substantial as Finney's, and she drew strength from it.

It's his ball game for now, but let's see how this plays out, lovely Rita. Remember: situational awareness. Situational awareness.

"We talked about the appendectomy," Finney continued. "Do you remember what you told us?"

"Good morning, Dr. Wu." One of the nurses, seated at the nurse's station in the center, waved to her. "Your patient is in bed 8."

Rita took a deep breath, plastered on her best, reassuring-surgeon smile, and peeled herself off the doorframe. There was a single number printed on a sign hanging over each cubicle. On lead feet, she headed toward the one marked "8."

"You told us everything was going to be fine," Finney said. "But it wasn't."

She gritted her teeth and kept walking.

"What are you going to tell this patient, Dr. Wu? Are you going to tell her everything is going to be just fine?"

Easy, lovely Rita.

"Look. Do you want me to operate on her, or not?" she muttered. "You're distracting me."

He didn't answer. His ensuing quiet struck her as sullen. She tried to picture him. She remembered a tall, reserved man with a boyish face and light brown hair. He'd never met her eye when they spoke, choosing instead to stare over her shoulder, or at his wife.

The curtain to cubicle eight was open. Mrs. Sanchez was lying on a gurney, in a hospital gown, an IV dripping clear fluid into the back of her left hand. Her husband sat to her right, in a chair with orange-vinyl cushions next to the gurney, holding her hand. A nurse was bent over her other hand, taping the IV line into place. She finished and eyed the IV bag approvingly with its steady *drip drip drip* of clear fluid.

"Here she is," she chirped, announcing Rita's arrival.

In med school, Rita had learned *the five f's* of a typical patient with gallstone disease: female, forty, fat, fair, and fertile. Except for the female part, Mrs. Sanchez was none of these. She was fifty-six, trim, Hispanic, and had, to Rita's knowledge, only one daughter, who was in college up in LA. She'd been a handsome woman once, with cheekbones that leaned forward like the prows of two sleek sailing ships and big dark eyes. But the years had worn her face down, gravity pulling the skin downward, like a flower wilting. Despite rolling out of bed at God-knew-what-hour to make her 5:00 A.M. hospital check-in, she'd applied a modest amount of makeup, and her medium-length hair, dark with a few grey roots, was in a neat, age-appropriate style. She was lying underneath a blanket drawn up to her midsection, exuding quiet resignation.

The hand with the IV rested on top of the blanket; the other lay in the grip of Mr. Sanchez, who held it tightly, as if she might float away. Mr. Sanchez had a kind face and the bearing of a man who'd slouched into middle age without protest. His hair was snow grey, thick and wavy. He was wearing a collared blue golf shirt, tucked, and his belly drooped over his belt and settled over his starched tan slacks.

"Good morning," Rita said, smiling.

"Good morning," they each replied. Mr. Sanchez dropped his wife's hand long enough to give Rita's a polite squeeze. His was soaked with sweat.

"There you go, sweetie," said the nurse. "We're just going to slip this over that gorgeous head of yours." She leaned in and gently guided a blue surgical cap onto Mrs. Sanchez's head.

Mrs. Sanchez smiled uncertainly and touched the cap.

"I'm going to leave you with Dr. Wu now. You know, she's one of our favorite doctors."

Rita knew that wasn't true—

(*Spencer, Spencer is one of their favorites*)

—but that at least most of the nurses liked her because she treated them with respect. The nurse winked at Rita and was gone.

Rita pulled the second chair up to the head of the gurney and sat. She placed her hand on Mrs. Sanchez's shoulder.

"How are you feeling today?"

"I feel . . . good." Mrs. Sanchez spoke with deliberation and a Mexican accent. She started to open her mouth again, and then shook her head and turned to her husband. An unspoken signal flashed between them.

"She feels okay," he said, gazing at his wife and massaging her hand. His English, too, was accented, but less than hers. "The pain—*aqui*." He pointed to his right-upper quadrant, just underneath the rib cage, the location of the gallbladder. "It's still there. No better." He shrugged. "No worse."

"Well, after today, it's going to get better. A lot better." She stretched her smile as wide as it would go and pointed to her own abdomen. "*No mas.*" Rita's Spanish was atrocious, but she wanted to show that she was at least trying.

Her husband nodded politely and, following his lead, so did Mrs. Sanchez. Rita joined in, and all three nodded together.

"So," Rita said, and pursed her lips. "I've got something I need to tell you."

Mrs. Sanchez looked at her husband, who stared intently at Rita.

"We're all good to go this morning. But we have some—um, equipment issues." Mr. Sanchez's eyes widened, and Rita quickly added, "But everything's okay! Just fine. We just want to . . . check everything over again."

"Why? Is the . . . robot—broken?" Mr. Sanchez asked suspiciously.

"No. Everything's fine. Really. I just want everything to be perfect. So we're going to delay the operation. Just for an hour, maybe two, to do some additional safety checks. Okay?"

He digested this, then leaned in close to his wife. They shared a brief exchange in Spanish.

"Excuse me, but do you have to use the robot, Doctor?" Mr. Sanchez asked.

"Yes," Finney said.

Yes, Rita thought. She bit her tongue to prevent the word from leaving her mouth. She tasted warm, salty blood.

What would make her say such a thing?

Because, *no*, she *didn't* need to use the robot.

She had to choose her next words carefully. "Well—as we've talked about, Mrs. Sanchez will be part of something exciting. Something that is going to make surgery better."

"Yes, Doctor. But will it make *her* surgery better?"

"Yes, it will," Finney said.

Yes, it will, Rita almost said, but stopped herself. She knew that wasn't true.

Mr. and Mrs. Sanchez were looking at her expectantly.

Finney, in her head: "Yes. It. Will."

"No . . . it . . . won't," Rita responded, as much to Finney as to Mr. Sanchez. She was surprised at how difficult it was to speak. Like her tongue, bloodied and sore from where she'd bitten it, was trying to obey two masters at once.

"Is that really what you want to tell them, Dr. Wu?" Finney pressed.

Rita said, "What I mean to say is that she's going to do great no matter what. Robot, or no robot."

"I don't want her to be a—guinea pig. No offense, Doctor."

"She won't be a guinea pig. I promise. I would never experiment on a patient."

"Experiment." Mr. Sanchez frowned and pursed his lips, as if the word had left a bad taste. "But . . . no disrespect, Doctor: That's what this sounds like. An experiment."

Mrs. Sanchez's eyebrows drew together. She posed a question to her husband in rapid-fire Spanish. He shook his head and patted her arm.

"Look," Rita said, spreading her hands. "Mr. Sanchez. I've done this operation over five hundred times. The robot is simply a tool to help me. A tool that we've tested literally thousands of times."

She didn't add that these tests had been conducted in computer models, simulators, live pigs, human cadavers—everything other than a living, breathing human being.

Until now.

Mr. Sanchez let go of his wife's hand and folded his arms. "This robot is . . . safe?"

"Yes. Absolutely."

"Would you let the robot operate on your family? Your husband?" He held both of his palms up in front of him. "No disrespect, Doctor."

Your husband. She knew he didn't mean anything by that, and she tried not to let it irritate her. She heard that a lot. People always assumed she had a husband. She didn't need a husband.

(*But Spencer, she needed Spencer*)

"Yes." She truly believed the auto-surgeon was safe. She hoped, *desperately*, that it would be safe in her hands, this morning.

Mr. Sanchez glanced at his wife, and in that one look Rita glimpsed so very much. Love. Devotion. Loyalty. Fear.

Would Spencer look at me like that, under the same circumstances? After how I've treated him?

(*No, can't think about Spencer don't think about him not now*)

He interlaced his fingers in his lap, peered down at them, and sighed.

She leaned over and touched his arm. "Surgery is

scary. I know. I've had it myself. It's one of the reasons I became a surgeon—I wanted to help people."

He nodded and turned to his wife. More exchanges
in rapid Spanish, at the end of which Mrs. Sanchez
smiled faintly and nodded.

Mr. Sanchez's posture relaxed. He offered Rita a re-
signed smile.

"Okay, Doctor. She'll have the robot surgery today.
You're a great doctor, and we trust you."

His smile widened as hers faltered.

You told us everything was going to be fine, Finney
had said. *But it wasn't.*

"Now, just to go over everything again: You understand what I'm doing today?"

"You're removing her—vesícula biliar." Mr. Sanchez gestured toward his abdomen. Mrs. Sanchez
nodded.

"Her gallbladder," Rita agreed. "Correct. And you
understand that there will be observers in the operating room? People who aren't directly involved in the
surgery?" Mrs. Sanchez had signed a form acknowledging her approval of observers but could still back
out if she wanted to. In which case, they'd go forward
with the surgery but not allow any visitors.

And Chase would freak out.

Mr. Sanchez translated, his wife nodded, and he
said, "Teaching is important. As long as you're the one
doing the operation."

"I will be. And you're okay with the delay?"

An exchange of Spanish. They both chuckled. "She's
wondering if she can have a snack. She's hungry."

Rita forced herself to laugh. "Unfortunately, no." She then asked Mr. Sanchez, "Are you going to be here after the surgery?"

"Yes. In the waiting room. Our daughter will be here, too. She's driving down from college."

"Oh? From where?"

"UCLA."

"Good for her. That's a great school."

"Yes, it is. Thank you, Doctor." His chest expanded to temporarily dwarf the soft prominence of his belly. Mrs. Sanchez beamed her approval. "She wants to meet you. She's heard a lot about you."

"All good things, I hope."

"Oh, yes, Doctor." He grinned. "All good."

You told us everything was going to be fine.

But it wasn't.

She shook each of their hands again, indicated that she would visit with Mr. Sanchez and their daughter after the operation, and left them. At the door to pre-op, she cast one last glance over her shoulder.

Mr. Sanchez had stood up and was leaning over the bed, pressing his forehead against his wife's. They were holding hands.

She was really going to do this. Operate this morning.

A part of her—an unpleasant, foreign-seeming part—was pleased.

The rest of her was dismayed.

God help me.

"Well done, Dr. Wu," Finney said. "Well done."

What am I doing?

SEBASTIAN

Well.

That was that. It had worked. So far, so good.

The tiny receiver nestled in his ear (*not* one of Finney's devices, thank Christ) crackled. "Sebastian."

"Yeah, boss."

"Dr. Montgomery is delaying the surgery. We have some extra time before execution of the primary command. Unexpected. But not problematic."

Execution of the primary command. Finney sounded like a goddamn automaton. "Agreed. I think I should join the tour group, though. Keep an eye on Montgomery. Make sure he doesn't switch anything else up on us. I'll follow the tour and end up in OR 10, as we'd planned."

"I agree. And Sebastian?"

"Yeah, boss?"

"I'm going to switch off your feed to Dr. Wu."

Again. Sebastian sucked on his teeth. "For how long?"

"Until you reach the OR."

"Why?"

"You need to concentrate on the tour. And Montgomery."

Bullshit.

The tour would be a goddamn dog-and-pony show. No reason he couldn't focus on both Montgomery and Wu at the same time.

What the hell are you really *up to, boss?*

"In the meantime, I'll take care of the good Dr. Wu," Finney said.

Sebastian sensed there was no point in debating. "Okay. If you say so, boss."

"Inform me immediately of any new developments. Otherwise, I'll speak to you again in a few hours, Sebastian." Static spat in Sebastian's ear, and Finney was gone.

SPENCER

"Good morning, Dr. Cameron."

"Good morning, Wendy." Spencer backed into OR 2 through its swinging double door. He kept his freshly scrubbed hands up in the air in front of him at shoulder height. Without dropping his hands, he turned around and approached the sterilized instrument table where Wendy, the scrub nurse, was waiting. She was already gowned and gloved. "How are you today?"

Wendy dropped a sterile towel over his hands and winked with an understated sexiness Spencer found appealing. He assumed she was winking at him: The nurses and anesthesia resident here were all women, and Bogart was unconscious. There weren't any neurosurgery residents or med students around this morning because they were at a lecture. "I'm great today, Dr. C, because I get to be in *your* room."

He chuckled as he dried his hands with a towel. "Oh, I bet you say that to all the surgeons."

"No," she said in a low voice. She kept her blue eyes fixed on his face. "I really don't."

Chrissy, the circulating nurse, was standing several feet away yet clearly keeping close tabs on their conversation. He caught her rolling her eyes. He couldn't look like he was playing favorites, so he said: "Well, thanks, Wendy. I appreciate that. Good morning, Chrissy!"

"Good morning, Doctor!" she called back enthusiastically.

"Always a pleasure to be working with you."

The crow's-feet around Chrissy's eyes lengthened. "Thank you, Doctor!"

The skin around Wendy's eyes remained smooth. Her eyes moved briefly to Chrissy, then settled back on him. He found this appealing. How could he not? Her eyes were big and blue.

"Extralarge gown, right, Dr. C?"

"Yes."

She dangled the sterile gown in front of him like a matador goading a bull with a cape. Spencer dropped the towel on the floor and stepped into the gown, pushing his arms into the sleeves. It was the biggest gown available yet so snug it barely fit him; he had trouble sliding his arms and shoulders into it. He always did. Chrissy helped secure the gown behind him as Wendy slipped on his (extralarge) sterile gloves.

He began to prepare Bogart for the biopsy. Next to him, Wendy turned to gather instruments from the sterile tray. Reflected light from her nose stud glinted from the gap between her cheek and the hem in her face mask.

"I just can't believe the way these extralarge gowns barely fit you," Wendy cooed. "It's like you're going to rip right out of it! Do you work out, Dr. C?"

"I, uh, try to stay in shape. I guess," Spencer said.

"Oh please. Were you, like, a football player, or something?"

"Nah. Never appealed to me. I boxed. In high school."

"Boxed! Wow."

"Yeah. Well, there was this retired Olympic boxing coach in my hometown in eastern Washington who worked with some of us kids. Great way to stay in shape and out of trouble." Although he hadn't been the kind of teenager who'd had trouble staying out of trouble.

"How about college?"

"I played rugby at the University of Washington. Proud Huskie."

"Rugby. Well, it shows," she said, laughing. She touched the back of his hand, letting it linger briefly.

Spencer noticed. *Of course* he noticed: he was a heterosexual man with an intact libido and a pulse. Wendy was a little on the thin side, and he wasn't into the way she highlighted her hair, or the blue eye shadow, or the body piercing. But she was cute. And available, she and her first husband having ended their short marriage last year, without acrimony or kids.

Plus, Spencer was lonely. Not that there hadn't been *any* women since he and Rita had split. But they'd come and gone, placeholders to fill the void left by Rita. A lawyer. A personal trainer at his gym. A woman who described herself as a "life consultant." All nice enough, especially the consultant, who was about the most cheerful person he'd ever met. But none could hold a candle to Rita. Lately, he hadn't had the energy or interest to go looking for more.

Or was it the misguided hope that Rita might yet come to her senses about the two of them?

He knew in his gut that a fling with Wendy would lead only to temporary parole from his loneliness. Plus, he didn't need the aggravation of innuendo. The OR break and locker rooms trafficked heavily in gossip. Exhibit A: the idiot who'd passed out naked in the OR. People like Ray were eating that stuff up; and even if, by some bizarre circumstance, the naked surgeon had a reasonable explanation, the guy's reputation was still toast. Once his identity was out, it would be just as well for him if he never showed up here again.

As if reading his mind, Wendy said, in a low voice, "So. Dr. C. Did you hear about what happened this morning?"

Spencer chuckled. "You mean the naked guy?"

Chrissy, standing behind Wendy, squealed. "Wendy's the one who found her!"

Her?

"Her?" Spencer asked, forcing casualness into his tone.

Wendy's eyes gleamed with the joy of secret, salacious knowledge. "I'm not supposed to talk about it. Dr. Montgomery told me not to tell anyone." Her eyes darted briefly to the anesthesia resident, who was absorbed in a medical textbook on her iPad. "But, yes. A woman, Dr. C. Can you *believe* it? Lisa Rodriguez and I found her while we were setting up OR 10." She glanced at the anesthesia resident again. "But you didn't hear it from me."

Rita operated in OR 10 on Mondays.

In fact, she was supposed to be operating there right now.

Easy, Spencer. That doesn't mean anything. It could have been anyone.

"A resident?" he said casually. "Drape, please."

Wendy handed him the sterile drape. "No." He couldn't see her lips, but it was like he could *hear* her smirking. "An attending."

His mouth went dry as he unfolded the drape and placed it over Bogart. That narrowed it down to about ten women, including Rita.

"Ahh," he said. "The plot thickens. So who was it?"

"I'm not allowed to tell you." But it was so obvious she wanted to. All she needed was a nudge.

"Come on. You're leaving us all in suspense here."

Wendy put her elbows on the scrub tray and leaned toward him. "Well, what do *I* get?"

"Umm . . . my undying gratitude?"

She threw back her head and laughed. "You can do better than that, Doctor," she said. "I was thinking along the lines of food." Toying with him now.

"Coffee? The cart in the lobby is first-rate."

"You know," she purred, "I have a condo down on Mission Bay. Small, not a big deal, but sunsets from my balcony are *gorgeous*, and I make a mean paella. I'm having some friends over this Saturday."

"Kelly clamp, please."

She handed him the clamp. "You should come."

Chrissy raised her eyebrows.

Careful, Doctor.

"Ah . . . how can I turn that down?" He was careful not to actually *say* yes.

"You can't," she said.

"Okay, then. Done. Who was it?"

Eyeing the anesthesia resident, Wendy wrote a name on a surgical towel using a sterile marking pen and slid it toward him.

Dr. Wu.

With a little smiley face underneath it.

"Ah . . ." He picked up the pen with an unsteady hand and wrote back: *R U SURE?*

She nodded emphatically. *Yes.*

"Saturday?" she murmured. "Spencer?"

"Sure," he said absently, his mind now running in five different directions, some of them leading to the strange car parked in front of Rita's house. "Saturday."

"Margaritas at five. I'll text you my address after the case. Okay?"

"Sure."

Rita. Naked in an OR.

Impossible.

He did his best to concentrate on Bogart's biopsy.

It wasn't easy.

SEBASTIAN

It was remarkable, Sebastian observed, how easy it was to walk unchallenged into the operating room of a major university hospital, in a major U.S. city.

Embarrassing, really.

You couldn't board a commercial airliner these days without a goddamn body-cavity search, but you could write down a name in black Sharpie on an adhesive paper name tag (or, better yet, use a printer, which is what Sebastian had done), slap it on your chest, claim to work for some surgical device manufacturer (any of the big ones that had contracts with the hospital would do), and stroll right the hell in, unchallenged, thank you very much.

After changing into a suit and tie he'd stowed above a ceiling tile in a little-used men's room, Sebastian had slipped unnoticed into a group of about twenty observers gathering near an entrance to the construction area at the end of a long corridor on the third floor. All the commotion, with the handing out of hard hats and review of safety rules, had provided perfect cover.

He'd had a brief, tense moment when the harried hospital public-relations team organizing the tour— a caffeinated pair consisting of a pretty, dark-haired, dark-skinned young woman in a formfitting blue dress and an even prettier, blond-haired young man sporting a grey skinny suit with red skinny tie—had realized the number in the tour group was higher than what they'd been expecting. Several people, including him and a woman who identified herself as a reporter for the *Wall Street Journal*, were not on the list.

Anxious to stay on schedule, the flustered pair had ignored the discrepancy and scrambled to procure more hats. Shit, they hadn't even bothered to write down his fake name. With a vacant smile, the pretty PR man had thrust a hard hat and Turner Hospital promotional brochure into Sebastian's hands and shooed him through a door (normally locked, Sebastian knew), which opened onto a bridge that led into the heart of the construction site. When construction was complete, the bridge would (Sebastian also knew) be one of the main thoroughfares connecting Turner with the new wing.

The top of the bridge was covered, but its sides were not; and now, as the tour group strolled across it, a strong, salt-tinged breeze blew in from the ocean. It ruffled his hair, fluffing it like a blow-dryer, and blew his tie over his shoulder.

He noticed that the precise blond hair of the PR guy, who was walking in front of him, remained in perfect lockdown, not a strand out of place, and his tie remained safely ensconced under the buttoned-down coat of his wrinkle-free suit. Suddenly self-conscious, Sebastian ran his fingers through his hair and carefully repositioned his tie underneath his suit coat before securing it with a button.

A trio of men behind him were having a lively discussion about liver transplants. Visiting surgeons, probably. Another alias he'd considered for today was that of a surgeon, visiting from another hospital. He might have been able to pull it off, he thought. Back in the day, he'd done double duty as his unit's corpsman, so he had some solid working knowledge of medicine—one of the skills that had landed him this job with Finney.

His medical abilities were the real deal. He'd hit the books hard during training, when he'd been selected as a corpsman. But it was the combat experiences that had honed them, sharpening them to the point he felt comfortable doing most anything short of major surgery. Some of the medical procedures he'd performed by himself, without support, in shit holes all over the world, had terrified him. But he'd had no choice. Shit happened.

Oh Jesus this one time: a kid (*kids, they'd all been kids*) shot to pieces, fucking *pieces*, the flesh of his neck and head torn away; alive but unconscious, goddamn blood everywhere; and from somewhere in the middle of the mound of raw hamburger that had a few seconds earlier been the kid's face (*Gary, his name was Gary, and he was from Indiana, and the guys had called him* Gary Indiana, *like the song in that old corny musical*), he'd sucked air through what had remained of his mouth.

It had become clear, fast, that Gary Indiana was suffocating. The pipe leading to his lungs—the trachea—was collapsing, clogging with blood and thick, pink chunks of God-knew-what. The evac helicopter had been ten minutes away; Gary Indiana had maybe a quarter of that left to live.

So Sebastian had made a decision, and he'd done what he'd never done before, or since: he'd slipped a plastic breathing tube into what was left of Gary Indiana's trachea to prop it open and maintain the precious flow of oxygen until help arrived. He'd done it right there, out in the open, in a desert in the middle of fucking nowhere.

But he'd done it right.

God*damn*, but that had been one scary experience: his hands shaking, fumbling at the sterile packaging of the plastic tube; Gary's wet, rasping breaths driving him to distraction. He'd managed it, somehow, and positioned the tube correctly, and kept him alive until the helicopter had arrived.

He'd never found out what had happened to Gary Indiana: if he'd made it in the end and, if so, what he looked like now. Sebastian didn't like to think about that, tried not to imagine him on a respirator in a VA-hospital chronic-care ward.

As confident as he was, Sebastian also knew his limitations, and doubted he could bluff his way through an extended conversation with a surgeon. No, too risky.

Speaking of surgeons: Dr. Chase Montgomery was at the front of the group, walking slowly backward, bragging about the new state-of-the-art operating rooms in the new wing.

What an asshole. Sebastian had Montgomery pegged from the get-go: the kind of leader who ped-dled his garbage about team or higher purpose or what-ever in order to promote himself. Grade-A-prime bullshit.

They reached the end of the bridge, and Mont-gomery led them into the skeleton of the new hospi-tal. Sebastian looked around, admiring its size and complexity. It was going to make one hell of a nice hospital, someday—especially if Montgomery and the bullshit promotional packet were to be believed. Not so much a hospital as a five-star hotel.

Right now, though, it was still a construction site: ex-posed wiring and plumbing elements, half-completed walls, and piles of raw materials—wood, wallboard, stacks of pipes, sheets of glass, bundles of steel rods, clusters of paint cans—all stacked in corners and hallways. The innards of a large building laid bare.

The smell of plaster and fresh paint lingered in his nostrils, and the air resounded with hammering, saw-ing, and shouting, some in English, some in Spanish. Lots of welding, too, and the group intermittently had to wind its way around cascades of sparks. The workmen didn't so much as look twice at them; maybe they were used to well-dressed gawkers tramping through every day.

Montgomery explained that the new hospital was being built in stages, which was why some sections were already encased in glass and cement, while others remained windowless and open to the air. Sebastian spied workers covering the exposed sections with large blue tarps.

"Preparing for the big storm tonight," Montgomery explained, gesturing to two workers as they unfurled, like a sail, a large blue tarp over an empty window and secured its corners with ropes and buckets of gravel. "We have a lot of materials in here we need to shelter from the wind and rain. Supposed to be a really big one. It'll be nice to finally get some rain. We need it here in California. Drought, you know."

Montgomery then led them into the new operating-room area, not far from the bridge they'd just crossed. He took them into one of the larger operating rooms (at least three times the size of Sebastian's entire apartment), and the group listened politely as he pointed out its features. Sebastian observed that the operating rooms had come along faster than most of the other sections. All twenty were more or less complete, each forming its own cavernous, enclosed space with four walls and a ceiling, sheltered from the elements and placed well away from the open, windowless sections. No blue tarps needed here.

Sebastian's practiced eye noted how the interiors of the new operating rooms were hidden not only from other areas of the construction zone but also from Turner, the adjacent buildings, and the nearby street. Without the construction workers around, some serious shit could go down in here without anyone's suspecting it—even Turner employees, or the security guards who kept watch over the construction site.

This didn't matter to him, or to Finney, but what the hell, it was impossible for Sebastian to turn off the professional side of his brain; so he made a mental note of it, anyway, just in case.

These features jibed with the blueprints Sebastian had acquired and memorized, and with the reconnaissance surveys he'd undertaken of Turner, both at night and during the day. He and Finney's plans didn't involve the construction site, but always best to be prepared.

Security, he'd noticed, focused on preventing theft of construction materials and was pretty decent but by no means insurmountable. A twelve-foot-high chainlink fence, covered with green-vinyl screens, surrounded the perimeter. At night, exterior floodlights spaced at intervals along the perimeter transformed these sections of fence into pools of day; more lamps strung throughout the building's infrastructure did much the same for the interior.

Competent and well trained, the nighttime guards concentrated mostly on the single gate in the fence, which was where most of the cameras were directed. But they also intermittently walked the entire perimeter at random times.

All this made perfect sense, since if someone intended to jack the valuable crap lying around, like building materials and power tools, the perimeter gate and the fence (under, through, or over) were the only ways in or out.

Except for one other place.

The bridge to Turner Hospital, across which the group had just walked.

Not a viable option for your run-of-the-mill thief with, say, an armful of stolen plumbing fixtures. But, in a pinch, a feasible route for him to access the new wing.

Again: didn't matter, but what the hell, options were options. He couldn't turn that part of his mind off, the one always considering tactical possibilities.

Montgomery droned on, fielding the occasional question. Blank smiles affixed to their bland faces, the PR team maintained silent vigil, flanking him, one on each side, like sentries plucked from a fashion-magazine spread. Sebastian checked his watch and scanned the other members of the tour, among them the chancellor of the university, the dean of the medical school, and the chief medical officer. Big shots. The others he didn't know.

The *Wall Street Journal* chick—who, like him, hadn't been on the original guest list—seemed to him one of those eternally pissed-off types, her expression frozen in disdain, one half of her lip elevated in a lazy semisneer. He liked that in a woman: Something about the whole attitude thing appealed to him. Clad in a conservative grey skirt and white blouse, gliding along on fashionable shoes, she projected boredom and dis- interest.

Sebastian was good at reading people and wasn't fooled for a second. The boredom was an act. Each of the questions she lobbed at Montgomery was a feint, designed to draw him out of the shelter of his scripted monologue, a little at a time. Montgomery, no dummy, parried these with a witty remark and the grin of the media-savvy shark, even as her dark eyes, sharp and bright, roamed everywhere, absorbing every detail.

Good-looking, too, he decided (he couldn't always turn off that part of his brain, either, so why bother?). She was black, with short, stylish hair shorn close to her skull. Well-defined chin. Nice neck without a hint of flab. Svelte, but curvy in the right places. Probably worked out, judging by the well-defined calves. Yeah. She was all right.

The PR man leaned over and whispered in Montgomery's ear.

"Right!" Montgomery said brightly. He clapped his hands once and rubbed them together. "Right. Well, it's time to head back. We're going to have everyone change into scrubs for the operating room, then we have a brief presentation before the actual operation. So let's go!"

Sebastian and the others followed him back across the bridge.

So far, so good, Sebastian thought, walking behind the *Wall Street Journal* chick.

Trying, but failing, not to admire her ass.

FINNEY

Dr. Wu had returned to the locker room to clean herself up, and he had let her.

No reason not to. He'd also permitted her to remove her glasses to use the toilet, and to take a shower, in (relative) privacy. Because, why not? He was feeling generous. Overall, everything was proceeding as he'd planned. She wasn't going anywhere.

Now he was listening to the steady *thrum* of shower water against her skull, which to him, through his audio feed, sounded like the drone of jet engines in the cabin of a passenger plane.

Finney was sitting in a small, windowless room in an anonymous office building next to Turner—a building that he owned, and which at present was unoccupied. He'd seen to that months ago, quietly clearing out the business tenants through intermediaries and expired leases, so that he'd be far from any prying eyes this morning.

The room was spare but suited his purpose just fine. There was a large desk on which to place the electronic tablet that tethered him to Dr. Wu and a rolling desk chair with padded arms and a high back for reclining.

He pushed himself away from the desk, leaned back in the chair, and stared at the ceiling. The water thrummed in his ear, as if he were standing in the shower with her.

Sebastian.

He assumed the man was climbing the walls right now, wondering what he was doing, suspecting that Finney was holding out on him, perhaps laying plans Sebastian wasn't privy to. Which, naturally, Finney was.

Plans that involved killing Dr. Wu.

But those would come later. For now, he simply wanted to be alone with her. Because, really, this whole thing was between only the two of them.

Without taking his eyes off the ceiling, he pulled the worn-leather notebook from his front shirt pocket, the same one he'd written in the day of Jenny's funeral. He held it up to his face. A frayed cloth bookmark, attached to the binding, flagged a page near the back. He opened to that page and studied the name he'd written there in mechanical pencil a year ago.

Dr. Rita Wu.

He replaced the bookmark, closed the book, and hugged it to his chest.

When Jenny had still been alive, people had wondered what she'd seen in him.

Oh, they didn't come right out and say it to his face. But Finney knew they were thinking it. Talking about him behind his back. He wasn't *stupid*.

Most, he knew, thought it was his money. With good reason. He had a lot of it. And he, being careful with his money, had always regarded the women who pursued him with suspicion.

He'd dated before Jenny, of course. Like most men, he had physical needs. Close companionship hadn't interested him. But satisfying those needs had, and he'd never been one to *pay* for that kind of thing.

So he'd dated, but never without a thorough background check of the woman in question, during which his investigator invariably turned up material that confirmed his suspicions (at least in his own mind), and prevented the development of a longer-term entanglement. Which was fine. There was always another woman.

And then Jenny.

From the beginning, she'd been different. An accountant by training, she'd worked for one of the smaller biotechs he controlled, one developing new treatments for diabetes. He'd met her at one of the company meetings he occasionally attended, and she'd intrigued him.

It had begun with her hand.

He disliked shaking hands. People's hands were *dirty*. Coated with disease and filth. He tolerated hand shaking only because it was good business, and politeness demanded it. But he kept a small bottle of liquid hand sanitizer in his pants pocket at all times; and he would slip his hand in his pocket to surreptitiously cleanse it after each offending, germ-soaked shake without removing the bottle from his pocket.

He hadn't done that after shaking Jenny's hand, not one squirt of lemon-scented, bacterial death. He hadn't felt the urge, hadn't pictured in his mind, the way he normally did, the millions of microbes teeming across the surfaces of her palm and fingers. He didn't understand why.

He'd also had no clue as to why he was able to look her straight in the eye when they first met. Looking people in the eye usually made him uncomfortable. Hers had been beautiful eyes. Green, to go with her red hair.

He'd observed during that first meeting, and subsequent ones, how other people were drawn to her warmth, as if she were the sun, and they the planets orbiting around her. She had a positive energy she transmitted to those around her. To him, she was unflaggingly kind and professional, but otherwise hadn't shown the extreme deference, bordering on sycophancy, as the others who worked for him did. He liked that.

And her laugh. God. Her laugh had been like a drug to him. Other people's laughter often annoyed him, grated on his ears, like a knife scraping against a glass bottle. Her laughter was music.

The more he was around her, the more he'd wanted to *be* around her. He'd started to schedule more meetings at her company just to have an excuse to be in the same room with her. And, privately, he'd fallen for her. It didn't occur to him to ask her out. He'd simply watched her, content to admire her from a small distance, delighted to have joined her orbit.

Until the thing happened with the comic books.

Finney was a comic-book fan. Science fiction, too. As a kid he'd been a fanatic, had spent all his free time (and, without friends, he'd had a lot of it) poring over comics and science-fiction novels. He'd loved and collected the classic comics—kept them in special airtight plastic bags with cardboard backing, and would handle them only with white-cotton gloves—but he'd devour whatever he could get his hands on: old, new, valuable, worthless. It hadn't mattered.

As a child, he'd dismissed the action figures and other toys that went with them as, well . . . childish, because it was the stories he loved. He'd steeped himself in their arcana with the seriousness of a professor. He'd even tried his hand at writing a few though he knew he wasn't any good. He could wax poetic on the dif-

ferences between steampunk and cyberpunk, expound
on the history of Japanese manga, or recite the origins
of even the most minor characters in the most insig-
nificant, short-lived series.

The thing with Jenny had happened at Comic-Con,
an international convention of comic-book, science-
fiction, and fantasy fans. Each July, tens of thousands
of Comic-Con conventioneers seized San Diego by
the throat. Legions, shuffling from one exhibit to another, dressed in absurd costumes, clutching tote bags
full of free tchotchkes, clogging sidewalks and streaming across downtown intersections in packed, multicolored lines like army ants on the march through the
jungle. To him, it was the biggest Halloween party ever
for grown-ups.

But it hadn't always been like that. Finney had attended Comic-Con for years. *Decades.* Each year,
growing up, he'd *begged* his parents to drive him the
hundred-odd miles south from their home in Los Angeles to San Diego until he was old enough to make
the trip on his own; and, each year, his bemused parents had acquiesced.

He was old enough to remember a time when
Comic-Con was just him and several hundred fellow
true believers sifting through cardboard boxes of comics in a hotel basement—not the obscene carnival it
had become. He missed those days. As a kid, he was
only rarely happy; and his happiest times were there,
among his fellow fans. He'd looked forward to seeing
them each year. Especially the adults, who'd treated
him like an equal. How they hadn't judged him, or

cared where he came from—this skinny, awkward kid with acne so bad it looked like he'd tossed tomato sauce on his face each morning.

At Comic-Con, the dark and disturbing thoughts that had plagued him, that would steal into his head, especially at night—

(*yes dark and disturbing he knew he'd always known that but didn't know how to control them not until he'd met Jenny*)

—the ones he'd nursed toward his tormentors through middle school and high school, would dissipate like morning mist in the rising sun.

Staring at the ceiling, listening to the shower water, he stroked the leather cover of his notebook and reflected that he'd never, *not once*, written down a fellow comic-book fan's name in it. He'd never needed to.

The comics had sustained him: kept him company during the long, lonely hours of his childhood, nurtured his dreams of scientific things that did not yet exist, and inspired him to a career in which he invented them for real. Because of this, he'd continued to attend Comic-Con every year, like a sacred pilgrimage—well after he'd become a grown man who should have known better.

And then, one year, there she'd been.

On the sidewalk outside the convention-center entrance.

One hundred thirty thousand fans converging on eight square city blocks, and there she'd been. Total, random chance. Serendipity.

Or had it been?

He'd long been convinced that the universe had

been telling him something that day. He didn't believe in a benevolent deity guiding his destiny. But he did believe in a cosmic clockwork, unseen cogs and wheels, spinning under the influence of a divine, orderly plan. The cosmos had deemed that he and Jenny should be together, and its interlocking parts had spun to that purpose.

This had been several months after he'd met her. She'd been wearing a pair of jeans and faded I GROK SPOCK T-shirt. He'd been walking in, she out. He'd stood there, slack-jawed, his brain trying to process the image of her red hair glowing in the summer sun, of believing that she was really there, at *his* Comic-Con.

She'd spotted him standing there at the door, gaping. She'd done a double take, and blushed; and then she'd laughed, and bathed him in a beautiful smile. He'd grinned, smitten in a way he'd never been, or would ever be again.

They'd talked there by the door for fifteen minutes as the costumed crowd pressed around them. She was alone. It turned out she was as big a fan as he, had been since a teenager, but embarrassed to share it with friends and colleagues because she'd wanted to be taken seriously. He'd laughed and told her he understood, and that her secret was safe with him. He invited her to join him, his stomach turning somersaults, and she'd followed him back inside.

Finney's status among the old-timers granted him special access to quiet, privileged places. That day, and the next few that followed, he'd brought Jenny to these places. They'd watched from the wings as groups of Hollywood actors appeared onstage before screaming throngs, mugging for the crowd, like British royalty waving from high palace windows. They'd wandered among the exhibits, and chatted with artists and writers in intimate VIP-only meet-and-greets. They'd shared their favorite stories and comics with each other, and talked for hours over long dinners.

And they'd fallen in love.

Through unspoken agreement, they'd never told anyone about the seed of their relationship. It was their secret: a shared connection that was (and always would be) theirs alone. He was sure that the others, the ones who had *mocked* him behind his back, would have snickered and sneered.

Comic books? Pathetic. And she seemed so normal. *Just goes to show you can never tell, though. Can you?*

He squeezed his eyes shut.

God, how he'd been pulled, helpless, to her life force, like a moth to light. He'd been carried along by blind devotion. It was exhilarating and terrifying, as if he'd been trapped on a tiny raft shooting down a white-water river.

He'd become a different person with her. Before Jenny, he'd thought of love as a biological construct, electrical impulses firing in the circuitry of the brain, neurons communicating through tenuous biochemical conduits in simple, reproducible patterns. She'd shown him that it was something much more. Something he was incapable of analyzing.

Or resisting.

He opened his eyes, wiped a tear from his cheek, and cocked his head to one side.

Something was happening.

The sound of the shower water had stopped.

He leaned forward and scooted his chair toward the desk. On his tablet, a new signal had appeared in the top right corner of the screen. Dr. Wu was using her phone, in which Sebastian had installed a tiny monitoring chip while she'd lain unconscious in the operating room.

He saw the number she was calling.

It made him want to smile.

But he still didn't permit himself the satisfaction. He didn't deserve it.

Not yet.

Instead, with a tap of a finger to the tablet, he opened his link to her brain.

RITA

Rita was in the shower, staring at the drain, thinking about nothing but the warmth of the water hitting her neck, when she realized she'd forgotten to call Darcy back.

Again.

She rapped her forehead gently against the tiles below the showerhead.

Dammit.

Finney was *really* messing with her brain. She couldn't keep her thoughts straight. Darcy had called her to say she wasn't feeling well—

Oh God.

She jerked her head up so that the jets of water were slapping her in the face.

Oh God, oh God, oh God.

What had Darcy said?

I woke up with a horrible headache this morning.

And Finney had said: *Ask her where her head hurts.*

Her left side. Her left *ear*.

Just like Rita.

He'd done something to Darcy, too.

With new dread—

(*don't panic*)

—she turned off the water, wrapped herself in a towel from a nearby hook, and stepped out.

Finney had been quiet since she'd returned to the women's locker room. Not a word as she'd nibbled on a granola bar and a couple of ondansetron antinausea pills she'd scrounged from her locker; or when she'd announced she was going to pee and then hop in the shower, then removed her glasses and stuffed them in her locker before undressing. She'd taken her time, especially in the shower. Screw the drought. It was supposed to rain tonight anyway.

But she knew he was still there, listening. She could sense his presence. The air around her seemed heavy and electric, like before a summer thunderstorm.

The locker room was busier now. Surgeons and nurses periodically filed by her locker. She wanted to ignore them, wished she could crawl into a hole somewhere. But they all knew her, so she managed the obligatory smiles and hellos, scanning their expressions and wondering how many had already heard about her . . . *situation*. But none acted like they had.

She opened her locker, took out her phone, and dialed home.

"Checking on your sister, Dr. Wu?" Finney said in her ear.

Shut up, she thought back. She wondered how he knew what she was doing, with her glasses still tucked in the back of her locker under a spare pair of scrubs.

Monitoring my phone calls, maybe?

The line rang several times, then: "Hi, this is Rita. I'm sorry I can't take your call right now—"

She hung up and tried Darcy's phone.

It went immediately to voice mail.

She took a deep breath.

Calm, lovely Rita. Stay calm.

She dialed home again.

"Hi, this is Rita. I'm sorry—"

Dammit!

She stabbed the redial key with her index finger.

"Hi, this is—"

She hung up. Sweat broke out all over her body, mingling with the drops still clinging to her skin.

"I wonder what's happening?" Finney said.

Shut. UP!

She sat down on the bench in front of her locker and dialed home once more.

Another cycle of rings. It seemed to stretch for hours.

"Pick up, pick up, *please* pick up, kiddo," she whispered.

And then Darcy's voice, thick with sleep. "Hello?"

"Darcy." Rita's stomach, which had risen into her throat, dropped back into its normal position.

Thank you thank you thank you God.

"Ah. There she is," Finney said.

"Ree. Sorry. I went back to bed." Darcy yawned. "Didn't hear the phone."

"No—*I'm* sorry, kiddo. You wanted to talk earlier, and I . . . totally forgot to call you back. I'm so sorry. Things here have been, um—" She groped for the right word. "Crazy."

"That's one way to describe it," Finney said.

"S'okay." Darcy yawned again.

"How are you feeling?" Rita asked.

"Um . . . better. My head's better. When I first woke up, it felt like someone had taken a *sledgehammer* to it, Ree. And there was some dried blood on my left ear." Rita's stomach lurched back into her throat. "Isn't that *weird?* I must have slept on it wrong. Or something. The weirder thing—actually, the thing that kind of freaked me out a little . . . what I was trying to tell you earlier—"

"What?"

"Well . . . I swear to God, I've been clean, Ree. Swear to God. Three months this time. You know that. Totally clean."

A nurse in street clothes, carrying a set of folded scrubs under her arm, smiled at Rita as she went to the locker next to Rita's and started dialing the combination. Rita smiled back, stood up, walked to the opposite end of the room, and cupped her hand around her mouth. "What do you mean?" she said quietly.

"Three months. Clean. Swear to God."

"Okay, yes. Clean. I believe you, Darcy. What are you talking about?"

"I just felt a little . . . I don't know. Kind of, like, *out* of it? Like I had a hangover, or something? Like I had partied last night? But I *didn't* party last night. I *know* I didn't. After you left for the hospital, I just watched a really dumb movie, some lame Adam Sandler thing, and went to bed. Swear to God. So it kind of, like, freaked me out a little?"

Oh God. Just like me.

Rita swallowed hard.

Calm, lovely Rita. Situational awareness.

"Have you noticed, uh, anything else, Darcy? Any other . . . uh, symptoms?"

"No."

"Are you hearing any strange sounds?"

"Sounds? No. Why?"

So Finney's not talking to her. Why is that?

Rita stared at the floor and quickly processed this. She saw no other option but to keep Darcy in the dark until she could figure out what to do next.

Problem was: She hadn't the faintest idea.

Except that I have to operate on Mrs. Sanchez.

"No reason. I'm sure it's nothing," Rita said.

Besides, what would she tell Darcy? That the bitter, vengeful husband of a former—

(*and dead, don't forget dead, she's dead because of ME*)

—patient had apparently snuck into her house last night and done some kind of bizarre surgery on her head while she slept? Trying to explain that to Darcy would be no less likely to land her in the psych ward than trying to explain it to Chase.

"You've been through a lot, kiddo," Rita said. "You're probably having some, uh, withdrawal symptoms, or something. Delayed withdrawal symptoms." Rita well knew there was no such thing as "delayed" withdrawal from the substances Darcy used to take.

"You think?" Darcy said brightly.

Rita tightened her grip on the phone. "Absolutely, kiddo."

"Oh, Dr. Wu. Such lies," Finney breathed. "Are you as disingenuous with your patients as with your family?"

Bastard, she shot back at him in her mind.

Darcy said, "Okay. That makes me feel better."

"Good."

Wish it made me *feel better.*

A brief silence, then: "Hey, uh . . . Ree?"

"Yeah, kiddo?"

"Can I ask you something?"

"Sure."

"Did you come home last night?"

"Um." Rita tightened her towel around her body and glanced back toward her locker. The nurse was almost done changing into her scrubs, her head turned the other way. "Why do you ask?"

"When I woke up this morning, your bed looked like it hadn't been slept in."

Rita sighed and pressed a hand to her forehead. "No, Darcy. I didn't. I . . . was working late and fell asleep at the hospital."

"Oh. The big operation today?"

"Yeah."

"How's it going?"

"We'll be starting soon."

I need to operate on Mrs. Sanchez this morning.

"Oh. Well. You should probably go then, huh?"

"Yeah."

Because I need to operate on Mrs. Sanchez.

"What time will you be home?"

Something inside Rita felt like it was dying. *Home*, and everything that went with it, seemed so remote now that it might as well be on the far side of the moon. "Don't know yet," she said mechanically. "Late, probably."

"Okay." Darcy yawned. "I'm going back to bed. Call me when you're on your way and I'll throw something together for dinner. Okay?"

They were chatting as if today were like any other day, and *God*, what Rita wouldn't give for that to be so.

"Okay." She could barely push the word out of her mouth.

"Good luck, okay? Love you, Ree."

"Love you too, kiddo."

As Rita hung up and leaned against a nearby wall, a horrible thought seized hold of her.

She would never speak to Darcy again.

"Your sister has had some bad times. Hasn't she, Dr. Wu?"

Leaning there, Rita supposed that, in a morning filled with the most disturbing things imaginable, the realization that Finney could not only listen in on a private conversation with her kid sister but had somehow rigged Darcy's head with the same *thing* he'd implanted in Rita could crush whatever was left of her. Stamp out her will completely.

But it had the opposite effect. What had been simmering anger became hatred. She balled her hands into fists. She was a doctor, had taken an oath to protect human life, but in that moment, she wanted to hurt Finney, hurt him *badly*, in all the ways possible for one person to hurt another.

"What have you done to my sister?" she growled.

No answer.

"Coward. You're a coward. Hiding behind your microphone."

No answer.

She staggered back to her locker as if in a dream (*nightmare*). The nurse with the locker next to hers had finished and was gone. Rita loosened her towel and began to change into fresh underwear (she always kept at least one extra pair for call nights) and scrubs. She was careful to leave her glasses facing away from her, toward the back of the locker.

Finney said, in barely more than a whisper: "What do you know about cowardice, Dr. Wu? Pilots go down with their planes. Captains go down with their ships. But surgeons get to walk away from their disasters. Just like you walked away from Jenny."

Bastard, she fumed.

Yeah, okay, she *did* feel guilty about his wife. Of course she did. She always would. More than he could ever know, for reasons he could never fathom. But, to hell with him: What the hell did he know about being a surgeon? About what that meant? About complications, and living with the ghosts of patients who'd died under your care? Each day, she made countless decisions that altered people's lives. Operate, or don't operate? Big incision, or little one? Cut out more of an organ—a colon, perhaps, or a liver—and risk serious

complications, or cut out less and not cure the disease?
And always, *always*, there were consequences.

"What do you know about anything?" Rita mumbled.

"A lot, actually. Take your sister. Darcy Rose Wu, aged twenty-two. Mother, Rose Wu, died shortly after birth, from unexpected complications of delivery. Correct? Raised by your father, Kevin Wu—"

"Don't you say my father's name," she hissed. An orthopedic surgeon she recognized but had never spoken with, seated on a nearby bench, paused her texting to eye her curiously. Rita turned the other way and placed a hand over her mouth. "Don't you *dare* say either of my parents' names. Ever."

"—and, after his death, by your grandmother, Peggy. And yourself. It must have been hard to be orphaned, at such a young age. I imagine it's one of the reasons why all of those bad things happened to your sister when she was at Brown."

Rita pursed her lips and tried to take some comfort in knowing he didn't have the story quite straight. Because the bad things with Darcy had started long before Brown, when she was in high school: after their grandmother had died, and Rita, in her late twenties, scarcely more than a teenager herself, had become Darcy's guardian. They'd been little things, at first. Typical teenage things. No big deal. Open the teenager textbook, flip to the *moodiness* chapter, and there they were. Shouting matches. Slammed doors. Sullen looks. Missed curfews. Provocative clothes.

Then the escalation when Darcy was sixteen: sneaking out for a secret night of clubbing in Tijuana with

girlfriends. An awful early-morning phone call; Rita
signing out her duties and leaving her shift early to
drive thirty miles to the U.S. Border Patrol office in
San Ysidro, its front windows glazed brown with the
grimy sediment accumulated from the exhaust of millions of idling cars waiting their turn to cross into the
U.S.

The *humiliation*. Picking up Darcy—dazed, reek-
ing of booze and puke—from a meaty, uniformed female agent with judgmental eyes and stringy hair the
same dirty shade of brown as the front windows of the
office, who pushed forms at Rita across a pitted For-
mica counter. *Sign here, please. And here. And here*.

Furious, she'd let Darcy sleep Tijuana off for most
of the next day, then let her have it over dinner. Really
got into it with her: like what the hell had she been
thinking; and didn't she know how lucky she was that
she hadn't landed in a *Mexican* jail, for God's sake; and
what would Mom and Dad have thought.

Darcy, her face blotchy and pitted and pathetic, had
cried: chunky tears of guilt, or anger, or both, and then
fled to her room, where she'd remained most of the
next week.

Looking back, Rita knew that was when she should
have made herself more involved with Darcy. Active
intervention then might have prevented what came
later. But Rita's insane work schedule had left her no
time to be a single mom to a teenage sister.

No. That wasn't completely true.

She *could* have devoted more time to Darcy. By
then Rita was a doctor—not yet a fully trained one, but
she had her MD, which made her employable. She

could have opted out of the punishing schedule of a surgeon and found a well-paying job with normal hours in a research lab.

But she loved surgery too much, couldn't imagine life without it. She hadn't been willing to choose between surgery and Darcy. And after Tijuana, Rita had fooled herself into believing Darcy would figure things out on her own. Why? Because Darcy was bright and talented and sweet. Because she was a gifted writer and a beautiful singer; because she was active in the drama and glee clubs, had plenty of (normal-seeming) friends, and her grades were superb. Junior year, she'd placed second in a statewide playwriting competition for high-school kids. Second! In a state of 40 million people. How could a kid like that *not* figure things out on her own?

And hadn't *Rita* figured things out on her own, as a teenager, after Dad had died? Hadn't *she* gotten by okay, with only a well-intentioned but clueless grandmother? Hadn't *she* navigated adolescence, parentless, without so much as a tardy slip at school?

Rita had provided food, shelter, clothes, and money for random teenage-type crap. She'd helped out with homework when she could (which was precious little); had arranged for a sitter to clean, cook, and drive Darcy to school when she couldn't (which was most of the time). She'd attended (some) of the school plays and glee-club performances, and watched the videos of the ones she couldn't.

Otherwise, she'd pretty much left Darcy—smart, sweet, and vulnerable—to her own devices.

To find her own way.

But Darcy had not found her own way.

Rita understood the concept of ADHD. She grasped the pharmacology of its treatment. She could recite from memory the physiological effects of drugs like Adderall on adolescents, knew from her experiences in the ER why kids without ADHD sought them out.

Smart pills, one gorked-out college kid had told her one night in an ER bay. Right before she'd shoved a tube down the kid's nose to pump out his stomach. Totally safe, those kids believed. An easy, nonaddictive way to finish a big term paper—or study for final exams—in a single night.

Bullshit.

Amphetamines. Stimulants. Speed. Steroids for concentration. Addicting as hell. Readily available in high-school hallways and college dorm rooms.

Rita knew all of this.

So why hadn't she recognized these things in Darcy?

Rita had never figured out where the pills had come from, and Darcy had remained tight-lipped. It didn't matter. Not in the end: not after the heart palpitations, and dizziness, and the projectile vomiting, and the late-night rush to an ER that, much to Rita's relief, was not the one in which she'd worked.

Things had turned out fine, thank God. Darcy recovered quickly and, unhinged by the ER trip, had sworn off the pills. Rita arranged for therapy. Darcy righted herself, blazed across the finish line of her senior year, and graduated near the top of her class, chemical-free. The therapist declared success and signed off. That summer, the one before college, had passed in a haze of optimism and relief.

But no, too easy.

In retrospect, it had all been much too easy.

The following fall, Rita would have loved to have dropped Darcy off at Brown herself. Over the summer, they'd talked excitedly about the two of them trekking cross-country in Rita's battered Honda Civic. They even took out a map one night and traced a route, complete with stops at national parks, and at Graceland, which Darcy had always wanted to see.

But the talk remained just that: talk.

There was the important research paper on robotic surgery Rita had to present at the American College of Surgeons. And the extra shifts Chase had asked her to work, as a personal favor. And the auto-surgeon. *Always* the auto-surgeon. Chase had handpicked *her* to lead the auto-surgeon project, which back then had been just getting off the ground. How could she possibly get away, with all of that going on?

Darcy was a big girl, she'd told herself as she helped Darcy pack her things and ship them to Rhode Island. *She'll be okay.*

Rhode Island.

So far away.

Would it have made a difference if Rita had gone with her to help move in? Or if she'd insisted that Darcy stay closer to home for college? She'd never know.

A little independence. A little distance. It'll do her some good, Rita had reassured herself as Darcy, her wide dark eyes spilling with tears, had cast one final, uncertain wave over her shoulder before passing through the TSA checkpoint.

Done with the pills forever. That's what Darcy had told her.

Promises made. Promises broken.

Three thousand miles away, in the dark of a bitter New England winter (*the worst one in years, she now remembered, she'd heard it on the news*), it began again. She'd done okay during her first year, but then stumbled through her second, and fallen flat on her face in the middle of her third.

A year ago, when so much in Rita's life all went so wrong all at once.

Darcy. Spencer. Jenny Finney.

A perfect storm of crappiness.

"Am I correct?" Finney asked.

And now, a sudden insight: She was inching toward insanity.

"Dr. Wu?"

Yes. Insanity.

Definitely.

She felt its approach as if she were groping blindly down a darkened train tunnel, and somewhere up ahead, unseen, a speeding freight train—the insanity— was bearing down on her. She wanted to go back, out of the train tunnel and away from the train, but she could not; Finney's voice in her head kept nudging her forward, toward the speeding train. Toward insanity. And she had no way, no way at all, to stop the train, or herself.

No way out.

"Dr. Wu."

Still.

It might not be so bad, she thought. *Insanity.*

It would hit her head-on, knock her into oblivion; and then she wouldn't care about any of this, and she could hang out with Moses, her former patient, on the psych ward. Talk Scripture, or something. It'd be nice. They could become buddies.

Then she heard her father in her mind: *Situational awareness, lovely Rita.* He sounded calm, and the calmness pulled her out of the pitch-black train tunnel. *Keep him talking. Gather more information. There are always options. You can get through this. Your kid sister needs you. Darcy needs you, lovely Rita.*

She took a deep, shuddering breath. *Right.* Darcy. She needed to think about Darcy.

The train tunnel receded.

"Dr. Wu. Answer me, please."

She now was done dressing. She glanced at the orthopedic surgeon, who was absorbed in her texting, and took a seat on the bench in front of her locker. She bent over to tie her sneakers.

"The two of us got by okay," she said to her sneakers.

"*You* may have, Dr. Wu. Darcy's path has been somewhat . . . shakier, it seems to me."

"Darcy has done fine. Not that it's any of *your* business."

Situational awareness.

"Oh, but I think it's very much my business."

"The hell it is."

Rita finished tying her sneakers and sat straight up. The orthopedic surgeon was staring at her.

"Hi," Rita said.

The woman went back to her texting.

Rita stood up, grabbed her glasses, and slipped them on as a text came through on her phone. They were ready for her in OR 10. Her stomach clenched.

I need to operate on Mrs. Sanchez.

"Ah," Finney said. "Excellent."

But *why* did she need to operate on Mrs. Sanchez? Where was this urge coming from? Why must she operate, even though she still knew in her heart it wasn't the right thing to do? *Operate. Don't operate.* It felt like a mental tug-of-war, pulling her brain apart, like taffy.

Operate.

Don't operate.

The image of the train tunnel was returning, like a fade-in at the beginning of a movie.

"Dr. Wu?" Finney said after several seconds. "Let's not keep them waiting." Pause. "For Darcy's sake."

Darcy.

The train tunnel faded again.

She slammed the locker door closed.

Startled, the orthopedic surgeon dropped her phone.

"Sorry," Rita mumbled as she picked the phone up off the floor and handed it back to her. The woman eyed her warily. "I mean, well—just, sorry."

Rita felt the woman's eyes drill into her back as she walked away.

SEBASTIAN

Once the tour group had changed into scrubs, everyone settled into plush seats in a pristine amphitheater adjacent to the main entrance of Turner's operating rooms. In all his reconnoitering, Sebastian had not been in here before and was struck by its newness. It had the look of having been built, or perhaps remodeled, recently, with clean walls and shiny fabric on the chairs, and possessed a new-car kind of smell.

Montgomery took position on the dais in the front of the amphitheater. He wore an immaculate white coat over his scrubs, with his name embroidered in cursive over the left front coat pocket, and the Turner logo—a modified caduceus in which a trident replaced the staff—stitched across the right. A large, high-def monitor stretched the length of the wall behind him, on which floated the logos for both the University of California and Turner, tracing random paths across the screen. As he moved across the dais, the fabric of his white coat wobbled, so crammed was it with starch. He reminded Sebastian of a CEO launching a new product.

"Several years ago," Montgomery said, his voice amplified by a small cordless microphone on the collar of his white coat, "a group of us surgeons here at the University of California asked ourselves how we can do things better."

The lights in the auditorium dimmed. The logos on the screen disappeared, replaced with a picture of a group of surgeons wearing long white coats, scrubs, and broad smiles. They were standing in front of the main entrance to Turner. One was Wu; another was Montgomery. The camera panned across them in an unhurried, diagonal arc, like a documentary.

"Surgeons are creatures of perfection. We obsess

about it. We don't accept *average*, or even *good enough*. We strive, always, for *perfection*. In that spirit, we here at Turner didn't ask ourselves: How do we lead the pack? We asked ourselves: How do we get so far out in front of the pack, we change surgery forever? To paraphrase the great hockey player Wayne Gretzky: We decided we didn't want to go to where the puck *is*—we wanted to go to where the puck *is going to be*."

Montgomery stalked the stage, waving his hands in the air. "We asked ourselves, where is the puck going to be in five years? Ten? How do we control the puck? How do we, in essence, *become* the puck?"

Sebastian shifted in his seat.

Okay. Jesus. We get it. It's all about the goddamn puck.

"Becoming the puck meant fundamentally changing our way of thinking," Montgomery said. "Surgeons have been doing things essentially the same way for over 150 years. But we are about to change all of that. Forever."

On the screen, the picture of the surgeons transitioned into one of a sleek aircraft cockpit with high-tech digital control panels. Two pilots, both men, one black, one white, sporting multistriped epaulets affixed to white dress shirts with the sleeves rolled up, were turned in their seats toward the camera, flashing thumbs-ups signs with virile, affable charisma.

"Automation. That's our puck, folks! To automate an operation the same way one would automate a plane flight. Autopilots use computer-controlled systems to mechanize the finely coordinated movements of an airplane and guide it safely through all aspects of its flight. Takeoff." Below the pilots appeared a smaller picture frame in which a video clip showed a passenger jet soundlessly lifting off from a runway. "Flight." The takeoff picture transmogrified into a view of the same jet cruising at high altitude among sun-dappled clouds. "Landing." The jet glided in for a routine landing on a different runway.

"Autopilots fly tens of thousands of us around the world every day. They flew many of you here today. Why, then, not *auto-surgeons*? Machines that perform the surgeries for us, the same way autopilots fly our planes?"

"But surgery is an art!" thundered a man in the front row. He had a shock of white hair, stooped neck, and haughty bearing. He had no microphone, but the acoustics were exceptional, and Sebastian could hear him quite well from his seat in the back. "A machine can't do what a surgeon does! We are human beings, laying hands on other human beings! A machine can't do that! We are *artists*!"

Montgomery nodded in a way that communicated both agreement and polite dissent. "Yes, Dr. Linton. We surgeons are indeed artists. And you, sir, are a master. We have, all of us, benefited from your pioneering work. There is no doubt, sir, that you have forgotten more about the art of surgery than I could possibly ever hope to learn."

Linton bobbed his snowcapped head in regal concurrence, accepting Montgomery's compliment as the pope would a kiss to his ring.

Sebastian wanted to laugh out loud.

Jesus *Christ* but was this Montgomery guy slick.

"But," Montgomery continued, "surgery is also a science, Dr. Linton. Why not combine the science *and* the art? Why not have surgeons program machines to execute the same tasks they otherwise would, but without the imperfections of the human condition? To map out every nick of the scalpel and tie of the suture, then have machines perform them?"

"Bahhh!" Linton exclaimed, pawing at the air in the manner of a baseball fan dismissing a bad call by an umpire.

"Your skepticism is completely understandable, Dr. Linton. But if I may—"

"No, sir, you may not!" Linton tilted his chin up and sniffed through cavernous nostrils guarded by thick white hairs. "I would remind you that we *lay hands* on people, Doctor. Every stitch I threw, in every single operation I ever performed, was *perfect*. Because it *had* to be, Doctor. No *machine* can do that!" He snorted. The white nostril hairs cowered.

Montgomery smiled indulgently and spread his hands wide. "But if I may, sir: Does not aviation also deal in matters of life and death? We place our lives in the hands of autopilots every time we board a commercial flight. As you did, sir, when you flew here from Boston."

"Bahhh." Linton discovered a spot on the auditorium wall off to the right of the stage on which to fix his sullen gaze.

Montgomery gestured to the image of the grinning pilots in their gleaming, computerized cockpit. "Whether it's a commercial flight or a combat mission, any pilot these days will tell you that automation has

become essential. Computers haven't replaced pilots—
they've only taken over certain aspects of flying. Made
it more precise. *Safer.* Our auto-surgeon functions
much like an autopilot. The surgeon designs a surgical
plan and programs it into the auto surgeon. The auto-
surgeon then executes the plan under the surgeon's
supervision, much like the flight plan for a plane. We
believe that most of the steps for basic operations—
like removing an appendix—can be automated."

"An autopilot has direct connections to the controls
of the airplane," the woman from the *Wall Street Journal* interrupted from her seat near the front. "How
does a computer perform an operation on a person?"

Definitely a smart chick.

Montgomery was unruffled. He grinned. "Ms. . . .
Grant. Correct?"

She nodded.

The pilots disappeared, and gasps rippled through
the audience as behind Montgomery the screen lit up
with a 3-D image of a mechanical device composed
of a sleek, central cylinder that sprouted six smaller,
cylindrical projections with tapered ends that reached
toward the floor. Wrapped in a gleaming, silver-colored
casing, the object looked like a gigantic, six-armed jel-
lyfish, or an octopus.

Sebastian had seen it hundreds of times before; and
the thing looked so damn real, floating up there in the
air, the graphics rendered so precisely, that Sebastian
felt that if he climbed up on the dais and pressed his
hands to it, unbending metal would press back.

All in all, Sebastian had to admit, a goddamn impressive show.

The hologram hovered behind and above Montgomery, spinning in slow revolutions. One end of it came within a few inches of Montgomery's head, appearing as if it would give him a good whack across the skull.

"The answer to your question, Ms. Grant, is robotics. We built the world's first fully automated surgical robot."

RITA

Rita was waiting in OR 10 when Mrs. Sanchez—
(*whom she needed to operate on*)
—arrived.

She'd been running equipment checks with her handpicked, two-person surgical team: Lisa Rodriguez, and a physician's assistant named Thomas—a gruff, large man of few words, many tattoos (some of which ran across the top of his bald head), and extraordinary surgical competence who was a die-hard Oakland Raiders fan and rode a Harley-Davidson. Had the hospital allowed for such things, Rita was sure he would wear black scrubs in the OR, maybe accessorize them with some shoulder chains and make the whole ensemble look good.

Chase didn't much care for Thomas. Rita suspected it was some kind of guy-testosterone thing because Thomas was so completely not her type but exuded a manly charisma that she nevertheless found sexy, and which probably set men like Chase on edge. Whatever. To Chase's credit, at least he hadn't interfered with the composition of Rita's team.

Spencer, on the other hand, liked Thomas. He always had.

Finney hadn't said a word since the locker room. That could be good or bad. Rita decided probably bad. She knew he was still there, could sense his presence. She wanted to ask him why he'd stopped talking, but the company of so many others precluded doing so.

And, at any rate, all that couldn't be helped, because she needed to operate on Mrs. Sanchez.

Her eyes swept the room, across the operating table and all of the equipment, verifying everything was in its place. OR 10 was enormous: three times the size of the other operating rooms and designed to accommodate large groups of observers for teaching. An outsize video screen, seven feet high by nine feet wide, dominated one wall, its purpose to project live images of the operation being performed. Sort of a Jumbotron for the OR.

She shifted her gaze from the screen to the door as two anesthesiologists, Dr. Henry Chow, the affable head of anesthesia, and a young assistant professor, Nikhil, wheeled Mrs. Sanchez to the operating table—

(*The same one I woke up on this morning but don't think about that now, can't think about that now.*)

—located near the room's center.

For a routine operation, Nikhil would be the senior anesthesiologist, and Dr. Chow would be off in administrative meetings, or maybe overseeing several different operating rooms at once. But this was no routine operation.

A young woman and man, their ID badges and timid postures identifying them as med students, followed a few respectful paces behind the gurney, as if trailing a hearse in a funeral. Rita sensed it was their first time in an OR: Their eyes were wide, and their movements as stiff and rigid as wooden puppets.

Rita had no med students with her today. Or residents. Chase had decreed that the auto-surgeon project was too important to allow for the presence of surgical trainees.

Nikhil and Dr. Chow took position at the anesthesia station located at the head of the table, amidst an array of video monitors, a wheeled cart containing a pharmacy's worth of drugs, a few IV poles, and several cylindrical steel tanks full of gas.

Rita thought Nikhil a good guy: young and inexperienced, in only his first year of practice, but smart. Confident, but not too confident. He knew when to ask for help and wasn't self-conscious about doing it. Better still: He spoke fluent Spanish, in which he was now talking to Mrs. Sanchez in reassuring tones. She nodded, and Nikhil, Thomas, and Lisa helped her scoot from the gurney over to the operating table—

(*The same table the EXACT same table I woke up on NAKED but don't think about that now because I need to operate on Mrs. Sanchez.*)

—and lie down on her back. Lisa drew warm blankets up over her as Thomas pushed the empty gurney out into the hallway.

Rita stepped up and took Mrs. Sanchez's hand. As always with surgery, Mrs. Sanchez was the only person in the room not wearing a surgical mask. She smiled bravely, but her jaw muscles looked tensed.

"Okay, Doctor?" she asked. "Okay?" She squeezed Rita's hand, and a few tears spilled from the corners of her eyes. Gravity tugged them down toward her ears, and they left silvery wakes over her crow's-feet before disappearing underneath the elastic rim of her scrub cap.

To hell with sterility.

Using her free hand, the one not locked in Mrs. Sanchez's grip, Rita pulled down her surgical mask and rallied a feeble smile. "Yes. Okay."

Oh, God, please let that be so.

"*Está bien,*" Mrs. Sanchez said. Nikhil placed a clear plastic mask over her nose and mouth.

"*Respire profundo por favor, señora.*"

Mrs. Sanchez inhaled and exhaled, in and out, deep and slow. Her chest rose and fell.

"*Muy bien,*" Nikhil said.

Mrs. Sanchez closed her eyes.

Please, God, don't let it be for the last time.

To distract herself from the churning in her stomach, Rita concentrated on what Nikhil was doing. She watched him depress the plunger of a syringe filled with milky white fluid, which sped through an IV line and into Mrs. Sanchez's arm. She groaned and jerked her arm.

"*Lo siento, señora,*" Nikhil murmured in her ear. He glanced at Rita, then at the students, observing with wide eyes a few feet away. "That's propofol. Related to barbiturates. We use it to induce amnesia. It burns sometimes, going into the vein."

The students nodded solemnly.

Mrs. Sanchez stilled, and her closed eyelids fluttered. Her hand went limp, and Rita laid it gently on the table at her side.

Nikhil chased the propofol with a syringe full of clear fluid.

"That's rocuronium," Nikhil explained to the students. "A neuromuscular blocking agent. Takes effect in about forty-five seconds. It will paralyze her muscles. All of them, including her diaphragm. Which means she won't be able to do what, Leah?" He pointed to the young woman.

"Um. Breathe?" Leah said.

"Yes. Excellent. Breathe. On her own, at least. We'll have to do the breathing for her, with this respirator." He pointed to a steel box the size of a small refrigerator, to which several gas cylinders marked O_2 FLAMMABLE were attached with hoses. "The paralysis will allow us to control her blood oxygen levels and keep her from moving. And this—"

He held up a drug vial containing a clear liquid. "This is sugammadex. It will reverse the paralysis, within about three minutes of injection, at the end when we want her to wake up."

Nikhil laid the sugammadex vial aside and hefted a metallic instrument composed of a handle attached to a long, curved hook with a tapered end.

"Nathaniel," he said. The other student snapped to attention. "What's this?" Nikhil wiggled the instrument back and forth.

"A . . . laryngoscope?"

"Correct. What's it for?"

"To help you, ah—put in the endotracheal tube. So she can breathe."

"Correct. Nice work. Both of you."

The students exchanged looks, and Rita didn't need

to peek underneath their masks to know they were grinning.

"Now watch, because eventually I'm going to expect you to be able to do this on your own." Leah and Nathaniel pressed in closer. Nikhil pried open Mrs. Sanchez's limp jaws with his left hand; with his right, he slipped the curved tip of the laryngoscope between her teeth, yanked the handle up toward the ceiling, then pointed into the inside of her mouth with his left. "See that? The circular opening with the white bands?" Leah and Nathaniel nodded. "That's her trachea. Goes straight to the lungs. That's where the endotracheal tube goes."

Dr. Chow, who'd been observing silently, stepped forward and pressed a plastic tube the length of a grade-school ruler into Nikhil's free hand. He slid the tube into Mrs. Sanchez's mouth and pulled the laryngoscope free.

Nikhil had wielded the laryngoscope with a deft touch, as fine as any of the anesthesiologists Rita had seen; but when he removed it, a thin coat of blood stained its silvery tip, where the metal had scuffed the soft skin lining the inside of Mrs. Sanchez's throat.

"Nicely done," Dr. Chow observed.

Rita agreed. She also wondered, not for the first time, whether patients would ever agree to surgery if they knew, really honest-to-God *understood*, the kinds of things doctors did to them in operating rooms.

Nikhil connected the endotracheal tube—a few inches of which stuck out of Mrs. Sanchez's mouth, as if she were sucking on a length of PVC pipe—to the respirator and glanced at his monitors. He placed a stethoscope on Mrs. Sanchez's chest and listened through it.

"Good to go?" Rita asked.

He flashed her a thumbs-up. "You're all set." Using a fabric harness, Nikhil fixed the endotracheal tube in place, so that it wouldn't pull out of her mouth, and taped her eyelids shut with strands of silk tape.

Lisa drew the operating-table restraining straps around Mrs. Sanchez—

(*The same straps the EXACT same straps that were around me this morning*)

—one across her upper thighs, another across her chest, and buckled them into place.

The straps. She couldn't take her eyes off them.

Lisa gave each of the straps a good firm tug—

(*Naked I was NAKED*)

—to make sure they were snug.

A wave of nausea accompanied a sour taste in her throat as she thought of herself stretched out on that table. God, what was she *doing* here?

I need to operate on Mrs. Sanchez.

Yes, but why? The urge was irresistible and incomprehensible. Her heart pounded in her ears; sweat broke out across her body. She was panicking, spiraling again toward madness.

Darcy. No matter what else happens, think about Darcy.

She had no choice. She had to keep going. Because of Darcy.

And because I need to operate on Mrs. Sanchez.

Nikhil was still lecturing the students. Rita took deep breaths and focused on what he was saying, trying to keep her mind occupied with something, *any-thing*, other than those damn table straps.

"This is isoflurane," he said, patting a large metal canister located next to the respirator that, like the oxygen tanks, was fastened to it with hoses. "Isoflurane, and gases like it, produce the profound unconsciousness—a kind of reversible coma—needed for surgery. Paralysis drugs, like rocuronium, don't induce unconsciousness. You need the gas to knock a patient out."

"Can isoflurane, or any of these other tanks of gas, explode?" Leah asked.

"No. Isoflurane is completely inert." He waved toward the oxygen cylinders. "But oxygen can burn."

He twisted a valve on the top of the isoflurane canister and chuckled. "I mean, surgery's weird, if you think about it. You know? For most of human history, you couldn't operate on a person without pretty much killing them. Then along come these inventions that change everything. Sterilization. Antibiotics. Anesthesia. These days, we take them for granted. Like it's no big deal. Especially anesthesia. Have you guys ever seen one of those old Western movies? Or *Gone with the Wind*, maybe? No? When a guy—a soldier, or cowboy—has his gangrenous leg cut off with only a hacksaw, a shot of whiskey, and piece of leather to bite down on? In the movie, it's dramatic, but, like, no big deal. Well . . . consider the fact that amputation means *sawing through bone*. The pain would be *inconceivable* if you were awake."

"I like him," Finney pronounced loudly in her ear. *Shit!*

She jumped so high she felt like she almost hit the ceiling, then looked around to see if anyone had noticed. Thomas and Lisa were preoccupied with sorting surgical instruments in the back of the room, and Dr. Chow and the students were absorbed with Nikhil's informal lecture.

"Your anesthesia colleague there," Finney added. "I like him quite a bit and what he has to say about things."

She wondered what it was about Nikhil—and what he had to *say about things*—that Finney found so appealing. She waited for Finney to elaborate. He didn't. As suddenly as he'd spoken, he fell back into silence. Which heightened her unease.

"Does anybody ever wake up accidentally? In the middle of surgery?" Nathaniel asked.

"Theoretically, yes. It's called intraoperative awareness." This was Dr. Chow. "Very rare. One in every twenty thousand surgeries performed, supposedly. But I've been doing this for over twenty-five years, and I've never seen it, or heard of it. Or run across another anesthesiologist who has."

Lisa tapped Rita on the shoulder and flashed her a meaningful look. Rita followed her to a far corner of the room. Lisa glanced at Thomas sitting in front of the computer, mumbling to himself as he scratched at a hairy forearm sporting more ink than bare skin; and then at Nikhil and Dr. Chow, who had launched into an animated discussion of drug dosages and blood oxygen levels with the students. Chase and the visitors hadn't arrived yet.

The quiet before the storm.

"You look . . . much better than you did earlier, Dr.

Wu," Lisa said in a low tone. A diplomatic observation. Lisa was nothing if not diplomatic.

"Thanks, Lisa. I'm okay." She leaned in. "Does anyone, uh, know? About . . . you know."

Lisa's sharp eyes swiveled to Thomas, the anesthesiologists, the students, then back to Rita. "Dr. Montgomery told me not to tell anyone. He was angry. Calm. But angry. He implied I might get in trouble if I talked to anyone."

She cocked a hip to one side and folded her arms. "Frankly," she said coldly, "I could have done without the lecture. He should know me better than that, after all the years I've worked here."

Rita nodded. Lisa was smart and tough. In the realm of life experience, a stern lecture from Chase wouldn't even be a blip on her radar. Or, probably, discovering a naked surgeon on an OR table at the start of an otherwise normal working day.

Lisa added in a whisper, "Wendy, well . . . you just can't tell about her. You know what I mean?"

"Yeah. I do. It's okay. I'll—deal with that later." Rita placed a hand on Lisa's arm. "Can you do me a favor, Lisa?"

"Of course."

"Can you . . . keep an eye on me, this morning? Just to make sure that I don't do anything . . . stupid?"

Lisa's eyes were somber above her mask. "Sure. I'll do that."

"I'll have my eye on you as well, Dr. Wu," Finney said.

The sound of his voice was as abrupt as a slap to her face.

"Dr. Wu?" Lisa said, studying her expression. "Are you okay?"

"Yeah. I'm okay, Lisa."

Lisa's eyes oozed skepticism.

(*She doesn't understand. That I need to operate on Mrs. Sanchez. How can I make her understand?*)

"I'm okay," Rita repeated, as if saying the words out loud would make it so. She took a deep breath and nodded toward Mrs. Sanchez, lying on the operating table. "Let's do it."

Thomas joined them at the operating table, and the three of them set to work preparing Mrs. Sanchez, and the auto-surgeon, for what was to come.

SEBASTIAN

"But there are other robotic surgery systems already on the market," Grant, the *Wall Street Journal* reporter, said. "How is yours different?"

"Those FDA-approved robots are terrific," Montgomery replied. "We use one of them here at Turner. But they depend on the surgeon, who performs the operation by directing the robotic arms with joysticks from a control station. Our robot is unique *because it doesn't depend on the surgeon*. Think of robots on car assembly lines, performing intricate series of preprogrammed movements. Instead of building cars, our robot performs surgeries."

The crowd tittered as Dr. Linton stormed noisily from the amphitheater. He loped down the center aisle from the front row, arms swinging in wide arcs, muttering. Sebastian caught the words *insanity* and *crimes against humanity* as Linton passed him.

Montgomery squinted and smiled at the audience, his hands clasped in respectful repose until Linton had completed his exit, and the sniggers had ceased. He said, "Change is hard. Innovation is scary. BUT . . ."

He gestured grandly toward the device on the screen. "Robotics offers us the way forward. To make surgery *safer.*"

He pivoted and strode to center stage. "Consider: Unlike human surgeons, robots will never get tired. Their attention for every fine detail of every operation will never waver. Their hands will never shake from too many cups of coffee, or from even, God forbid, the ravages of old age!" He thrust out his right hand—its back wrinkled as crepe paper and dotted with the brown-spotted calling cards of excessive ultraviolet exposure—and made exaggerated quivering gestures.

Slick bastard.

Once the good-natured chuckles had died down, Montgomery said, "I'd now like to introduce you to Delores."

The video screen image stopped rotating. Montgomery stepped to one side to afford the audience an unobstructed view.

"Ladies and gentlemen, meet Delores. Delores, say hello, please."

"Good morning, Dr. Montgomery," the 3-D image replied. The audience stirred. The feminine voice was pleasant and conversational.

"I'd like to tell you that her name is a witty acronym," Montgomery said. "Like, *Dynamic Elegant*

Original Robotically Engineered Surgeon. But we're not *quite* that poetic. Delores is named after the great aunt of a senior engineer on the project, with whom she bears an unfortunate resemblance."

There were a few guffaws. Montgomery smiled. "Delores processes the software code that we input into her system—the surgical plan—and then translates that code into a series of coordinated robotic movements. Delores, tell the audience about yourself."

"Of course, Dr. Montgomery. I am an automated robotic surgical system, capable of performing surgery based on programmed sets of instructions."

On the screen, the perspective zoomed in on the central cylinder.

"My central core houses a sophisticated onboard computer and guidance system that connects wirelessly to a secure server. My onboard system downloads the appropriate software for performing the operation. However, I am also capable of interpreting real-time input and adjusting my actions accordingly."

"In other words," Montgomery interjected, "Delores can automatically react to unexpected things that might happen during an operation."

"Can the system be hacked?" Grant asked with half-hooded eyes. "Could somebody reprogram it? Make it perform a different kind of operation?" A sly grin. "Or worse?" Sebastian admired the back of her neck, which was very smooth.

Montgomery's smile was indulgent. Sebastian wondered if Montgomery was getting tired of smiling. Shit, Sebastian's cheeks were starting to ache just from watching the guy.

"In theory, Ms. Grant," Montgomery said. "Yes. But our encryption algorithms were designed by an acclaimed University of California computer-science professor. A smart, persistent hacker *might* gain unauthorized access to Delores's system within, oh, one or two *hundred* years." He winked.

Bullshit. No system was hack-proof. Something Sebastian knew for a fact about Delores.

Because he and Finney had hacked it.

"Now," Montgomery said. "Delores, please show us your feet."

"Of course."

The image rotated, its focus shifting to two of the smaller silver cylinders that budded from Delores's cylindrical core, one on the left and one on the right. Smaller objects, shaped like small vises, sprouted from their ends.

"A *wonderful* presentation, to be sure, Chase, of a truly *impressive* device," the Turner CEO said. "Does the *real* Delores respond to voice commands?"

"Oh, yes. The speech recognition is state-of-the-art. Don't be fooled, though, by her friendly persona. Delores can't think. She's simply been programmed to respond within a range of straightforward questions and commands. Delores, is it correct that you can't think on your own?"

"I think that's subject to opinion, Dr. Montgomery."

"These two mechanisms," Montgomery said over the resulting laughter, "a right one and a left one, secure Dolores to the operating table. We affectionately call them the feet—the left foot goes on the patient's left side, right foot on the right. Small, magnetized clamps at the bottom of the feet attach Delores to the operating table. Gyroscopic stabilizers keep everything completely steady. We estimate that the stabilizers can handle up to a magnitude 7.0 earthquake without Delores's moving so much as a millimeter. A convenient safety feature here in Southern California."

There were a few approving chuckles. Montgomery said, "In addition, Delores's feet can adapt themselves for use on any type of surface. Even on rough ground."

"Why incorporate that kind of feature into its design?"

"Because, Ms. Grant, we envision a day when Delores will be used routinely outside of the operating room. The world's first fully mobile surgical robot."

"Seems awfully complicated to cart around."

"On the contrary. Delores is small, light, and portable. Easily assembled by a single person. And battery-powered for up to eight hours of use."

"I understand you've received funding from the Department of Defense," Grant pressed.

"Yes. We're proud of that. Think how many of our brave young men and women in uniform we could eventually save with Delores deployed on the front lines. But that's only a fraction of Delores's potential. Humanitarian medical missions. Routine care for remote communities or ships at sea. The possibilities are limitless."

Damn, but the man can really shovel it.

Sebastian glanced at his watch and sucked his teeth. By now it was clear that nothing else in this morning's schedule was going to change, and Montgomery's spiel was wearing thin. Sebastian knew all about the goddamn robot. Delores was key to the job at hand. Finney had provided him with detailed schematics, and a working model, and he'd studied them inside and out. Hell, he could have delivered the presentation better than Montgomery. But if he left now, he'd attract unwanted attention.

He shifted in his seat and wondered what was going on with Wu.

Montgomery stretched his smile wider, and said, "Now. Delores, tell us about your camera."

"Of course."

The image zoomed in on a single cylinder.

Delores said, "My camera combines high-definition digital video with state-of-the-art ultrasound technology. The images are beamed to video monitors so that operating personnel may observe and supervise my movements. My onboard computer creates a real-time, three-dimensional map so that I may adjust my movements in accordance with variations in anatomy and blood flow."

"Delores analyzes the patient's individual anatomy more accurately than any human surgeon," Montgomery said. "Delores can detect structures, like blood vessels, that can't be seen by the human eye, which enhances precision and safety."

Montgomery's eyes darted to the side. The PR man and woman materialized from the shadows at the front of the amphitheater. Each held a silver cylinder the length of a baseball bat with circumferential joints spaced along their entire length at two-inch intervals. The man went to the back row of the room; the woman remained in the front.

"Now. This part I'm *really* excited about. Delores, tell us about your arms."

"Of course." The image zoomed in on the three last cylinders, which projected from the central body in parallel. Several small objects—including a small pair of scissors, and a scalpel—protruded from their tips.

"My arms are flexible, precision surgical platforms, each of which contains all of the basic instruments necessary for the performance of any operation: scalpel, electrocautery scissors, needle driver, retractor, suction, irrigation. The microservers in my arms allow me to instantaneously switch from one instrument to another."

"We call them Swiss Armies," Montgomery said. The man sitting next to Sebastian chuckled and bobbed his head in understanding. "We're quite proud of them. There's nothing else like them in the world. The circular joints allow the arms to bend in *any* direction. They can work around *corners*. And, for the first time, *ever*, every surgical instrument combined into a single tool. Amber and Paul are handing some examples out. Feel free to have a look, then pass it along to your neighbor."

Amber distributed a few Swiss Armies to the front row, Paul some to the back.

"Based on the software, Delores selects the specific instrument needed and deploys that instrument from the arm—similar to choosing an individual tool from the handle of a Swiss Army knife."

"I had a Swiss Army knife when I was a girl," the university chancellor, a former engineering professor, cracked. "There's not a corkscrew on one of those things, is there, Chase? Or a toothpick?"

"No, ma'am," Montgomery said through his grin. "No corkscrew or toothpick. But everything a typical surgeon needs. Medical-grade scalpel. Scissors, with built-in electrocautery, to stop bleeding. Needle drivers, for sewing tissue together. The suture—the thread for sewing—automatically feeds into the needle driver, another unique innovation.

"Having all of these different instruments combined together into a single package increases efficiency. Each instrument is instantly available whenever needed. It takes only a few seconds to flip from one to another—much faster than deploying one manually. In some cases, it could mean the difference between life and death."

"Chase, what's this for?" the CEO asked. He was holding one of the Swiss Armies, which had been rigged to display several of its surgical instruments at once. He pointed to one of them: a turquoise, flyswatter-shaped object, composed of soft, interlacing meshed fibers.

Montgomery smiled. "That's an extendable retractor, for holding organs and tissues out of the way during surgery. We call it a fan because it resembles a hand fan."

The thin, bespectacled man next to Sebastian handed him one of the Swiss Armies. This one displayed a scalpel, its surface dulled to prevent injury. The Swiss Army was light. Sebastian knew that the composition of its ceramic alloy was similar to that of advanced body armor.

Sebastian touched the tip of the dulled scalpel.

He thought about what would soon transpire and felt sorry for Wu.

Not to mention, a guilty corner of his conscience confessed, her patient.

Paul the PR man's cell phone chirped an electronic variation of "Ode to Joy." He signaled Montgomery.

"Okay," Montgomery said. "They're ready for us over in the OR. Any more questions?"

There were none.

Montgomery clapped his hands once and smiled a shark's grin. He looked hungry. "Okay, then! Let's head over to the OR and the future of surgery!"

The audience rose as one and shuffled toward the exits.

RITA

Rita heard them before she saw them: the murmur of many voices, Chase's radio-deejay rumble rising above the rest.

With the help of Thomas and Lisa, she'd already prepared everything for the big show: had slid Mrs. Sanchez into proper position on the table and inflated her abdomen with carbon dioxide, pumped through a hollow needle stuck in the skin, until she'd resembled a fat Buddha, the normal contours of her body flattened into soft, convex curves.

She'd made four incisions across her shaved, sterilized abdomen, and sunk through each incision an object shaped like a large screw, with a flat circular head on one side and sharp-tipped cone on the other. Finally, through one of the screws (or *ports*), she'd inserted Delores's camera, which was beaming a live image of Mrs. Sanchez's internal organs to the operating-room Jumbotron.

Rita was now sitting next to Mrs. Sanchez, in sterile gown and gloves, her hands resting lightly on a table covered with sterile instruments, Lisa sitting next to her. Thomas, who wasn't scrubbed, hovered in the back of the room, ready to help on a moment's notice. Nikhil and Dr. Chow were in position at the anesthesia station. The med students had been dispatched to other operating rooms.

Finney had again lapsed into silence.

Rita gazed up at Delores. The young project engineers who had helped design Delores used words like *cool* and *retro* to describe the metallic curves and jointed arms. But to Rita, Delores was . . . *unnerving.* Even a little sinister. A gigantic metallic insect, straddling Mrs. Sanchez, a leg secured to each side of the table, with the camera and three-jointed arms pointed at her abdomen like four enormous stingers.

The protuberance from the central cylinder looked like a misshapen head, complete with colored dials for beady eyes, and a panel that could pass for an ogling mouth. She hoped the next version, Delores 2.0, would be less intimidating. Because if she was a patient and caught a glimpse of this damn thing perched over her, she thought she'd never set foot in a hospital again.

No turning back now, lovely Rita.

She drew a deep breath.

Please, God.

She stood up as Chase led the visitors into the room. *Please. Let everything turn out okay.*

She counted about twenty of them, more than Chase had been expecting, and they fanned out in a rough semicircle facing the operating table.

"Well, here we are, ladies and gentlemen. Step right in, there's room for everyone. This is our biggest operating room, designed to comfortably accommodate up to thirty visitors. Can you hear me in the back? Sir? Wave your hand if you can hear me. Good. Can you see me? Good. Now. I'd like to introduce you to one of our star faculty members and our auto-surgeon team leader, Dr. Rita Wu."

As part of the prearranged routine she and Chase (well, Chase, mostly) had worked out, Rita waved to the group. She was grateful for her mask, which covered her mouth, so she didn't have to muster a fake smile.

"Good morning!" she called out with an enthusiasm she was not experiencing. She felt like a tour guide addressing a high-school field trip. "Thank you all for being here today. Delores and I are excited to demonstrate the world's first fully automated surgery." She laid her hand on Delores's cylindrical core, which was covered by a transparent, disposable sterile cover. "This is Delores. Delores, say hello."

"Hello, Dr. Wu." Delores's stereophonic speakers were located on the central core, close to the panel that looked like a mouth.

"Delores, how are you feeling today?"

"I feel like a million dollars, thank you, Dr. Wu."

"Which is almost how much she costs!" Montgomery added (right on cue), to much laughter.

God, Chase has them eating out of the palm of his hand.

"Delores, what kind of surgery will you be performing today?" Rita asked, staying on script.

"I will be performing a laparoscopic cholecystectomy, an operation in which the gallbladder is removed through small incisions in the abdomen."

"Gallbladder removal is a very straightforward operation," Chase said. "One of the first our surgical trainees are able to perform on their own."

"What does the gallbladder do?" someone asked.

"It stores a digestive enzyme called bile. Bile is made in the liver and helps absorb fat. The gallbladder can be removed without any long-term consequences."

"Are there any other operations you've been developing for the robot?" the hospital CEO asked.

"Yes, as a matter of fact: a laparoscopic appendix removal. We've already written the software for it, and we're currently searching for a suitable patient. Now. I'd next like to introduce you to Dr. Chow, our chief of anesthesiology, who will discuss a second system we're testing today: a machine that automatically delivers anesthesia."

Dr. Chow took a step forward, his hands clasped primly behind his back. "Thank you, Chase. In concert with our surgical colleagues, we've developed a robot for administering anesthesia medications. We've nicknamed it Morpheus, after the Greek god of dreams." He placed his hand on a nondescript black-and-silver box the size and shape of a laser printer, sitting on a metal table a short distance from Mrs. Sanchez's head. "This is Morpheus. I'm sorry to say Morpheus doesn't talk! But Morpheus has an important job: to automate the job of the anesthesiologist."

"In a way, replacing the anesthesiologist is even more straightforward than replacing the surgeon," Chase said. "Anesthesiologists usually don't have as much to do during operations as surgeons."

"Hey!" Dr. Chow hammed it up by placing his hands on his hips. Also prearranged. By Chase, naturally.

"Don't worry, Hank, you guys won't be out of a job anytime soon!"

"That's because we're the ones who actually keep patients alive while my surgical colleagues here rearrange their insides! Seriously. Much of what we do as anesthesiologists depends on gathering information about the patient—temperature, pulse, blood pressure, oxygen levels—and acting on it appropriately to ensure the patient remains comfortable, asleep, and safe throughout the surgery."

Chow didn't possess Chase's easy command of an audience. But he'd always been a good lecturer: clear and articulate, capable of delivering complicated information.

Chow said, "Morpheus collects this information, interprets it, and automatically fine-tunes the levels of anesthesia medications the patient receives. We humans keep control over everything else, including putting the patient to sleep before the surgery."

Chase nodded. "The concept behind Morpheus is the same as behind Delores: to automate routine portions of the operation."

"Could these robots, working together, perform an

operation entirely without people?" someone from the back asked. "Without any doctors?"

"In theory, yes," Chase said. "All of the components are there. We just haven't tested them together yet."

"Autopilots on planes can automatically make corrections to prevent disasters," a black woman standing in front said. "Are there safety features like that on your robots?"

"Yes, Ms. Grant," Chase said. "Delores is programmed to recognize problems and take immediate and appropriate action without the need for direct human intervention."

"What kinds of problems?"

"Bleeding. Delores is programmed to stop bleeding." Nobody could see it because of his mask, but Rita was certain that Chase's smile would have dazzled and reassured. "But we're not going to worry about any bleeding here today."

SEBASTIAN

"Sebastian? Can you hear me?"

"Yeah, boss," Sebastian murmured. Finney had switched his signal back on.

"No problems, I assume?"

"No. None." Standing with the observers, Sebastian shifted his weight and touched Alfonso's dog tag through his scrub shirt as Montgomery walked up to the large video screen, placing himself to one side so that he could simultaneously face both it and the assembled group.

The boredom Sebastian had felt earlier in the auditorium was gone. Everything over the past year had been leading up to this. He felt tense but calm: supremely focused, adrenaline surging through every part of him, like it used to right before a combat mission. He scanned the room, taking it all in, searching for anything that might interfere with what was about to happen. Observers. Anesthesiologists. Wu and her assistants. Robot. Everything in its place.

His eyes lit briefly on the patient: a vague lump hidden beneath sterile blue sheets, the robot's arms pointed at its center.

He forced himself to look away.

He wouldn't think about what came next.

Alfonso, he knew, would not have approved.

"Gorgeous picture," Montgomery said. A red dot, projected from a laser pointer Montgomery held in his hand, danced across the large video screen on the wall. "Thanks, Rita. Okay, folks. This is the live picture from Delores's camera. You are now seeing exactly what Delores is seeing. For you nonsurgeons, carbon dioxide is currently flowing under pressure into the patient's abdomen, pushing everything out of the way. That's why we see her organs so clearly."

"Would the carbon dioxide hurt? If you were awake?" Grant asked.

"Most definitely! The pain would be excruciating. Good thing the patient's asleep! Now. Here's the liver."

The red dot moved over a glistening, brown, wedge-shaped object that took up three-quarters of the screen. "You can appreciate how big it is, relative to everything else. Very healthy-looking in this patient, I might add. A remarkable organ, the liver. It has many crucial functions, mostly involved with digestion and detoxification."

"Can you live without it? Like the gallbladder?" It was the same guy who'd asked about the gallbladder earlier.

Idiot. What kind of an asshole would ask a dumb-ass question like that?

"Oh, no. Without your liver, you'd die. Quickly." The laser pointer circled a small swathe of green just visible underneath the brown edge of the liver, like a Manzanilla olive lying in dirt. "See that little hint of green there, toward the right? That's the gallbladder, tucked underneath the liver. The gallbladder is tethered in place by its blood supply and by a hollow tube called the bile duct, both of which need to be safely cut. We'll see more of them soon."

The laser pointer slid over the remainder of the screen as Montgomery pointed out more anatomy. Falciform ligament. Omentum. Small bowel. Large bowel. Diaphragm. "Oh, and if any of the nondoctors feel the need to sit down, or step out, we've provided plenty of chairs for everyone."

No one moved.

"No? Terrific. Strong stomachs all around. Now, you can see that Dr. Wu completed the first part of the operation this morning, before we arrived. However, Delores is fully capable of performing the same tasks. Delores can even use a scalpel to make an incision in the skin, just like a human surgeon."

"So why didn't it do that today?" Grant asked.

"We want to gradually test Dolores's capabilities under real-world conditions."

Montgomery looked at Wu and nodded. She nodded back.

"Are we ready, Dr. Chow?" Wu asked.

"You are good to go, Rita. Everything looks perfect up here." He turned and gave a thumbs-up to the group. "Morpheus is working beautifully. Just as expected."

"Wonderful," Montgomery crowed. "Dr. Wu, please commence."

Sebastian thought himself a hard man. A professional. He'd seen and done some . . . *distasteful* . . . things over the years. But he'd owned up to what he'd done and didn't apologize for it. Any of it. He'd done what he'd done to survive. The world was shit, and he'd made of it what he could.

Still . . . what he knew was coming made his insides squirm. Was it with guilt? But guilt was unprofessional. So why was he feeling this way?

Because Alfonso wouldn't have been down with this shit.

He shifted his weight and pushed the thought from his mind.

Wu pushed a button on the robot's central body. The three arms entered into a coordinated sequence of movements, buzzing and humming and spinning, flexing their joints like octopus tentacles.

They reminded Sebastian of a Spider-Man movie. He'd seen it with Sammy, and it had been pretty good, with this villain with big metallic tentacles fused to his body, which he moved around like extra arms and used as weapons. That's what these things looked liked: metallic tentacles.

Montgomery explained: "Dolores's arms are now orienting themselves. Recall that each of those arms has a Swiss Army at its tip: the instrument with the multiple tools that we demonstrated for you earlier."

The arms moved themselves into position over the remaining three ports, one arm per port. They halted above them, hovering centimeters away, as if waiting for something.

"Delores, initiate manual-positioning protocol for Swiss Army numbers one, two, and three," Wu said.

"Of course," Delores responded. "Initiating manual-positioning protocol for Swiss Army numbers one, two, and three."

He heard a click, followed by the tinny droning of multiple gears in all three of the arms. A pause, then each slid smoothly forward, seeking its corresponding port.

Now Sebastian thought the arms looked like silver snakes, slithering toward the patient; all they lacked were hissing, metallic tongues. The tips of each of the Swiss Armies extended through a circular opening in the top of its port and disappeared into the patient. The spinning stopped, and all three instruments paused, again, with their tips in the ports.

Montgomery said, "Dr. Wu will now move each of the Swiss Army instruments into its final position manually."

"Why?" Grant asked. "Why not have the robot do it?"

"Again, out of caution, Ms. Grant. It's the first time we've done this with a patient, and we decided it was the absolute safest way to proceed. Once Dr. Wu has personally positioned each of the instruments, Delores will assume control."

RITA

Rita grasped the first Swiss Army.

"I think it's fair to tell you, Dr. Wu," Finney said. "I'm quite familiar with Delores, and the auto-surgeon program. I have been for some time."

Rita jerked her hand away from the Swiss Army and suppressed a yelp.

"Dr. Wu," Lisa whispered. "Is everything okay?"

"Yes," Rita whispered back.

"My apologies. I didn't mean to startle you in front of all of these people," Finney said.

Rita reached a tentative hand back toward the first Swiss Army as Finney said, "I'm the majority investor—the owner, for all intents and purposes—of the privately held company that designs and manufactures Delores. Were you aware of that, Dr. Wu?"

Oh, shit.

What's he talking about?

"But of course you wouldn't know that," Finney said. "It's not a matter of public record."

Rita's surgical gown suddenly seemed too hot. Sweat gathered in her armpits and trickled down her sides.

I need to operate on Mrs. Sanchez.

She gripped the Swiss Army and gently pushed it farther into Mrs. Sanchez, as she'd done hundreds of times in the simulations, sliding it through the port and into Mrs. Sanchez's abdominal cavity.

The pointed tip emerged on the screen of the Jumbotron, magnified to the size of a lamppost.

"And there's the first Swiss Army, inside the patient's body," Chase said. "Now coming into our camera's field of vision."

Rita took care to not push it too far, too quickly— to keep its tip a safe distance from the liver. Even without its scalpel deployed, the Swiss Army was a potential deadly weapon: a spear that could impale Mrs. Sanchez's liver, or other organs, if Rita extended it a few centimeters too far.

Rita stopped advancing the tip, and said, haltingly, "Delores, initiate laparoscopic cholecystectomy protocol for Swiss Army number one."

"Initiating laparoscopic cholecystectomy protocol for Swiss Army number one." An affable gyration of gears.

"Hear that spinning sound?" Montgomery said. "That means Delores has activated the first Swiss Army and is ready to use it."

"For almost a year now, I've monitored your progress keenly," Finney said.

Oh, God.

"You could say I've been a silent partner of yours. I'm most interested to see how things turn out with Delores this morning."

"Oh, God," Rita breathed.

"Did you say something, Dr. Wu?" Lisa whispered.

"No, nothing, Lisa," Rita whispered back.

She reached out and grasped Swiss Army number two.

SPENCER

His operation over, and his insides knotted with worry over Rita, Spencer slipped a mask over his face and padded into OR 10, right behind one of the cardiac-surgery guys, who held the door ajar for him. It seemed that he and the cardiac guy weren't the only ones interested: The room was packed, almost to the door. Spencer had been in OR 10 many times, but had never seen it this crowded.

He saw Montgomery holding court next to the main video screen. Rita was scrubbed—

(*Damn but it was good to see her, if only from a distance*)

—and appeared to be making adjustments to the auto-surgeon. He knew it was the auto-surgeon because he'd seen pictures of it: practically everyone in the damn hospital had, what with all the publicity.

"Dr. Montgomery, do you think it's really safe? Entrusting people's operations to machines?" he heard a woman ask as he inched around the back of the group, hunting for a gap so he could see the video screen. Mindful of his size, he didn't want to block other people's views. He settled on a reasonably good position behind everyone else, where his height afforded him a decent angle. But he couldn't see Rita from here. He wanted to see Rita.

"Absolutely, Ms. Grant," Montgomery replied. "And I'd like to make one thing absolutely, crystal clear here: the surgeon—the *human* surgeon—is always in charge. *Always.* We've even designed a fail-safe mechanism to ensure that."

Montgomery used a laser pointer to draw attention to a large red button mounted prominently on the side of a silver cylinder Spencer recognized as the main component of the robot. It looked like a fire-alarm knob mounted on a wall, the kind you needed to break glass to access, and about the same size.

"That's Delores's emergency stop button," Montgomery said. "The fail-safe. Pushing it immediately shuts Delores down, allowing the human team to take over. I'd call it the *kill switch*, but we don't like words like *kill* in the operating room."

Montgomery paused so as not to step on his own punch line. There were a few polite chuckles. Otherwise, stone-cold silence.

Montgomery cleared his throat.

"So. The fail-safe instantaneously shuts Delores down."

With the laser pointer, Montgomery indicated another red button—much like the one on the robot—mounted on the side of a printer-sized object sitting on a table near the patient's head. Spencer saw Hank Chow and a younger anesthesiologist he didn't know standing next to it.

"We've also incorporated a fail-safe into Morpheus," Montgomery said. "It shuts off the infusion of anesthetic gases and injects paralytic-reversal drugs to wake the patient up."

Right, Spencer thought. *Morpheus. The automated anesthesia machine.* Hank had been bragging about it in the OR break room the other day. A lot of the other anesthesiologists, Spencer knew, thought it was total bullshit.

He pursed his lips and frowned, uneasy, taking it all in, trying to process the calmness of the scene with his unnerving conversation with Wendy.

Everything seems *okay . . .*

He wanted a closer look at the robots, and at Rita. He spotted another location nearer Rita, from which he judged he would have a better view without disturbing anyone else. He slipped to one side of the audience and took up a position there, much closer to the operating table.

Better.

Rita's hands were wrapped around a slender, silver cylinder about the length of a seven iron. She was slowly pushing it forward through one of the laparoscopic ports.

Probably one of the robot's operating arms. From where he was standing, everything seemed to be going fine.

Maybe Wendy had gotten her story wrong. Maybe the naked surgeon hadn't been Rita.

He inched a little closer.

RITA

"Yes," Finney said to her. "I'm *very* interested to see how Delores performs. I think—"

Rita winced as a high-pitched whistle sounded in her ear, replacing Finney's voice. It lasted for a few seconds.

And then silence.

Rita froze. She shook her head and listened for him. Nothing.

She waited for Finney to finish whatever it was he'd been telling her.

He didn't.

Which was . . . weird.

As was the silence inside her head.

FINNEY

Finney frowned and tapped the side of his tablet with a single slender finger.

That's odd.

The precise, elliptical patterns that had been dancing across his screen a moment earlier, the ones that had indicated a strong connection between his control tablet and Dr. Wu's implant, were gone, replaced by a fitful series of jagged peaks and valleys.

"What was that?" he said aloud.

He tapped the side of the tablet again.

"Boss," Sebastian whispered over their link, "I think we have a problem."

"Well that's—huh. Strange. Strange. Um. I believe I just lost contact with Dr. Wu."

"Interference. Something's blocking your transmission, boss. We've seen this before. During the tests."

"Yes," Finney said, drumming the fingers of his right hand on the desk, a cheap, lightweight type found in office cubicles. The man had an infuriating talent for stating the obvious. The pertinent issue was: What was causing the interference? And the runner-up: How do we fix it?

Finney placed his hands on the desk, interlaced his fingers, and stared at the *ugly* interference patterns, squeezing. His knuckles turned red. Then white. His hands shook. They knocked loudly on the desktop.

No.

"I don't think I need to emphasize that this is a *very* inopportune moment for this to happen, Sebastian."

The knocking of his hands escalated into a violent rattle.

Not now.

"Right. I'll try to figure it out from my end, boss," Sebastian said.

I've waited too long for this.

"Please, Sebastian."

NOT . . .

. . . NOW.

RITA

She stood there, still as a statue, listening to the silence.

It was a silence different from the one she'd experienced while taking a shower, when Finney hadn't been talking to her. It seemed to her a *quieter* kind of silence. Was it her imagination? She also found it strange that he'd cut off midsentence, as if in the middle of a phone conversation, and the call had dropped.

For the first time since he'd so disturbingly reentered her life in the locker room, she sensed his *absence*.

She cocked her head to one side. *Yes.* She was growing more certain of it. Like being on an airplane, growing numb to the steady *thrum* of the engines as you drank your Diet Coke at thirty-five thousand feet, then arriving at your destination and realizing later, on the car ride home, that the *thrum* was gone.

Her heart hammered against the back of her sternum and ribs.

Could he really be gone?

And to where? And why? Was this thing in her head no longer working? And if not, how about the one inside Darcy?

"Dr. Wu?" Lisa whispered. "Why are you stopping?"

Chase had also noticed the pause. "Rita?" he asked. "How are things going over there?"

"Everything's perfect!" she sang back.

And, for the moment, it almost felt like it was.

Because he's gone.

She pushed the second Swiss Army a little farther into Mrs. Sanchez's abdomen. On the video screen, its tip appeared next to the tip of the first one.

He's gone! She wanted to shout it.

Feeling almost euphoric, Rita took her hands off of the Swiss Army, and said, "Delores, initiate laparoscopic cholecystectomy protocol for Swiss Army number two."

She waited for Delores to respond.

Nothing happened.

SEBASTIAN

Sebastian's eyes searched the room, trying to iden-
tify a source of the interference.

What the hell was going on?

"Delores, initiate laparoscopic cholecystectomy
protocol for Swiss Army number two," Wu repeated.

A flashing red light on the side of the robot's central cylinder appeared.

"System error," Delores said. "Wireless connection
broken."

Interesting. Whatever was screwing up Finney's signal also had to be messing up the robot. *Good.* It gave
him time to size up the situation.

Which would not be easy. *This goddamn crowd.* It
had swelled a lot, with curious hospital employees trickling in to watch. Had to be upwards of thirty people
here now, all angling for a glimpse of the action. *Like
the mosh pit of a goddamn rock concert.* Locating
the source of the interference would be a bitch, if not
damn near impossible.

"Sebastian?"

"Working on it, boss," he said quietly, swiveling his
head this way and that.

Where's that goddamn interference coming from?

SPENCER

"System error," the robot said again. "Wireless connection broken."

Shifting of feet. Murmurs. Someone coughed.

Spencer caught Rita and Montgomery sharing a look.

Montgomery said, "Ah. Is anyone, perhaps, carrying some kind of electronic device with them? Certain kinds of energy waves can interfere with Delores's wireless signals. Microwaves, for example. Anyone have a microwave oven on them?"

Chuckles.

"Are cell phones okay?" someone asked.

"Normally, yes. But perhaps for today, if everyone could just please turn theirs off . . ."

More murmurs. Hands patting pockets and digging into them; phones powering down with electronic chirps and musical cues. Spencer dutifully shut his off.

The red light on the robot continued to flash.

"System error. Wireless connection broken."

Montgomery said, "Yes. Well. Anything else? Is everyone sure they've turned off everything?"

People looked around at each other, shook their heads, shrugged.

"Does anyone have any medical implants, perhaps?" Montgomery asked.

Murmurs, shaking heads, and more shrugs.

Implants. Spencer's right hand stole to his right ear. The portable EEG lead was still measuring his brain waves and beaming an electromagnetic signal back to the server in Raj's lab. Its signal had been powerful enough to screw up his satellite car radio. Could that be it?

Spencer reached up underneath his scrub cap and behind his ear, as if scratching it. Probing with his fingers, he located the electrode, and ran his finger along its flat, smooth surface until he located the small knob on its border. Using his fingernail, he slid the knob from one side to the other, shutting off its transmitter.

The red light on the robot stopped blinking.

"Wireless connection reestablished," Delores intoned. "Operative systems online."

Well, what do you know? He'd have to tell Raj about that. More bugs to fix.

Montgomery rubbed his hands together with relish. "All right, then! Thank you, everyone, for your cooperation. Please continue, Dr. Wu."

"Delores, initiate laparoscopic cholecystectomy protocol for Swiss Army number two," Rita said.

"Of course," Delores said. "Initiating laparoscopic cholecystectomy protocol for Swiss Army number two." The gears of number two signaled their approval.

SEBASTIAN

Like a radar dish searching for a target, Sebastian shifted his gaze from one end of the crowd to the other, hunting for anything, any*one*, looking suspicious.

Proximity. Whatever it was, it must be near both Wu *and* the robot: That's why it was interfering with the robot, and their connection with Wu, but not their connection with each other.

There was this one guy.

Standing near the robot. Sebastian's eyes couldn't help but be drawn to him because he towered over everyone else. A *big* motherfucker who had been scratching behind his right ear. Flirting with middle age, maybe a shade shy of forty but in good shape. The guy folded his arms, and his biceps looked as if about to rip right through the short sleeves of his XXL scrubs. Something about him made Sebastian twitchy.

He started to inch toward him.

But then a man standing next to the big guy pulled out his phone, which was supposed to be turned off, and furtively snapped a picture of the robot, which they'd been instructed repeatedly not to do.

Then he saw *another* dude, also near the robot, texting on *his* phone. Jesus, couldn't people pull their heads out of their electronic asses for just one second?

Goddamn hopeless.

No way to tell for certain where that interference had come from, or whether it might come back: too many people, too many possibilities.

He was turning his attention back to the screen on the wall when Finney spoke up.

FINNEY

Ah. There we go. Much better.

The signal on his tablet had returned to its proper pattern. The implant was working again.

Finney unclenched his hands.

"Sebastian. I'm back online. What did you do?"

"Nothing, boss," Sebastian whispered. "Must have been interference from an electronic device in the room. The signal returned as soon as Montgomery had everyone power their devices down."

"Intentional?"

A pause. "No. I don't think so."

"Good. Let's continue then."

Finney reopened his audio to Dr. Wu.

RITA

She knew, even before he'd said a single word.

He was back.

She could sense it.

Her heart sank.

"So. Dr. Wu. I'm very interested to see how Delores performs. " Finney was picking up where he'd left off, acting as if nothing had happened. But she was sure, *absolutely certain*, that he'd been gone, if only temporarily.

She bit at her lower lip. Was he unaware of what had happened? Or covering up a mistake? She suspected the latter and was struck by the realization that his absence had coincided with Delores's shutdown.

Coincidence?

She didn't think so. She had no idea what it meant but made a mental note of it anyway.

Situational awareness.

"Having some expertise in this particular field, I've availed myself of the opportunity to add some of my own ideas to Delores's design and development," Finney said.

His own ideas?

"Rita?" Chase said. "You may continue."

"Yes. Of course." Rita wrapped her trembling hands around the third Swiss Army.

"Surprised to hear we've been working as a team, you and I?" Finney said. "Don't be. You and I have much the same goals. You can't imagine my delight upon discovering you were working with the company manufacturing Delores's prototype. And how fortuitous for me that, at the time, its founders needed a major cash infusion."

She didn't like the way this was headed.

But I need to operate on Mrs. Sanchez.

"The idea of replacing flawed human surgeons with exacting machines is admirable. Your views align with my own on this. In fact, my opinion is that machines would make far better—and safer—surgeons than humans. Wouldn't you agree?"

What does he mean?

Rita froze.

"Dr. Wu," Lisa whispered.

"How well do you think a machine like Delores would have done with my wife's surgery?" An agonizing pause. "Better than you?"

Oh God, oh God, oh God . . .

"Dr. Wu," Lisa whispered fiercely. "They're all waiting."

"Rita?" Montgomery asked. "Is everything okay?"

She glanced up. Chase was staring at her.

So was everyone else.

So many people . . .

God, how she wanted to stop.

But she HAD TO OPERATE ON MRS. SANCHEZ.

"Yes." She inched the instrument forward.

Farther into Mrs. Sanchez.

And closer to her liver.

Finney said, "I think we both know that Delores can perform quite well under routine conditions, Dr. Wu. The simulations proved that beyond any doubt. What I'm *really* interested in knowing is how well Delores will perform during an emergency. That's a more interesting question. Wouldn't you agree?"

Rita had a wretched feeling in the deepest pit of her stomach. The worst she'd had, maybe, since the two grim-faced men in uniform had shown up at their door to tell her that her father's plane was a smoking pile of debris scattered across ten square miles of desert and that she and Darcy—

(*Darcy, oh God Darcy, hope she's still okay*)

—were orphans.

Her heart pounded. Sweat gathered in large drops underneath her surgical cap.

The tip floated into view on the wall screen.

"So. This is what I propose we do, Dr. Wu. I propose we test the true limits of Delores's capabilities. Here. Now. For this audience."

Oh, God.

Out of the corner of her eye, Rita saw that Chase had turned his attention from the screen and was chatting with a member of the crowd.

"Deploy the scalpel for Swiss Army number three," Finney said.

"Dolores, deploy scalpel for Swiss Army number three," Rita said.

It was her voice, all right, but the words seemed to have come out of someone else's mouth.

What made me say THAT?

With a click of gears, the scalpel materialized from

the tip of the third Swiss Army, its sharp tip shining menacingly.

Like a switchblade.

"Scalpel deployed for Swiss Army number three," Delores responded.

One badass switchblade.

As one of the young male engineers on the project liked to describe it.

Delores, unflappable, observed, "Please note that scalpel deployment is in violation of this operative protocol."

Yes, Rita thought. *It most definitely is. SO WHY THE HELL DID I JUST DEPLOY IT?*

"Dr. Wu?" Floating above her surgical mask, Lisa's eyes were wide, and fixed on the scalpel, which on the monitor was as big as her hand.

"Good," Finney said. "Now, I want you to push the scalpel into the patient's liver."

"You want me to do *WHAT*?" Rita hissed.

SPENCER

Spencer's right knee was starting to throb. He'd been standing too long. He placed more of his weight on his left leg and folded his arms. His attention meandered from Montgomery, who was chatting with the hospital CEO and university chancellor (*Damn, how many VIPs are here today?*), to the video screen.

He saw a scalpel pop out from the tip of the instrument and heard the robot announce its arrival.

What? The butterflies in his stomach, the ones that

had been fluttering around since his conversation with Wendy, suddenly exploded into a frenzied swarm. This did not seem right.

Violation, the robot had said there was a violation.

Not right at all.

What's she doing?

He opened his mouth to speak. Nothing came out.

He wet his lips and tried again. "Rita?" he said softly. "What are you doing?"

No one heard him.

RITA

"Dr. Wu? Why did you do that? Why is the scalpel out?" Lisa sounded remarkably calm. Much calmer than how Rita felt.

"It's nothing, Lisa," Rita whispered. "It must have, uh, accidentally deployed. I'm working on it."

She ordered herself to say the words to retract the scalpel, but her mouth and tongue refused to respond.

"Push the scalpel into the middle of the liver, Dr. Wu," Finney said.

She almost laughed out loud.

Is he kidding? Absurd. Finney was asking her to deliberately impale a vital organ—one of the *most* vital—in Mrs. Sanchez's body, as if it were some kind of slab of meat for a shish kebob. The scalpel would tear through Mrs. Sanchez's liver like a butcher's knife through cottage cheese.

Has any surgeon in history, totally on purpose, caused a major complication during an operation?

Probably not. She did not want to become the first, or violate every moral fiber in her being.

And yet . . .

There was something ugly inside of her that did.

Some terrible nameless *thing*.

It *wanted* her to plunge the scalpel into Mrs. Sanchez's liver. It wanted to *so badly*. It was an awful, rapacious urge. Not a specific thought, or emotion.

It simply *was*.

She felt her hands, which were still resting on the third Swiss Army, the one holding the scalpel, twitch, as if of their own accord.

No.

They twitched again.

No!

Her hands relaxed.

She imagined what would happen if she were to follow through on Finney's command.

Fun fact, she thought, with sudden, inexplicable giddiness. *The liver is filled with blood. Up to fifteen percent of all the blood in your entire body, at any one time, is in the liver. A three-pound, blood-soaked sponge. Every second, of every day, blood constantly streaming in and out.*

"Do it," Finney urged. Into her ear. Into her *mind*. "Push the scalpel into her liver."

On the gigantic screen, the liver appeared as big as a queen-size bed, and throbbed with every beep of the cardiac monitor.

Throbbed with blood.

With life.

If she punctured her liver with the scalpel, Rita knew, Mrs. Sanchez would bleed.

She would bleed, and almost certainly would die.

"No," Rita murmured.

"Do it!"

She felt a hand on her arm. "Dr. Wu?"

Rita flinched and pulled her eyes away from the screen. It was Lisa. "Dr. Wu? What's wrong? What are you doing?"

Before Rita could answer, the bored-sounding black woman standing in the front row—

(*Grant, Chase had called her Grant*)

—asked, "Dr. Montgomery? Why is the scalpel sticking out? From the instrument? Is Delores about to use it?"

Upon hearing the word *scalpel*, Chase's head snapped around. He squinted at the screen.

"Dr. Wu? What are you doing?" he said sharply.

"Do it," Finney repeated. "Push the scalpel into her liver."

"*No!*" Rita whispered fiercely.

"Rita!" Montgomery was practically shouting. All pretense of formality for the benefit of the visitors was gone.

He moved toward her.

SEBASTIAN

Damn.

Goddamn if Wu still was fighting it!

Practically goddamn inhuman, how she was resisting. None of the experimental subjects, all men, had ever fought back with such tenacity.

"Do it," he heard Finney whisper to her. "Push the instrument into her liver."

"No," she said.

And *still* she fought it.

Incredible!

With the signal strengths Finney had been using all morning, all that juice he'd pumped into her brain, she should be Finney's goddamn zombie mind slave by now. Or lying facedown on the floor in a puddle of her own drool.

God*damn* but she was tough.

If Finney wasn't careful, Sebastian worried Wu would soon be screaming like some nut job: like the ones in the videos, whose brains had been carpet-bombed with commands, and who'd then developed the thousand-mile stares.

The ones who'd died.

He sucked on his teeth.

Maybe that's what Finney had intended for Wu all along.

Insanity.

And death.

FINNEY

Finney's eyes narrowed to slits.

She was resisting him.

She was resisting him, and he would not have it.

He was in charge. Not her. She would not deny him

the fruit of his labor, or frustrate his plan to set right the order of things. The order she'd ripped apart when she'd *murdered* Jenny.

No.

She would not.

He swept an index finger from one end of the tablet to the other.

RITA

The buzzing she'd experienced earlier, in the locker room, then later in the alcove with Chase, slammed its way back into her head.

But this time it was different.

It was worse.

Much worse.

This time, it *hurt*.

God, how it HURT!

Agony. A thousand barbed needles lancing the inside of her skull: digging, burning, *ripping* into her head. She'd never experienced anything like it.

She gasped and staggered.

She reached out to the OR table with one hand to steady herself, and . . .

SEBASTIAN

Holy shit.

Finney had turned up the signal strength *again*, to the highest levels so far—the highest Sebastian had ever seen—way beyond the safety parameters the designers had established in the test subjects; and he'd fired a huge pulse of energy into her brain.

"Jesus, boss. *Careful,*" Sebastian whispered into his link.

Finney ignored him.

"Do it," Finney said to Wu. "Do it now. Push it into her liver."

She would do it, Sebastian thought. Or it would rip her fucking brain apart.

Or maybe it already had.

RITA

. . . in that moment, that moment of grabbing the side of the OR table with one hand, Rita felt as if she were being split in two, like a coconut sliced in half by a machete.

Suddenly, the pain, the thousand sharp objects piercing her brain, were gone.

Thank God.

The pain had been excruciating. She doubted she'd be able to hold herself together if it came back.

With one hand on the edge of the operating table, and the other still on the Swiss Army, she looked around. Another Rita, an exact twin of herself—complete with sterile gown, gloves, cap, and mask—was standing next to her, looking at her; and she experienced a strong sense of déjà vu.

The other Rita said, in Finney's voice, which was in her left ear only, *Push the scalpel into the liver.*

Rita took her hand off the table and placed it on the Swiss Army. With both hands, she began to advance the Swiss Army toward Mrs. Sanchez's liver, using the image on the screen as a guide. Because, well . . . why not? The other Rita, the one standing next to her, had told her to. It seemed a reasonable thing to do.

That's it, the other Rita crooned in Finney's voice. *Good.*

But then Rita stopped, the tip of the scalpel centimeters away from the liver.

No, she said to the other Rita, the one speaking in Finney's voice. *I can't do that. It would kill her.*

Then, suddenly, Rita wasn't in the OR anymore, but at her medical-school graduation, clutching her diploma, reciting the Hippocratic Oath with her class, when she promised that she wouldn't ever intentionally hurt any of her patients.

An instant later and in her mind she was in the hallway, outside the room of the patient who was coding, watching that commanding surgeon with Mediterranean-blue eyes puke into the sink.

And then she was in pre-op, with Mr. and Mrs. Sanchez, Mr. Sanchez clutching his wife's hand and talking about his daughter at UCLA.

Not pre-op now, but her bedroom; and Spencer was there, lying next to her, on the bed, naked, his enormous, gentle hand running through her hair, down her cheek. He cupped her chin and brought his lips close to her left ear. His breath was warm and inviting and tickling her earlobe.

Do it, he murmured, but it was Finney's voice, not Spencer's. *Do it now. Push the scalpel into her liver.*

No, Rita said.

And then she was back in OR 10. The other Rita who had been standing next to her, the one who had been speaking in Finney's voice, was gone.

The pain in her head was back.

She wanted to scream.

She wanted to throw up.

She wanted to *die.*

"Do it!" Finney yelled. The sound of his voice crammed her head, violating her mind in a way that felt more vulgar and obscene than if he'd violated her body.

Then from a distance, a long distance away, Rita thought she heard Spencer say, "Rita! What are you doing?"

Spencer? But it couldn't be Spencer. Because what would Spencer be doing *here*?

"Rita! What's going on? Rita!" That was Chase. *Why was Chase here again?* She couldn't remember. It didn't matter, anyway, because she was thinking about something else.

She was thinking about her eyes. How she wanted to cover them.

She wanted to cover her eyes because she knew what was about to happen, and she didn't want to see it because it was going to be terrible, and she had no power to stop it.

She felt her hands jerk forward.

In an instant, on the screen, the scalpel tip crossed the small gap remaining between it and Mrs. Sanchez's liver.

Someone in the room gasped.

Was it her?

Then, just before the scalpel hit the glistening, pulsating brown surface, she said, "God help me."

SEBASTIAN

Sebastian saw her hesitate, hands trembling, as if struggling with herself.

He watched, stunned, as Finney turned up the signal strength *again*.

"Do it," Finney screamed.

She did.

And Sebastian watched as their plan, the one they'd been mapping out for nearly a year, was executed.

Flawlessly.

Sebastian couldn't tell whether he felt good about that, or bad.

But he didn't want to see any more. He slipped from the room as everything went to hell.

SPENCER

"Rita!" Spencer bounded toward her.

She mumbled something he couldn't make out, something about God, as the scalpel entered the patient's liver and disappeared beneath its undulating surface.

Spencer had known Chase Montgomery for a decade. In all that time, he'd never seen the man at a loss for words. Until now. Montgomery made a guttural, caveman grunt. Then said: "Well, we, uh—*huh*." Or some variation of that.

Spencer was just as stunned. He'd never seen anything like this, never even *conceived* of anything like this.

But he'd seen it with his own eyes.

Rita.

The liver.

The scalpel.

Rita pushing the scalpel into the liver.

What on earth had possessed her? Pure craziness. He knew that for Rita, a surgical complication was a personal affront by God and Nature. She never gave up her fight for absolute perfection, and Rita's complication rates were some of the lowest around.

Until this insanity.

So now what?

He stared at the screen. For the moment, at least, there wasn't any bleeding.

Which was good. Because the astonishing illogic of what they'd just witnessed had left all the surgeons stunned and speechless. Between himself, Montgomery, and the other surgeons here, Spencer estimated there was at least one hundred years of combined clinical experience. This patient's life was now in danger. They all should have been rushing forward to help Rita.

But, instead, there they were, standing around like idiots, waiting for something to happen.

RITA

After the tempered, diamond-tipped steel of the scalpel had buried itself in Mrs. Sanchez's liver, Rita couldn't remember exactly how it had gotten there.

She knew that she was responsible. That she'd been the one to stab the liver. But she didn't understand why—

(*Finney, it had to have been Finney*)

—she'd done it. Staring at the video screen, she felt as if she'd just emerged from a horrible nightmare—

(*Finney had made her do it, somehow*)

—except that the nightmare wasn't ending. The ugly image on the screen, of the Swiss Army sticking like a skewer out of Mrs. Sanchez's liver, horrified her.

But she couldn't worry about any of that now.

Chase made a loud noise. A strange sound; and, oddly, one of the things Rita would later remember most about the whole horrible morning. It reminded her of the dolphins at Sea World she'd seen with her parents when she was little, blowing air through their blowholes as they'd surfaced.

She gritted her teeth, steeling herself for the inevitable, her hands still wrapped around the Swiss Army. And she waited.

She waited for the bleeding.

Nothing happened.

Five seconds went by.

Nothing.

Ten improbable seconds.

Still nothing.

The room, crammed as it was, remained silent except for the beep of the cardiac monitor, which broadcast the steady beat of Mrs. Sanchez's heart.

Hope. Or a sliver of it, at least.

Maybe the scalpel had managed to miss the big blood vessels. Or, maybe it hadn't, but the Swiss Army was now holding pressure against whatever bleeding was occurring under the liver's surface. Both scenarios were manageable.

God, could she really have been that lucky?

Fifteen seconds.

Dumb luck.

It happened sometimes. This one time, a drunken frat boy climbing over a wrought-iron fence had slipped and impaled his thigh on an arrow-shaped ornament. The firefighters who'd found him, dangling from the top of the fence like a fleshy flag from a flagpole, had given him hefty doses of painkillers before cutting him free, but smartly left the metal strut sticking through his leg.

Good God, what a freak show *that* had been in the ER, with two feet of iron bar sticking out of the kid's leg. But when Rita had rushed him to the OR, she'd discovered that the bar had missed every single vital structure in his leg—blood vessels, nerves, bone: sparing his leg, and maybe even his life. Dumb luck.

Rita was all for dumb luck. She loved dumb luck. She prayed that dumb luck was smiling upon them now and that maybe Mrs. Sanchez would still walk away from all of this.

Twenty seconds.

No bleeding.

Behind her, she sensed Lisa and Thomas moving quickly, opening additional sterile packages of surgical instruments, the kind needed to fix big holes in major organs and big blood vessels.

Good.

Rita allowed her hands holding the Swiss Army to relax. She started calculating ways by which she could salvage this, her mind flipping through potential treatment algorithms, calculating her next, best move.

"Lisa—" she began.

That's when the bleeding started.

SPENCER

On the giant wall screen, the blood fountained around the Swiss Army like an enormous red geyser.

Christ, Rita! What have you done?

Someone gasped. Spencer couldn't tell if it was a man or a woman: either a man with a high voice, or woman with a low one. Except for the pulsating blood on the screen, though, it was a moment frozen in time. No one moved.

Until, as if from some agreed-upon, unspoken cue, everyone moved at once.

RITA

The blood shot up and away from the liver in high-pressure spouts timed with each beep of Mrs. Sanchez's heart on the cardiac monitor. Droplets hit the camera, splattering across the lens, like red paint—

(*like red rain just like that old Peter Gabriel song red rain coming down red rain pouring down over me what's wrong oh God what's wrong with me concentrate dammit concentrate . . .*)

—on to a window, clouding the field of vision.

She shook her head, trying to sweep it clear of these addled thoughts— thoughts that seemed to be coming from outside of her, from *elsewhere*, and tried to focus on the video screen, and on saving Mrs. Sanchez's life.

From out of her peripheral vision, she saw Chase rushing from the room. He was shouting to Lisa and Thomas that he was going to scrub, and to grab him some sterile gloves and a gown, and the laparotomy tray with the vascular clamps.

(*Laparotomy tray that's for emergencies that's for making big incisions in people's abdomens to stick your hands inside to stop bleeding . . .*)

She shook her head again, more forcefully: *Concentrate!*

Then a rushing sound in her left ear, and the room spun at crazy angles; slowly at first, then faster and faster.

She staggered away from the OR table and vomited into a nearby trash can.

(*In the trash can at least and not all over the floor in front of all these people . . .*)

Then the dark closed in from the margins. Embraced her; enveloped her mind. It was . . . soothing, like sliding into a warm Jacuzzi when you had aching muscles, or climbing into bed at the end of a really, *really* long day: maybe the very longest day of your life.

So she gave in to the dark because it felt good. Besides, she was too tired to fight anymore.

But as she slid into unconsciousness, one thought— a terrible, sickening one—raced through her mind: Mrs. Sanchez was going to die.

She had killed Mrs. Sanchez.

God help me, I killed that poor woman.

The blackness was all but complete when she heard Dolores say: "Initiating laparoscopic cholecystectomy protocol for Swiss Army number three."

That's strange, she thought.

Delores was beginning the operation on its own.

Why? What had made Delores do that?

And then Delores said: "Iatrogenic hepatic injury detected. Initiating emergency hemostasis safety protocol."

Rita raised her head from the trash can, vomit dribbling from her chin, and as if through a haze, saw the video screen.

Dolores's camera was fixed on the middle of the bleeding liver. The three Swiss Army instruments were moving with blinding speed and singularity of purpose.

Dolores.

What are you up to?

She puked again into the trash can.

"Rita!" Spencer's voice, approaching.

(*Sorry, Spencer, I'm so sorry for everything . . .*)

SPENCER

Rita vomited again, into the trash can, then knocked it over as she collapsed, spilling its contents across the floor, her body jerking in violent spasms.

She was seizing.

He ran to her side and shoved a pillow behind her head to keep her from fracturing her skull on the tile floor. On her scrub pants, a dark, damp stain spread outward from her pelvis and down her thighs. *Urine.* The sharp smell of it filled his nostrils. He held her hand and grimly waited for it to end.

She seized for a long time.

FINNEY

Finney watched as Dr. Wu toppled to the floor. Her glasses fell from her head and landed with the camera lens facedown on the floor, so he could no longer see what was happening.

But that was all right.

He no longer needed to.

Listening to the shouting and commotion, as Mrs. Sanchez bled and Dr. Wu seized, he leaned back and interlaced his fingers behind his head.

And, at long last, he allowed himself to smile.

It had been a gamble, to be sure. He'd had to push her to the brink of mental collapse. Yes, he'd underestimated her resilience. But, in the end, it had turned out *magnificently*, exactly as he'd planned: In one fell swoop, she'd been disgraced, and the robot's full potential realized.

He took the small, worn-leather notebook and the mechanical pencil from the front pocket of his shirt, opened the notebook, placed it on the table in front of him next to the tablet, and clicked the pencil three times.

The lead tip hovered over the empty box next to Dr. Wu's name for a full minute as he considered putting an *X* through the box and an end to his business with her. He pondered the quality of mercy, and what Jenny might have done in this situation. Perhaps, he mused, he'd now exacted his pound of flesh and should abort the rest of the plan. Maybe allow both Dr. Wu and the sister to live.

He touched the pencil tip to the paper.

Jenny.

It had all been for her. Of course it had. He would have doused himself with gasoline and burned himself alive if she'd asked it of him. He would have died for her.

No.

Instead of marking an *X*, he ground the pencil tip into the page until it snapped.

NO.

Dr. Wu would have no mercy.

Because she deserved none. That scalpel-wielding *whore* had *butchered* his wife and child.

As for the sister, well . . . that couldn't be helped: Before he killed her, Dr. Wu needed to experience the full extent of his pain, what it felt like to have the one closest to her suffer, then die.

He laid the notebook and pencil on the table and touched an icon on the tablet. A new window appeared on the screen. It had a clock in it, and the clock began to count down toward zero, as if to the launch of a rocket. He continued jabbing at the icon with his finger, over and over, for no good reason other than he felt like it.

He would have died for Jenny.

Now he would kill for her, to atone for her suffering.

And mine.

And he would restore balance to the universe.

RITA

Through the darkness, Rita heard the trill of a pulse oximeter, bleating rhythmically in time with an unseen patient's heart as it measured the blood oxygen levels; and the hum of far-off conversations; and the muffled, intermittent murmurs of an overhead PA system.

Rita opened her eyes. She was in a bed. The patient with the pulse oximeter was she; the oximeter sensor was taped to her left index finger. She was wearing a hospital gown. An IV line ran into her left arm, attached to a bag of clear fluid. She peered at the small lettering on the side of the bag. She didn't have her glasses, so the lettering was blurred, but she could make out it was normal saline. For dehydration.

She looked around. The bed was in the middle of a hospital room, which she recognized as one of the private rooms in Turner's ER. A heavy, sliding-glass door, like a patio door, with a large number 5 printed on it took up one entire wall. The door was ajar, and voices drifted through. Chase was sitting in a chair at the foot of her bed, texting.

"Chase?"

Chase squinted at her with red-tinged eyes. He appeared spent, as exhausted as she'd ever seen him.

"Are you all right?" he said.

God, and his *voice*: It sounded like gravel rattling in the bottom of an empty metal can. No trace of TV anchorman at all.

Am I all right?

She wasn't sure.

"What . . . what happened to me?"

"I was going to ask you the same question, Rita. You're in the ER. What's the last thing you remember?"

She twisted the bedsheet in her hands. "The bleeding. Mrs. Sanchez. My patient. Is she . . ."

"Dead? No. Remarkably enough, she's fine." He placed his phone on the arm of his chair. "Extubated and resting. Didn't even need a blood transfusion, if you can believe that. Her biliary tree is intact, thank Christ, but we're going to keep a close eye on her for a few days, just to be sure she doesn't develop a delayed bile leak."

"So . . . you were able to stop the bleeding?"

"Oh, yes. Yes we did. With some unexpected help." He shook his head. "If I hadn't seen it with my own eyes, I never would have believed it. After you . . . *harpooned* . . . that patient's liver, Delores's safety protocols kicked in."

"The—safety protocols?"

"Yes."

"I didn't know we had turned them on."

"Neither did I. We'd loaded the software into the onboard system but hadn't activated it, or been expecting to use it. The engineers are sifting through the data, trying to figure it out. But it looks like Delores recognized the bleeding and automatically engaged the safety routines."

"The safety routines worked?"

"Oh, *God*, yes. Did they ever. Better than we ever could have hoped. I'll be damned if the goddamn thing not only repaired the liver laceration but managed to finish most of the cholecystectomy before we shut it down, and I got in there. It worked *that* fast. I couldn't believe it. *Christ*. It was goddamn eerie. Like it had a mind of its own."

He grunted. "You didn't have to be a doctor to appreciate how . . . *impressively* Delores performed. That reporter from the *Wall Street Journal* was poking around afterward, insinuating we had somehow staged the entire thing to show off Delores's safety features. Goddamn conspiracy theory, of course . . . but strangely, Rita, your complete, incomprehensible incompetence made Delores look even better than we'd intended."

"Chase, about what happened—"

His hand shot up, palm out. He turned off his phone (she'd never seen him do *that* before), and put a finger to his lips; then he rose from the chair, slid the glass door closed, and drew a curtain across it. The glass was thick, and save for the trill of the pulse oximeter, silence enveloped them.

He sat back down with a severe expression. "Rita. Listen to me. Listen very, *very* carefully. God knows why you did what you did. But I'm not joking, and I'm not fooling around—"

"I realize that, Chase, but—"

"—because you are in *really* big trouble. Before you say anything, anything at all to me, would you like to talk to a lawyer?"

"Why would I want to do that?"

He dragged his hand down his face, leaned forward, and squinted harder.

"The tox screen, Rita."

She shook her head. "I don't understand. What tox screen?"

"The tox screen we sent here in the ER. On you."

A tox screen. So: They'd tested her blood for alcohol and drugs. And, come to think of it, they'd probably checked her urine, too—an unpleasant half memory now surfaced of someone catheterizing her bladder.

"Why on earth would you send a tox screen?"

"Dammit, Rita. Why *wouldn't* we? It was medically indicated. We didn't know what the hell was going on with you. I mean, first you impaled that woman's goddamn liver." He guffawed. "In front of the goddamn chancellor of the university. Oh, and don't forget the *Wall Street Journal*. Then you puked all over yourself, collapsed, and seized. What a *goddamn* mess."

"*Seized?*"

"Yes." He got up and started pacing at the foot of her bed. "Grand mal. You stopped breathing. Scared the shit out of us. We called a code and brought you down here. A tox screen is part of the workup." He sat back down on the edge of the chair. "You know that."

"What did it show?"

Chase glanced over his shoulder at the closed sliding door and the drawn curtain. He scooted the chair closer to Rita's bed. Its four legs screeched unhappily across the floor.

"What *didn't* it show, Rita? Traces of cocaine. Methamphetamines. Heroin. Some benzos. A blood alcohol level of 0.04%—not enough to be legally drunk in California, but with everything else, it kind of adds a what-the-hell-were-you-thinking twist. You know?"

She said, in a small voice, "What?"

"Booze and illegal drugs, Rita. In your body. While you were *operating*."

"But, that can't be, there must be a mistake—"

"No."

"But, I—"

"Is that what you were doing here last night?"

"What?"

"Is that how you ended up in OR 10 this morning? Did you take off your clothes and pass out?" He drew his hand down the length of his face, slow and hard, and laughed bitterly. "Sleepwalking! Sleepwalking. You said you were sleepwalking. *Goddammit*, Rita. If we inventory the drugs in the anesthesia cart, in OR 10, will some of them come up missing?"

"What? No, Chase!"

"The narcotics, maybe? Or the benzos?"

"No! That's . . . absurd. I never did any of those drugs. I've never done drugs in my life."

"Then how did they end up in your blood?"

"I don't know. Are you sure it was *my* blood? That there hasn't been a mistake? Maybe you should have the lab check again—"

"We already have. Twice."

"Maybe somebody, I don't know—put them there, somehow, in the samples—"

"Please, Rita," he said, his face flushing with anger. "Now you're sounding ridiculous. Why would someone have done that?"

"I—" She broke off, because she suddenly knew there was no point in debating this anymore. The realization, the comprehension of her terrible predicament, crashed over her, and she knew exactly how the drugs and the alcohol had gotten into her body. It all made sense: elegant and horrible sense.

Finney.

The hungover, sluggish feeling she'd had all morning, and her inability to remember what had happened last night. Finney had somehow drugged her and left her on the OR table naked. He'd set her up, in the nastiest way possible, in front of her colleagues and Chase.

In front of *everyone*.

Oh, dear God, how could she ever talk her way out of this?

"I thought you'd stayed sober, Rita." A note of hurt had crept into Montgomery's voice. Of confidence betrayed. "Since that business with the appendectomy. I thought you'd been sober since then."

"I have, Chase." She laid her head back on the pillow. God, but she was tired. "I have."

"I helped you—" He glanced over his shoulder and leaned in so close she was afraid he would fall off the chair. "I helped you," he whispered. "I helped you with the understanding that it would never, *ever* happen again: that business with the drinking. Put my own reputation and career on the line. For *you*, Rita. Buried that report so that it would never see daylight. Had that nurse transferred to another hospital."

"I know, Chase. I know."

"I can't help you, Rita. Not this time. What a mess. What a goddamn mess you've made. This is all going to come out. Negligence is a given. There may even be criminal charges. Assault and battery . . . who knows? There's no lack of evidence, that's for sure. Hell, aside from the thirty goddamn people standing in the room, we got the whole goddamn thing on tape."

She didn't say anything. What was there to say?

"Given the circumstances, you realize that the hospital and university will wash their hands of you. They're going to leave you twisting in the wind."

"What about you, Chase? What are you going to do?"

He sighed and stared at the wall above her bed. "Do you really want me to answer that, Rita?" he said softly. "Honestly, I shouldn't even be talking to you right now. I can't help you this time. I really can't. Hell, I've already called my *own* lawyer."

"What did he say?"

"He told me not to talk to you." With a grunt, he pushed himself out of the chair. "Look. It's out of my hands. It's already gone straight to the top—because *the top* was standing right there in OR 10 when you put the goddamn hole in the liver. By law, the hospital must notify the California Department of Public

Health and the Medical Board. Based on the information at hand, the CEO has already placed you on paid administrative leave pending an investigation."

"Will I lose my license?"

He grasped the handle of the sliding-glass door. "That may be the least of your worries. Just—please, Rita. For God's sake. Get a lawyer."

Chase slid the door open. The distant clamor of the ER, the rustlings of sick humanity, intruded, then died away as Chase slammed the door behind him, hard enough to make the glass rattle.

Finney crooned in her left ear, "I knew about the drinking, you know."

Oh, God.

The drinking.

How could he know?

"I'm curious. When did it start?" Finney asked.

A few months before your wife died, she almost said out loud, but caught herself.

Her mind drifted back to more than a year ago, when Darcy had dropped out of Brown. A surprise text from the airport one Sunday morning, a few more from the cab—and then there she was, at Rita's front door, having hit the wall, emotionally, physically, in every way one could. Standing there at the door, Darcy hadn't said anything. She'd just dropped her bags, and wrapped her arms around Rita's neck, and started sobbing, her emaciated frame—

(*God, she'd lost so much weight*)

—wracked with dry heaves. She'd smelled of cigarettes.

"Was there a particular reason why you drank?"
Finney said

*Because it was my fault. Because I hadn't been
there for my baby sister when she'd needed me.*

As Darcy had cried uncontrollably, her face buried
in Rita's neck, it had dawned on Rita how selfish she'd
been over the years. No, not just selfish. *Weak.* Weak
because she'd let it all happen, had let it come to this.

She would fix it, Rita had decided. She was a *surgeon*, goddammit. She'd been trained to fix things.
Worse things than this. She might not have been there
for Darcy before, but she could sure as hell fix her now.
She'd resolved, right there in the doorway, to double
down, reprioritize, to excise from her life, with surgical precision, all the nonessentials, the *selfish* and *weak*
things, and focus on Darcy.

And then she'd jettisoned, like ballast tossed from
a hot-air balloon, all of her other serious personal relationships.

Spencer.

God, breaking up with him had hurt *so* much.

Harder still was not telling him why. That had been
her decision, not Darcy's. She was a private person
who in her mind organized life into compartments:
Darcy in one, Spencer in another; Darcy unaware of
Spencer's existence, and Spencer only vaguely of
Darcy's. Explaining Darcy's sudden appearance to
Spencer would have smashed this orderly arrangement. Besides, Spencer would have insisted on helping
Rita, because helping people was his nature. Fixing
Darcy was something she'd needed to do on her own.

When, a few days later, she'd broken up with him with some canned speech about there not being room in her life for a serious relationship—

(*His eyes. God. So sad.*)

(*Like a big, hurt puppy. Like she'd kicked a puppy.*)

—it had killed her.

She supposed she'd come across as an ice-cold bitch, the stereotype of the driven professional woman without the time or inclination to settle down with a proper man and play house. *Fine.* Maybe she really *was* a ruthless bitch. In which case Spencer deserved better anyway.

You don't believe that, Rita. You never have.

When she'd told Chase she'd be taking some time off, having accumulated over the years enough unused vacation to practically retire, he'd squinted at her from across the expanse of his desk, considering her silently for several moments before saying in his smooth baritone: *Don't worry. We'll keep the lights on for you. Do whatever it is you need to do.* He'd never pressed her for more information.

"Dr. Wu? Can you hear me?" Finney said.

Darcy had agreed to cut out the pills, and the wine she'd needed to bring her down from them, but flatly refused to enter therapy. Rita had shrugged and let it go. The two of them had eased into a sedate routine, Rita indulging in the small luxuries she'd denied herself since . . . well, pretty much ever. Sleeping. Sunbathing. Long brunches. Hikes. Day spas. Reality TV. Movies.

They'd talked about everything, and nothing. Mom. Dad. Gram. Darcy's boyfriends. Spencer. Rita's career. Darcy's fears and failures. Weeks passed. Darcy gained weight, cut down to a quarter of a pack a day, and started to take long walks for exercise. She began to talk about writing again, and of transferring to State, or maybe the University of San Diego.

Then, just as Rita had been getting ready to head back to work, and Darcy was perusing college catalogs, a call came from the friend in Portland, inviting Darcy for the weekend. Darcy, who had no money, asked Rita for some.

Just enough for the plane ticket, Ree. And some food.

Rita had hesitated, her instincts nudging her to keep Darcy close for a bit longer. But it was just a weekend, after all. What could a weekend hurt?

She'd given Darcy the money.

A weekend in Portland had stretched into a week. A week into two, two weeks into two months. And then . . .

Rita was alone again.

That was when the drinking had started.

With Darcy gone, she'd considered going back to Spencer, who'd continued to pursue her like a lovesick teenager, but rejected the idea. It wasn't pride. She'd had no pride left to swallow.

That was when the drinking had started.

No. She didn't *deserve* Spencer. Besides, Spencer was a luxury she couldn't afford: When Darcy came back again—

(*If she came back,* she'd worried.)

—she wouldn't have room for both in her life.

Darcy had not come back. Not then.

That was when the drinking had started.

Portland didn't work out. But Darcy had met a boy there—

(*Simon? Steve? Something that started with* S.)

—who'd convinced her to go with him to Seattle. She and S-something had moved in together. Darcy had landed a waitressing job, but during infrequent calls had asked for money: to help, she said—

(*Pay for the partying.*)

—find time to write a novel.

(*In between the partying.*)

"Dr Wu?" Finney said.

Rita closed her eyes . . .

SEBASTIAN

Sebastian was feeling—

(*guilty*)

—crappy.

That lady. The patient. She hadn't deserved that. No one deserved that.

It was one thing to have planned the whole thing out on paper and to imagine how it was part of a bigger picture, a grander plan. But to have actually seen it play out, with the scalpel, and the blood . . .

But guilt was unprofessional.

As for Wu: It was a wonder she wasn't a raving lunatic by now. Or dead.

When did I become one of the bad guys?

He was not a murderer. He was a professional.

It's a job. Like all of the others before it. One last goddamn job.

Fine. Just a job. He had to keep reminding himself why he was doing it.

After leaving OR 10, he'd turned down the receiver in his ear, changed his clothes, stuffed his phone in his pocket, and wandered out to a small park behind Turner, on its west side, with a sweeping view of the Pacific.

He sat alone at a cement picnic table, away from the others in the park, and faced the ocean. He stared at it for a long time, thinking, then glanced at his watch. Late afternoon on the East Coast.

He dug out his phone and thumbed a number, a special one, buried under layers of software security. Real black-hat-type shit, with enough encryption to leave even the NSA guys scratching their heads should they ever stumble across the signal.

"Hello?"

"Hi, Sis."

"Brother." He heard surprise, mixed with affection. "It's been a while. Are you okay, Brother? Staying out of trouble?"

"Trying, Sister. Trying." The last time someone had mocked (to his face, at least) Sebastian for addressing his twin as *Sister*, and her for addressing him as *Brother*, had been back in seventh grade, and that kid had ended up with a shattered jaw. It had cost Sebastian a stint in Juvey, the first of several. But it'd been totally worth it.

"Well. I guess that's an improvement over not trying."

He smiled. "How're the kids?" His hand tightened around the phone. "How's Sammy?"

"Good. Real good. Straight A's so far this semester. Again. The teacher—she's real young, but nice. And knows her stuff. Teach for America. She says Sammy's real smart."

"Naturally. He takes after his uncle."

"She says that he treats the other kids good, too. Helps them with their schoolwork. She says he could go far, but that he needs stimulation. *Stimulation.*" She snorted. "I'm doing my best, Brother. Not a lot of *stimulation* around here. Not the good kind, at least. They closed the library in our neighborhood, which wasn't for crap, anyway. I've been taking the kids to the central library downtown, on weekends. When I can. Central library's real nice." She paused, and then added quietly, "He had a checkup at Children's Hospital last week."

Sebastian's stomach clenched. "And?"

"Pretty good. I think. But they didn't say *cure*. They said . . . *remission*. Yeah, remission. That's what they called it. They told him he was a *survivor*. He loved that." He could hear the smile in her voice. "Survivor."

Survivor.

You and me both, kid.

"They never say *cure*, Brother," she said. "The doctors. Why is that, do you think?"

His palms suddenly felt sweaty. "I don't know, Sis. You know, uh, how doctors are. He, ah . . . there with you now?"

"No. He's down at the Boys and Girls Club. After-school program. He'll be back soon. The counselor always walks him home."

Through the receiver, Sebastian heard a far-off siren, followed by what might be the nearby jangle of breaking glass, and hoarse, angry shouts in what sounded like Russian.

"Sierra?" his sister said. "Sierra. Get away from the window, baby. That's my big girl. Mommy wants you to go to her bedroom, okay? And sit on the bed. Turn on the TV and sit on the bed. Mommy will be right there, baby."

Sierra asked her who she was talking to. She told her.

"Hi, Uncle!" a tinny voice called from the background.

He laughed. Goddamn, it felt *good*. "Hi, Sierra."

"He says *hi* back, baby. Now do what Mommy says. Thank you, baby."

"What's going on?"

"Nothing," she said curtly.

He ignored her lie. *Jesus. I've got to get them out of that shit hole.* "How's Sierra?"

"Good. Except her parochial school raised the freakin' tuition. Again. You believe that crap?"

"It's the Catholic Church, Sis. They've been robbing people blind for thousands of years."

She laughed. "Yeah. I suppose."

"How much you need?"

She hesitated before saying, "There's, um . . . something else."

"What?"

"The . . . medical bills. Thought the problem was fixed. But when I took Sammy to his appointment, they almost didn't let him see the doctor. I had to practically beg."

Begging was not in his sister's nature. He could only imagine how hard that must have been for her. "The fifty grand I sent six months ago—"

"Was a start. But those damn co-pays piled up, Brother. MRIs, chemo, surgery, hospital stays . . ."

He wanted to smash his phone to pieces on the cement picnic table. *Mother fucker! Wasn't goddamn Obamacare supposed to take care of this shit? He's just a fucking kid!*

He said calmly, "How much you need?"

A pause. "It's not dirty, is it? I don't want your money if it's dirty. You know that."

"No. It's clean." *Clean enough,* he thought, gazing at the horizon. Clean as he could make it. "How much?"

She told him. *Shit.* A hundred thousand more. That was a lot of goddamn money. Much more than he'd suspected. Plus, he knew she was lowballing him, asking for much less than what she really needed. She was a proud woman—she worked two goddamn jobs, shitty jobs with shitty pay, because it was all she could get.

He sucked his teeth. *Jesus Christ. The sick kid of a single mother.* Couldn't they give her a goddamn break? He couldn't let them end up on the street. But paying off those bills, even in part, would burn through much of what was left in his account. Most of the payment for Finney's job—this *goddamn shitty* job—was on the back end. Thank Christ it was over. He needed what Finney owed him. Now.

I need that money.

He promised to transfer more than enough to her by the end of the day.

She thanked him, and said, "So. You sound okay."

"Yeah. I'm all right."

"Can you tell me where you are?"

"No."

A pause. "Can you tell me when we're going to see you again? Sammy keeps asking about his favorite uncle."

His *only* uncle. His only family, besides his mother and sister. Sammy and Sierra's dirtbag father had split years ago. Sebastian had toyed with the idea of tracking him down, so he could kill the asshole (slowly, of course), but decided the prick wasn't worth the effort. The boy needed a father figure, something Sebastian had never had. The girl, too. "Soon, Sis. Soon. I'm finishing up a job now."

"What kind of job?" Her voice was thick with suspicion.

"Just a job." He added quickly, "Legit, Sis." *Legit enough.*

"Don't bullshit me, Brother."

He sighed. He knew changing the subject wouldn't help. She was a fucking pit bull: Once she grabbed ahold of you, no force on God's earth would make her let go. "Look. It shouldn't take more than a few weeks for me to set my shit straight. Then I'm coming to see you guys. And I'm staying, Sis."

"How long?" she said after several seconds.

"Long enough for me to find the boy some goddamn proper *stimulation.*"

She laughed, and he knew he had her. They spoke for the next half hour, then, only as twin brother and sister could. And then, when exchanging good-byes, she said something odd—something she hadn't said in years, not since he'd re-upped after his first combat tour.

"Just, be careful, Brother. Please. Be careful."

She hung up.

Be careful.

His arm holding the phone went slack and dropped between his legs. He stared at the dark clouds gathering over the ocean.

Sick.

He was sick to death of this whole goddamn business. Thank Christ he was about to be done with it.

It was time to check in with Finney and get his final payment. He sighed and tapped the Fruit Punch Drunk icon on his phone. The audio in his earpiece crackled to life.

RITA

. . . and when Rita opened her eyes again, another Rita was lounging in the chair next to the bed, the same chair in which Chase had been sitting. She was wearing a hospital gown, just like hers, and staring at her. Her legs—muscular and firm, the legs of a runner—were crossed. Her hands were interlaced in her lap, casually, as if the two were having a chat over coffee. Just-us-girls.

"I knew, Dr. Wu," the other Rita, the one sitting in the chair, said. She spoke with Finney's voice, which Rita could hear only in her left ear. "I knew that you were drinking before my wife's surgery."

Rita stared at the other Rita in the chair, and replied, "It was all you, wasn't it? That weird compulsion I had to operate this morning, and the bleeding. All of it. I don't know how you did it, but you've destroyed my career. My life. Everything that means anything to me."

The other Rita said, "You set yourself on this path, Dr. Wu, when you operated on my wife drunk. Besides. You fail to see the bigger picture. Your self-immolation has ensured the success of the auto-surgeon. Delores performed magnificently in front of very important people."

"I wasn't drunk," Rita grumbled.

The other Rita said nothing.

"I wasn't drunk," Rita insisted, and propped herself up on the pillow.

"The report Dr. Montgomery alluded to suggested otherwise," the other Rita said.

Rita said, "The report of one disgruntled nurse, who accused a lot of women at Turner of totally bogus things before he was fired. None of his complaints ever went anywhere."

The other Rita said, "Dr. Montgomery arranged that, though, didn't he? At least in your case?"

Rita looked away.

The other Rita said, "I've read the complaint. The nurse accused you of drinking before you operated on Jenny. He claimed he smelled alcohol on your breath."

Rita pressed her lips together, and said, "That doesn't prove anything." It didn't. It was in fact one of the reasons why Chase had been able to make the complaint go away.

The other Rita said, "I must admit that I, myself, didn't smell alcohol on your breath when you spoke to us before the operation. Neither did Jenny, as far as I know."

That was probably because, by the time she'd gone to see the Finneys in pre-op, Rita had sensed the suspicion in the sour glare of the scrub nurse that night: the creepy little guy with the scrawny arms, weasel eyes, and swatch of dark peach fuzz coating his upper lip, like a hairy caterpillar; the guy she was sure hated taking orders from a woman surgeon. According to Lisa the scrub nurse, Caterpillar Guy had put his hand on Lisa's butt once, during an operation, and after Lisa had matter-of-factly informed him that the next time it happened, he'd draw back a stump, Caterpillar Guy had complained to the head of surgical nursing that Lisa had a *hostile attitude*.

So, after seeing the look on Caterpillar Guy's face that night, she'd loaded up on two boxes worth of breath mints, and frantically scrubbed her face and hands clean of any incriminating odor. Just to be sure.

The pulse oximeter on Rita's finger whined in a slow, steady tempo, like a truck backing up, as she remembered that ill-fated Sunday night. She'd been on call, from home, and she'd been alone. It'd been a slow night—not much going on, not a single call from the hospital for hours. She'd figured a few drinks would be okay. One glass of wine, maybe two. No big deal. So she'd pulled out some Chardonnay.

First time she'd ever had a drink on call. She'd known other doctors who drank on call routinely. She'd seen them at parties and book clubs, phone in one hand, a glass of wine or beer in the other, chatting on the phone with another doctor, or a nurse, or maybe even a patient. How might one of those docs responded if she'd asked them about boozing on the job? Probably that it was no big deal, like driving home after having a drink or two with dinner. One just had to be responsible. Discreet.

Which is what she'd told herself that night, as she'd poured herself the second glass. *No big deal. Just be responsible.* Right? She'd once overheard a surgery professor claim to another, only half-jokingly, that he thought he operated better with a buzz on. Sipping the Chardonnay that night, she'd wondered if that was true.

She'd never been much of a drinker: too focused on school, and cross-country, and work. And then there was Darcy. Rita had learned in med school that drug dependency was hardwired in the genes, passed from one generation to the next. Their parents hadn't had any such problems, as far as she'd known; but after watching Darcy go down in flames, she'd worried that she and Darcy might both be carrying some recessive gene, and that she might well be destined for a similar fate if she wasn't careful. Besides, doctors were especially susceptible to drug and alcohol problems. Statistics showed it. So, other than an occasional drink during the holidays, Rita had avoided alcohol.

Then Darcy had stayed in Portland.

The night she called to tell Rita she wasn't coming back, Rita had been sitting at her kitchen table after getting home late from the hospital. She'd put the phone down and stared out the window into the night, then gotten up to rummage around in a cabinet in the living room. She'd pulled out the fine Cabernet a grateful patient had given her, and a dusty wineglass. She'd uncorked the wine and washed out the glass.

After the first glass, things hadn't seemed so bad. After the second, they'd seemed downright agreeable. After all, she didn't need Darcy. Right?

The headache she'd woken up with (*After only two glasses—jeez, had I really been that much of a lightweight?*), one that had plagued her through morning clinic and the two routine operations that had followed, hadn't dissuaded her from stopping off at the Costco on the way home to pick up a case of Chardonnay. Much cheaper to buy in bulk, and she'd once read that white wine was less likely to cause morning-after headaches than red. Not true, it turned out, at least not for her—but her alcohol tolerance soon increased, which helped.

She *always* remained in control. She'd told herself that repeatedly, night after night. Besides, studies showed you lived longer with a daily glass of wine, right? The health benefits were scientifically proven.

One drink a night after work had become two, occasionally three. She drank alone, which the sensible part of her tried to point out was *not* okay. In fact, it was pretty far away from okay. But she was in control. *Always.* She could stop anytime; she just didn't feel like it. And she never drank on call. Ever. That was a line she would *NEVER* cross.

Until that Sunday night, a few weeks after Darcy's call, when she'd crossed it.

Spencer.

It had been all about Spencer.

Not that it was his fault. She didn't blame him. They'd run into each other in a hallway at Turner that morning, each of them on weekend rounds. She hadn't seen him for a few weeks. They exchanged awkward hellos; and then Spencer had just looked at her. Just for a moment. He hadn't said anything. He hadn't needed to. Had just gazed at her—

(*Like a sad puppy I'd kicked.*)

—with those big blue eyes, and walked on past. In her mind, as she went about her day, his eyes floated in front of her. Like that book she'd read in high school, *The Great Gatsby*, and his eyes were like that billboard near the road where the lady got hit by the car. The eyes of God, their English teacher had told them.

When she'd gotten home that night, Rita had kept seeing his eyes. She couldn't get them out of her head. So she'd poured herself a glass. Then a second. She'd been reaching for the third when the ER called: an appendix in need of emergency removal.

She'd panicked because she'd definitely had a slight buzz on. Frantic, she'd brushed her teeth hard enough to make her gums bleed, then driven, *carefully*, to the hospital, well within the speed limit, hands at ten and two on the wheel the whole way. Dismissed the chief resident who would have otherwise assisted in the OR. Loaded up on enough coffee and Red Bull to keep her jacked up for a week.

I was stone-cold sober by the time I operated on her, Rita thought. *Insisted* to herself. It had been a rare complication that had killed her. *Even if I hadn't been*

drinking earlier, it wouldn't have made a difference.
Jenny Finney would still have died.

And that was that.

Was it, though?

It had been one tough case. One of the worst Rita
had ever seen, the woman's abdomen a mess: appendix ruptured, pus everywhere. Rita had to all but chisel
the appendix out, so inflamed were it and the surrounding organs.

So had the drinks mattered? Slowed her reaction
time during the operation, if only a little? Messed with
her judgment? Dulled her perception just enough to allow her to miss the hole lurking in Jenny Finney's in-
testine? The one that would leak poison into her
abdomen for the next three days, before Rita diagnosed
it, and rushed her back to the operating room?

By then it had been too late. After the second operation (the *take-back*, in surgeon-speak), Jenny Finney
had lasted another week, the longest of Rita's life, dying in the ICU, her life ebbing with each failed organ,
and with each additional plastic tube inserted into her
body by the ICU doctors.

An unusual complication. But not unheard of. And,
as an expert panel of Rita's surgical colleagues had de-
termined, an unavoidable one. Had Chase had a hand
in that? Rigged the composition of the committee, perhaps, and its exhaustive report? Maybe. If so, he'd
never let on. In any case, they'd exonerated her completely. Jenny Finney's death, in their official opinion,
had been the worst kind of luck. Or, in the dry verbiage
of the report: *an unforeseen, catastrophic complication occurring within the standard of care.*

And yet.

How many sleepless nights since? How many hours spent marking the headlights of passing cars that tracked across the ceiling of her darkened bedroom? Wondering what she could have done, *should* have done, differently. The woman had haunted her for the last year, her own personal ghost.

Rita hadn't touched a drop of alcohol since.

She considered telling Finney (or, rather, the twin version of herself sitting in the chair talking in Finney's voice) all of this.

Instead, she said, "I wanted to come to her funeral. You wouldn't let me."

In her left ear, a new edge crept into Finney's voice. "Your presence there would have made a mockery of it. You were DRINKING, Dr. Wu."

Rita winced. "I tried. I tried so hard to save her—"

"LIAR!" Finney screamed.

The word was pain. It lanced through the substance of her brain.

And again: "LIAR!"

Agony.

There was nothing else.

Rita clutched her head, rolled over, shrieking, and fell off of the edge of the bed.

Again into darkness.

SEBASTIAN

"Liar!" Finny screamed a second time.

Jesus! He's going to kill her!

"Mr. Finney," Sebastian said. "*Stop*."

"What?"

"Stop. *Now*. You need to get out of her brain for a while, boss. She can't take much more of this. You're going to kill her." The display on his phone, and the sounds over the audio feed—crashing noises, and people rushing into the room—indicated she was seizing again.

"Sebastian." Finney regained his normal, calm self. "She was drinking. The night of Jenny's death."

"I know, boss. We've talked about this. But you need to stop. She's going to die."

"What does it matter? She's as good as dead already."

"What?"

Silence.

"What do you mean she's *as good as dead*? We're done. It's over. I'm due my back end, Mr. Finney. I'm ready for my payment."

Sebastian didn't like how much time elapsed before Finney responded. "You and I need to talk, Sebastian."

Something, then, caught Sebastian's eye.

A new icon had appeared on his phone, displaying a signal from the device inside Wu's *sister's* head. The one he'd implanted shortly after implanting Wu's. The device they'd meant to use only as a backup—leverage against Wu in the event Wu's device malfunctioned.

The new icon was a timer, running backward.

A countdown.

What did you do, boss? What the fuck is counting down inside that girl's head?

Sebastian sucked his teeth. He didn't like this development. Not one goddamn bit. Finney was up to something, and Sebastian needed his goddamn money.

Sammy and Sierra's money.

"Okay. Let's talk. But face-to-face, boss." *In a public place, you cagey bastard. Where everyone can see us.*

"Fine. Where shall I meet you?"

"Higdon Park." Without waiting for Finney's response, he flicked off his audio and thought things over. He'd hear what Finney had to say. Feel the bastard out. Play along, for now at least.

And, if necessary, buy some time to set a backup plan in motion.

FINNEY

Nestled between Turner to the east, low-lying office buildings to the north and south, and the ocean to the west, Higdon Park was a small patch of green extending from the chain-link fence enclosing the construction zone to the edge of the tall cliffs over Black's Beach.

That's where, as agreed, Finney found Sebastian.

He walked toward him, across the grass. The grass was the rough-hewn variety common to municipal parks throughout San Diego, its resilience to dry heat attractive to small communities with limited park-maintenance budgets. Most San Diegans chose to forget, or at least overlook, that they lived in a desert that happened to sit next to an ocean.

Finney thought this type of grass comfortable
enough, but scratchy, if you walked over it in bare feet,
or stretched out on your back on it. But it smelled good,
particularly after being mowed, and its smell evoked
fond memories of long-ago afternoons spent in solitude, in Southern California parks like this one. His
hours alone back then were oases, times when he could
hide from the other kids and the shrill drumbeat of
their shouting and screaming and shoving so that he
could bury himself in his comic books.

The buildings along the north and south sides
housed a few small biotech companies and university
laboratories. Finney (or, rather, one of his companies
run through a third party) owned one of these buildings, in which sat the windowless room from which
he'd directed this morning's activities.

The clear blue sky was breaking into grey, intermittent clouds that blotted out the sun in bursts of shadow.
But the temperature was still balmy. A few clusters of
people were at cement picnic tables, enjoying the erratic sunshine, eating lunch, or just chatting. Two were
throwing a Frisbee on the grass.

Sebastian was sitting on top of one of the tables,
gazing out over the Pacific. The table was otherwise
empty. It was the one farthest away from the others and
the one closest to the ocean. Sebastian had his feet up
on one of the benches, his hands in his pockets.

Finney approached him from behind.

"Mr. Finney," Sebastian said, when he was about
five feet away. He didn't take his eyes off the ocean.

The two of them, Finney noted, were a nondescript
pair. Sebastian had changed into a torn, untucked

T-shirt (LIFE IS GOOD the back of it proclaimed in cheerful lettering over a surfing stick figure), jeans, flip-flops, a baseball cap, and sunglasses. At least half a dozen other men strolling around the park, or between the adjacent low-lying buildings, were in similar gear—typical for any public area in San Diego all times of year. Finney, in khakis, a collared shirt with a nondescript striped pattern, and casual black loafers, could have passed for any of the cubicle dwellers or lab personnel from the surrounding buildings.

In one fluid motion, Sebastian hopped off the table and began to amble across the grass, toward the cliffs and the ocean. He didn't wait for Finney to follow.

Finney struck out after him. "So. What do you think, Sebastian?"

"About what, boss?"

Finney pulled abreast. "The auto-surgeon. It performed exactly as I'd planned."

"Yes." The hems of Sebastian's T-shirt flapped in the stiff breeze. The wind had picked up in the last few hours. "It did."

"Beautiful. Wasn't it? Today was the first step in replacing flawed human surgeons, like Dr. Wu, with automated surgical systems. Systems immune to poor human judgment."

Sebastian didn't respond.

Where is he going?

They reached the edge of the grass, crossed a sidewalk, and walked over several feet of dry, packed dirt to a waist-high metal railing. A bright yellow sign affixed to the railing in red lettering warned:

DANGER!
UNSTABLE CLIFFS
STAY BACK!

A weathered placard next to the sign provided pictures and text about the California grey whale, which Finney knew sharp eyes could sometimes spot several miles offshore from vantage points such as this during the whale's winter migration from Alaska to Mexico. Beyond the railing were several more feet of hard dirt, followed by cliff edge and empty space. Finney could now hear the roar of powerful waves smashing against the base of the cliffs, hundreds of feet below.

Finney knew these cliffs thrust some four hundred feet skyward from the eastern edge of the beach below in sheer, crumbling towers of unsteady sandstone. In some places, as here, the Pacific licked the base of the cliffs with regularity at high tide; in others, there were wider expanses of beach that offered up safe, dry spots of sand for beachgoers who wished to remain high and dry.

"Big waves," Sebastian remarked. "That storm off the coast is moving in faster than they thought. Supposed to be a big one. Heaviest rainfall in years, they're saying. Supposed to set all kinds of records with the storm surge. Flood and mudslide warnings. El Nino. Extreme weather. Global warming."

Finney watched as Sebastian ducked under the railing and stepped to the edge of the cliff. He peeked over the side, then squatted with the grace of a cat dropping to its haunches, inspecting the ground a foot away from the cliff's edge, probing in the dirt with his fingers.

Finney glanced around, but nobody in the park seemed to notice. "Do you mind if I ask what you're doing out there?"

Sebastian stood up and brushed the dirt off his jeans. He had an odd smile on his face.

"Keeping my options open," he said. He reached his right hand up and touched the middle of his chest, as if he was clutching at something underneath his shirt. He did that often, at least several times a day, ever since Finney had first met him. It was an inexplicable habit. "Apparently, just like you, Mr. Finney."

He came back toward Finney, moving with deliberation, measuring out each of his steps, as if counting paces. He ducked back under the railing.

"What's that supposed to mean?"

Sebastian placed his elbows on the railing and stared out over the ocean, toward the dark clouds gathering on the horizon. "The countdown. In Wu's sister's head. That's how long she's got left to live, isn't it?"

"Yes."

"What's it counting down to?"

"A conformational change in the nanoparticles. The batteries will release their remaining stored charge all at once, causing them to scatter at high velocity."

Sebastian's expression didn't change. "A bomb."

"Of sorts. Yes. Of sufficient power to induce a cerebral hemorrhage. She'll be dead in minutes."

Sebastian grunted. "Painful, I would imagine. Those particles. Like shrapnel."

"Yes." *Excruciating. I'm counting on it.* "An autopsy, should it be performed, would later suggest a

spontaneously ruptured blood vessel, consistent with
a congenital malformation."

Sebastian nodded. "A natural cause to explain everything. I assume Wu's device is similarly rigged? If you
opted to . . . activate it?"

"It is."

"In Wu's case, it'd also explain the bizarre behavior leading up to her death. Cover our tracks."

"Yes."

"And if Wu were to have an MRI in the ER before
it went off—"

"—it can be altered."

"Why a countdown? Why not just detonate it now?"

"I'm not ready to. The countdown is a fail-safe. In
case something happens, to either of us, the bomb will
still go off early tomorrow morning."

"But *why*? Why the bomb?"

Finney said nothing. He watched as Sebastian took
two steps back away from the railing, in front of the
whale sign, and kicked at the dirt. He turned and stared
at a tree, a lone, gnarled Torrey pine, about thirty feet
away, and then kicked the spot in the dirt again.

"Okay. Then, why not tell me, boss? Why keep me
in the dark?"

Finney had suspected Sebastian was going to be
peeved about this. He didn't understand why, though.
Wasn't Sebastian always talking about careful planning? About not limiting options? About having alter-
natives? Finney's plan adhered to those principles. This
man—an *employee*—was questioning his methods.

"I didn't think you needed to know."

"Well, that's where I would disagree with you, boss. That kind of information is helpful to me."

"Well," Finney said. "Perhaps we can agree to disagree on that point, then." Sebastian had bent over and was pushing at the dirt. "What are you *doing*?"

"Options." He stood up and, for the first time since Finney had joined him in the park, met his eye. "Look. I didn't sign up for this, boss. We had an arrangement. All of these months, we've been working toward two specific goals: destroy Wu professionally and ensure the success of the auto-surgeon. We've accomplished both." He gazed at the Torrey pine. "The plan I agreed to didn't involve killing the sister. I did what you asked: implanted the nanoparticles in Wu and her sister and pumped Wu full of extra drugs and booze. Left her naked on the OR table. You've achieved your objective: disgraced Wu and boosted the profile of the auto-surgeon. Why kill the sister? The nanoparticles are untraceable, and if Wu ever tries to tell her story, no one will believe her. I mean . . . damn, boss. She'll never practice medicine again. She'll probably be facing criminal charges. Maybe even jail time."

"Are you losing sight of our purpose, Sebastian?"

"No. Are you?"

Finney sighed. The man was not without his skills, but he could be so damn *exasperating* sometimes.

I don't need to explain myself to you, Sebastian an impulsive, undisciplined part of him wanted to say.

Oh, but on the contrary, his rational side replied. He very much did. Sebastian was judging him. Judging his actions. Judging his decisions. Finney couldn't have that, couldn't abide it. Sebastian very much needed to know why Finney had pursued this particular course of action.

"Have you heard of the Code of Hammurabi?" Finney asked.

"Sure. King Hammurabi of Babylon. An ancient set of laws, inscribed in a language called cuneiform on a large stone pillar about 2,000 B.C."

"Yes." Even after working with the man for almost a year, Sebastian still managed to surprise him, now and again. How could a man in Sebastian's . . . well, *unsavory* line of work demonstrate such familiarity with topics as esoteric as ancient Middle Eastern history and culture?

"Oldest written law on record," Sebastian said.

"Technically, no—not the oldest." Finney took some measure of satisfaction in one-upping Sebastian on this point. "There are reports of at least two others, both from ancient Sumer, with a similar content of laws that predate Hammurabi's by at least two centuries."

Finney turned to the horizon, on which black clouds were tumbling angrily. "Nevertheless. Remarkable achievement, Hammurabi's Code. I've seen the original surviving record, carved into a diorite stele—or, as you say, stone pillar—on display in the Louvre. I traveled to Paris just to see it." *Right after Jenny's burial. I had to see it. I had to see the Code with my own eyes. To burn it like a brand into my brain.* "Over seven feet tall. Remarkable."

Sebastian folded his arms and waited.

"Steles with the code were, it's believed, placed on prominent display in Mesopotamian cities so that their citizens would be familiar with the laws. Laws covering every aspect of human civilization and behavior. Murder. Marriage. Trade. Sex. They're all there." He turned away from the horizon and fixed Sebastian with a cold stare. "Including the penalties for breaking them. For meting out punishments for transgressions, Hammurabi's Code was built on the basic principle of *lex talionis*. Do you know what that is?"

"Law of retribution. Eye for an eye, tooth for a tooth. That sort of thing."

Finney's eyes narrowed. *The man could be simply exasperating.* "Yes. Rather grim, some of the punishments in Hammurabi's Code. Looking back, we might even say barbaric. But I would counter that they corresponded to both the nature and the severity of the crime. If a son struck his father, for example, he had his hands cut off."

Finney gripped the railing with both hands. "It's very detailed, you know. There's even a section covering what was to happen if someone caused the death of a pregnant woman. Do you know what was to happen then? In that particular case?"

"Something that involved death, I would imagine."

"Yes. Death." Finney twisted his hands back and forth on the railing, like he was gunning the accelerator of a motorcycle.

"Boss. We don't live by Hammurabi's Code."

"Don't we, though? Don't we exist in a criminal-justice system whereby we exact punishments in proportion to the crime? What about the death penalty? Isn't that a form of *lex talionis*? Eye for an eye? She killed my wife and unborn child, Sebastian."

"Not intentionally."

"No. Not intentionally. But through her negligence. Criminal negligence, since she'd been drinking that night. The system allowed her to walk away from it. But Jenny did not walk away from it." He felt the veins along the back of his hands pop into sharp relief as he clutched the railing. "I'm a man of my conviction, Sebastian. And I abide by the spirit of Hammurabi's Code."

Finney now made a decision. He let go of the railing and pulled his leather notebook from his pocket. .

Sebastian looked at it curiously. "What's that?"

Finney had never before shown his notebook to anyone. Not even Jenny. Had never told her of its existence; had sealed it in his safe-deposit box, shortly after their engagement.

For good, he'd thought at the time. He'd almost destroyed it, in fact: went so far as to turn on the propane-fueled fireplace in his living room one morning for that very purpose. Twice that morning he'd thrust the book over the flames, his hand trembling; and twice he'd changed his mind. In the end, he'd decided to keep it as a reminder of his past life. Of his past self. Of what he had been before Jenny.

Now it was a reminder of what he'd become since her death.

He opened it to the first page, yellowed with time, which was filled with legible, but immature, handwriting. Not the script of an adult but of an older child. At the top of the page was written a date from thirty years ago. Underneath it was a large, hand-sketched box with a big black *X* drawn through its center, beside which was written a single name: *Tucker Steele*. Below the box and name were smaller, denser sentences that resembled a cooking recipe or assembly instructions for a home appliance.

"What's this?" Sebastian asked, staring at the name, and the crossed box sitting next to it.

"Tucker Steele was a boy in my eighth-grade class. Immensely popular. Good-looking. Athletic. You're familiar with the type, I'm sure. I was, needless to say, none of those things."

Finney touched Tucker's name with his finger. "Tucker enjoyed tormenting boys like me. He and his popular friends. Adolescents can be unimaginably cruel, and the school administrators could not have cared less. This was a long time ago, Sebastian, when prevention of bullying among schoolchildren was not all the rage, as it is now."

He ran his finger along the lettering of Tucker's name, beginning with the *e* at the end of *Steele*, from right to left, toward the *X*.

"We had cheap, plastic-backed desk chairs in our classrooms. Uncomfortable. The plastic backs were thin, and it was easy to stick sharp objects, like tacks, all the way through them. The sharpened point would stick up from the back of the chair, waiting for an unwary occupant to lean back into it."

Finney's finger reached the *X*. "I sat in front of Tucker in English. Assigned seating. I was in the front row. The entire class could see me. I was late to class that day. Rushed. Distracted. Tucker must have primed the rest of the class, let them in on the joke, before I got there."

Finney's finger lingered over the *X*. "When I sat down, I didn't simply lean back in the chair and onto the tack. No. I was in a hurry, and I was distracted, so I *slid* into the chair, with my back flush against the plastic."

He tapped his finger on the *X*, as if keeping time with a beat. "The tack caught on the bottom of my shirt and the skin of my back, ripping both open. It gouged a big gash all the way up, in both my shirt and my skin, from the small of my back to just below my shoulder. Tucker and his friends—the whole class—thought it was hilarious. Erupted into laughter. The teacher yelled at me for the disruption and, when it became apparent I was bleeding all over myself and the chair, scolded me for my carelessness and ordered me to the nurse's office."

He glanced at Sebastian. "It was, for me, a crowning indignation in a series of them at the hands of Tucker and his friends. We'd just read about Hammurabi's Code in history. The principle seemed apropos. I considered its practical applications, and I formulated an appropriate response to Tucker based on *lex talionis*. It wasn't challenging." He shrugged. "There was a dog. I poisoned it."

It took a moment for this to sink in with Sebastian. "You *poisoned his dog*? When you were in *eighth grade*?"

"No. Not Tucker's dog. His friend's dog. One of his friends who'd laughed at me in English. Another popular boy named Ryan. The specifics aren't important. It was rat poison, and I made it look like Tucker had poisoned Ryan's dog as some kind of practical joke in response to a slight from Ryan. And quietly—very quietly—I made sure the entire school knew it. No one suspected my involvement, or doubted Tucker was responsible. That's how well I set things in motion, Sebastian."

Finney smiled faintly at the memory. "It was a big deal. Animal cruelty—things like that simply didn't happen in our school, or our community. Ever. Bullying, yes. Animal cruelty, no. It was a scandal."

"So you set this boy up."

"Yes."

"Did the dog die?"

"Yes." Finney shrugged. "Not my intent. The dose was higher than I'd anticipated. What does the military call it? *Collateral damage?* At any rate, Tucker's popularity, the one thing in the world that mattered most to him, was destroyed. *Dog poisoner.* Can you imagine? He became an outcast. He tried to tell people it wasn't him, that he would never poison a dog. Cried, and begged. Nobody believed him. Not Ryan, or Ryan's parents, or the administration of our school. Tucker and his entire family were humiliated."

Finney pushed his finger hard against the *X*, as if trying to push it all the way through the paper, then drew it away. "One day, Tucker didn't show up for school, and the news spread that he'd been expelled. That was the day I put an X through the box next to his name."

"Did Tucker ever find out it was you?"

Finney shook his head. "No. I wanted him to. Badly. I wanted to take satisfaction in having him know it had been me. You can't imagine how tempted I was to mail him a package (anonymously, of course) with a tack, and my ripped shirt, and some rat poison. But I wasn't stupid. I knew it could be traced. So I had to take my satisfaction in the outcome. Which, believe me, Sebastian, I did."

He turned a page. "I did." He flipped carefully through the remaining pages of the book, which were filled with many more names, and many more boxes. All of the boxes had been marked with an *X*.

Except for the last one.

"Others followed, over the years. I would write out a name, and draw a box, and sketch out a plan for implementing *lex talionis*."

"Lots of names," Sebastian observed quietly.

"Yes. Well." Finney snapped the book closed and returned it to his pocket. "One makes enemies when running a successful business. I've made my fair share."

The wind coming in off the ocean seemed to grow stronger.

Finney pursed his lips. There was one final phase of his plan to kill Dr. Wu and the sister for which he needed Sebastian's help. Now was the time to broach it. He would need to choose his words carefully so that Sebastian would agree to it. He sensed the man was beginning to question his methods.

"Sebastian. There's something else I require of you before all of this is done. Something I've never mentioned before, and for which I'm prepared to compensate you. Handsomely."

Sebastian's face was impenetrable. "Go on."

Finney explained what he needed from Sebastian. When Finney was done, Sebastian said, so softly that

Finney could barely hear him over the wind, "I didn't sign up for that, either, boss."

"I have plans for her, Sebastian. She needs to atone for what she did to Jenny. I just need you to get her in position."

"But what about *after* she's in position? What are you going to do to her then? How are you going to explain how she ended up there in the first place?"

"You don't have to worry about that. You can leave. Never look back. I'll wire the remaining money to your account, on the spot. Ten times what we originally agreed upon, Sebastian. *Ten times*. Think of it. You'll never have to work again. You can confirm the account transfer, using whatever independent method you've arranged, then leave us. Leave, and never look back."

"What if I refuse?"

"Then I pay you the agreed-upon amount now, the original amount, and we part ways. I'm a man of my word, Sebastian."

Sebastian stared at him, the wind whipping at his T-shirt.

"Twenty. Twenty times the original amount."

"Twenty? No. Absolutely not. Out of the question."

"Twenty. Or I walk. With the original amount. Right now."

Finney considered it. He needed the man for the final part of his plan. And he knew that Sebastian was capable of unpleasant things should he walk away now with the perception he'd gotten a raw deal. Finney didn't need that kind of aggravation.

Besides, in the end, Finney would see to it that Sebastian got nothing.

And Sebastian would never see it coming.

"Fifteen." He had to make it appear as if he was haggling. Cave in too quickly, and Sebastian would grow suspicious.

"Eighteen."

"Done."

"Half now."

"No. Nothing until everything is in place."

Finney watched as Sebastian turned and studied the dark clouds on the horizon. He hadn't revealed this part of his plan to Sebastian until now because he hadn't been certain they'd ever get this far. Confident, but not certain.

He'd also sensed—rightly, it seemed—that Sebastian would have qualms. Sebastian possessed an inexplicable sentimental streak. Witness his reluctance to boost the power to Wu's implant, and his incomprehensible concern for her life. It was an unexpected weakness in a man of Sebastian's qualifications. Finney had thus far chosen to overlook this but wondered now if Sebastian would in the end balk at his offer.

Which would be disappointing but not disastrous: Finney would pay him his fee, and Sebastian would go on his way; and Finney would set off the devices (*bombs*, Sebastian had called them—an apt enough description), and then place an *X* through that final, empty box.

And harmony would be restored to the universe.

Albeit a harmony he would find less satisfactory.

Sebastian seemed to sense Finney's willingness to walk away from the deal. "Okay, boss," he finally said. "Just this last thing. For 18 million. Paid in full, immediately on completion of the task." Sebastian's hands remained at his sides. He knew how Finney felt about handshakes.

"And you're confident you can accomplish this?"

"Yes."

"Are you sure?"

"She's not going anywhere. I checked: They're keeping her in the hospital for the time being. Overnight at a minimum." He stole a glance at his watch. "Just give me a few more hours of prep time before I drive you home. Okay?"

Reasonable enough. Besides, Finney liked the solitude of the windowless room in his building. A few more hours there, alone, sounded appealing. "Yes."

As Sebastian walked away, back to Turner, Finney gripped the railing and watched the gathering storm. By the look of things, the weather reports were right: It was shaping up to be a big one.

No. Dr. Wu certainly wasn't going anywhere.

Nor would she, ever.

One way or another, she would never leave Turner alive.

SPENCER

Spencer and Raj were at one of the cement picnic tables in Higdon Park, a take-out lunch from a sushi place located in one of the adjacent office buildings spread out on the table in front of them. Raj's opinion was that, for sushi, hole-in-the-wall was the only way to go. Raj's favorite place in San Diego was the size of a broom closet, located in a random strip mall next door to a 7-Eleven. But Raj thought this place was pretty good, too, and Spencer agreed.

Raj's shoulder-length hair was wet. His wet suit, draped over the bench next to him, was drying in the fitful afternoon sun. His generous belly spilled through the gap of his unbuttoned Aloha shirt and over the waist of his swimming trunks. His surfboard lay in the grass nearby, upside down, its three triangular fins aimed toward the sky.

Spencer, still in scrubs, sat in front of his untouched lunch. At first, Raj dug into his with his usual enthusiasm, but slowed as Spencer brought him up to speed on the morning's events, starting with what Wendy had told him. The further Spencer got into his story, the slower Raj ate.

Raj put his chopsticks down when Spencer reached the part about Rita's sticking the scalpel into the liver.

"Fuck *me*," he observed.

"You've got that right," Spencer replied, then went on to describe Rita's seizure, and the robot's mind-boggling repair of the liver laceration; and about his helping the code team stabilize Rita and transport her to the ER, and making sure she was stable before he came to Higdon to meet up with Raj.

What he didn't say was that he'd rather have stayed over in the ER at Rita's bedside. But he'd had no business being there, as far as anyone else knew.

Once he'd finished, Raj said, "Holy shit, Spencer. Holy *shit*. That's . . . wow. Wow, man." He shook his head.

"I know. Right? I mean—have you ever heard of anything like it?"

"No. No way." Raj shook his head emphatically. His wet hair whipped around his neck in thick cords. "Not even close. It's . . . surreal, man. So . . . what do you think?"

"I don't know."

"Psychotic break, maybe?"

"I don't know. Maybe. But she seemed pretty lucid in the OR. Right up until the—you know . . . scalpel thing."

"Psychotics can seem perfectly lucid when they want to."

"Yeah. I know."

"Had she woken up yet? When you were still in the ER?"

"Kind of, but not really. Her vitals were stable. She opened her eyes about ten minutes after we transported her down there. She started talking, but not making any sense."

"Psychosis. Definitely."

"No. I don't think so." He frowned. Raj, he thought, was a little too eager to write her off as deranged. "Classic postictal state. I've examined lots of patients after they've seized, and her behavior was typical. She didn't recognize me or anyone else. She kept mentioning Delores—that's the name of the surgical robot—and someone named Jenny. While they were stabilizing her, and cleaning her up, she kept telling Jenny that she was sorry. I checked: Jenny was not the name of the patient she was operating on." *I wish I knew who Jenny was and what Rita was so sorry about.* "In any case, she won't remember any of it once she's fully awake. Patients rarely remember anything after a major seizure."

"So what now?"

"Well, nothing else scheduled for me today, so I thought I'd go back over and check on her once we're done with lunch." By then, Spencer figured, the ER guys will have gotten a head CT, or maybe an MRI.

I hope she doesn't have a tumor. Please, God, don't let her have a brain tumor.

But a brain tumor would explain a lot.

Raj picked up a California roll, considered it, then dropped it. "Do you—still have a thing for her?"

Spencer reached back to scratch his head and felt the nub of the EEG electrode behind his right ear. He'd forgotten it was there. He slid the button back into the ON position as he watched two guys standing near the safety railing overlooking the ocean. One had medium-length dark hair and was wearing jeans, a T-shirt, sunglasses, and a baseball cap. A little on the short side. He looked Hispanic. No, Asian. Both? He couldn't tell at this distance. The other, tall and lanky with sandy hair, had on a striped dress shirt with comfortable-looking khakis, like a pair you'd buy at the Gap. They were chatting, the one in the khakis showing the dark-haired one a little book.

A perfectly ordinary scene: just two friends hanging out in the park. Why couldn't his life be more like theirs? More, you know . . . normal?

"Shit," Raj breathed. "Does anyone else know? Anyone else burdened with the details of your weird love life?"

"No. We kept it secret. You know that. That's the way she wanted it. She was afraid that—she said that she didn't want people talking, passing judgment on her. She didn't want people to think she was sleeping around to advance her career."

"God. And you're otherwise so *vanilla,* man. So normal." Spencer couldn't help but scowl at him. "Really. I mean it. I'm serious. It's been, what: a year? More than that? She told you things were over between you two. Why can't you just move on?"

"I don't know."

Raj sighed. "It's just weird, man. You haven't been stalking her again, or anything, have you?"

Spencer didn't answer.

"*Have* you?"

He dropped his eyes.

"Oh, shit. You are."

"It's not stalking, Raj."

Raj leaned toward him over the table. "The *hell* it isn't. Shit, I mean, *listen* to you, man. You should hear yourself. Are you still running by her house?" Raj peered at Spencer's face. "Oh my God. You are. That is *so* disturbing."

"No, it's not."

"Yes, it is."

"We live in the same neighborhood. My . . . route just happens to take me along her street. That's all."

"You're stalking your ex-girlfriend, and now she's had a psychotic break." He picked up the California roll again and bit into it. "That's a pretty fucking disturbing coincidence, Spencer." Rice flecks flew out of his mouth.

Spencer balled his fists. "I'm not stalking her. It's—
you— You wouldn't understand."

"You're right. I wouldn't. I don't. Because it's *weird*,
Spencer. Normal people don't do this kind of thing."

Spencer rarely got angry. But his nerves were frayed
by what he'd seen that morning, and his temper flared.
He struggled to keep it under control. "You never liked
her, did you?" he growled.

Raj defiantly chewed on the roll. "No. I didn't."

"Why?"

"Because she never treated you right, man. She's a
cold-hearted *bitch* who didn't deserve you. Keep things
between you a secret?" He guffawed. "I mean, really—
that sucks. It's like she was *embarrassed* about you,
man. She knifed you in the gut. Practically ripped your
heart out and held it up to your fucking face."

Over the years, his parents had often remarked to
Spencer that, the angrier he got, the softer he had a
tendency to speak. Raj had to bend way, *way* over the
table to hear him when he said: "What do you know?
Who the hell do you think you are?"

Raj finished the remains of the roll and said, "Your
friend, man."

"My friend." Spencer nodded. "My friend."

He stood up and pushed his uneaten lunch toward
Raj.

"Here," he said coldly. "Just keep shoveling food in
your face, my fat *friend*."

"Where are you going?"

"What the hell do you care?"

Spencer stalked away.

"Spence," Raj called after him.

Spencer didn't turn around.

"Come on, Spence. Hey. I'm *sorry*, man. Come back."

He pointed himself toward the OR to check on his patient, who'd be awake in recovery by now, and to change out of his scrubs.

His next stop after that would be the ER.

SEBASTIAN

Sebastian was suspicious.

He was sitting in his car in a quiet section of the Turner parking garage, thinking.

I'm a man of my word, Finney had told him.

With a straight goddamn face!

The hell he was. Sebastian sensed something was up. No way that what he had in store for Wu—what he wanted Sebastian to do to her—was the whole story. *Plans within plans.* Finney was a cold, calculating son of a bitch, and there was little doubt now in Sebastian's mind that Finney was playing him. Or at least trying to.

But that was okay, because the gears in Sebastian's brain were spinning. Planning options. Hedging against nasty surprises. Calculating endgames. Bastards far craftier than Finney had tried to play Sebastian before. And regretted it.

Sebastian wanted his money. He needed his money. *Sammy and Sierra's money.* And he'd be goddamned if he didn't get it. Sure: He'd considered taking the million and just walking, right there, in the park. *Maybe*

I should have. That would have been the smart thing. The safe thing. Money enough for the co-pays, and the damn parochial school; money enough to find a decent place for the kids in the suburbs.

The problem was: It wouldn't last. A million didn't go far these days. Even if he made it stretch, within a few years he'd be right back where he'd started: scratching out a living doing this shit.

And then there was Sammy.

They never say cure, *Brother.*

Why is that, do you think?

He clutched Alfonso's dog tag through his shirt. How many more goddamn co-pays in Sammy's future? Maybe none. Hopefully none. But if there were, he and his sister would need deep pockets. Sammy deserved the chances the kid who'd killed Alfonso had never had.

Eighteen goddamn *million* dollars.

Now *that* was decent money. He'd be set up for life. They'd *all* be set up. It would once and for all get him out of this shitty line of work. Chump change to Finney, a billionaire a few times over. The bastard probably netted that much in interest in the time it took him to take his morning piss. Sebastian would be a fool to turn it down. So he'd rolled the dice, taken a calculated risk. He'd play Finney's game. For now, anyway. The trick was making sure he'd get paid, in the end. For that, he needed some insurance.

Sebastian was a problem solver. Methodical. Professional. Good at improvising solutions on the fly, trained to expect the unexpected. Finney had altered the rules on him. *No big deal.* A proper response would simply require fresh preparations, and he'd bought himself some time by telling Finney he needed a few more hours to finish Finney's stuff, which he didn't really: Finney's plans, as disturbing to Sebastian as they were, were straightforward.

He had a good idea of what he needed to do next.

He'd studied the tapes.

(*The teenager in her cell.*)

He'd studied the device.

(*The teenager curled up in her cell don't think about her.*)

And though he couldn't grasp all of the theory underlying it, he knew the device as well as anyone, including its inventors, and Finney. He just needed a little help to figure something out.

He muted his line to Finney, picked up his phone, and made an encrypted call. Three rings, then an electronically altered voice answered: "Blade."

"Blade. It's Scepter." His own voice, he knew, would likewise be unrecognizable on the other end, transformed by the electronic filter.

"Scepter." The electronic distortion could not hide the surprise of the person at the other end. He wondered, as always, if Blade was a woman or a man. The distortion made it impossible to tell. "Been a while."

"Yes." Six months, in fact, since he'd last hired Blade, when Blade had helped him hack into Turner's electronic medical record and security systems.

"What've you been up to, Scepter?"

"This and that."

"What can I do for you?"

"I need some help getting around a firewall. It's a rather . . . unique . . . system." He explained.

"Sure. By when?"

"By 8:00 A.M. GMT." Midnight tonight California time.

Blade chuckled. The electronic filter made Blade sound ominous, like a horror movie villain. "For you, my friend, I'll clear my calendar. But it'll cost you."

"It always does."

Blade named the price. Sebastian winced: Between his sister, and Blade, before the end of the day, his slimming bank account was going to be a whole lot slimmer: like, zero. Except for the cash he was carrying, he'd be out of money, and in dire need of the 18 million. *This had better goddamn work.* "Okay. Ten percent down. The other ninety on receipt of the algorithm."

"Twenty. Twenty down."

"Fifteen."

"No. Twenty."

Sebastian sighed and briefly considered taking his hacking business elsewhere. But Blade was the best and always available on short notice. "Fine. Twenty, then."

"You know what I'll need."

He did. Sebastian transmitted the data, including electronic payment, to the IP address Blade provided, routing it first through five separate overseas servers, to be safe—although, given Blade's formidable skills, he had to assume Blade had already traced him. Couldn't be helped: The risk came with the territory.

Blade confirmed receipt of the data and hung up.

Sebastian tossed the phone onto the front passenger seat and leaned back, listening to the audio feed from Wu's device.

She was sleeping, as best he could tell. He heard her steady breathing and the background hum of the Turner ER. Nothing much had happened since her last seizure: a few more blood tests; a brain MRI; her glasses with the camera confiscated and in storage, so they were useless.

There was a rustling.

He sat up straighter.

Something was going on.

SPENCER

Back now in his street clothes, Spencer was studying the large digital screen mounted over the ER nurses' station, searching for Rita's name. Roughly the size of a twin bed, the screen displayed all of the ER patients—their last names, working diagnoses, and beds in which they resided—and appeared like the departures and arrivals board in an airport.

One hand was behind his right ear, touching the EEG electrode; the other was in his pocket, idly fingering the extra electrode Raj had given him—the one he'd grabbed from his bag during his morning drive to work. The one that Raj wanted him to test on someone else.

He knew now who that was going to be.

There. Room 5. They'd moved her since he'd helped the code team bring her to the ER.

"Spencer! Hey, man." Spencer turned to the man in

white coat and scrubs who'd appeared at his side: Brian Ford, one of the head ER docs.

"Oh, hey, Brian. What's up, man?"

Brian was black, with two hypnotizing rows of the straightest, whitest teeth Spencer had ever seen. He liked Brian; but, as always when around him, Spencer experienced a twinge of envy as the two bumped fists. Brian was one of those guys who projected effortless, intelligent *manliness*. A man's man. Women loved him; men wanted to be more like him. He was tall and lean, but strong. He and Spencer played in a rugby league, and routinely bought each other beers at their favorite brew pub after games.

"Thanks for coming down. Jeez, that was fast."

Huh?

"What do you mean, 'fast'?" Spencer said. "Were you expecting me, or something?"

"I just paged you guys for a consult. Aren't you here about Rita Wu?"

With great effort, Spencer kept his face straight and his voice even, as he replied that no, he wasn't, but how could he help?

"Do you know her? Dr. Wu?"

"Dr. Wu? Yeah. I know her. I mean, you know, not too well. I've seen her around. I happened to be in the OR today when she had a grand mal, so I helped the code team bring her down here. Scary stuff. She seemed okay after we got her down here, though."

"Yeah, well, she had another grand mal after she got here. One of the nurses heard her talking and yelling, then found her on the floor next to her gurney, seizing in a typical tonic-clonic pattern."

Spencer folded his arms and did his best imitation of professional (*not personal, definitely not personal*) concern. "Huh. How is she now? Is she awake? Is she . . . okay?"

"Yeah. Fine, actually. A little postictal, but otherwise okay. Resting comfortably. Vitals are stable. Alert and oriented times three. Dehydrated and a little acidotic, but her electrolytes otherwise look good. EKG was within normal limits. I hung some normal saline and was able to fast track her for a head MRI. We're still waiting on the results. No hard indications for antiepileptics, so I'm not loading her up with Dilantin yet. We're going to admit her for observation and a workup. I've called Neurology, but they're crazy busy, and haven't been able to make it down here yet to see her."

"Why'd you call us?"

"Because I was worried she'd taken some head trauma when she fell off the gurney. I think she's fine, but you know how it is." He rolled his eyes. "Liability crap. Even with a fellow doctor."

"I hear you, man. Did you get the MRI before or after the fall from the gurney?"

"After."

"Good. Happy to have a look and leave a note in the chart."

"Thanks, man. You're a rock star. Listen. Spence." Brian looked uncomfortable. "You should know that, uh, when you look over her labs, you're going to see some, uh, well . . . sensitive stuff."

Spencer's stomach rolled over. "What do you mean?"

"The tox screen," Brian said quietly. "Well, it's . . .

it's pretty positive, man. She had some hard-core stuff on board."

(*Poker face, Spencer. Poker face.*)

"Huh. Like what?"

Brian shrugged. "Coke. Meth. Some others, any of which on its own could have conceivably kicked off her seizures."

DRUGS? RITA?

(*Poker face, remember the poker face*)

"Huh. You're sure."

"Absolutely.

Absolutely NO way.

Spencer nodded and said, with appropriate somberness and neutrality (*because he was, after all, just a colleague discussing sensitive information with another colleague in a somber and neutral way*): "Is that what you think happened?"

"She doesn't have a history of seizures, or any risk factors for them, and her workup is otherwise negative, so—pending the results of the MRI, yeah. That's at the top of my differential. Montgomery has already been down to see her. He was in there alone with her, talking. I, uh, don't know what about."

"I understand. I'll have a look."

"Thanks, Spencer. Oh, and one more thing: She keeps mentioning her left ear. Not sure why." His gaze now wandered toward a harried-looking nurse waving at him from across the room. From the doorway of one of the patient rooms, an ancient woman in a stained hospital gown, towing a wheeled IV pole, was screaming racial slurs at the nurse, who was Filipino. All over the ER, heads were turning to see what the noise was about.

Brian made a face. "Ah, I see the lovely Mrs. Thorn is back in my ER. *Delightful* woman. An absolute pleasure. She adores *me*."

Spencer appreciated Brian's sense of humor, dry as a fine wine.

"I think I'm the reason she keeps coming back." He clapped Spencer on the shoulder, flashed his gorgeous teeth, and winked. "Every day's better than the last, my friend. Damn, how I *love* this job. Let me know how things go, Spencer. And thanks again."

As Brian approached, the knobby Mrs. Thorn immediately redirected her venom and bigotry toward him, screaming insults and poking her gnarled, arthritic fingers into his chest. The grateful Filipino nurse turned her attention to more important matters.

Spencer texted his partner, the one on call for neurosurgery, telling her that he would be taking care of this particular consult.

At the entrance to room 5, Spencer's breath caught in his throat.

She was in bed, asleep, the room lights turned low.

Sure, he'd seen her around the OR, and the hospital, but only from afar. Fleeting glances, averted eyes. This was different. Now, he could just *look*. Absorb every photon of her, drink her in. God, it had been *so* long. It felt like he was seeing her again for the very first time. He felt as if he could stand there and stare, all day.

He took a small step forward, then another. She

looked pale and haggard but, to him, beautiful. He'd always thought she was beautiful. Her black hair tumbled over the pillow and draped across her slender shoulders.

Her eyes popped open, and she gasped, as if she'd awakened from a bad dream. Her eyes darted around before fixing on him.

"Spencer?" She sounded like she didn't believe he was real.

He moved to the head of the bed and gave a little wave. "Hi, Rita."

She jerked her head off of the pillow and touched her left ear. She seemed to be listening for something, from that ear; then her eyes met his again, and they clouded with what looked to him like fear.

"Spencer."

She reached out and gripped his arm, then his hand. Her touch gave him palpitations.

She hadn't touched him in so long.

SEBASTIAN

It sounded as if someone was in the room with her.

She said, "Spen—"

Static.

The feed went dead.

He sucked his teeth, listening to the static, then snatched his phone from the front passenger seat and frowned at the jagged lines of interference lurching across the screen, identical to the ones he'd seen that morning in the OR.

His gut twitched. He hated being blind *and* deaf. Whatever was happening, it deserved a closer look.

"Sebastian?" Finney said.

He unmuted his audio link as he climbed out of his car. "Yep. I see it, boss. I'm on it."

Sebastian hurried toward the ER. It took him a while, longer than he liked, because he first had to change back into scrubs. He paused at the ER entrance to fish out his hospital ID badge—

(ROBERT RODRIGUEZ, PERIOPERATIVE TECHNICIAN)

—and present it to a bored security guard (*goddamn, but she's a big one*) reading a paperback novel.

"Hi there."

Sebastian looked up, his hand just emerging from his pocket with his Rodriguez name tag.

It was Grant, the *Wall Street Journal* reporter.

RITA

"Hi, Rita," Spencer said.

The plastic chair next to her bed groaned under his weight as he sat. He scooted closer and, using the control panel on the side of the bed, raised its height and elevated its head, so that her eyes were on the same level as his.

She touched her left ear.

Strange.

She felt that distinct and peculiar sense, again, of Finney's *absence.*

The same feeling she'd had earlier in OR 10.

Was he *really* gone? She thought so. If so, this time,

she *so* hoped it would last. Because if she heard him again in her mind, she thought she'd walk to the edge of the park behind Turner, the one overlooking the ocean, and jump off the cliff.

"How're you feeling, Rita?"

"I've been . . . better." Her throat tightened.

Don't cry. Crying is weak.

She felt a tear glide down her cheek.

Don't. Cry.

He reached out with one enormous, gentle hand and wiped the tear away. He smiled, in that crooked, unguarded way of his: the same smile that made him look like a little boy, despite his huge physique; the smile she'd fallen in love with. The smile she still loved, she realized. And everything that she'd been through that day now didn't matter so much. With Finney gone, and with Spencer here, she felt, well . . . *safe.*

"I'm really glad to see you, Spencer."

She reached out and took his hand. He glanced over his shoulder, toward the door, and gave one brief squeeze before letting go. She found herself wishing he hadn't let go, or looked behind him, but she understood why.

I haven't exactly invited public displays of affection.

"I'm glad to see you, too, Rita. I would have, you know, preferred slightly better circumstances."

"Yeah." She smiled weakly.

"Rita." He cast another look behind and, in a hushed, urgent tone, asked, "Rita. What's going on? What happened up there today?"

"I can't—I don't know where to begin, Spencer."

"How about at the beginning? I've got time."

He grinned again. It felt like warm sun on her face. *Why not?*

He might end up thinking she was crazy . . . but, then, it wasn't like anything worse could happen to her at this point. Besides, she felt . . . disinhibited. The drugs and alcohol, maybe? Something they'd given her here in the ER? Or—and this thought made her blood run cold—was it what Finney had done to her brain?

So she told him.

Everything.

Beginning with the OR table—

"Which ear?" Spencer interrupted.

"What?"

"Which ear was bleeding?"

"Oh. Left. The left one."

"Okay. Go on."

She did, leaving out nothing. When she had finished, she said, "Well. What do you think?"

He frowned and scratched his head. "Rita—"

"You don't believe me." She felt betrayed, like he had sucker punched her in the stomach. "You don't believe me."

"I believe you think that's what happened." He was studying his hands, each the size of a child's baseball glove.

"That's not an answer. That's a platitude, Spencer." *That's what you say to a paranoid schizophrenic when you're trying to talk her down off the ledge.* "Don't *patronize* me."

"Rita—"

"No." She folded her arms and rolled over in the bed, away from him.

He sighed and rose.

"Wait." She rolled back over and grabbed his arm. "You're leaving?" He paused. How solid and indestructible he looked. She could smell him. His Old Spice. She'd always liked Old Spice because her dad had worn it. She wanted to take refuge in his solidity, to press her face into the crook of his shoulder and bury herself in Old Spice.

"I don't think it's a good idea for me to be here right now. Maybe later—"

"Please. Spencer." She clutched his arm. "When you're around me, I can't hear him. *I can't hear him, Spencer.*" It was true. Finney was still gone.

His eyebrows drew together. "Okay. How about this." He pulled something from his pocket: a flesh-colored circle a few inches in diameter. "Let me put this on you."

"What is it?"

"A new EEG electrode Raj and I have been working on. Remember my friend Raj?"

"Raj? Yes. He never liked me."

"Yeah, well." He shrugged but didn't disagree. "It's totally portable. Wireless."

"Why? Why should I wear it?"

"Please. Just do it. Look." He showed her one stuck to the skin behind his right ear and grinned. "I've got one of my own. Functional *and* stylish."

She scowled.

"Seriously," he said. "They're going to run an EEG on you eventually anyway. Who knows? Raj and I might come up with something useful. Something that might, uh, bolster your story."

Why not? "Fine."

She let him press it to the skin behind her ear. He took care not to trap any of her hair underneath it, and explained it had reinforced adhesive backing and was very durable. She could smell his Old Spice as he leaned over her.

Using an app on his phone, he verified that her patch was activated and working. "Think of it as a good-luck charm. That's what I do, at least, when I'm wearing it." He stood there awkwardly. "Get some rest, Rita. Okay? I'll come by and see you tomorrow morning."

"Spencer."

He stopped halfway to the sliding-glass door.

She was going to ask him, again, if he believed her. But she already knew what his answer would be.

"Nothing. Never mind."

"Get some rest, Rita."

And then he was gone. He left the door open.

She shut her eyes to keep the tears from rolling down her face. But the tears didn't come because she was too tired to cry. As she drifted off to sleep, she realized that she still couldn't hear Finney.

She was too tired to be grateful.

SPENCER

Paranoia.
Delusions.
Schizophrenia.
Psychotic break.
Spencer considered these terms and others while

walking, as if in a dream, back to the ER nurses' station, and squeezing into a chair in front of one of its many computers.

She's hearing voices.

Good God Almighty.

Voices.

He felt numb—

(*And drugs! She'd taken drugs! Before operating!*)

—as if he'd been dropped into a bathtub full of ice.

At least maybe the EEG will give us more information about her diagnosis. The MRI, too.

He located Rita's head MRI on the hospital server and displayed its images on the screen, as he'd done thousands of times with his patients. He scrolled over the images in cross section, starting at the top of her brain and working his way down to the bottom, scrutinizing the anatomy.

Frontal lobe, normal.

Parietal lobe, normal.

And so on. Nothing. Everything completely normal.

His mind began to wander.

I forgot to ask her about the Ford Fiesta in front of her house. Probably nothing, but . . .

Still scrolling through the images. Down to her brainstem now, everything still looking normal—

What?

He leaned forward, all thoughts of the Fiesta gone. He traced his finger along the left side of her brain, near the brainstem. Along the vestibulocochlear nerve: the conduit along which sound signals travel from the ear to the brain.

Something was there.

Something that definitely did not belong.

What the hell is that?

SEBASTIAN

"Uh, hi." Sebastian took his hand out of his pocket, leaving his badge in it.

"You were on the tour, right?" Grant said. "In the operating room this morning?"

Goddamn. He knew she'd been observant. But he hadn't realized *how* observant.

"Um, I think you're mistaken, ma'am."

"No, I'm not." A sly smile. "I saw you looking at me."

"Uh, well . . ."

Stupid. Unprofessional. She should not have noticed that. He was slipping.

Still. She had gorgeous teeth.

Her vulpine smile widened. "It's okay. I get it. So. Who sent you? Halsted Robotics? Or that European group?"

Ahhh.

So she thought that he was some kind of corporate spy.

Excellent. Yes. A very reasonable explanation. He couldn't have come up with a better excuse himself. In fact, there likely *had* been some snoops there today, scoping things out for the competition.

He slipped on a puckish grin and, with it, the role of corporate mole.

"You know I can't tell you that. The last thing I need is to end up on the front page of the *Journal.* Bad for business."

"What kind of business?"

"Consulting."

She threw back her head and laughed. "I'm Constance." She offered her hand. Sebastian took it. It was warm and inviting, like a spot by the fire on a cold night. "Call me Connie."

"Sebastian." No harm in telling her. It wouldn't be his name for much longer.

"First name, or last?"

"Both."

She laughed and leaned toward him. He caught a whiff of her perfume. *Poison.* Very nice. "Come on," she said in a hushed tone, as if the two of them were hatching a conspiracy. "Tell me who you're working with, Sebastian. Strictly off the record."

Sebastian glanced around.

"Off the record?"

"Strictly."

"Off the record, Connie: I know there's no such thing in your business as *off the record*." Such beautiful lips.

"Fair enough." The beautiful lips turned downward. "But I'd bet you're down here for the same reason I am."

She pulled her phone from her purse and started checking messages. "You're not going to get much else either, I'm afraid," she said matter-of-factly. "I saw Montgomery leave here a while ago, all in a huff. I tried to talk to him, but he wouldn't give me the time of day. I think he's hiding something." The phone was back in her purse, and she was staring off in another direction, as if something had caught her attention.

"Right. Well, I thought, couldn't hurt to try, I guess—"

"So. I've got this deadline. You understand. Good luck, Seymour."

Sebastian, he thought indignantly, watching her glide away without so much as a glance back at him. *The name's Sebastian.*

For a little while longer, anyway.

He stood there like a jerk for ten seconds before coming to his senses. *Goddamn unprofessional.* His exasperation with himself was matched only by his admiration for her and how well she'd played him. *Now* there's *a professional.* This distraction had cost him time. His ear buzzed with static from Wu's feed. He flashed his ID to the big security guard with the paperback novel and hustled into the ER.

At the nurses' station, an enormous guy in a long white coat, blue polo shirt, and grey slacks was rising from a chair in front of a computer screen. Sebastian recognized him immediately.

He was in the OR this morning.

Yeah. The one standing near the robot, scratching his ear. Coincidence? Maybe, but Sebastian wasn't a big believer in coincidence. As the guy made for the exit, Sebastian's eyes swept over the words embroidered on his white coat.

SPENCER W. CAMERON, M.D. NEUROSURGERY.

He'd have to follow up on that. But no time now. He made a mental note, strolled toward room 5 and (*careful, don't let anyone notice you*) peeked in as he passed by the open door.

Wu was in there, alone, resting in bed. Her eyes were closed.

Well. Nothing going on here.

"Sebastian?"

Sebastian moved to a quiet corner of the ER. "All clear here, boss. Everything looks fine."

"I still don't have a signal."

"I know. Me either."

"Why?"

"Don't know. Wouldn't be the first time a device failed, though. Does it matter?"

A beat, and then: "No. No, I don't suppose it does."

"So we continue with the plan?"

"Yes."

SPENCER

After walking to his office—a small, comfortable space on Turner's fourth floor with a nice view of Torrey Pines golf course to the north—it took Spencer a full hour to work up the courage to call Raj.

"No worries, man." Raj shrugged off Spencer's repeated apologies. "It's all good, 'brah. I just . . . I don't want to see you get, you know—hurt. Again. But I understand. Totally. If I'd been you, I'd have taken a slug at me."

Spencer laughed. "Fair enough. Listen. Raj. I went to see Rita over in the ER, after I talked to you. It turned out they wanted a neurosurgeon to evaluate her."

Silence.

Had the call dropped?

"Raj? Can you hear me?"

"Yes."

"Did you hear what I said? About Rita?"

"Yes," he said flatly.

"She, uh—she had kind of . . . some strange things to say. An interesting version of this morning's events."

"Uh-huh."

"You mind if I bounce it off you?"

"I'm all ears." But the coolness in Raj's tone suggested otherwise.

Spencer filled Raj in on all Rita had told him. Waking up in the OR. Her ear. Finney. The irresistible urge to operate, her ER conversation with Chase. When he was done, Raj said, cautiously, "Spence, man . . ."

"I know, I know—an elaborate delusion of a paranoid schizophrenic. Right? But there was something about her MRI that bothered me, Raj."

"What?"

"It looked like she had punctate hemorrhages around her TM and vestibulocochlear nerve, tracking medially toward her brain. On the left. Very subtle."

"So? What did the radiologist think?"

"That it was nothing."

"Well, there you go."

"But the left ear is the one she was hearing the voice in."

"Oh, come *on*, Spencer." Raj no longer hid his exasperation. "Maybe she stuck something in her ear. You know, like a pencil, or wire coat hanger. I once saw a schizophrenic in med school who pulled out one of his molars with a pair of pliers because he thought there was a radio transmitter in it, and—"

"*No.* This was different, Raj. I know foreign-body head trauma, and this was not it. This was something else. Something much more subtle."

"Subtle enough for you to have imagined it?"

"No."

"Then what are you saying, Spencer? That something really *is* inside her head? Making her do and say weird things?"

Spencer chewed that over. *Yes. I guess that is exactly what I'm saying.* And to prove it he needed Raj's help: something Raj would not be falling all over himself to offer. No, a straight-up plea wouldn't work. But maybe a more devious approach—an appeal to his friend's scientific curiosity, and intense pride in his work—might.

"No. What I'm saying is that she might have a neurological diagnosis that hasn't yet been identified. A diagnosis that could explain her behavior."

"Oh!" In an instant, Raj's attitude transformed from confrontational to curious. "Ohhhhh. And you're thinking we could make the diagnosis if we run her MRI through our software filters."

"Exactly."

"Huh." Raj sounded thoughtful. "Now *that's* an idea. All kinds of potential problems on the differential diagnosis. Infection. Nascent AVM. Subtle neoplastic lesion. White matter disease." He added, with a hint of justifiable conceit, "Any of which I bet we could detect with our software."

"Exactly."

"And you said you placed our extra EEG electrode on her?"

"Yes. Hopefully she'll leave it on for a while—"

"—so that maybe we can correlate her brain wave data with the MRI."

"Exactly."

"Huh. Well . . . with that storm coming in, lots of people are leaving early. I've already sent my grad students home and shut down the lab for the rest of the day . . . I suppose I've got nothing better to do."

Spencer smiled to himself. "How fast could you have me some results?"

In his mind's eye, Spencer imagined Raj's big, shit-eating grin as he said, "How fast can you get me her MRI?"

SEBASTIAN

A few hours later, Sebastian and Finney were driving north on I-5 under a sullen grey sky. Though he hadn't heard back yet from Blade, the rest of his preparations were almost complete. Sebastian gave a report as he maneuvered through the thickening traffic.

"The ER attending consulted neurosurgery, after the second seizure," he said. *After you screamed in her head,* he didn't add. "Name's Dr. Spencer Cameron. Neurosurgeon at Turner. Thirty-nine years old. Undergraduate and medical degrees from the University of Washington. Trained in neurosurgery at UC San Diego, and stayed on as a professor. Apparently, a popular, well-liked guy. I saw him in OR 10 this morning, watching the surgery."

"Does this Dr. . . . . Spencer—"

"Cameron. Dr. Cameron."

"—have any direct connections with Dr. Wu?"

"None. At least, none I'm aware of."

"What's that supposed to mean? Can't you be sure?"

"No, I can't. Especially now that she's gone dark and we're not receiving any signals from her device." He still had no idea what the source of the ongoing interference was but was well past worrying since it couldn't be helped; and, besides, it shouldn't affect his plans. "They haven't had any formal professional or personal interactions that I know of."

"Fine. Anything else?"

"The ER did a head MRI, as expected," Sebastian said. "The usual nonspecific, minor findings around the tympanic membrane. Nothing to raise the suspicions of the radiologist. Or, I'm sure, the good Dr. Cameron."

"Fine."

They drove on in silence, exiting the freeway and heading north along winding, hilly roads. Sebastian tried not to dwell on the fact that *he was supposed to be going in the other goddamn direction*; that by now he should have been *halfway down the goddamn coast of Baja*, high-fiving himself over the completion of the longest, most complex job he'd ever pulled off. Breaking out the fucking champagne. Counting the number of zeros to the left of the decimal point in his overseas account, and preparing to transfer a hefty chunk of it to his sister.

But, no, here he was: babysitting Finney, sitting next to him in Sebastian's nondescript Volkswagen, driving him home to Rancho Santa Fe, fifteen miles northeast of Turner, a community of rolling hills and isolated, enormous estates. One of the richest fucking zip codes in the U.S. Perfect for a guy like Finney.

He clenched his teeth.

Finney.

What an asshole. His poker face, around Sebastian at least, sucked. He obviously still thought of Sebastian as some kind of a chump. Like that thing with Hammurabi's Code. Like Sebastian was incapable of cracking a fucking book.

Whatever.

The more important issue was that Finney was getting less predictable. A *lot* less predictable. Pretentiousness he could deal with; irrationality could be dangerous. That business with Wu, and her drinking: unfortunate, sure. And Sebastian knew all about revenge: the primitive desire, after being hurt, to lash out and hurt back.

Alfonso. God, how he'd wanted to hurt somebody after what happened to Alfonso.

But still.

Sebastian from the beginning had been disturbed by Finney's readiness to gamble with the life of an innocent patient. Now, this business with the bomb in the girl's head. He wondered if he somehow could talk Finney into disarming it—

"Goddammit!"

A pack of teenagers on skateboards darted out in front of the car. They turned in sharp circles down the middle of the street, leaping into the air, flipping and spinning their boards in complex twists and turns before executing perfect landings with a clatter of wheels on pavement.

Sebastian slammed on the brakes. The car squealed to a halt inches from the nearest of them.

Christ! That was close. He sized them up. Skate rats, in the local vernacular. Four of them. Torn T-shirts and plaid flannels. Baggy jeans with belt lines slung low over slender hips, revealing glimpses of tanned, armadillo-plated abdomens. Knit caps pulled low over sullen eyes. Black-and-white-checkered sneakers. Shaggy, salted locks of hair. Haphazard patches of nascent mustaches. Skating well out of their normal area, which usually was closer to the coast.

The first three didn't so much as glance in the car's direction. The one bringing up the rear was different. He carried a camera mounted to a selfie stick, with which he'd been filming the others. He stopped long enough to glare at Sebastian from beneath hooded eyelids.

"Fucking *watch* it, dude!" He banged his fist on the hood of the car before shouldering his camera and following after the others.

Sebastian turned to Finney.

Finney was staring straight ahead. He pursed his lips, and he nodded.

"Are you sure, boss?"

A second nod.

Goddammit. We don't need this right now.

"I don't recommend this, you know." Sebastian nudged the accelerator and pulled the car to the side of the road. By now the camera kid had fallen half a block behind his friends. Sebastian opened the driver's side door.

"Sebastian."

"Yeah, boss."

"I want you to hurt him." Finney was gazing through the windshield. "I can't abide disrespect."

Sebastian sighed. Neither could he, but he was willing to let this one go. They had too many other things to worry about. He beeped the horn, long and loud, and climbed out of the car.

"Young man," Sebastian called. "Excuse me! Young man!"

The horn grabbed the kid's attention. He stopped about ten feet away, just short of a steep downhill stretch, his smooth, adolescent features twisted in rage, and sized Sebastian up. He must have concluded that Sebastian's unassuming appearance did not merit retreat.

A conclusion he would soon regret.

"What the fuck," the kid snarled. A declaration, not an interrogative.

He was standing on one side of the road, about a foot away from the curb, in the shade of a broad, tall evergreen, at the base of which grew a stand of thick, high bushes. The kid's three friends were out of sight, having sped down the hill. The estates on this road were big, few, and far between. City ordinance, or something: You couldn't divide land into parcels below two acres, or some such shit. Aside from the kid, Sebastian, and Finney, this stretch of road was deserted.

He approached the kid with slow, deliberate steps, keeping himself stooped slightly at the hip, with his hands up and palms out in a nonthreatening gesture: a skittish good citizen confronting a skateboarding hooligan.

As he'd intended, Sebastian's meek body language emboldened the kid, convincing him that he was the alpha here. The kid puffed out his lean chest. Perfect.

"Look. Young man," Sebastian said, hands up and palms out. "Look. I don't want any trouble. But I think you did some damage to my car back there."

"Oh yeah? That piece of shit?" He laughed and pointed at the Volkswagen.

Sebastian slowly closed the gap between them.

They were six feet apart.

"Yes. There's a small dent in my hood where you hit it. You and your friends are being very unsafe."

Braces glinted from inside the kid's mouth. "Oh yeah? Well screw *you*, dude. Go fuck yourself."

What a fucking mouth! This kid really *could* use a serious attitude adjustment. Fifteen, maybe? Sixteen, tops?

"There's no need for that kind of language, young man."

"Oh yeah? Well, *fuck*. And, *you*." The kid chortled, then coughed, as if choking on his own wit.

They were three feet apart.

The kid was tall. He had about three inches on Sebastian, and immense, rounded shoulders—broadened, no doubt, by years of paddling a surfboard. *Skate rats* and *surf rats*. Sebastian had learned soon after moving to San Diego that these kids were one and the same. In between surfs, the surf rats skated; in between skates, they surfed.

Sebastian waved his hands in supplicating loops as his appraising eyes roamed up and down the kid's lanky frame, then to a gap in the nearby stand of bushes. Yes. That would do nicely.

Sebastian considered using the small device in a holster, strapped for ease of access to the small of his back, hidden underneath his untucked T-shirt. A nifty bit of engineering: Finney had discreetly procured it from one of his business interests—a company quietly developing the next generation in law-enforcement products. Urban pacification, that kind of shit. They called it a conduction gun. Like a Taser, it fired electrodes that delivered shocks. Except it was smaller than a Taser and able to render its victim both helpless *and* temporarily unconscious.

Sebastian, however, rejected it as an option. This road was sparsely traveled, but they were out in the open, and why chance some random passerby spotting him? Besides, Finney wanted to teach the kid a lesson, and the conduction gun was ill suited for that. He needed it to be more personal.

Two feet apart now. Sebastian caught a whiff of weed from the kid.

The kid's eyes narrowed, perhaps sensing something amiss, and he leaned forward, shifting his weight toward Sebastian.

But it was already too late.

"Look, young man—"

It was easy.

Too easy.

So easy it gave Sebastian a sick feeling in his stomach.

Add beating up stoned teenagers to the lengthening list of things for which he'd never signed up.

It was all over in seconds.

Sebastian moved like a ghost. He dropped toward the ground as his right foot swept out toward the kid's legs. At the last possible moment, before striking the kid's exposed right knee, he coaxed—*begged*—his leg to swing a hair too wide, to harmlessly redirect the force of what would otherwise have been a crippling, bone-splintering blow that would have shattered the kid's leg and likely ended his skateboarding and surfing days forever.

A few blurred movements later, the kid was lying on the ground in the bushes, Sebastian's knee planted on his chest, the selfie stick in Sebastian's hand. The kid's board lay on the ground next to them, wheels up. The wheels spun for a few plaintive revolutions and stopped.

The kid stared up into Sebastian's face. His mouth was open in a perfect *O* of surprise.

Then the pain hit.

His expression changed. His mouth remained a perfect *O*, but the kid's eyebrows shifted. That's what did it, all that was needed to transform the *O* of surprise (eyebrows up and separated) to an *O* of pain (eyebrows down and drawn together).

The kid clutched his right leg and started to moan.

"My knee. You broke my *fucking* knee, man! You broke it!"

The kid *had* gone down awkwardly.

Sebastian examined the kid's leg while keeping his knee on the kid's chest. He ran his hands along the leg's length and across the knee. The kid moaned a little louder when he squeezed the patella, the circular bone at the front of the knee joint, but otherwise checked out just fine. Everything was still connected and in the right place.

Sebastian bent over him, his nose inches from the kid's face.

"No, I didn't," he growled. "Your leg's not broken, junior. But your knee's sprained. You're going to have some swelling, and a nasty bruise. Might even be on crutches for a few days. But you'll be just fine. Too bad for the rest of us."

The kid started to cry.

Typical bully bullshit.

What a pussy.

"Listen, junior." Sebastian slipped on his best badass-motherfucker glower and pushed his face way down into the kid's. Got right up into it with him.

The kid's tears were replaced with an expression of terror.

"That leg is nothing compared to what I could do to you for real," Sebastian hissed. "I tried to be nice, but you had to show me some attitude. Fine. That dude in the car with me back there?"

The kid's eyes, wide as dinner plates, swiveled toward the road and back. He nodded.

"That's right, junior. He's an important dude. And you were disrespecting him. He wants me to hurt you. *Really* hurt you. Like, make sure you're sipping-your-meals-through-a-fucking-straw-for-the-next-six-months kind of hurt you."

The kid cringed and slid his jaw back and forth.

Sebastian almost laughed.

"But I'm not doing that today, junior. I could. And

I will, if I ever catch you and those buddies of yours riding your boards around here again. I will personally disassemble you, piece by piece, if I so much as see you riding a fucking *tricycle* down this street. Do you get me, junior?"

"Yes," the kid whispered.

"Good. Same goes with talking to anyone about our conversation. Don't even *think* it, junior. Make up whatever story you like, as long as it doesn't involve me, or this little chat we're having right now."

The kid started to sob.

Sebastian left him there, bawling, and stepped out from the bushes. He glanced up and down the still-deserted road and brushed the dirt from his clothes.

The kid's buddies would come back for him, eventually, once they'd realized that their cameraman had dropped off the grid. The kid would make up some story: no doubt something involving an impressive skateboard maneuver gone awry.

On some level, he admitted to himself, an unexpectedly satisfying encounter. There was even a small chance he'd turned the kid's attitude around. But it mostly made him uneasy: another potential loose end, another variable in the equation.

He climbed back in the car and started the engine.

"Okay, boss?"

Finney's window was down, through which the kid's muffled sobs floated from behind the bushes.

"Yes."

About half a mile along, at the bottom of the hill, the kid's three friends were standing at the side of the road, staring back up the hill wearing varying expressions of pissed off. One was holding his phone to his ear.

Sebastian gripped the wheel tightly.

There were bad people in the world. He knew that. Bad people who did bad things for no good reason.

So when exactly had he become one?

Thick drops of rain were beginning to splatter across the windshield. He turned on the wipers, and in his head again ran through the plans he'd made for tonight.

Including the ones Finney did not know about.

RITA

"Rita?"

She knew the voice. She followed the sound of it out of the blackness and opened her eyes.

She was lying in a hospital bed, a different one, so she knew she wasn't in the ER anymore. Darcy was in a chair next to the bed.

"Darcy. Hi." Rita swiveled her head to meet her kid sister's gaze. She was, she realized, feeling better. Marginally. Her head seemed heavy but didn't hurt; her tongue felt thick but moist. Little things. She felt grateful for both. She would take whatever she could get.

Even though the room was dark (*Was it night already? Same day, or the next?*), Rita could tell Darcy had been crying. The light slipping under the closed door, and radiating from the control panel of the IV pump next to her bed, was enough for her to make out the streaks of tearstains on Darcy's cheeks, like silvery trails on a sidewalk in the wake of a snail's passage.

"Oh my God, Rita." Darcy sniffled liquidly and rubbed her nose with the back of her hand. The large gold ring perforating her right nostril wiggled from side to side and flashed in the anemic light. "Oh my God. Oh my God." Her eyes welled with tears, and she flapped her hands in front of her face. "Oh. My. *God*."

Rita heaved a mental sigh.

Here we go.

Darcy had barely opened her mouth and already Rita was experiencing a familiar irritation that made her want to roll over and go back to sleep. Darcy was upset, and scared. Rita got that. But please. The *drama*.

Rita hid her exasperation under a blanket of self-control. It was misplaced, even selfish. What more could she expect? Darcy had never been a pillar of emotional support, or a safe harbor for weathering one of life's storms. She wasn't equipped for it, had in fact caused more than her share of nasty storms in Rita's life and her own. Which was why she was now crashed in Rita's spare room, without any plans other than to remain there until something better came along.

Still. The last thing Rita needed now was to deal both with her own problems and her infantile sister's reaction to them. What she wanted most was someone who would listen to her crazy story, and believe her, and tell her everything was going to be okay, someone to help her find a way the hell out of this, preferably with her career and sanity intact. Or at least someone to pretend that these goals were achievable. But that wasn't going to happen with Darcy.

Darcy sniffled again. Her plump lower lip quivered, and she pulled at it. Her fingernail polish, electric pink, was chipped, and her nails looked gnawed on.

The two of them, Rita mused, were a study in contrasts, their appearances and personalities so opposite that the two left people scratching their heads when they were introduced as sisters. Where Rita was willowy and firm, with coils of muscle, Darcy was compact and voluptuous; where Rita's features were hard, Darcy's were soft: all blurred lines and hazy borders, as if Darcy's face was a picture, and she'd been moving when it was taken. Pudgy cheeks. Wide-set, wide-open eyes that made her appear perpetually surprised, or, when listening to someone speak, like she was hanging on their every word.

Dad's eyes.

Dad.

It was because of him that she was named Darcy. Not because her father had come up with the name. He'd had nothing to do with it. Their parents hadn't settled on a name before she was born; and then everything had happened so fast with Mom that she and Dad had never had a chance to confer on it.

Afterward, when her baby sister, pink and healthy, was lying in a crib in the newborn nursery, and Mom was laid out on a steel slab in the hospital morgue, their father, in a fit of grief, had delegated the naming task to thirteen-year-old Rita, for reasons he never made clear.

Once she had gotten over her surprise, Rita had approached it quite seriously. Even before her mom's death, Rita had been an intense kid. Born old, her parents and teachers would say; reading grown-up books during lunch in middle school rather than gossiping with friends. During those miserable days, she'd welcomed the distraction of coming up with a name. It filled some of the void. Meanwhile, Dad had numbly attended to the funeral arrangements, and Gram fussed over the baby; and the two, preoccupied with their own grief, ignored Rita.

Darcy.

As in Mr. Darcy.

Since reading *Pride and Prejudice* (the first time) when she was twelve, Rita had been a rabid Jane Austen fan. The name had slipped into her mind one morning when sitting and staring out the window, trying not to be sad. She'd at first favored *Emma*, but then rejected it, along with a bunch of other choices. Her opinion at the time was that the world was already too full of Emmas, Elizabeths, and Janes.

Darcy, on the other hand, had flair. Panache. Some uniqueness. And when, on the morning of her mother's funeral, she'd told her father what she'd decided on, and why, he'd hugged her and told her that *Darcy* was perfect.

And what about her middle name? he'd asked.

Middle name?

She'd forgotten about a middle name. His instructions hadn't been that specific.

Your sister needs a middle name, lovely Rita.

The gears of her mind had spun, and she'd blurted out:

Rose.

Mom's middle name.

Dad hadn't said anything but had nodded solemnly, his big eyes (*Darcy's eyes*) moist, and had hugged her again, long and hard.

So Darcy Rose Wu it was.

Over the years, as she'd pondered where she'd failed Darcy, Rita sometimes worried that naming her after Mom had been a huge mistake. Had she unintentionally saddled Darcy with a reminder of how her entry into this world had shoved their mother out of it?

"Are you okay, Ree?"

"Yes. I'm fine." Rita propped herself up on the pillow.

"Bullshit. You're lying." Darcy was a much better liar than she.

"Darcy—"

"No, Ree. How can you even say that to me?" Locks of black hair streaked with strands of pink fell into her eyes. She pushed them away. Darcy's previous hairstyle had been a half-shaven head. Literally: the hair on one side scraped raw down to the follicles, the other side untouched, the two in perfect symmetry. Rita had wondered if she'd used a tape measure, or maybe a protractor, to cut her hair, so perfectly was her scalp divided: bald versus not bald.

That had been over a year ago, when Darcy had dropped out of college and hadn't cared about hats, or sunscreen; and Rita remembered Darcy's gleaming half cranium (*right? or left? she couldn't recall*)— offset on the opposite side by voluptuous, crow-black hair worn in a tight braid that hung to her shoulder— turning first pink, then red in the California sun. It had looked painful, especially after it had blistered and peeled. But Darcy had never complained. Always stubborn that way.

"God, Ree." Darcy blinked her big eyes and shook her head. "You really look like shit. Are you sick? Oh, God. Do you have *cancer*, or something? Oh my God!" She placed her heels on the seat of her chair and hugged her knees. "Do you have a brain tumor? Oh my *God*. You have a brain tumor."

"Darcy—"

"You have a brain tumor, don't you?"

"I don't—"

"If you have a brain tumor, just tell me now."

"I don't have a brain tumor."

"What happened to you today?"

Where to begin?

"I—"

"If it's not a brain tumor, what is it? What are they going to do with you now? What's going to happen to you?" And the unspoken question: *What's going to happen to me?*

"I don't know, Darcy," Rita said quietly.

Darcy searched Rita's features, her own screwed up in worry. Rita experienced a rush of affection, mixed with shame over her initial annoyance. Darcy was a good person. She always had been. Rita had refused to call her selfish, even when so many others had, because Darcy was immature and confused. Plenty of confused kids were self-focused.

"God. I need a cigarette." Darcy winced and tugged at her ear.

Her *left* ear.

Rita's stomach did a somersault.

Ask your sister about her head, Dr. Wu.

"How's your ear?"

"Hurts." She rubbed it. "But less." She squirmed and scooted to the edge of the chair. "You're the doctor. You have any idea what's going on?"

"No."

Darcy stared at her hard. "Yeah. Okay."

"Have you noticed, uh, anything else? Any other . . . uh, symptoms?"

"No." Darcy had turned her attention to the window. "Popped a few Tylenol, drank some Gatorade, and by lunchtime felt almost good as new." A bitter laugh. "Then they called me about you."

Rita felt herself relax a bit.

Thank God.

She hadn't heard any voices.

She hadn't heard *his* voice.

Had Finney been bluffing? If it *was* the same kind of implant, if Finney really *had* put something in Darcy's head, maybe they'd gotten lucky, and the damn thing wasn't working.

Even so: Why would Finney have put it in Darcy's head in the first place? Rita remembered the overwhelming impulse to operate on Mrs. Sanchez. Finney must have brainwashed her, somehow, with the thing in her ear. There was no other reasonable explanation.

What else did he have planned for them?

The thought made her stomach churn.

It was raining outside. Hard. The two sat and listened to it beat against the window.

"Raining still," Darcy mumbled. "Maybe it'll help the drought." She hugged herself and shivered. "Shit. Just one smoke. That's all I need."

With her pink-laced hair, designer jeans, a faded white HELLO KITTY T-shirt, high-top Converse sneakers with the laces untied, and several gaudy plastic bracelets on each wrist, she looked like a little kid.

So vulnerable.

But different, Rita sensed, than when she'd last left San Diego.

When things with the boy in Seattle had ended, she'd moved to Santa Cruz with another boy, a surfer, who'd blown through Darcy's meager savings and then disappeared. Before she'd arrived last week from Santa Cruz driving a wheezing Ford Fiesta, Rita suspected there'd been a humiliating denouement at a Planned Parenthood clinic, but hadn't pressed Darcy on it. She'd parked the Fiesta out front, offering no explanation as to how she'd acquired it, and had since spent her time sleeping and watching TV, shuffling back and forth between her bed and the family-room couch, with occasional forays outside for a cigarette.

Rita had been laser-focused on work. But in their snatches of time together, Darcy had seemed . . . tougher. Sturdier. For years she'd been groping for something, as a person lying in bed might fumble for eyeglasses on a nightstand in a darkened bedroom. Maybe she'd finally found what she'd been looking for.

Sometimes, Chase had told her in the terrible days after Jenny Finney's death, *the only way out is through.* That had been before the review committee had exonerated her, and she'd felt paralyzed with guilt.

Maybe Darcy's finally made it through and out.

An affectionate smile crept across Rita's lips. "You and me, Darcy. The two of us. Aren't we a piece of work?"

Darcy's head snapped around. "What?" She saw Rita's smile, and her face relaxed. "Oh. Yeah. I guess."

"You were a horrible crier when you were a baby. You know that?"

"Jeez, Rita. What the hell has *that* got to do with anything?"

"You never stopped crying."

"I *know.* You've told me. Like, a hundred times. I cried when I was a baby. I get it. Lots of babies cry." She glanced at the door and tapped her feet on the floor. "Do you think they'd notice if I had a quick smoke? I could open a window. Just a crack. You know?"

"I think you actually met the clinical definition of colic."

"What does *that* mean?"

"That even your pediatrician took your crying seriously. There was this one night. You were maybe . . . three months old. Dad was on deployment, his first after Mom died, and you kept on crying. I thought Gram was going to jump off a bridge. She used to drive you around because it was the only time you'd ever shut up. And then the car would stop moving and—*bam!*— you'd start crying all over again."

Darcy cocked her head and brushed a pink strand of hair behind her ear. "What about you?"

"I was in *eighth grade*, Darcy. Mom was dead. God. I had my own problems. What did *I* care if you cried? I put my headphones on, cranked up the music, and locked myself in my room. You weren't my problem. Until that night."

Rita looked out at the rain.

It's really coming down.

"My girlfriend's mom had just dropped me off after cross-country practice. I remember being *so* tired, and stressed about homework. Gram was waiting for me at the door. With you. You were screaming like a banshee, no surprise. But Gram . . . was crying, too. Which was scary, because I'd *never* seen her cry. *Ever.* Not even after Mom died. You remember how she was. So she must have been at the end of her rope."

Darcy leaned toward her.

"'Here,' Gram told me, pushed you into my arms." Rita mimed the motion. "'Take her. Just take her.' Then she went to her room and shut the door. Didn't say another word. I didn't see her again until the next morning."

"So what happened?"

"You stopped screaming. I mean, not all at once. It wasn't like I could turn you off, like a light switch. God, how I'd wished I could! But you calmed down after a while. And then you . . . smiled. It was . . . *beautiful.* Like this tiny, private smile you'd been saving. Just for me. You'd smiled before. But this one seemed different. And suddenly I wasn't tired anymore. Or stressed about homework."

Rita's throat tightened. She twisted the bedsheet in her hands and watched the rain slap at the window. She knew that if she looked at Darcy now, she'd start crying. "I took you upstairs, gave you a bath, got you ready for bed. I didn't know what else to do. Then we sat in the rocking chair together, across from your crib . . ."

"That old rocker in the living room?"

"Yeah. We kept it in your room back then. Anyway, after you fell asleep, I tried to put you down in your crib, but you started to cry. So I sat back down in the rocker with you, and you quieted down."

"Then what?"

"I fell asleep. Woke up in the middle of the night, still sitting in the chair, with one hell of a stiff neck. You were out cold in my arms. I laid you down in the crib. You didn't cry, so I snuck back to my room, did my homework, slept for a few hours, then went to school. After that, well . . . I helped Gram out more, and started sleeping in your room. Things got better."

A gust of wind rattled the window.

"Things got better," Rita murmured.

She reached out and grasped Darcy's hand.

Darcy started crying.

So did Rita.

Which made Darcy start bawling. She launched herself out of the chair and seized Rita. Rita hugged her back as best she could, but one arm got tangled up in her IV line, so she draped it over Darcy's shoulder while she squeezed her with the other arm. The two held each other, crying, until Darcy's shoulders stopped heaving up and down, and her breathing slowed.

Darcy settled on the bed next to Rita. "I just—when I got the call, from the hospital, I was so scared. *So* scared. I don't know what I would do without you, Ree."

"We're going to be okay, Darcy. Whatever happens."

"You're lying."

"Darcy—"

"*No.* No. You don't believe that, Ree. Don't try to tell me for a second that you do."

Rita pursed her lips. "Well," she admitted. "It *is* fair to say I'm not sure what's going to happen next." Her urge to smile at the absurdity of this caught Rita by surprise. In fact, she felt strangely—*remarkably*—calm and clearheaded. Darcy's presence (and Finney's continued absence, which she still sensed) seemed to be having that effect on her. One thing had now become clear.

I need to protect Darcy.

Everything else around her could collapse—

(*shit, it pretty much already had*)

—but she had to guard her little sister.

I wasn't there for her. Now I need to protect her.

No matter what.

"What are your doctors going to do?" Darcy asked.

"Well . . . I'm not exactly sure. Has anyone come by since you've been here?"

Darcy shrugged. "A nurse. Around eight. She took your blood pressure and temperature. You seemed pretty out of it, so I just let you go back to sleep. You don't remember?"

"No."

"You've been talking in your sleep. Mentioned some guy named Spencer. Isn't he the guy you used to date?"

"Something like that. Have any of the doctors talked to you?"

Darcy shook her head. "None have come by."

Nor would they anytime soon, Rita suspected. She

had a feeling that, short of a medical emergency, Chase had declared her room a no-fly zone for her doctors—at least until tomorrow, when he and his bosses could figure out what the hell they were going to do with her next.

She could imagine the stories that would soon emerge. *Alcoholic druggie surgeon butchers patient before collapsing in cocaine-induced stupor.* People would eat it up. She almost felt sorry for Chase. How the hell was he going to spin *that*?

"So . . . you're going to stay here in the hospital tonight?" Darcy asked.

Am I?

She gazed at the rain hammering away at the windowpane.

"Ree?"

The only way out is through.

"Hmmm?"

"You're going to spend the night here?"

"Ummm . . . yes."

Or . . . maybe not.

"Do you want me to stay?"

She turned to Darcy. "What?"

"Do you want me to stay? Here? With you tonight? One of the nurses told me I could." She pointed to a vinyl-cushioned chair visible in the dimness on the other side of the room. "It folds out into a little couch, I guess."

"Oh. What time is it, anyway?"

Darcy looked at her phone. "Almost ten."

"And you said the nurse came by around eight o'clock to check my blood pressure?"

"Yeah."

Which means she'll next be back around midnight. If she follows the routine.

She took both of Darcy's hands in her own. She knew now what she had to do. She wasn't sure how she would pull it off, but first she had to get Darcy out of here. "No, kiddo. Why don't you go home."

"Are you sure?"

"Absolutely." She gave Darcy's hands a squeeze. "I'm fine. All I need is some sleep. So do you. And you're not going to get much here, lying in a chair, with nurses waking us up every four hours to check my vitals."

Darcy's lower lip trembled, but she nodded, and this time her eyes remained dry. "Yeah. Okay, Ree. But . . . what if I want to get ahold of you? Do you have your phone?"

"It's in my locker." *Along with the other stuff I need, including my clothes.* Rita pointed to a cordless phone on a table next to the bed. Like a hotel, Turner provided each room with its own landline. "Tell you what. Go home. Call the hospital operator as soon as you get there and ask to be connected to my room. Okay? We'll talk again then."

"Okay."

"Just . . . go straight home. Promise me, okay? I need you to be home tonight, Darcy. Promise me you'll go straight home."

"Okay, Ree. Sure."

"Call me the moment you walk through the door."

"I will. Love you, Ree."

"Love you, too." She kissed Darcy on the cheek, and

they hugged. Darcy broke away and made her way to the door. Light and sound splashed across the room as she opened it.

"Darcy?"

"Yeah?"

Rita smiled. "No smoking in the house, kiddo."

Darcy grinned and wiped her nose. "Right." The door closed behind her with a gentle click, and Rita was alone.

She picked up the phone and called the operator. She told him she was expecting an important outside call from a family member and to please put the call through. He promised he would.

Thirty minutes later, she picked it up on the first ring and clutched it to her ear. Her hand was shaking.

Please let it be Darcy.

It was. She was home, and okay.

Rita promised to call her first thing in the morning—a lie, but it couldn't be helped. She hung up and settled back, cradling the receiver against her chest, and watched the rain beat against the window.

And she waited.

SPENCER

Spencer was reclining in his favorite easy chair: a great big La-Z-Boy in front of the TV, perfectly broken in, its cushions molded to his body. Rita was standing in front of him, smiling. She was naked.

Which was nice.

She was gorgeous: thick dark hair, svelte frame,

dark eyes bright above lush, smiling lips. He drank her in. He could feel his hardness pressing against the inside of his pants, so hard it was almost painful, like when he'd been a teenager.

She took a few steps toward him. He realized, then, that he was naked, too: which was weird, he could have sworn he'd been wearing clothes a second ago, but that was okay, he wasn't going to complain or anything.

Without prelude, she wrapped her hands behind his neck and straddled him in one deft motion, as she'd done many times in this same La-Z-Boy; as she'd done that first night when, after he'd patiently (*and sweetly, don't forget sweetly*) worn her down, pursuing her through two months of chaste coffee and lunch dates (never at the hospital, she was always afraid someone would see them together), she'd texted him on a Friday night to see if he was home; and when he replied that he was, had shown up twenty minutes later, admitting that she'd fallen for him. Five minutes after that, they were naked and entwined together in the La-Z-Boy, like they were now.

He slipped inside her, and her warmth and wetness enveloped him. She gasped, and he did, too.

Oh, God.

Reflexively, he lifted his hips.

Rita, he panted. *I really love you. God, I love you so much.*

As she started to rock up and down on him, she leaned forward and kissed him deeply, her tongue exploring his mouth; and then moved her lips to his ear, as if about to whisper in it, as if about to tell him that, yes, she still loved him, and always would.

But electronic rings, not words, came out of her mouth.

Spencer tried to ignore the rings, tried to concentrate on Rita moving on top of him; he'd missed her so much and wanted desperately to go on with what they'd started.

But the rings kept coming. The damn rings wouldn't be ignored.

He opened his eyes. Rita was gone. He was alone in the La-Z-Boy. The ringing was coming from his phone on the arm of the chair. He reached for it, blinking away the dream.

"Hello?"

"Hi, Spence. Sorry to call so late. How are you, honey?"

He went limp instantly. "Uh—hi, Mom." Blushing, he groped for the lever of the La-Z-Boy and yanked it out of the recline position. The open medical journal lying on his chest, the one he'd been trying to concentrate on when he'd drifted off to sleep, and the sealed Ziploc bag of ice (now slush) draped across his aching right knee, toppled to the floor. "Is everything okay? How's Dad?"

"We're fine, dear. I was calling to check on *you*. I was watching the Weather Channel just now and wanted to make sure you were all right."

"Why?"

"The storm, dear. There are mudslides in Malibu. Bad ones. Entire houses *sliding down cliffs*, Spencer. Isn't Malibu close to you?"

He rubbed his eyes and yawned. "No, Mom." His folks still lived in the same small town in eastern

Washington they'd called home for forty years, and his mother phoned every time a California wildfire, mudslide, or earthquake made the news. None of these had ever occurred within fifty miles of his home, and no matter how many times he'd explained it to her, his mother would never understand that California was 800 miles long and 250 miles wide. "Malibu is 150 miles from here."

"Oh." She sounded mildly disappointed, like her life would have been more interesting if her only child was imperiled by tons of choking mud. "Well. Thank goodness. Is it raining where you are?"

He peered out the window. Night had fallen, and hard rain was beating against the glass. Blasts of wind rattled the pane. He lived in a one-story house, and could hear the rain pounding on the roof.

Man. How long have I been out? He checked his watch: two hours.

"Yeah. Pretty hard. About as hard as I've ever seen it in San Diego."

"Exactly! They're saying this storm—something about El Niño—is the biggest one in years. Isn't there a hill behind your house?"

"No, Mom."

"When your father and I were out visiting last summer, I distinctly remember a hill."

"Mom. That was my friend Greg and his wife Sarah's house. We had brunch there one day."

"Oh. Well. Maybe you should check on them."

The hill behind Greg and Sarah's house was a five-foot-high, gently sloping rise covered with dense foliage—hardly a mudslide waiting to happen. "They're fine, Mom. So how are you and Dad?"

"Oh. Well. You know—"

His mother launched into a summary of recent happenings: the kidney stone she'd passed (*"The pain, Spencer! Worse than childbirth!"*); the bridge tournament she and Dad had won; the married town councilman caught up in a sex scandal with a girl half his age. They kept busy and were (mostly) healthy: She was a retired elementary school teacher who volunteered at the local library, his dad a retired cop who still worked their thirty-acre farm and rode a tractor every day. But they weren't getting any younger. Dad needed a new knee, and had agreed (grumpily) to spend a month in San Diego this winter getting one installed by an orthopedic surgeon handpicked by Spencer.

She eventually handed the phone off to Dad, who repeated much of what Mom had told him, but from his dad's (not-all-that-different) point of view. They refused to adopt any social media, including Facebook, so when they were done, he hung up with promises to call them tomorrow and let them know everything was all right.

He put his phone down and shifted his sore knee, and his thoughts turned back to Rita.

Spencer, I can't hear him, I can't hear him when you're around.

He remembered her left ear, and the MRI, and about the way the auto-surgeon acted in the OR this morning: how it responded almost *too* well to that bleeding.

Spencer, I can't hear him, I can't hear him when you're around . . .

His phone rang again. He looked at the caller ID.

"Hey, Raj. What's up?"

"Spence." Raj's excitement spilled through the receiver. "Dude. I finished the analysis of the MRI."

"Yeah?" Spence sat up straighter. "And?"

"You have *got* to see this."

SEBASTIAN

Preparations.

Preparations, and plans.

Sebastian was again sitting in his car in Turner's parking garage. A half-empty Thermos of coffee lay in the cup holder next to him. Although the corner of the garage he'd chosen was deserted, he'd covered himself, and his phone, with a thick blanket, away from prying eyes.

Preparations.

After he'd dropped Finney off, Sebastian had stopped at his shabby apartment in Pacific Beach to retrieve his few possessions, brew a pot of coffee, charge his phone, and change into an all-black outfit: jeans, boots, long-sleeve shirt, and formfitting waterproof windbreaker—along with a few extra items he thought he might need tonight, including the conduction gun.

And plans.

From there he'd driven back here. By then, night had descended, the heavens had opened up, and it was pouring. He'd parked the Volkswagen (untraceable to him) in Turner's garage, which was near empty, most people having fled ahead of the storm. Still, it would be a few more hours before Turner would be deserted enough for him to kidnap Wu.

Kidnapping. He'd never signed up for that. What would Alfonso think?

Or Sammy?

Enough time to finish off what he still needed to do.

Using his phone, and a hacking program Blade had provided him six months ago, he'd accessed the Turner security network and disabled the nearby garage cameras. Then, using the same network, he'd located Wu's room and confirmed that she was there because the nurses had entered her 8:00 P.M. vital signs.

Around this time, Wu's sister, who they'd been tracking with the implant, had arrived at Wu's room. That was when *her* signal had cut out in a burst of interference identical to Wu's. Finney had noticed the signal change on his tablet and, agitated, ordered him to Wu's room to investigate.

But Wu and her sister weren't going anywhere soon, and he had other priorities now. His own ones. Finney had changed the rules on him, and had no way of knowing where Sebastian was. The sister could wait. So he'd first trotted through night and rain to Higdon Park (*another preparation*), and crept past the security guards huddled inside a tiny trailer, and into the construction zone (*more preparations*).

It'd taken him longer than he'd planned. By the time he was done, the interference had gone: disappeared at the same time the sister had left Wu's room.

Interesting. He'd have to remember that.

At that point, he'd conferred briefly with Finney, who'd agreed that the interference was no longer an issue. He'd reassured Finney that he would send word when ready, and then had returned to his car to wait for Blade to make good on his (*her?*) word.

Which, as he took a sip of coffee from the Thermos, Blade did: a soft chime of his phone announced that Blade was ready to forward the completed hacking program, pending receipt of payment. Sebastian sighed and hit SEND, imagining the numbers in his bank account spinning down to zero. Several seconds later, the program arrived, with instructions on how to use it.

He read the instructions but didn't open the program—not the right time yet. He didn't quite know what he was going to do with it but felt confident that its value would soon make itself clear.

Assuming, of course, it worked.

Twenty minutes later, at 12:10 A.M., Wu's 12:00 A.M. vitals appeared on his phone, indicating that Wu's nurse had come and gone on her midnight rounds. Barring the unexpected, the nurse would not return for four hours.

It was time.

Back now into Turner: where, in an out-of-the-way broom closet, he again donned the guise of Robert Rodriguez, perioperative technician. He went to Wu's room on the seventh floor and slipped unseen past a couple of nurses trying to wrestle some demented old hag in a patient gown back into her room. *Goddamn*, the mouth on her: filthier than the skateboarding kid.

He reached room 738. Wu's room, according to the hospital network. The door was cracked open. He nudged it open and crept inside, his eyes soon adjusting to the semidarkness. He dropped to a crouch and glided toward the bed, the conduction gun in his hand.

The bed was empty.

No Wu.

He stood up and searched the room. No one there.

He dug his phone out and double-checked the room number—*738*. Yep. This was it, all right.

All of her stuff was gone—except for her glasses, which he found stuffed in a plastic bag underneath a blanket, on the empty bed.

Shit.

He glanced toward the door and checked his phone for the signal from Wu's device. Still blocked, useless for tracking.

Shit!

Where could she have gone?

If he didn't find her soon, he was as good as fucked.

SPENCER

The picture on his computer screen looked like ones Spencer had seen of the Milky Way from space, the way it could no longer be seen in the night sky unless you were somewhere like Antarctica, maybe, or out in the middle of the Pacific: countless tiny white dots, merging together into random bunches and blobs flung against a dark background.

"What is that?" Spencer asked, almost jumping out of his chair. He could barely contain his excitement.

"Hell if I know," Raj said from the small frame in

the upper right-hand corner of Spencer's desktop computer screen, the only portion of the screen not occupied by Rita's brain MRI. "Millions of tiny particles, clustered around her left tympanic membrane, vestibulocochlear nerve, and lateral brainstem. Very small. I played with the contrast settings to make them look bright white. Easier to see that way."

Spencer pulled at his chin. "How small?"

"Each no bigger than a small protein. With some associated hemorrhage and inflammation. We'd never be able to see them unless I'd scrubbed the images with the latest version of our software."

"What are they made of?"

"Not sure. Best guess: mostly organic, but with bits of synthetic material as well."

"What are they doing there?"

"Hell if I know. Infection, maybe?"

"Well . . . prion diseases *are* protein-based, I suppose. Spongiform encephalopathies."

"You mean, like mad cow? Creutzfeldt-Jacob disease? That could explain it. Doesn't Creutzfeldt-Jacob cause dementia?"

"Yeah, it does, but not like this. CJD doesn't fit the clinical picture. This"—Spencer tapped the screen with his finger—"is just plain weird. Especially if these things are not entirely organic." Her MRI was now raising more questions than it was answering. "Maybe something will come up in her blood tests. And the portable EEG."

"That's another weird thing about this: the portable EEGs."

"What do you mean?"

"Well, your EEG signal got totally screwed up to-day. Twice. The first time around"—Raj's eyes flick-ered downward, and Spencer heard paper shuffling over the link—"10:00 A.M."

"That's when I went to Rita's OR."

"Correct. Bad interference. Until you turned it off. And when you turned it back on—"

"—by then I was in Higdon, with you—"

"—it was fine. Until the same thing happened again about three hours later—"

"—when I was visiting Rita in the ER—"

"—and the signal went completely on the fritz again."

"So . . . my EEG went haywire whenever I was around Rita?" Spencer asked.

"Correct."

"Why?"

"High-energy electromagnetic waves interfering with your signal."

"Where from?"

"From Rita."

"*What?*"

"Let me show you what I mean." Raj reached to his right. A picture of a horizontal squiggly line replaced Rita's MRI on Spencer's screen.

"What's that?" Spencer asked. "Looks like an EEG pattern."

"It is. Yours. The one your brain was transmitting today."

"Looks normal."

"It is. Beta activity predominating. Completely normal." Spencer expected Raj to make some wiseass comment—like how it was indistinguishable from a

chimp's, or something—but Raj's tone was somber.
"That's what it looked like throughout most of today.
What it *should* look like. But *this* is what your EEG
looked like when you were in the OR." The squiggly
line degenerated into a mass of scribbles, as if it had
been drawn by an angry four-year-old with a black
crayon. "All interference. Gibberish."

Spencer leaned forward. "Huh."

"And *this* is what your EEG looked like when you
were in the ER, visiting Rita." The angry scribbles disappeared, and then reappeared. "Interference."

"Holy shit. The same exact pattern."

"Yep. And there's more." Another EEG pattern appeared on the screen, with black scribbles identical to
the first two.

"My EEG again? With interference?"

"No. Rita's EEG. In real time. The output transmitted from her patch at this very moment." He paused.
"It's been that way since you put it on her."

"It's the same—"

"The same *exact* interference pattern," Raj said quietly. "And, whatever is interfering with her EEG signal, and yours, seems to be coming *from* Rita. Which
makes me—well, I wonder if it has something to do
with those tiny particles."

"*Holy shit.* Yeah."

"And here's another thing, Spence: whatever it is,
whatever's coming from Rita, the EEG interferes with
it. Cancels it out. Kind of the way noise-canceling
headphones work: waves in opposite phase knocking
against each other."

Whenever you're around, I can't hear him.

I can't hear him, Spencer!

"Did anything else happen when you were in the OR?" Raj asked.

"Well . . . the robot shut down, when I got close. I had to turn off my EEG before it would turn back on."

"Is the robot wireless?"

"I think so."

"I bet the EEG blocked the robot's wireless signal, too."

Spencer thought of the way his car radio had cut out when he'd put on his EEG patch on the drive to work this morning. He nodded. "So, let me see if I understand what you're saying: some weird electromagnetic signal is coming from Rita, which is interfering with our EEG."

"Correct."

"We don't know what the signal is, but it may or may not be linked to millions of protein-sized *things* in her brain."

"Correct."

"And the EEG patches are blocking this signal. Canceling it out, like with the surgical robot, or my car radio."

"Yes." Raj cocked his head. "So . . . what do you think?"

Spencer's palms were slick with sweat. He felt like he was going to throw up, his triumph over being proven right about Rita—

(*I knew something was up!*)

—trumped by dread.

What the hell is going on?

"I think I need to go back to Turner, Raj."
Right now.

RITA

Rita had waited until after the night nurse had taken her midnight vitals.

She'd pretended to be asleep when the nurse arrived. The nurse was young and surly, and Rita didn't know her. She'd announced her arrival with a shrill *hello* and a blast of overhead fluorescents that suggested passive hostility. Did she know who Rita was? Did she know what had transpired that morning down in the OR? Did she suspect her of being a coke-addled drunk?

Probably not. The nurses on night shift were often young (*i.e., lack of seniority meant they had no choice but to work unpopular hours*) and surly (*i.e., pissed off about it*). Temperature. Pulse. Respirations. Blood pressure. Tasks performed with minimal personal interaction.

Nurse Surly entered Rita's vitals into the room's computer, grunted good night, turned off the lights, and shut the door, leaving Rita alone in the computer-screen-illuminated semidarkness.

Rita disengaged herself from the bag of IV fluid, pulled the IV catheter from the back of her hand, and stood up—a little unsteadily at first, but soon gaining her balance. The belongings she'd had with her in the OR—underwear, socks, scrubs, sneakers, hospital ID, and glasses—had been delivered here and left in a clear plastic bag next to the bed. She pulled them out, everything except for the glasses, and slipped them on. She stuffed the bag with the glasses underneath a blanket, in case Finney was watching.

But she still sensed his absence.

In fact, her thoughts as she dressed were the clearest they'd been since she'd first woken up on the OR table. Probably the sleep, and the IV fluids.

Her hand lingered over the EEG electrode Spencer had placed behind her ear. She began to peel it off, then changed her mind. It made her feel like Spencer was close by, keeping tabs on her, and she found the thought comforting.

She glanced out the window. Still an ugly night outside. All she saw was water, hitting the window in angry sheets, smears of orange-yellow light from scattered streetlamps, and a few trees buffeted by the wind, which made a faint, high-pitched whistle as it gusted through the window cracks.

If Nurse Surly followed hospital routine, Rita had about four hours before she returned. She opened the door a crack and peeked out. The hallway in front of her room was empty. Turner kept only a skeleton crew on the night shift. Rita had spent many hours making rounds in this patient area, and she knew that, at this hour, it was staffed with only two nurses.

Luck was with her: About ten doors down, a demented old lady named Mrs. Thorn (Rita knew this because the woman kept screaming that she was *Mrs. Thorn, goddammit, so show some goddamn respect, you goddamn white-trash bitches*) was rooted in the middle of the hall, flapping her arms at Nurse Surly and another young nurse, raging that the *goddamn filthy spics* were stealing her money, which was *so goddamn typical*. The nurses' backs were to Rita.

More luck: One of the exit stairwells was immediately opposite Rita's room.

As the two nurses tried to corral Mrs. Thorn, Rita dashed through the stairway door. Mrs. Thorn caught sight of her, and pointed, and shrieked that *the thieving chink bitch was getting away*, but the harried nurses didn't even turn around.

She sprinted down the stairs two at a time. She hadn't yet figured out where she was going, or what she was going to do. All she knew was that she and Darcy had to get *away*: away from Turner and from Finney. She had no idea if Finney could follow them; and, at this point, she didn't care. She didn't have time.

First things first. She needed her car keys, phone, and wallet, all of which were in her locker.

So, hospital ID affixed to her scrubs, she headed downstairs, toward the OR locker room, hoping to avoid anyone who knew her.

More luck still: The only person she encountered on her way was some maintenance guy waxing the floors, who didn't see her, and when she reached the locker room, it was empty.

She quickly pulled out her keys, wallet, and phone, and exchanged her scrubs for the jeans, T-shirt, and sweater she'd worn the previous night. She crept out of the locker room and hurried back to the staircase.

Still no one.

She felt a surge of manic energy as she reached the first floor, elated at the prospect of escape. She flew through a door that deposited her in the parking garage and jogged to her car.

Almost there.

She slipped behind the wheel, started the engine, put the car in gear, and breathed a huge sigh of relief.

She was almost to the garage's gated entrance when it happened.

SEBASTIAN

Sebastian skidded to a halt, panting, at Wu's parking spot in the garage.

It was empty.

Goddammit!

Wu was gone, and with her, his chances of getting his money (*Sammy and Sierra's money*) from Finney. With her signal jammed, he had no way to track her.

Idiot!

Most of him was pissed. But a small part of him felt relief that Wu might yet escape.

Focus, idiot: What the hell do you do now?

His best bet would be to try to pick up the trail at her house. He'd started to walk to his car when a sound near the garage exit caught his attention.

RITA

Dammit.

She stopped the car short of the garage gate and rapped her forehead gently against the steering wheel.

Mrs. Sanchez.

She'd forgotten about Mrs. Sanchez.

Dammit! She pounded her fists on the wheel. She needed to go see her. She'd otherwise never forgive herself. She had no idea when she'd be back. Or even *if* she'd ever be back.

She backed away from the gate, parked in an empty spot, then logged on to the Turner network with her phone and skimmed through Mrs. Sanchez's electronic medical chart. The good news: Her blood tests and vital signs looked great. The bad: Her room was on the ninth floor. Rita had to avoid people, and therefore elevators, so it looked like she had some climbing to do. She grimaced. This would take time.

Finney was out of her head (*for now, at least*), but he might yet be coming after her. Her self-preservation instinct screamed for her to put the car back in gear and get the hell out.

But she couldn't.

Not without seeing Mrs. Sanchez first.

She killed the engine, retraced her steps to the stairwell and, after opening the electronic lock with her ID badge, began the long climb up. She paced herself, resting at each floor; but, in her weakened state, it was exhausting, and by the time she reached the ninth floor, her chest was heaving with the effort. At least her luck still held: No one, it seemed, was using the stairs tonight.

Rita paused in the room's open doorway. The overhead light was on, and Mrs. Sanchez was asleep in a bed in the center of the room. A young woman wearing a blue UCLA Bruins hoodie, headphones, and white sweatpants was in a window seat, legs crossed Indian-style in front of her, intent on her phone. She was thin and graceful-looking, with long dark hair and a pretty face, a younger version of the sleeping patient.

The girl laid her phone aside and took off her headphones. She sized Rita up with tired, but shrewd, eyes.

"Yes?" she whispered. "May I help you?" Her eyes shifted to Rita's hospital ID, which Rita had pinned to her sweater, then contracted to hostile slits.

The girl leapt from the chair, maneuvered a startled Rita by the arm back into the hallway, and planted herself between Rita and the door, which she gently closed behind her.

"Yes?"

"I'm Dr. Wu." Rita offered her hand. The young woman glanced at it coolly and folded her arms. Rita dropped her hand and felt heat rushing to her cheeks.

"I'm Mrs. Sanchez's doctor—"

"Yes. I know who you are," the girl said. There were dark circles under her eyes. "Can I help you?"

"You are—?"

"I'm her daughter. *Can I help you?*"

"I just wanted to check on her."

"Why?"

"I wanted to make sure she was okay—"

"Why? So you can, like, experiment on her again?"

"*What?*"

The girl fished a crumpled copy of the surgery consent form from her hoodie pocket.

"My father showed me this. This says you did some kind of experimental surgery on her?"

"Well . . . no, not really. It was a standard—"

The girl flapped her arms in the air, exasperated. "Why can't I get a straight answer from any of you guys? First my mom's surgery is delayed. Which in a way is good, because at least it gives me time to get here. And then it takes, like, three hours longer then we were told it would. Then some old guy in scrubs, who's wearing foundation, which I think is totally weird but okay, *whatever*, comes out and tells us that everything is okay, but that my mom's going to need to stay in the hospital for a while. My dad said he wanted to talk to you, but the old guy said you were really sick. Why did you operate on my mom if you were sick?"

"That's not what— Look, things didn't go as we'd planned, but—"

"Did you think you could take advantage of my parents because they don't speak good English?"

"What? No! Look—"

"Because that's just *twisted*. They *trusted* you. And now my mom is, like, *really* sick." A single tear spilled down her cheek. "My mom is my dad's *life*. You don't understand. You don't know what it's been like. I finally convinced my dad to go home and get some sleep—" She drew herself up straight. "I don't want you. I want the other doctor." Her voice rose, then broke, like a wave on the shore. "I want the old guy. The one with the makeup."

Rita glanced toward a nearby nurses' station. One of the nurses, who she didn't recognize, was staring at them with an arched eyebrow. The last thing Rita needed now was a scene.

The girl said other things. A man in an expensive suit who said he was from the hospital had come to see how her mom was doing, and what was *that* all about? A lady from the *Wall Street Journal* had left a message on her voice mail, and sent her a bunch of e-mails—and maybe she should be, like, talking to *her*? She said her boyfriend's mom was a lawyer, a *really important* one in Beverly Hills, and that she was going to talk to her first thing tomorrow morning . . .

The nurse with the arched eyebrow was walking toward them.

Chastened by a college kid.

The girl was still talking as Rita slunk back to the staircase.

Any other humiliations I can look forward to today?

She headed downstairs, dazed, wondering where her body was going to take her next. It seemed to be going toward the parking garage. *Good as anywhere, I guess.* From there, who knew?

Darcy. I need to go get Darcy.

Yes. Her thoughts sharpened with each step. And then the two of them would get out of here. Pick up some cash, empty as much as the ATM would let her. Then leave. She hadn't worked out the details yet, but that's what she was going to do. Leave.

Rita had just planted her feet on the first-floor landing when she heard a loud *pop*, and felt a sharp pain in her back, like a jab from four hot needles. Then all her muscles seized up, and she dropped, helpless, to the floor.

FINNEY

Finney sat in his favorite leather armchair, in his study, in his twelve-thousand-square-foot hacienda-style house.

The house was too big for one person. He knew that: When they'd been house hunting, Jenny had fallen in love with it because she'd wanted to fill it with children. He hadn't gotten around to selling it because he liked his privacy. And he had plenty of it here: in big, empty, echoing rooms on three acres surrounded by high walls. He had little contact with other people. There was Sebastian, and a few other intermediaries, and the (carefully vetted) house staff who'd left for the night. Since Jenny's death, he'd otherwise withdrawn from the world.

The rain streamed down the windows in waterfalls. What had Sebastian said earlier? Something about a flash-flood warning? Mudslides? The storm seemed to be dumping as much water, in as short a period of time, as they'd predicted.

He stroked the cover of his notebook as if it were a cat sitting on his lap; and, like the purring of a cat, the worn-leather dimples of its cover transmitted soothing vibrations to his fingertips. His skin tingled, and he felt alive with anticipation.

He'd been sitting in this chair since arriving home several hours ago. He hadn't eaten or slept. He'd wanted to sleep, to rest up for tonight—had every intention of sleeping. But how could he? He was too keyed up. The universe was on the verge of righting itself. Just one more piece to put in its place, one last nudge in the right direction, and everything would be as it should be. As it had been before. The imbalance that had existed since Jenny's death would be gone, and with it his pain.

And yet . . . would it?

Would the pain *really* be gone?

He wasn't so certain anymore.

His eyes moved to the large, framed portrait of Jenny on the wall: the same one he'd given a copy of to Dr. Wu (*murdering whore*), the one of her sitting on the grass and smiling. A lifetime ago.

He closed his eyes; and in his mind the beautiful face in the picture transformed into what it had been when the ICU doctors came and told him she was brain-dead, and that it was time to pull the plug: a grotesque mockery of its former self, puffy and pale and lifeless. Like a corpse.

He opened his eyes, laid the notebook aside, and picked up the gun from the table next to the chair.

He chambered a round and put the barrel in his mouth.

The steel was cold, but he was expecting that, because this was not the first time he'd done this. Sitting in this chair, staring at her picture.

What he'd never done was pull the trigger.

Which, gazing at Jenny's portrait, he did now.

Nothing happened.

The trigger didn't yield.

The gun didn't fire.

He frowned, took the gun out of his mouth, and examined it.

Yes: There was the round in the chamber. He'd done it properly, exactly as the man who'd sold him the gun had shown him. So why hadn't it gone off? And ended his pain?

Ah. The safety. It was on. You could tell because the little lever above the trigger was pointed toward the word *safe* etched in small letters in the metal, and away from the orange dot. He'd never owned a gun, and was still getting used to it. He supposed he should have practiced with it. Maybe gone to a firing range. But he hadn't wanted to attract attention. Especially Sebastian's.

With his thumb, he flipped the lever toward the orange dot (*safety off*) and put the gun back in his mouth.

His finger twitched on the trigger.

No.

He took the gun out of his mouth, flipped the lever back to *safe,* and carefully placed it back on the table.

This was no coincidence. The universe had *stopped* him, left the safety on the gun, for a reason. He wasn't *meant* to pull the trigger. The universe *wanted* him to finish this task. To bring order out of the chaos.

The tablet on his lap hummed with an incoming text: Sebastian, telling him it was time for him to come back to Turner.

He glanced out the window and sighed. He didn't relish driving in the storm. He didn't drive much anymore, paid other people to do it for him. It was so dark, and rainy, and some of the low-lying roads between here and Turner might be flooded.

But.

A small price to pay for cosmic retribution.

RITA

Rita was lifted onto something soft, flat on her back . . .

. . . and then she was on something that was moving, gazing upward as brightly lit ceiling tiles slid smoothly by . . .

. . . still moving then, but the tiles had been replaced by darkness, and a cold wind, and drops of water splattering her face, and she smelled rain, heard it falling as . . .

. . . she woke up.

God, but I'm getting tired of waking up today.

She realized she was propped up against a concrete wall, her legs lying on a concrete floor. The room was dry, but the sound of pouring water was everywhere. Every muscle in her body, every part of her, ached.

Her nose itched. She tried to scratch it . . .

. . . but she couldn't move her hands, which felt like they were tied behind her back with some sort of plastic straps. Tight, but not too tight, and not all that uncomfortable.

There was a man with straight, medium-length dark hair sitting cross-legged on the floor a short distance away. He looked to be a man of mixed ethnicity (*Asian? Hispanic, maybe?*) and intense dark eyes.

He was staring at her.

Situational awareness, lovely Rita.

SEBASTIAN

Her first question was the most predictable one.

"Who are you?"

"My name is Sebastian. I work for Mr. Finney."

"Sebastian." She licked her lips. "Sebastian." Her mouth seemed to be taking his name for a test drive. "Is that your first name, or your last?"

"Just call me Sebastian."

"Okay. Sebastian. What have you done to me?"

"Which parts do you want to know about?"

She considered that. "My ear. And Finney talking to me through it."

He gave her this: She was one tough lady. Calm, cool, collected. He knew combat-hardened soldiers who'd be blubbering like babies by now, crying for their mothers. But what *she* wanted was answers. Sebastian had already decided, before she woke, that she deserved them. No harm in telling her. It wouldn't make any difference.

"Implants. Placed through your ear. Millions of microscopic machines, the size of small proteins, composed primarily of biodegradable compounds. Injected into your tympanic membrane."

"My eardrum."

"Correct. The particles implanted into your vestibulocochlear nerve. They're like a radio receiver: In response to energy waves beamed to your ear, the particles vibrate. Or give off electrical pulses. Or cause the release of neurotransmitters. Or all of those. I'm not sure. The physiology and biochemistry are

way above my pay grade. Anyway. The nerve trans-
mits the signals to your brain, which interprets them
as speech. Finney was, literally, talking directly into
your brain."

"Why did he stop?"

"The particles in your ear stopped responding to his
transmissions."

"Why?"

"I don't know. They do that, sometimes."

"Are you lying to me?"

"No."

"How do I know?"

"You don't. But there's no reason for me to lie."

She went quiet for a while.

"Did those—things, have anything to do with . . .
in the operating room today, when I . . . when the
scalpel—"

"Yes."

"How did he make me do—"

"Does it really matter, Doc? The point is that he did.
He used the particles. Used them against you." Sebastian tapped his forehead with his finger. "Used them
against your mind. Got into your head. Tricked you
into stabbing that woman."

She nodded, then examined her surroundings, as if
it were the first time it had occurred to her to do so.
"Where am I?"

"The construction area next to Turner. In one of the
new operating rooms." He paused before adding,
"Don't bother to scream. The only reason I didn't gag
you is that no one can possibly hear us." The din from
the rain, and from the heavy runoff as it rushed loudly

through gutters and down the sides of the building, made his point.

"Or see us," he said. They were in a semicompleted operating room, one of the ones he'd visited with the tour group, the inside of which was impossible to see from the outside. To be safe, Sebastian had also inactivated the lights in selected areas of the building, betting that no one would come until the storm blew over.

Wu looked down at the ground and nodded.

So calm.

She'd looked calm in the second-floor stairwell, too, when he'd shot her with the conduction gun.

He'd gotten lucky.

Again.

Fortune favors fools, Sebastian.

That's what Alfonso would have said.

He'd stumbled upon her getting out of her car, near the exit of the garage, and shadowed her to Mrs. Sanchez's room, watching as the Sanchez girl had unloaded on her before he'd followed her back down the stairs.

Afterward, it had been easy enough to get her here. He'd placed her on a gurney, drawn a sheet up to her chin to make her look like a patient, and wheeled her away. The storm had chased away almost everyone. Except for the patients, the minimally staffed night crew, and the odd family member, the hospital was empty.

He pointed to her chest. "Those dog tags around your neck. Whose are they?"

She looked at him quizzically. "My father's."

"What'd he do?" His research on her hadn't included that.

"Flew planes. In the Navy."

"What'd he fly?"

"The P3, mostly."

"The Orion." Sebastian nodded. "Sub hunter."

"Yeah." She tilted her head to one side. "Were you Navy?"

Sebastian hesitated, then said, "Let's just say we were a . . . mixed-branch unit."

"I didn't know there was such a thing."

"It's not something my bosses advertised. Why are you wearing his tags?"

"Why are you asking me about my father?"

"Why not?"

"What are you going to do to me?"

"I don't know." Which was a half-truth.

"Are you going to kill me?"

"I don't know." Another half-truth.

She shifted position on the wall, and said, "Do you expect me to cry, or something? Because I won't. I won't give you the satisfaction."

I know you won't.

"No. I don't expect you to cry."

When did I become one of the bad guys?

But for the sound of the rainwater, there was silence.

"He died," she said finally.

"What?"

"My father. His plane went down in the desert, east of San Diego. Catastrophic mechanical failure." She shrugged. "They gave us a flag, and his tags. The flag is in a box, somewhere, in storage. The tags, well—I like to wear them."

"Wearing them makes you feel like, what—he's still with you?"

She shook her head, in a way that a woman does when a man's stupidity has left her speechless, and shot him a look brimming with vinegar. "Something like that. But when *you* say it, it makes it sound . . . cheap."

Sebastian reached inside his open collar and pulled out Alfonso's tags. They clinked together, like wind chimes, as he dropped them down the front of his shirt.

Rita's eyes traveled over them. "If you're out, why do you still wear yours?"

"I don't. These are—*were*—a friend of mine's."

"He's dead?"

"Yes."

"How?"

Since the mission debriefs, he'd never told the story to anyone. No reason to. It wasn't his way, or the way of the men beside whom he'd fought. Not in their code. It was also in violation of federal law, he supposed. But when lately had he been concerned about lawbreaking?

When did I become one of the bad guys?

"We were on a mission," he said. "Even if I could tell you where, it doesn't matter." *Does it ever, really?* "The intel we'd been given was that the, ah, target was in a particular location." *A safe house. For psychopathic jihadist terrorists.*

"Problem was, the intel was incomplete. There were a lot of houses around the target, and they all looked the same. And they were all packed. Families. Babies. Old people. Things went all to hell. Lots of firefights. House-to-house, room-to-room. In-close shit—*stuff*. In-close stuff, ma'am." She deserved respect, so he tried to tone down the swearing. "One of those times you couldn't tell the good guys from the bad."

"Sounds complicated."

"Yes." *One big,* complicated *clusterfuck.* His hand squeezed and relaxed, squeezed and relaxed, around Alfonso's tags. "It was." He chewed on his lower lip. "Did you know that we invaded Russia once? The U.S.?"

"No."

"Yeah. Most people don't. In 1918, near the end of World War I. Eight thousand red-blooded American soldiers running around Siberia. The Russians had already gotten their asses out of the war back in 1917, after the Bolsheviks had lined the tsar and the royal family up against a wall. Remember the Bolsheviks?"

She looked at him stonily.

"You know. The Commies. Like Lenin. Anyway. The Bolsheviks started a civil war. The English and French were scared shitless—pardon me, Doc—were *disturbed* by the prospect of a Communist Russia, and they dragged President Woodrow Wilson kicking and screaming into the whole damn mess. So Wilson sends these Army pukes over there. Ships them right the hell over, and they spend the next three years squatting in the mud, freezing their butts off, getting shot at by Bolshevik guerillas.

"The real kicker of it was those poor bastards didn't

even know who they were supposed to fight. The smiling peasants who sold them vodka during the day were the same rebels taking potshots at them in the middle of the night. Sound familiar, ma'am? Vietnam. Iraq. Afghanistan." He chuckled humorously and shook his head. "*Siberia*."

He sucked in a deep breath. "Anyway. It was this kid who killed Alfonso. This little kid. No older than my nephew is now. I never blamed him. The kid. I mean, what kind of an asshole puts an AK in the hands of a twelve-year-old? What the hell does a twelve-year-old know about *anything*?"

He held the tags tight in his fist. "Alfonso was dead by the time I got to him. A head shot. Never had a chance." *Or much of a head left.* "Neither did the kid. By the time we sorted things out, the rest of us had already—well . . . Not sure it would have mattered if we'd known who'd been firing at us."

He shrugged. "The thing of it was, afterward, our, ah, leadership thought it best if that particular incident was never a matter of public record. The number of civilian casualties, all the ones that got caught in the cross fire . . . I mean, it was a slaughter. Leadership decided that they didn't want another, ah, *unfortunate* incident tarnishing the sterling reputation of the United States military."

"What does that mean?"

"It means that leadership never owned up to us being in that particular location, at that particular time. They blamed the whole thing on a local militia group. A rival faction."

"So it was . . . covered up?"

"Yes."

"That kind of thing really happens? Government cover-ups?"

He shot her a look. "You don't strike me as the naïve type, Doc. Or the hypocritical one, either. Didn't your boss pull the same kind of thing with you?"

She leaned her head back against the bare cement wall and stared at the ceiling. "Just doesn't seem right."

Sebastian shrugged. "Wasn't the first time. Won't be the last. Even though they never owned up to it publicly, my bosses needed a scapegoat. Alfonso had been our ranking noncom; our officer had died in a helicopter accident en route. Alfonso was also, conveniently, dead. So they blamed him. Made him the scapegoat in the official report that, officially, doesn't exist. And that was that. Disgraced him. *Dishonored* him." Even now, after all of this time, the bitterness flared. He wanted to punch his fist through the closest wall, not caring if he broke every single *fucking* bone in his hand. Instead, he spat into the white-plaster dust on the floor.

"So yeah, Doc," he said, his voice thick with emotion. "I wear his tags because they make me feel, if only a little, like he's still here."

They also help keep the nightmares away.

Sometimes.

Wu appeared unmoved. "Now you work for Finney."

In his nightmares, he always sees the kid with the AK-47. Except it's not the kid, but Sammy. His eyes are wide with terror, like a pair of small green headlights in the night-vision goggles.

"Yes."

"The things you do for Finney," she said with

unmistakable contempt. "Is that what your friend, Alfonso, would have wanted?"

The *balls* on this chick!

Passing judgment on *him*. Her life destroyed, Finney rummaging around in her goddamn head, and *still* she had the nerve to tell him what was what. He supposed he should be angry with her. But he wasn't.

He wanted to tell her how much more complicated it was. That Finney was his ticket to giving his niece and nephew better lives; that in giving them better lives, he could honor the memory not only of Alfonso, but of the kid who'd killed him, the kid Sebastian had been forced to kill and rob of his future.

But the thing of it was, she was right.

There were good guys in the world, and there were bad guys.

When did I become one of the bad guys?

"Sebastian," said Finney over the receiver in his ear. "I'm here."

RITA

The man who called himself Sebastian cocked his head to one side. He put his hand up to one ear and gave the appearance that he was listening to something. Or someone.

"Roger that," he said. "I've left the door across the bridge unlocked for you."

He rose, walked over, and knelt beside her. He was holding something in his hand. She couldn't see what it was.

His eyes were . . . sad. Yes. Most definitely sad.

"Sorry," he said.

"For what?"

"This."

And then the plastic mask he held in his hand was over her mouth and nose.

Cool air blew against her face. It smelled sweet.

Nitrous oxide.

Laughing gas.

His hand was around the back of her head and neck, holding her mouth and nose in place, against the mask.

She squirmed, tried to move her face away from the mask and its invisible slumber. But his grip was strong.

"Don't struggle," he said with surprising gentleness. "It'll only make it harder if you fight it, Doc."

She fought anyway. Tried to hold her breath, to ward off the sweetness.

Sweet smell.

Sweet darkness.

RITA

Disjointed sensations, disjointed images. Fragments of fragments.

She was lying flat on a hard surface.

She felt a pinch, in the crook of her elbow—

(the antecubital fossa it's an IV going into my antecubital vein an IV going into me)

—and then a burning sensation, spreading through her arm—

(is that propofol? but can't be propofol . . . why pro-pofol? why now propofol? why me?)

—shafts of fire racing along venous highways from her elbow to her shoulder—

—her throat something was in her throat she was choking on it, then . . .

RITA

. . . back to awareness.

Out of all the times she'd woken today, this time was the worst.

The worst time waking up *ever*.

The first thing she perceived, as she emerged from unconsciousness, was an awful sensation in her throat.

No.

Awful didn't begin to cover it. No adjective she knew of in the entire English language did. *Awful* was just a word. What she was experiencing was something else, entirely.

She wanted to cough.

And gag.

And puke.

And scream.

She wanted to do all of them at the same time.

Badly—more badly, it seemed, than she'd ever wanted to do *anything*, ever, in her entire life.

But she couldn't cough, gag, puke, *or* scream. She tried, God how she *tried*, but she couldn't do any of these things.

Why? Why couldn't she?

Bafflement.

Fear.

Pain.

Why?

She opened her eyes.

No, she didn't.

Because her eyes were already open.

When had that happened?

She didn't remember opening her eyes.

She looked to the left.

No, she didn't.

Because she couldn't look to the left.

She couldn't move her eyes.

She realized, then, that she was biting down on some kind of tube. It filled her mouth and poked out of her lips, so that she was sucking on it.

What is that?

It tasted like plastic.

One big plastic Popsicle.

She reached up, to pull the plastic Popsicle from her mouth. That's when things got worse.

Much worse.

Because she couldn't move her arm.

Really couldn't move it. Not because she was tied down, like this morning when she'd woken up in the operating room. She couldn't move it because her muscles weren't responding.

She knew, then, that she was paralyzed.

She sucked in her breath.

Which—

(*Oh my GOD!*)

—proved impossible, because *she couldn't breathe*, either.

She heard a familiar *whoosh*, the sound of a respirator, and, at the same time, felt her lungs expand with fresh, oxygen-rich air, as if she were inhaling deeply, but doing none of the work that normally came along with it.

Her lungs filled to capacity, the whooshing ceased; and then her lungs collapsed in on themselves, expelling the stale air through the tube in an agreeable barter of oxygen for carbon dioxide. There was a pause, then the respirator whooshed, and the cycle repeated itself.

Terror and *panic* were, like *awful*, only words. Abstract concepts. She felt as if she'd been buried alive, trapped, with tons of earth pressing down on her body.

Her torso was cold, very cold, from the top border of her pubic hair on up, and she suspected (*just suspected, after all, since she couldn't look or feel with her hands*) that she was naked from the waist north. Not so the southern part of her—the bottom of her hips, and her legs, and her feet—which felt, by contrast, relatively warm. Downright comfortable, compared to the rest of her.

She heard voices. The first one she recognized immediately, and it filled her with revulsion and dread.

"Is she awake?"

That one was Finney.

"Can't tell for sure. But I've disabled the isoflurane."

The second voice was . . . the man who called himself Sebastian, she thought. A little harder to be sure because she'd heard him talk only once. "There's no way to directly measure her level of consciousness with the paralytics on board." Yes, that was him. She was certain of it now. "But her heart rate and blood pressure are way, way up, just suddenly spiked like crazy. So, yes—I think she's awake. Let's try a noxious stimulus."

Something sharp (*a hypodermic needle?*) poked into her right side.

Ouch!

She couldn't say the word out loud, but the heart monitor protested for her by quickening the pace of its beeps in response to her pain.

"Okay. See the monitor? Her heart rated jumped when I stuck her with the needle. So as best as I can tell, boss, she's awake. Or at least as awake as she's going to be."

Oh my God oh my God oh my God

She was paralyzed and intubated.

And she was wide awake.

She was WIDE AWAKE.

WHAT ARE THEY GOING TO DO WITH ME NOW?

As if in answer, Finney pushed his face down into Rita's, inches away from her nose. It was weird seeing him in the flesh. It seemed less intimate somehow than hearing him inside her head.

"Dr. Wu." He looked much the same as she remembered. Perhaps a few more toes added to the crow's-feet around his eyes, a blush of grey at the temples. "I'm assuming you can hear me right now."

(*oh God oh God oh God*)

He was speaking toward her right ear. Her good ear. "You understand, now, I think, the depth of my feelings on the matters that have transpired between us."

He sounded calm, much calmer than the last time he'd spoken to her. And so formal. But then he was always formal, as if he were a college professor lecturing a large class. "So I see no need to draw things out. As you've probably realized, we've intubated and paralyzed you. Like one of your patients. I imagine you feel very helpless right now." A pause. "Just like Jenny was helpless."

(*oh God oh God oh God*)

Her heart rate, already elevated, went higher. The beeps on the monitor came fast and furious. The respirator blew air in, and her lungs pushed it out.

"Yes. I can see by the heart monitor that you can indeed hear me. So. Regarding these matters between us. I've been vexed, Dr. Wu, by the lack of a meaningful punishment for your actions. I've always believed that the punishment should fit the crime. I've spent a long time thinking about it. Jenny was helpless, like you are now. Jenny suffered from her surgery, then she died."

(*please no*)

"I tried to decide how you could experience something similar, as recompense for what Jenny went through. I thought long and hard. I'm not a doctor or a medical expert. But I read. I read voraciously. And I was interested to come across *accidental awareness during general anesthesia*. Also called, I believe, *intraoperative awareness*."

(*oh my God*)

The heart-rate monitor wailed.

His thin lips stretched into a thinner smile. "I see you're familiar with the concept. We all take it for granted, I suppose, that if we ever have to undergo surgery, and we need to go to sleep for it, we're not going to wake up in the middle."

(*please NO*)

"I was delighted to hear your anesthesia colleague refer to it earlier today in the operating room. Like he said, it's a rare event. But still: One is one too many for such an unpleasant experience. Don't you think?"

(*PLEASE NO*)

"Can you possibly imagine? What it would be like? To be completely awake as you undergo abdominal surgery?"

He leaned a little closer. They were almost nose to nose. "Take Jenny's surgery, for example. A laparoscopic appendectomy. A straightforward operation, from what I understand. Think of it. First the scalpel carving your skin up like a Thanksgiving turkey. Then those sharpened plastic ports, twisting into your abdomen, like giant screws. Stretching. *Tearing* you open. Then all of that carbon dioxide, filling you up, and your insides swelling like an enormous balloon."

(*I'M SO SORRY*)

"Of course, that's just the prelude, because then the surgery *really* starts. Metallic instruments, pushing and pulling on your intestines, this way and that. Cutting and stapling of bowel. The pain would be *unimaginable*."

(*I'M SO SORRY SHE DIED*)

"But not without precedent." He got a faraway look

in his eyes. "Japanese samurai called it *seppuku*. Ritualized suicide. Remarkable. Such *discipline*. Such *control*. The offending samurai made two large cuts across his own abdomen with his *katana*—his sword." He used his hands to mime the motions across his belly. "The ritual was intended to cleanse him of his dishonor. Appropriate in your case. The English Crown, on the other hand, took a different approach, hundreds of years ago. They called it drawing and quartering. Traitors were first hung until not quite dead, then disemboweled, then their intestines burned while they were still conscious. The subsequent beheading must have seemed to them the greatest mercy."

His attention returned, and he refocused it on her. "I for one can't possibly imagine what it would be like. Waking up in the middle of surgery."

(*I'M SO SORRY I'VE ALWAYS BEEN SO SORRY*)

"Although, in your case, you'll have never gone to sleep, so it's a little different."

He leaned even closer to her; and, for one absurd instant, Rita thought he was going to kiss her cheek. Instead, Finney reached out and gently repositioned her head and neck so that her eyes were tilted toward her feet, taking care not to move her tube out of place.

"That's better. I want you to be able to see everything, Dr. Wu. The operation you'll be undergoing tonight, compliments of Delores, is the appropriate one, of course: a laparoscopic appendectomy. The same one you performed on Jenny. Morpheus will keep you paralyzed and inject some stimulants into your bloodstream to ensure you remain completely awake for the duration."

(*OH GOD*)

"Oh. And one more thing, Dr. Wu. Your sister." Through her peripheral vision, she saw him lay an object next to her right ear, on the same flat surface she was lying on. "She has an implant in her brain. Similar to yours. It's a bomb."

(*OH GOD DARCY OH GOD*)

"I'm going to detonate it in a few moments, after Delores has started. I've put a speaker near your head: so that, before it's over for you, you can listen to your sister die."

(*NO YOU BASTARD SHE'S JUST A KID*)

"This will be the last time you and I speak. Or, rather, that you hear me speak."

(*PLEASE GOD THIS CAN'T BE HAPPENING*)

As he turned away, he said, "You'll want to scream. I'm sorry that you won't be able to."

Finney disappeared. There were shuffles, and a small grunt, and then Delores's silver form appeared above her.

Portable, Delores is portable, they carried Delores here.

She heard the familiar sound—two taps followed by a whir—of Delores's gyroscopic feet latching into place on either side of her abdomen, securing Delores into position.

"Power on," Delores said. "Systems check in process."

Battery-powered for up to eight hours.

Now all she could see was Delores, squatting over her, her four stinger-like appendages aimed directly at her bare abdomen. Rita saw a distorted reflection of herself in the bright silver of Delores's undercarriage.

Oh God.

This was really happening.

"Systems ready," Delores said.

This was *really happening to her.*

Delores was GOING TO OPERATE.

ON HER.

AWAKE.

"Delores," Finney said. "Initiate laparoscopic appendectomy protocol."

"Of course. Initiating laparoscopic appendectomy protocol."

With her head in its new angle, Rita could see everything. Delores's motors ground and whirred as the camera and the three Swiss Armies spun a foot above her bare torso.

"Deploying scalpel."

There was a loud click as one of the Swiss Armies extended its scalpel—

(one badass switchblade)

—and moved toward Rita's skin.

She tried to close her eyes. But her eyelids were paralyzed. She watched, terrified, as the scalpel snaked toward her skin, like an enormous stinger, and tried not to picture the sharpened steel biting through the fat, nerves, and muscle that lay underneath it.

Is this hell? she wondered. *Is Finney my own personal devil, punishing me for my sins?*

Now, from the speaker next to her head, she heard Darcy. It sounded like she was on the phone. *With the boy from Santa Cruz?* God, she hoped not, the guy sounded like such a loser—which was an absurd thought, because *what did it matter now?*

Even though she'd never been an especially religious person (*Spencer, Spencer was the religious one, he'd been praying the day we'd met*), Rita prayed.

Prayed that it would be over as soon as possible. For both of them.

Delores's scalpel moved toward her with inexorable precision.

Please God let this be over fast.

Closer.

Please God. I'm sorry.

Closer.

I'm so very sorry. I'm so sorry for everything.

She found herself wishing for second chances.

Spencer, I'm so sorry, for throwing it away, for treating someone as good as you so badly . . .

The scalpel was an inch away from her skin . . .

SEBASTIAN

. . . and then the scalpel stopped, hovering a fingernail's distance over her navel.

A red light flashed on the side of Delores's central unit.

"System error," Delores declared. "Wireless connection broken."

"What?" Finney frowned at Sebastian, who shrugged.

"It's the same thing that happened earlier today, in the operating room."

Finney opened his mouth and closed it, like a fish. He seemed incapable of processing this.

"Well," he snapped. "You were there. Fix it."

Sebastian looked at him.

He'd done everything Finney had asked.

He'd captured Wu and transported her here, without anyone's being the wiser.

Lucky.

He'd placed an IV in her arm and induced anesthesia without making her heart stop.

Lucky.

He'd managed to slip the endotracheal tube down her throat—

(*Like with Gary Indiana on that combat mission, just like Gary Indiana*)

—without killing her.

Lucky.

He'd successfully hooked her up to Morpheus, the anesthesia machine, and preset the proper infusion of paralytics.

Lucky.

His luck eventually would run out.

"This wasn't part of our agreement, Mr. Finney. As agreed, I got her into position for surgery. Now make the payment, and I'll consider fixing Delores for you."

"Fix it first. Then I'll make the payment."

"No." He had the advantage, and he'd be goddamned if he wasn't going to press it.

Sammy and Sierra's money.

Finney's lower lip quivered, both fists clenched. He looked like a little kid about to throw one hell of a tantrum.

"Fine." With his earpiece and tablet, Finney made

a terse phone call that lasted all of ten seconds, after which he nodded at Sebastian. Using his phone, Sebastian completed the transfer into his anonymous overseas account through a secure third party previously arranged for him by Blade. In a burst of text, the party confirmed the deposit.

Eighteen million *dollars.*

"Done," Finney said. "Now. Fix it."

Sebastian hesitated.

Should he screw Finney over and just walk? After all, he had what he needed: more than enough money to last a lifetime and to buy his family a better life. Getting the hell out now was one *hell* of a tempting proposition.

He gazed at Wu, stretched out helpless on the makeshift operating table, which he'd fashioned from a large wooden pallet (the same type used to board up windows) and two wooden sawhorses.

"*Fix* it," Finney repeated.

What the fuck are you waiting for, Sebastian? Just go!

Wu's sister was on the phone. He could hear her on the speaker he'd rigged, talking to some guy.

God*damn*, but she sounded young.

When did I become one of the bad guys?

Leaving the two women alone with Finney didn't feel right. He wasn't sure what he would do once he fixed (*if* he could fix) the robot. Hell, he wasn't sure of *anything* anymore.

But he still had the program Blade had given him.

Let's play it out a little longer. See what happens.

"Turn off your device," Sebastian ordered, powering his phone down and slipping it into his pocket. Finney switched off his tablet.

Delores's red light continued to flash. Sebastian stroked his chin as he studied Wu and Delores. *Electronic interference*. In the OR, their contact with Wu had dropped at the same time as the robot had frozen up. "Interference. Blocking both the robot and the signal to her brain."

"From where? Something in this room?" Finney asked.

"No. I went over every square inch and tested all of Delores's functions before I brought Wu over."

Nothing we're carrying, nothing in the construction site, nothing on Delores, so . . . what is it?

Sebastian stared at Wu, thinking.

Why had her device suddenly stopped working this morning in the OR? And then, just as suddenly, started back up? And then stopped again later, in the ER, for good? And what about her sister's implant? There had to be a pattern to it. What was he missing?

Something on Wu?

He walked toward her, stepping absently around several red, metallic gas canisters stacked on the floor, each of which was knee height and stamped in large white letters with the words:

ACETYLENE
NO SMOKING OR OPEN FLAMES!

He'd noticed them earlier while getting the room ready. Acetylene, he knew, was for welding. The construction workers had likely stashed them here to shelter them from the rain, probably in violation of a shitload of safety codes. *Whatever.* This was the best room he'd scouted out, and he hadn't had time to move the canisters. Besides, it didn't matter.

He started with her feet. He left her jeans on because he knew they'd be a pain in the ass to get off, as he inspected most every part of her, probing and prodding with clinical detachment, moving his hands 360 degrees around her body. Feet. Legs. Pelvis. Abdomen. Chest. Neck. Head.

Nothing.

He frowned, and was turning to say something to Finney when something caught his eye, nestled behind Wu's right ear.

What the hell?

It looked like a quarter, with borders too regular and smooth to be anything but artificial, and an off-flesh color that differed from the surrounding skin.

He reached out and gingerly scraped at it with his fingernail (*Maybe not such a good idea,* some part of his brain declared, *not knowing what it is, or what it might do to your finger*), testing to see if its edge would peel upward, away from the underlying skin.

It did. He coaxed the corner off a bit more, then peeled the entire thing off and held it up to the light. It looked like a circular Band-Aid, except stiffer, with flexible metallic fibers interwoven into its material.

"What is that?" Finney asked, staring at it over his shoulder.

"I don't know. But someone must have put it there on purpose."

"Why?"

"I've no idea."

Sebastian dropped the metallic Band-Aid on the floor and ground it underneath the heel of his boot.

Delores's red light stopped blinking and turned green.

"Wireless connection reestablished. Operative systems online."

"I'll be *damned*," Sebastian murmured.

"Resuming laparoscopic appendectomy protocol."

There was a beep, and an ecstasy of small gears spinning.

The scalpel resumed its course toward her belly.

The blade came into contact with the skin just above Wu's navel . . .

. . . and then stopped before it could apply pressure to it.

"System error," Delores said. "Wireless connection broken."

The red light on the central unit winked at them.

"What *now*?" Finney huffed, bending over the flashing red light.

That's when Dr. Spencer Wallace Cameron tackled him.

SPENCER

Spencer saw two men standing together over Rita. He didn't know them, or understand why they were here, but it was obvious that they meant to hurt her, and in the most horrific way.

He blindsided them, catching them by complete surprise, rocketing out of the surrounding gloom, a human missile of massive proportions.

Raj. Thank God for Raj. It had been Raj's idea to use her EEG electrode as a tracking device, tying it into her location like a GPS.

His first irrational impulse—after he'd gone to Rita's hospital room to check up on her, and discovered that she was gone and that the nurses had no idea where she was—had been to call 911 to report a missing person. The dispatcher had listened politely, then informed Spencer that an investigating officer would be out within twenty-four hours to take a report.

Twenty-four hours! Spencer had thundered.

To which the dispatcher had responded: Was it not possible that she simply had left the hospital and gone home without telling anyone?

Yes, Spencer had admitted.

And the dispatcher had asked him, quite reasonably: Why then, sir, do you suspect she's missing?

Spencer had hung up in a huff, thought, then called Raj, who was awake and hungry for more news. Raj was nonplussed, but game, after Spencer explained the situation, emphasizing that he suspected Rita was confused from whatever was going on in her head and that she may have wandered off, and why involve hospital security since they would simply give him the run-around, like the police had? Raj disliked authority, so avoiding hospital security appealed to him.

To their surprise, and Spencer's increasing sense of dread, Raj had led Spencer to the second-floor bridge connecting Turner to the new hospital wing, then under the yellow construction tape blocking its entrance and through a door someone had left ajar, and then across the bridge and into the darkened interior of the construction area. The signal had dropped at that point; Spencer had wondered if it had something to do with his phone, which was almost out of power.

But by that time, he could hear their voices, which, along with a faint glimmer of light, had led him here, to this bizarre scene straight out of some Hollywood slasher movie.

Now, he didn't think, or hesitate. He didn't care who these guys were. He simply attacked. A mindless machine, intent on taking them down and getting Rita the hell away from here.

He hit them hard, with a classic rugby tackle, low, using his shoulder.

The tall, sandy-haired one went down first. He appeared to be in the act of inspecting the robot. The wind Spencer knocked from him came rushing out of his mouth with a high-pitched yelp, and he went up and over Spencer, ass over elbows, spinning around and landing full on his back, onto the pitiless concrete.

Having not lost any momentum, Spencer then plowed into the other one, who was slim with dark hair. This guy was quick, and had already started to move out of the way, but Spencer's impact was still tremendous. The two went down together.

The man grunted as Spencer landed on top of him. Spencer immediately straddled him and, before the man could recover, punched him in the face, his fist sinking to a satisfying depth into the soft cartilage of the man's nose. There was a squirt of blood.

Spencer hit him again. It made a soft, wet sound, like a watermelon's hitting pavement and breaking open.

The dark-haired man groaned.

Spencer clamped one enormous hand around the man's throat and raised his other fist, which was now stained with the man's blood. The man struggled at the hand around his neck. Blood gurgled from his mouth and nose.

Spencer hesitated.

Finish him! some ugly part of him screamed.

Spencer had never in his life been so angry, so full of hatred.

He squeezed the dark-haired guy's neck harder. Two more well-placed blows, he knew, would smash most of the bones in the asshole's face.

Three more would probably knock him into a coma.

The guy sputtered and squirmed, pawing at Sebastian's hand.

Spencer's raised fist shook.

No.

He was better than that. A man of faith and conviction. This guy was down for the count. That's all that mattered.

For good measure, Spencer knocked him once more in the side of the head, with less force, before pushing himself up and off him. The man curled up into the fetal position and groaned.

Panting, Spencer glanced at the sandy-haired one on the floor. He wasn't moving.

Rita.

He'd worry about the two of them later. Right now, he needed to get Rita away from those damn machines.

The anesthesia machine was the closest one to him. Remembering Montgomery's spiel from the OR that morning, before everything went all to hell, he frantically ran his eyes and hands over its sides until he located a large red button.

The fail-safe switch.

The one that would shut everything off, wake her up, and reverse the paralysis.

He slapped it with his palm.

The machine emitted a low buzz, followed by a hissing noise. That was it: No other signals came, no other indications that it was doing what it was supposed to do. Spencer hoped pushing the button had done the trick.

Now, where's the one for the damn auto-surgeon . . .

There it was.

Beckoning like a red beacon on the side of the robot, several feet away.

He strode over to it.

He was reaching out for the button, his hand inches from it, when the dark-haired guy jumped on his back.

SEBASTIAN

Christ, but this guy was big!

Sebastian had learned long ago to trust his instincts.

Dazed, and half-blind from both pain and the blood streaming into his eyes from his ruined face, Sebastian's instincts were telling him that he wasn't going to get out of this fucking situation unless he dealt with this big bastard—

(*Cameron, he realized, that neurosurgeon in the ER*)

—who was, quite literally, standing between him and his freedom.

Sebastian's instincts had told him that jumping on his back was the thing to do: to buy time for him to recover his senses so that he could assess the situation, to temporarily throw Cameron off his game, maybe get him in some kind of choke hold.

He could have tried the conduction gun, which was tucked into its holster over the small of his back. But his instincts reminded him that he had just gotten his ass handed to him and that he could barely see straight, let alone aim and get off a clean shot.

With a surprised grunt, Cameron staggered backward, with Sebastian riding him piggyback, away from Wu and the auto-surgeon. Riding Cameron like a bull at a rodeo, the professional part of Sebastian's brain wondered why the hell Cameron hadn't beaten him to death when he'd had the chance. He should have. Because Sebastian had survived shit far worse than this, and he wasn't planning on giving Cameron any more chances at gaining the upper hand.

Christ, he was strong! Cameron jerked Sebastian this way and that until his teeth chattered. Holding on to him much longer would be impossible. A choke hold was out of the question.

But then Sebastian's instincts spoke to him again.

Clinging to Cameron with his left hand, Sebastian reached up with his right and clawed at Cameron's head behind both ears.

There.

Behind the right one.

As he'd suspected.

Then Cameron threw him off, and Sebastian landed hard on the ground several feet away.

SPENCER

Furious, Spencer spun toward the dark-haired man and approached him, trying to ignore the pain in his right knee, which had gotten worse. Much worse. Maybe something he'd done while tackling the two men.

Spencer stopped and frowned. The dark-haired guy was clutching a small circular object in his right hand. As Spencer watched, he threw it down and ground it into the floor with the heel of his boot.

"Wireless connection reestablished. Operative systems online," the robot said.

What?

Spencer whipped around. The red light on the robot's central cylinder, which had been flashing red a moment ago, was now green.

Spencer's hand flew to his right ear.

The EEG patch was gone.

His hand came away bloody. The dark haired guy had ripped it off his skin while riding his back. He was so jacked up, he hadn't noticed.

"Resuming laparoscopic appendectomy protocol."

Two beeps sounded, and gears whirred ominously from within the arm holding the scalpel to Rita's abdomen.

The scalpel resting on her skin.

No!

Spencer launched himself toward the fail-safe, but his injured knee (*damn, but it was really starting to hurt*) slowed him down, and the button seemed so far . . .

RITA

What the hell is going on?

Rita had heard Delores shut down and felt a surge of elation. Then she'd listened, confused, as Finney and Sebastian conferred, had felt Sebastian examine her body (*so meticulous and practiced, like a doctor*) and remove the EEG patch Spencer had given her from behind her ear (*what has that got to do with anything?*).

She'd listened as Delores had started back up, and then, mercifully, shut back down. Then she'd heard grunts and scuffling.

She perceived the metal of Delores's blade, pressed up against her abdomen, in alternating tactile waves timed with her breathing: sharp, but without enough pressure to break the skin, as the ventilator forced her abdomen up into it, dull as her lungs pushed her abdomen back down.

Sharp. Dull. Sharp. Dull.

"Resuming laparoscopic appendectomy protocol," Delores said.

Oh God.

It was crueler that she should anticipate deliverance, only to have it stripped away. Maybe that's what Finney had intended all along.

Two beeps, and gears whirred from within the arm holding the scalpel to Rita's abdomen.

It's happening Oh God it's really happening I'm getting operated on DELORES IS OPERATING ON ME . . .

The scalpel bore down and slid across her abdomen, and her skin began to part in its wake, like fiery red lips opening.

Finney had been right.

She wanted to scream.

But she couldn't.

SPENCER

. . . and then Spencer slammed the red button on the side of the robot with the heel of his palm.

"Emergency stop initiated. Systems shutting down."

With a gratifying mechanical hiss, the scalpel retracted away from Rita's belly, leaving only a small, superficial incision above her navel, from which streamed a slim rivulet of blood.

Relieved, Spencer glanced at the sandy-haired guy, prone and still, lying in the same spot on which he'd dropped, his chest falling and rising slowly. Meanwhile, the dark-haired guy, his face a bloodied mess, was watching him from the floor on the other side of the dimly lit room.

Something about this guy made him nervous.

Without taking his eyes off the dark-haired guy, he reached back and grabbed the Swiss Army with the scalpel: wrapped his enormous catcher's mitt hands around the slender robot arm and yanked as hard as he could.

Dolores protested with a shriek of tearing metal. The arm broke off at its thinnest part.

Spencer now held it up in front of himself as if he were some medieval knight, wielding the scalpel-tipped metallic tube like a sword. A few red-colored and yellow-colored wires dangled from the end opposite the scalpel.

Then the arm made a grinding sound that set his teeth on edge. There was a loud *pop*, and he smelled smoke.

The scalpel disappeared . . .

. . . and was replaced by a bright blue, flyswatter-shaped retractor.

Spencer looked at it, shrugged, and advanced toward the dark-haired man, swinging the robot arm in front of him.

His right knee now throbbed with pain.

SEBASTIAN

From his spot on the ground, Sebastian wiped the blood from his eyes and observed Cameron advance toward him, holding the robot arm.

The guy was *big*.

There was, Sebastian realized, a part of him grateful that Cameron had stopped the robot. He didn't care what Finney thought Wu had done to his wife—*nobody* deserved that shit.

But he had to get the hell out.

And Cameron was in his way.

Sebastian rose to a squat. He'd fought plenty of big guys, most of them big and stupid. This guy was big as they came—but not, he sensed, so stupid. He acted like he'd been in some honest-to-God bare-knuckle brawls. He'd boxed, probably, judging both by the efficient pounding he'd given Sebastian and his stance as he approached, clutching the robot arm with its ridiculous blue flyswatter. He seemed comfortable grappling in close quarters and knew how to use his size.

Still, he no longer had surprise on his side, and Sebastian had his weapon, tucked into its holster over the small of his back. Sebastian would have to wear him down, or find a weak spot. Or both. Something that would give him the chance to use the conduction gun. He would sooner die than spend the rest of his life in prison.

"Look. I don't want any more trouble," Sebastian said. It hurt to talk. His nose felt swollen to the size of a grapefruit.

Ignore it.

"Fine, then," Cameron said, in the halting tone of a man holding on to control of his rage by his fingernails. "Then lie down with your stomach to the ground and spread your arms and legs out."

"Okay, okay. Take it *easy*." He made as if to sit on the ground and stared at Cameron as he approached, his eyes probing for weaknesses, anything at all he could exploit to his advantage.

There.

Right there.

That was it.

That's what he needed.

Cameron was favoring his right knee.

RITA

Rita blinked.

Spencer?

Spencer!

Spencer was *here*. In this room, talking to someone—Sebastian, maybe? She wondered if Spencer had been the one who'd shut Delores down. But what the *hell* would Spencer . . .

Wait.

She'd blinked!

She tried it again.

Yes, most definitely a blink!

The paralysis was wearing off.

Morpheus must have injected her with the paralysis-reversal drug (*Sugammadex, was it? that's what Nikhil was using*), as it was programmed to do.

She tried wiggling her fingers. They felt heavy and slow, like big, thick sausages. But they responded.

Concentrate, lovely Rita.

You can do it.

She began to cough, quietly, around the tube. Her gag reflex, no longer stifled, was kicking in.

Her arms were lead weights. She strained to lift them toward her face—

(*Concentrate!*)

—and the tube sticking out of her mouth.

SPENCER

The man wasn't lying down.

Spencer was pissed but not stupid. He kept himself between the man and the closest doorway, brandishing the robot arm.

"I said, *lie down*!" Furious as he was, Spencer didn't want to hurt the guy any more than he had to—just keep him out of action and get the cops here. Let the cops take care of him.

"Okay, okay." The man waved his hands wearily. "Just, don't punch me in the face again, man. Okay?" He started to lie down.

Then, before Spencer could react, the guy was on his feet and moving.

Damn, he's fast.

The man shot to Spencer's left. Spencer threw the Swiss Army at him, but the big, metal cylinder went wide as the man abruptly reversed direction.

Which was okay. Spencer had thrown it as a distraction. Right after chucking it at him, Spencer launched himself low, toward the man's center of gravity . . .

SEBASTIAN

. . . Sebastian saw him coming and, at the last possible moment, dodged smoothly aside, sending Cameron off-balance.

Only for a moment.

But it was all Sebastian needed.

Cameron's right knee was moving more slowly that the rest of him. Exactly as Sebastian had anticipated.

Sebastian dropped to a crouch and kicked out with his leg in a move similar to the one he'd used on the skate rat earlier in the day.

Except this time, he didn't hold back.

This time, he didn't swing his leg wide.

His foot slammed into Cameron's right knee with the force of an industrial press.

The effect was more than he'd intended. Sebastian knew the outcome even before he felt the cartilage and bone and ligament collapse and heard the *snap*, sharp and loud as the crack of a whip.

The result was immediate. Cameron cried out, seized his ruined knee, and crumpled.

Sebastian rose, breathing hard, and watched Cameron writhe on the ground, clutching his knee in agony.

Such a waste.

He sensed movement to his right.

Finney materialized from the shadows.

He was holding a gun.

A gun?

A Glock. And he was holding it all wrong.

Which didn't matter so much because he was pointing it at Sebastian.

Where the hell had Finney gotten a goddamn gun?

"Boss?"

"Thank you, Sebastian."

Finney fired it four times into Sebastian.

FINNEY

The force of the bullets blew Sebastian off his feet and out of the pool of light they were standing in. He toppled over some stacked building materials and disappeared.

The gun shook in Finney's hand.

It wasn't too late. He could still salvage this. Set things right, make things the way they were *supposed* to be. The universe lusted for *order*. It craved *balance*. Every action needed a reaction. Why couldn't these people see that? Why couldn't he make them understand?

The gun shook.

He had to move quickly. Not much time. Someone would be here soon to investigate the noise.

The big man first. Then he'd finish off whatever was left of Sebastian.

Then Wu.

He'd save Wu and her sister for last.

He approached the large man, who was the same one Sebastian had pointed out to him today in the park. A neurosurgeon. Campbell, or something? How on earth had he found them? No matter. He'd take care of him. He'd take care of all of them.

The big neurosurgeon was on the floor, curled into a ball, clutching his right knee, moaning.

He looked up as Finney approached.

Finney raised the gun toward the man's upturned face, which was streaked with tears.

RITA

Finney was about to shoot Spencer.

He was about to shoot Spencer.

Without thought, Rita hurled herself at Finney. She didn't care about the blood dripping from her abdomen, and from the crook of her elbow where she'd pulled out the IV from her arm; or that she was drawing breath in painful gasps through her raw and swollen throat; or that she was shirtless.

Twenty years of anger management vaporized in an instant by the gun aimed at Spencer's head.

Finney, intent on Spencer, didn't see her coming. She crashed into him from the side, shoving his arm holding the gun away from her as he fired. The bullet went wide, striking the metallic casing of Morpheus, displacing a rubber hose—

(*The one connected to the oxygen tanks*)

—attached to its side. The bullet's impact produced a flintlike spark, a jangle of broken metal, and a hiss of escaping gas.

A flame appeared from where the bullet had displaced the hose: an orange tongue that licked the wooden pallet on which Rita had been lying. The pallet's edge began to smoke, then burn, the flames rapidly spreading across its surface.

Toward a stack of red gas canisters stacked on the floor next to the pallet.

As she struggled with Finney, a detached part of Rita's brain processed this—the bullet spark, the flame, the spreading fire, the red tanks of gas—and thought, *Oh, shit. That can't be good.*

Finney yelled and stumbled sideways. Not knowing what else to do, Rita kept a vise hold on his arm and bit the back of his hand holding the gun.

Finney screamed a second time.

SEBASTIAN

An indisputable fact: Finney had shot him.

Another indisputable fact: He, Sebastian, was a fucking idiot.

Idiot!

How could he have been so *fucking* stupid?

Finney had to have planned this from the very beginning. It made perfect sense. So fucking obvious now. He should have seen it from a mile away. Hell, part of him even admired the Machiavellian bastard for it.

Once the authorities discovered Wu's body hooked up to the auto-surgeon, they'd be investigating this clusterfuck for years, trying to figure out how she'd ended up on the wrong end of a scalpel. With Sebastian also dead at the scene, Finney could arrange for any story he wanted to tie Sebastian to Wu and plant additional evidence. He could have made Sebastian and Wu look like secret business partners whose relationship had soured, or lovers engaged in kinky sex. It didn't matter.

Finney would also have to bring Cameron into it now, of course. But three bodies instead of two would simply generate more orgiastic Internet speculation once the story broke. Totally plausible.

But that was all water under the bridge. Sebastian had more pressing concerns: like, the physics of bulletproof vests, and like, how-the-fuck-was-he-going-to-get-out-of-this-thing-alive?

Okay.

So he'd been an idiot. He'd dropped his guard for a moment. But he wasn't a *complete* moron. He'd slipped on body armor before tonight's activities, concealed underneath his windbreaker: an ultrathin state-of-the-art vest he'd obtained from a friend of his at DARPA, so slim and flexible as to be undetectable without close inspection. Perfect for not arousing Finney's suspicion. He couldn't say that he'd suspected Finney would shoot him, exactly—he'd just sensed the potential for a shit-storm, and prepared accordingly.

By no means was this the first time he'd been shot. And here was the thing that Sebastian had learned over the years about bulletproof vests:

They're not all that fucking bulletproof.

Most people had it in their heads that if you wore a vest, you were fucking Superman.

Bullshit.

Finney had shot him with a Glock 9 mm, the muzzle velocity of which was somewhere on the order of thirteen hundred feet per second. Sebastian had been standing close, well within ten feet. Two of the four shots had been direct hits: one to his abdomen and one to his chest. The other two had missed.

So, okay, yeah: The vest *had* stopped the two bullets.

But at that range, it had been like getting hit twice by a baseball bat.

Swung by a major-league home-run champion.

On steroids.

The abdominal hit had knocked the wind out of him, and now it hurt like a son of a bitch, nearly eclipsing the pain from his broken nose. It was going to leave one hell of a mark, for sure. But from what he could tell, at least it hadn't done major damage.

The chest was a different story. Maybe the angle at which the bullet had struck him: at the thin border of the armor's protective material, near his armpit. It felt like a broken rib, maybe two, on his right side. Each breath was an agony, a thousand knives sticking him in the side at once.

Ignore it. Suck it up. Move your ass.

Lying on the cement floor out of the light, he heard someone moving, back near the makeshift operating area, but couldn't see a goddamn thing from where he was.

Training and instinct had to be his guides. He slipped the conduction gun from its holster (*dammit, why hadn't I brought a real goddamn gun?*) and, staying low and quiet, using stacked construction materials as cover, stole through the shadows to reconnoiter and gain position on Finney.

He heard scuffling, a shout, more scuffling, a second shout.

He peeked around the corner of a large crate.

And couldn't believe what he saw.

Finney had picked the wrong chick to mess with!

Wu had pulled the goddamn tube from her own

throat! Jesus, was there *nothing* that slowed this woman down? Now, slippery with her own blood, she was grappling like a demon with Finney, trying to wrest the gun from him, her jaw clamped onto his hand. It was clear she didn't know the first thing about fighting, but he'd be goddamned if she wasn't wrestling him to a draw, and he had at least fifty pounds on her.

Neither one spotted him as he crept around the corner of the crate and raised the conduction gun.

Dammit.

Wu was too close. He couldn't get off a clean shot. The damn gun was like a crossbow—it could be fired only once before it required tedious reloading. He couldn't risk hitting her and wasting his one good shot.

So he tiptoed closer . . .

RITA

. . . *I'm not going to win.*

The thought came to her with remarkable clarity.

She hadn't been in a fight since high school, but she remembered what it felt like to lose. He was bigger and stronger. And, pumped as she was with fury and adrenaline, she knew she couldn't keep this up much longer: Weakened by the drugs, her lungs and limbs were starting to fail her. She wasn't scared: At least she would go down fighting. But she was sad, so *sad*, that she would fail Darcy.

Her teeth were still in his right hand. He tried to transfer the gun to his left as he reached with it to gouge at her eyes.

And then . . .

. . . the gun clattered to the floor!

She saw her chance and let go of him to grab it. He tried to push her away. She flailed out, and felt a thrashing of arms and legs. The gun slid away. He kicked her in the belly. Stunned, she coiled herself around his foot, and dropped to her knees. He drew back his foot and kicked her belly again, viciously. She gagged and coughed and fell on outstretched hands.

Then he was facing her, grinning with triumph, as he stooped for the gun.

So that's it, then.

She lay panting on the floor, waiting for it to end . . .

SEBASTIAN

. . . there.

Perfect.

Smile and say cheese, asshole.

Sebastian pulled the trigger.

The four electrodes of the conduction gun fired, like harpoons from the prow of a whaling ship, and embedded themselves into Finney's perfectly exposed ass . . .

RITA

. . . and she saw Finney suddenly jerk up, his hands on his butt, a ridiculous expression of surprise on his face.

Surprise collapsed into a bizarre grimace. His limbs launched into a violent dance, flailing this way and that, and he collapsed—no, *hurtled*—onto the cement floor. His arms and legs twitched for several seconds before becoming motionless.

Now, sprawled out on his belly, she saw four metal prongs sticking out of his butt, each attached to a wire. Her eyes traced the wires back to a black, gun-shaped device held by the man called Sebastian.

Sebastian strode over, grabbed Finney's gun, flicked a small lever above the trigger, and stuffed it into his belt.

"Didn't he shoot you?" Rita asked, hacking and coughing.

"Yes."

He offered no explanation but extended his hand. She took it, with some reluctance, and he helped her to her feet. He was wearing a dark windbreaker and a thin black vest underneath it. Wincing (*in pain?*), he removed first the windbreaker, which he draped across her shoulders, then the vest, which he dropped on the floor.

He gestured toward the wooden pallet. It was covered in flames. These were fast approaching the red gas canisters she'd spotted earlier. She now saw they had white lettering on the side that read:

ACETYLENE
NO SMOKING OR OPEN FLAMES!

"We have to go," he said, raising his left hand toward the red canisters.

"Maybe there's still time to put out the fire—"

"No! We have to go *right now*, Doc."

SEBASTIAN

Slipping her arms through the sleeves of the wind-breaker, and zipping it up to cover her bare torso, Wu rushed to Cameron's side and knelt beside him. She put her hand on his face. He moaned, but didn't move.

"Not without him," she said.

Sebastian looked at the acetylene tanks and the flames inches from their surface.

Fuck this.

"Suit yourself." He made for the doorway on the other side of the burning pallet, but the intense heat from the fire drove him back. The flames were voracious, consuming the flammable building materials, which in this section of the structure had remained dry. The sprinkler systems were either not installed or inactive.

Shit.

He wished her luck and spun toward the exit on the opposite side of the room, intending to loop back toward the bridge through one of the adjacent hallways.

"I can't move him by myself!" she called after him. "And what about my sister? Goddamn you! What about Darcy?"

He stopped in the entryway without turning around.

"*Help me*, goddamn you! You bastard. You can't leave him here. Help me get him out of here. Goddamn you. *Please*. God*damn* you . . ."

Is this what Alfonso would have wanted?

Shit.

When did I become one of the bad guys?

"Please . . ."

Shit, shit, shit, shit!

Sebastian ran over and knelt next to Cameron, opposite Rita.

"Come on," he growled. "Let's get him on his feet."

She put her lips to Cameron's ear. "Spencer, sweetie. It's time to go."

Cameron bit his lower lip and nodded, without opening his eyes.

"Count of three, Doc. One, two, three!"

An arm draped around each of their shoulders, Cameron screamed as they hoisted him up. So did Sebastian. The bastard was *heavy*, and it was like Sebastian could feel the jagged edges of his broken ribs rubbing against one another as he lifted him. Wu staggered under Cameron's weight but kept her feet.

They lurched through the doorway, out of the make-shift operating theater. Sebastian cast a final glance back at Finney, lying where he'd fallen, the flames advancing toward him.

Nice doing business with you, boss.

The adjacent area felt cool, the one after that cooler, and the one after that, farther away from the fire, cooler still, the same as the surrounding night.

"Stop," Wu panted. "I need . . . to stop . . . a second."

"We don't have time."

"Just . . . for . . . a second."

"A little farther."

"No . . . can't."

Bad idea, Doc. They needed to put as much distance as possible between themselves and that goddamn fire. But, Christ: She looked like she was about to drop, so Sebastian stopped. *Probably far enough away by now.* They laid Cameron out on the floor. He groaned without opening his eyes.

Sebastian lifted his right arm and pointed, then winced: God*damn* but that hurt. He could barely move his right arm. Those broken ribs were a bitch. "Okay. We go this way, skirt the fire, double around, and make it back to the bridge—"

The first explosion.

A tremendous *boom*, familiar to Sebastian from all of the combat zones in which he'd ever served, rippling outward, an expanding wall of heated and compressed air.

There goes the acetylene.

Instinctively, he dropped to the floor next to Cameron, pulling Wu down with him and covering her with his body. The explosion ripped through half-finished walls and ceilings and floors, and rained hot shards of metal and building parts around them.

The direction in which Sebastian had been pointing a moment ago, the alternate route back to the bridge, was now in flames.

Shit.

"Okay. Change in plan." He gestured toward a hallway leading from the opposite side of the room. "If we head—"

The second explosion.

Like an artillery shell, one of the red tanks blasted through the walls of the hallway he'd been pointing to, punching through the walls as if they'd been cardboard, leaving more flames in its wake.

Oh. Shit.

It was as if the goddamn fire had a mind of its own and was herding them in one direction: west. Away from the bridge, and Turner. Toward the other side of the construction area and the park.

Well, at least we'll be safe in the park.

"Okay. Come on. Only one way we can go now."

They struggled to lift Cameron up and got moving. Sebastian guided them down skeletons of corridors, grateful now for having memorized the blueprints. The floodlights for the construction zone had gone out, but the glow of the fire was enough to show them the way. Sebastian no longer worried about the security guards, who were no doubt preoccupied with the fire. A completed staircase got them to the ground floor, and a small hole in the green fence gained them the safety of the park.

They halted in the middle of the grassy area, which he and Finney had walked across today, well away from the fence. The rain had stopped, but the grass was soaked, and large puddles dotted the field. He felt a stiff, cold wind. Behind them he heard a din of sirens, fire alarms, and faint shouts. The lights in the other buildings around the park were out, their power a victim of the storm, the fire, or both. The sky was overcast. It was darker, away from the fire, and they appeared to be alone.

Cameron groaned. His pain was reflected in Rita's

face, just visible in the firelight. "He needs help. I'm going to go get it." She made to leave.

"No, you're not, Doc."

Wu gaped at the gun in his hand. "What are you doing?"

Wiping the sweat from his forehead, and ignoring the pain in his right side, he glanced in the direction of the sirens. The first responders would be preoccupied with preventing the fire from spreading to Turner and evacuating the patients. He still had some time, and there was something he needed to do.

He owed her that.

"Shut up and listen. We don't have much time."

"What the hell do you mean?"

"The bomb inside your sister's head, Doc. I can deactivate it. But I need you to sit tight and be calm. Okay?"

She stared at him, her expression unreadable, then pursed her lips and nodded.

Goddamn nerves of steel.

Sebastian restored the gun to his waistband and took out his phone. It was time to see if Blade's hacking program was worth the price he'd paid. He accessed the bomb's signal, which appeared on his screen as a pattern of sinusoidal waves undulating next to a timer. The timer was at fifty-one minutes, twenty-three seconds and counting.

Counting down to her sister's death.

"Look. There's a control system, with a timer: an automatic countdown Finney had rigged, in case something happened, and he wasn't able to detonate the bomb himself." *Much as the son of a bitch would have liked to, I'm sure.* "Finney locked me out of the system, but I think I've worked out how to bypass his security."

"How much time do we have?"

"Plenty. Fifty minutes and change."

By then I'll be in Mexico.

Using Blade's instructions, which he'd memorized, he initiated the hacking program. Three *beeps* sounded from his phone. *There. I'm in.* He rapidly inputted a series of commands, pushed the SEND key, and waited.

The screen flashed.

The timer halted its countdown.

He smiled. His shoulders, which he only now realized were hunched up to his ears, relaxed. "There. That should—"

The timer started spinning backward again, this time at a dizzying rate, the numbers blurring together as they spun toward zero.

What the hell?

He frowned and quickly began to restart the hacking sequence.

"Oops."

"Oops? *What do you mean, 'oops'?*"

"The countdown started again. But faster."

"*What?*"

"Just—hold on a sec, Doc. I'm working on it."

Goddamn you, Blade . . .

RITA

Rita didn't like this. She frantically patted her jeans, looking for her phone. It wasn't there. So she bent over and searched Spencer's pockets until she came up with his. He groaned but didn't open his eyes.

Luckily, Spencer hadn't enabled the phone's security lockout (*typical Spencer, always trusting that way*). She punched in Darcy's number from memory, ignoring the LOW BATTERY warning flashing at the bottom of the screen, and the multiple text and voicemail messages from Spencer's friend Raj.

The phone signal was weak, one bar only. The call connected briefly, then dropped.

She dialed Darcy's number again.

SEBASTIAN

Three more beeps from his phone as the hacking sequence finished its second run. Sebastian tried a slightly different command sequence, hit SEND.

The countdown slowed to its previous, normal pace.

But it didn't stop.

Shit.

The timer was down now to nineteen seconds.

Okay. Let's try this.

He started inputting more commands. Making things up as he went now.

"How much time do we have?" Wu asked. He registered out of the corner of his eye that she was now holding a phone up to her ear. Probably Cameron's, since he'd disposed of hers earlier.

"You don't want to know," he said calmly.

Fifteen seconds.

His fingers danced across the screen.

Ten seconds.

"Sebastian?"

"Working on it."

Tap, tap, tap went his fingers on the screen.

"*Sebastian?*"

Five seconds.

"Almost got it."

"SEBASTIAN!"

He transmitted the final command sequence and held his breath.

Three, two, one.

Zero.

The waveform transmitted by the bomb vanished.

Christ, he thought. *I'm too late.*

RITA

Sebastian rapped on the phone's side with his knuckles.

"Sebastian? What happened?"

He didn't answer.

The call to Darcy cycled through several rings.

Then Darcy's voice: "Hello?"

"*Darcy?*"

She'd never heard anything sweeter than that voice.

"Ree? What's up?"

"*Are you all right?*"

"I'm fine," Darcy said, sounding surprised. "Are *you* all right? Why are you calling—"

That's when Darcy started to scream.

Rita felt as if her insides had turned to liquid.

She dropped the phone.

SEBASTIAN

Wu fell to her knees and splashed about in the mud, fumbling for the phone. She retrieved it and, clutching it in one hand, glared up at him, her face streaked with soot, blood, and tears.

In all of his years of doing what he did, Sebastian didn't think he'd ever seen such an expression of pure, unbridled hatred.

All of it directed at him.

She hissed, "I promise you, you bastard, if anything has happened to my sister—"

RITA

She broke off as she brought Spencer's phone back up to her ear. The call was still connected, but the LOW BATTERY signal was flashing more quickly.

What?

What exactly would she do to Sebastian?

Kill *him?*

Maybe, she thought. If she could. If her baby sister really *was* dead.

"Darcy?" she said meekly into the phone, her heart pounding and sinking at the same time.

No response.

She wondered if she could somehow grab the gun from Sebastian and—

"Hello? Rita? Are you still there?"

"*Darcy?*"

"Yeah. Hey, Ree. Sorry I yelled. I was out in the backyard, having a smoke—you know, because you don't want me smoking inside. And this big-ass opossum just walks right up. Scared the living shit out of me. Big as a golden retriever. Swear to *God*. With that freaky long rat tail. And those teeth! It *hissed* at me, Ree. *God*, I hate those things. So. What's up?"

Rita started laughing hysterically as the battery ran out on Spencer's phone.

SEBASTIAN

Sebastian stared at the words scrolling across the phone screen—

SEQUENCE ABORTED
BATTERY DISCHARGE DISABLED

—and relaxed his grip on the phone, not caring why it had taken so long for the message to come through.

Christ. That was close.

"She's all clear, Doc."

Wu, laughing like a maniac, seemed to already know that. It was a bit surreal: her kneeling in front of him, caked in mud, soot, and blood, cackling in the firelight. Like she was in some kind of bizarre Satanic ritual or something. He hoped she wasn't losing it.

She suddenly dropped Cameron's phone, pressed her hands to her forehead, and stopped laughing, as if she'd forgotten what was so funny.

"Oh my God," she said. "Shit." He could see her trembling all over. "Holy shit."

Yes, he thought. *Holy shit indeed.*

Fueled by the acetylene explosions and a strong wind, the entire construction site had become a blazing inferno, despite the recent rains. The roar of the fire intermingled with an occasional crash of debris as a floor or wall collapsed. The air was heavy with the smell of smoke. His eyes swept from the fire, to Wu, to the darkness at the southern edge of the park, then back to Wu.

He was itching to get out of here.

But first: one last loop to close. He owed her that, too. Before stuffing his phone in his pocket, he carefully disabled the explosive in Wu's device—the countdown hadn't been activated, but he didn't want it to go off by accident.

"There. And now, Doc, you and I are, I believe, all square." *So you'll pardon me for getting the hell out of Dodge.* "This is where we part ways."

She was still on her knees, her hands on her forehead, breathing fast. She looked up at him with a hard glint in her eyes. "Those . . . things. In my head, and my sister's—what happens to them now? What will they do to us?"

"Nothing. I've permanently shut down the bomb in your head." Her eyes widened. "Yes. Just like your sister's. As far as the devices go: The particles will slowly dissolve over the next few months. Even the synthetic bits will disperse. Eventually. It'll be like they were never there. You and your sister are free and clear."

He turned to go.

"Wait!"

"Yeah?"

"Do you expect me to be . . . grateful, or something?"

He smiled faintly. "No. I don't."

I didn't do it for you, Doc. I did it for me. And for Alfonso. And for Sammy and Sierra.

And the kid with the AK.

And before she could say anything more, he headed south.

Toward freedom.

RITA

Oh God, she thought, as Sebastian vanished at the edge of the park.

Brain bombs.

Stabbing one of my patients with a scalpel.

Getting operated on awake.

Too much.

Too fucking *much.*

She took a deep breath.

Situational awareness, lovely Rita.

She got up and went over to Spencer. She glimpsed his ashen face in the firelight. His eyes were closed. His respirations were fast and shallow. She located the radial pulse in his wrist: weak and elevated. Her eyes moved to his injured leg, and she sucked the damp night air.

The wound was far worse than she'd thought: an open fracture, with a segment of jagged, bloodied bone (*distal femur, probably*) protruding through a rip in his pants leg, like the end of a gigantic candy cane snapped in half. He needed serious medical attention. Right away.

"Spencer. Listen to me. I need to go get help."

"No!"

He opened his eyes and gripped her arm. His terrified expression seemed out of place and a little absurd—a boy's frightened face pasted onto a grown man's body. "Don't leave me. Don't ever leave me again."

"Sweetie." She kissed his forehead (*cold and clammy, he's going into shock*) and held his hand. "I'm not going anywhere. I'm just getting some help. I'll be right back."

She kissed his hand once and stood up, ignoring his protests and those from her own aching body. She turned the collars of Sebastian's jacket up against the wind and ran toward the closest building, intending to make her way around the construction zone and to the front of Turner.

It struck her then like a spiked vise closing around every portion of her head at once.

Pain.

Oh, God.

"Dr. Wu," said Finney in her left ear. "You and I aren't done."

She staggered and fell, sprawling out in the mud at the side of the field, near one of the picnic benches, clutching at her head, thrashing and squirming.

THE PAIN.

"No, Dr. Wu," he whispered into her mind; and the pain, incredibly, grew worse. "You and I aren't done yet."

FINNEY

Finney stabbed the cracked screen of his tablet with his finger and sent another pulse of energy into her brain.

Twenty feet away, she splashed about in the mud like a caught fish flopping around on a dock.

He smiled. It hurt, because his lips were cracked and burned. He didn't care.

He'd underestimated them.

All three of them.

After he'd regained consciousness; after he'd yanked the conduction gun hooks from his buttocks; after he'd dragged himself through fire and pain, hobbled by the chunk of hot metal embedded in his left thigh; after the cool night air had soothed the burns covering much of the left side of his body and face; after he'd followed the sound of their voices (*he couldn't make out what they were saying but no matter*) through the gap in the fence and arrived at the park in time to see Sebastian leave the other two; after trying to detonate the bomb first in Dr. Wu's head, then her sister's, only to determine that someone else (*Sebastian, had to be Sebastian*) had already defused them—after all of these things, his folly was now clear to him.

Still, one card left for him to play.

Her implant had been robbed of its explosive capability, but it was still active. Sebastian had failed to shut it down.

Sebastian, who was now gone.

He plucked his notebook from his coat pocket. Or tried to: Its blackened pages crumbled in his hand. He let the ashes drift to the ground.

No matter.

Dr. Wu was motionless now.

"Dr. Wu." He spoke into the microphone of his tablet. "Rita." His tongue caressed the two syllables of her given name. It was the first time he'd addressed her by it. Its use seemed appropriate now, for reasons he couldn't fathom. "There's one way left to save him, Rita. Only you can save him."

"Spencer? You mean save Spencer?" she replied breathlessly.

"Yes. Save Spencer."

He started limping toward her.

RITA

The pain in her head was gone.

Rita blinked, and looked to the side . . .

. . . and locked eyes with a twin version of herself, who was lying next to her in the mud, on her hands and knees.

"You need to walk over to the cliff," the other Rita, the one on her hands and knees, told her in Finney's voice. She was wearing blue jeans, which were splattered with mud, and Sebastian's dark windbreaker. "At the end of the park. Overlooking the ocean. That's the only way to save him."

"Walk over to the cliff? But, firefighters, and paramedics—" She pointed in the opposite direction. It took a lot of effort. Her arm felt heavy.

"No. They can't help him. They won't get here in time. The cliff, Rita. The cliff will save him. Only the cliff will save Spencer."

"Why? How? How will the cliff save Spencer?"

"Everything will be obvious to you once you're at the cliff."

Of course. The cliff. The cliff will save Spencer.

She didn't know why, but this made sense. She needed to walk to the cliff.

"Walk to the cliff, Rita."

"Okay." Rita rose from the mud and walked west across the park. Her twin walked next to her, keeping pace, murmuring her approval in Finney's voice.

Rita reached a railing. There was sign with a picture of what looked like a whale on it (*dark, hard to tell in the dark*), and another sign that said something about unstable cliffs.

(*Unstable cliffs?*)

She hesitated at the railing. There was water on the ground everywhere, and her feet were soaked.

"Go under the railing."

"Why?" Rita asked.

"To save Spencer."

"Right. To save Spencer."

Of course. She needed to go under the railing to save Spencer.

She slid under the railing, splashing through water and mud.

"Take two steps forward, then stop."

Rita did.

There was blackness ahead, spreading out before her at her feet, devoid of any light.

There was the roaring of angry waves, far below.

There was a strong, cold wind.

It was like standing at the end of the world.

Rita shivered. "Now what do I do?"

There was no answer.

Her twin, the other Rita who had walked with her from the field, was gone.

FINNEY

He'd initially followed her from a distance, then closed the gap, dragging his injured leg behind him, to within a few feet as she approached the railing.

He knew he could convince her to keep right on walking, right off the edge.

But that didn't feel right.

No. It seemed more fitting that he be the one to push her over.

He ducked under the railing and picked his way among fast-moving rivulets of water, some a few feet wide and just as deep, little canyons carved into the soft clay as tons of runoff from the heavy rains raced toward the Pacific.

She was staring ahead, out over the dark ocean.

He stole up behind her.

His smile was thin and broad as he reached both hands toward her back . . .

SEBASTIAN

Sebastian was never able to explain what had made him look at the Fruit Punch Drunk app again on his phone.

Or —having looked at it, and perceived the reestablished connection between Finney and the still-active device in Wu's head, and realized that Finney had managed to lock him out of the command sequences again—what had made him turn around and come back.

He didn't need to do this. He'd gotten away clean, picking his way south along the cliff's edge, carrying the waterproof pack of supplies he'd hidden earlier near the Torrey pine in Higdon Park.

(*Options always options*)

He had all the money he and his sister's family would ever need.

He knew that Finney—

(*who had somehow managed to survive, he had to give the stubborn bastard credit*)

—even with all of his resources, would never be able to find him again should Sebastian not wish him to.

But he felt *glad* that he'd come back because he knew that Alfonso would have approved.

Now they were coming into sight, two dark silhouettes in front of the safety railing, near where he'd been standing earlier today with Finney. Sebastian

approached as quickly as the ache from his broken
ribs allowed.

What the hell are they doing?

As best he could tell, they were both right up near
the cliff's edge, like they were about to go off it, and
in this damn dark he couldn't tell for sure who was
who. The gun and conduction gun were useless here:
He might hit Wu.

No time for much of a plan.

In one swift movement—

(*Pain, ignore the pain*)

—he dropped his backpack and launched himself
underneath the railing. He grabbed both of them
roughly from behind (realizing only at the last moment
that Finney had been standing behind Wu) and yanked
them both back toward the railing. The pain from his
ribs flared and threw him off-balance, and he tumbled
backward, his right side crashing against the railing.

And against his cracked ribs.

His vision exploded into stars of agony.

One of them—

(*Wu?*)

(*Or Finney?*)

—fell against him. Instinctively, he grabbed for the
pistol in his waistband, but in his pain, he dropped it.

FINNEY

. . . and then someone (*Sebastian, who else but Sebastian could it be?*) grabbed him from behind, by the

shoulder, and pulled him back, before he could push her over.

Before he could accomplish his task and relish his moment of triumph.

His moment of triumph!

He staggered backward but, despite his injured leg, managed to keep himself upright. He felt something heavy land on his foot.

He looked down and, amazed, perceived it was his gun.

His gun.

Like manna from Heaven, his gun.

Then he had it in his hand, and he was pointing it at the two of them, both clutching the railing, mere paces away. They were panting, Wu draped across Sebastian, as if they were lovers.

This time he wasn't going to hesitate.

He pulled the trigger . . .

RITA

It was like the weirdest dream.

She'd been going for help.

Then Finney's voice, and the mud, and her inexplicable need to go to the cliff.

Now here, at the edge of the park, entwined with Sebastian on a metal railing.

Finney, too, just beyond the railing, standing between them and the cliff's edge, grinning wildly. Behind them, the fire suddenly flared and brightened; and his face, badly burned on one side, flickered in it, like a demon in the flames of hell.

He was pointing a gun at them.

She closed her eyes and waited.

Spencer. I love you.

Darcy, I'm sorry. I failed you.

I failed both of you.

FINNEY

. . . but the trigger didn't yield.

The gun didn't fire.

The safety was on.

Should have practiced more.

He was fumbling for the lever with his thumb—

(*Who knew it was so hard to fire a gun?*)

—when beneath him, the muddy ground gave way . . .

RITA

Her teeth rattled, and she heard an immense rumbling—felt it in her chest, as if a tractor-trailer truck were zooming by inches away.

But no gunshot.

She opened her eyes.

The ground on which Finney had been standing was gone.

So was Finney.

Before her brain could process this, the wet earth

she and Sebastian were standing on melted under their feet—

(*mudslide California mudslide those happen in California after heavy rains*)

—and she lost hold of the railing and started to fall.

No time even to cry out.

FINNEY

. . . and a roar.

His whole universe a huge roar.

He was falling.

Or was he flying?

Air whooshed across his ears, tickled his scalp.

As he fell (*flew*), he tumbled. No *up* or *down*. Only the roar and the tumbling. It was, he thought, like being in a gigantic washing machine.

He wasn't frightened. Just exhausted. *So it's over.* He was glad, relieved that he didn't have to worry anymore, and that this miserable existence was ending.

He'd believed that he could somehow single-handedly fix things and set the cosmos back on its proper heading.

But he couldn't.

He knew that now.

Now he realized killing Wu and her sister wouldn't have made a difference. The promise of cosmic balance had been an illusion. The emptiness, the absence of *her*, would have remained.

In the instant before he smashed onto the rocks, and tons of wet earth entombed his broken body, he spoke his last word, which disappeared into the rumble of the tumbling mud.

Jenny.

SEBASTIAN

The edge of the cliff, and Finney, had disappeared.

He clung to a twisted length of railing with his good left arm. The mudslide had dragged much of the surrounding railing down with it, but this bit remained, partially buried in the mud. His legs were swinging in space. He could hear the crash of waves breaking far below.

Wu was clinging to him, her arms wrapped around his waist.

The railing was too slick.

He started to lose his grip.

Through gritted teeth he told her this, and told her to climb, using his body as a ladder. She did, gripping his clothes as handholds, using his torso as a ladder for her hands and feet. Thank Christ she didn't weigh much.

His hand was slipping.

He cursed like he never had, a magnificent string of *shit*s and *goddamn mother fucker*s. He prayed and begged Alfonso, wherever he might be, to help him.

And then she reached the railing, and grabbed it to pull herself up to firm ground. Now, with one arm wrapped around it, she reached back down toward him with the other. "Come on," she implored, grabbing him by the shoulder and pulling. Streams of running water ran over the side of the cliff and splashed in his face, and he sputtered and coughed.

He counted down—*three, two, one*—to prepare himself; and then, like a monkey on a tree branch, he swung his right arm, the one on the side with the broken ribs, up and grabbed a piece of railing.

Agony.

The pain in his right side left him with just enough breath to scream.

He reached up and snatched her outstretched hand. With the added weight, her grip on the railing faltered, and she began to slide across the slippery mud toward the edge.

It was her turn to scream.

He let go of her hand and grabbed another length of rail poking out of the mud.

There. This one was less slippery. She stopped sliding.

Between her pulling and his, they got him up to the top. They threw themselves down and lay in the mud, panting, until it occurred to him that more of the cliff might give way.

RITA

"Come on," Sebastian gasped, dragging her up.

He pulled her to the grass. Across the park, beyond the fence, the construction site was a roaring blaze. She could feel its heat from here. She spotted distant figures around its perimeter. Spencer was lying where they'd left him, silhouetted against the firelight. He was waving his arms weakly toward the fire, up and down in unison, as if he was praying to it.

"I need to go help him," she said.

"Yes."

Sebastian limped over to his backpack a short distance away, pressing a hand to his side.

"You should come," she called to him. "You need medical attention."

"No. I'll get by." He pointed to the darkness past the twisted remains of the safety railing. "But I'd appreciate it if you told them I went over the side. With Finney."

She nodded. "Okay."

He faced south and took a single step before stopping and turning his head, so that he was in profile. The firelight danced across his bloodied, swollen face. "I'm sorry, you know. I'm sorry about all of this."

She smiled faintly. "I know."

He nodded.

Clasping his right side, he disappeared into the black ink beyond the edge of the firelight.

SEBASTIAN

3 months later
February

Sebastian (no longer his name, he reminded himself) had needed to disappear for a while.

With his talents, and connections, and newly acquired assets, he could have done so anywhere. A sandy beach in Bora Bora. Carnival in Rio. Safari in Africa, a Buddhist monastery in Tibet, a volcanic plain in Iceland. He'd considered all of these, and more, and rejected them.

So it was that he'd found himself huddled against the cold drizzle of a February in Paris.

He'd never been to Paris. He took his time. He marveled at Notre Dame, and wandered along the banks of the Seine and the Canal Saint-Martin. Drank fine wines, ate fine food. He could afford to, after all.

The Louvre.

Christ, how he loved the Louvre. He didn't know that much about art, but he couldn't get enough of it. One full day spent there had stretched into a week, and one week into two as he'd gazed at masterpiece after masterpiece, humbled before humanity's creativity.

Then one morning he stumbled across it. Just as Finney had described it.

The stele of Hammurabi.

He gazed up at its obsidian surface, clutching Alfonso's dog tag through his shirt. With his other hand he scratched his nose, which was crooked from where Cameron had broken it. He could have had it fixed. But he didn't. He wanted to remember. Plus, he thought it went well with his thick goatee and shaved head.

Tucked under one arm was a thick package containing all of his notes: everything he'd collected about Finney, and the device, and the events at Turner.

He'd been a professional, and his notes were meticulous. He'd be mailing the package that afternoon to an acquaintance in Budapest, who'd then forward it through a string of contacts in various cities across the world.

And, eventually, into the hands of one Ms. Constance "Connie" Grant of the *Wall Street Journal*.

The package's contents would, he knew, fill in all the gaps the authorities hadn't been able to—or at least those that didn't involve him. As far as the world was concerned, the man known as Sebastian was dead.

But the world had a right to know about everything else.

He hoped (*wishful thinking, he knew*) that he would see Grant again, someday.

He contemplated the stele as the tourists milled around him.

There would be no more jobs, he vowed it.

No more wasted days.

His phone rang. He smiled when he saw the caller ID.

"Hi, Sis."

"So. When are you coming home?"

He laughed. This was a running joke, the first thing she said at the beginning of every conversation. *Home.* She meant the new one—the nice, big house in the suburbs.

He replied as he always did: "Soon, Sis. Soon."

This time, he meant it.

For good.

SPENCER

1 year later
November

It was a magnificent day.

But then: wasn't it always, in Southern California?

Spencer held Rita's hand. He walked with a small limp, which his orthopedist had warned him he might have for the rest of his life.

Bullshit.

He'd accepted the prognosis as a challenge, a gauntlet thrown. He'd be damned if he was going to let himself hobble around like an old man. He'd flung himself into his physical therapy, which was a real bitch, and lately he was encouraged: There'd been some noticeable improvement. Plus, he was twenty-five pounds trimmer. Not too shabby.

Together they strolled, fingers entwined, among the headstones. They didn't say anything.

There was nothing to say.

When they arrived, Rita released Spencer's hand and knelt—not such an easy thing for her to do these days. She laid a small wreath over the grave. Spencer crossed himself.

After a few moments, when she didn't get up, Spencer said, "Penny for your thoughts."

"Trying to decide if I'm going to accept Chase's offer."

"Ah, yes." Rita's sly, squinting mentor had not only

managed to survive the robot thing, he'd thrived. The guy was Teflon. "Has he moved into his new office?"

"The CEO's office? Oh yes. It was supposed to have been in the new wing by now, of course. But with the fire damage, that's not going to happen until next year."

"He's moving quickly to, uh, consolidate his position."

"Well, you know Chase."

"Chief medical officer and Chase's right-hand man. *Woman*—sorry. Nice offer. Second-most-powerful person at Turner."

"On paper, at least. Yeah."

"With a huge salary to match."

"Yeah. I guess."

"You could be my sugar mama."

"Don't count on it, Doctor," she said, laughing.

Spencer understood her hesitation. It *was* a nice offer, but the job would be a lot of work. And there was Darcy to think of, who'd not only enrolled full-time at the University of San Diego (straight *A*'s so far this semester), but had already cranked out the first 150 pages of a novel. Rita had let him read them, and they were pretty damn good.

Then there was the matter of her swelling belly.

What a turn of events since last year. Thank God for that Grant woman at the *Journal*. God knew who her sources were, but the story she'd told in that series of articles! Sinister medical technology. Human experimentation in secret labs. Corruption. Murder. And she'd cast Rita as an ass-kicking heroine thwarting a brilliant psychopath. Rita had been on administrative

leave at the time, under the black cloud of an investigation, her future uncertain. Hell, they'd *both* been
on the hot seat.

The articles had changed *all* of that. For a time,
they'd been a national sensation, all anyone could talk
about. The rest of the investigation was expected to last
for months, maybe years. Especially the overseas stuff.
But Rita's part was done, for now at least, and her professional star was again on the rise.

He suspected there was more. They'd found Finney's
body, eventually, underneath all of that dirt on the
beach. But they'd never found the body of the man Rita
had called Sebastian. The authorities had shrugged it
off, said it must have washed away.

Had it really? Maybe. Rita wasn't talking. Spencer
had let it go. Because, even though this Sebastian guy
had almost crippled him for life, it wasn't important
to him. Bygones were bygones. It didn't matter.

She was important.

She was what mattered.

Rita pressed her hands to the small of her back, to
support it against the extra weight, and stood up with
a small groan. She gazed down at Jenny Finney's head-
stone, hands still pressed to her back, and blew a
strand of hair from her face.

She'd confided in him about the drinking, and the
guilt she still nursed: the quiet doubt that, but for that
Chardonnay, Jenny Finney would still be alive. Reminding her of the investigation that had cleared her, or
that she'd been sober by the time she'd started operating, would not make the guilt go away. Ever. It was, he
knew, her burden to carry, and always would be. Every

surgeon, including him, had lost patients. She had to make peace with it. Pick up the pieces and move on.

That's why they were here today.

"Okay?" Spencer asked her.

"Yeah."

She looked him full in the face and smiled. She took his hand and pressed it against her abdomen. He felt it quiver with the baby's kicking, as if signaling approval with her answer.

"Yeah," she repeated. "I'm okay."